THE
TRICKSTER'S
LOVER

Samantha MacLeod

Samantha MacLeod

THE TRICKSTER'S LOVER © 2016 by Samantha MacLeod. All rights reserved.

This book is a work of fiction. Names, characters, and locations are either fictional or are used in a fictional context. No academic careers were harmed in the making of this novel.

ISBN 978-0-9976898-1-5
ISBN 978-0-9976898-0-8 (ebook)

For my husband.
Thank you for sharing me with the voices in my head.

CHAPTER ONE

"You okay?" My brother tilted his head toward me. The breeze off the ocean ruffled his hair, which was bleached almost white from years of surfing and working outside.

I don't know, I thought. *Maybe I met a god last month. Or maybe I'm losing my mind.*

"Thanks for rescuing me this morning," I said, avoiding his question.

It was Christmas Day, sunny and a perfect seventy-five degrees in San Diego. We were walking along Coronado Beach, barefoot, my jeans rolled up to my knees. I'd flown in from Chicago last night, and Mom had given me a solid twelve hours of sympathy about breaking up with Doug. But as soon as the presents were opened this morning, she was back to her litany of suggestions about the various ways I could be less of a disappointment to the family.

"Caroline, you could at least wear a little lipstick,"

Mom said.

I nodded under the glare of the white aluminum Christmas tree. Mom had given me a Mary Kay makeup kit the size and shape of a cinder block, and I shifted it precariously close to my knees so I could reach my mimosa.

"You've just got to get back on that horse," she continued. "I'm sure there are plenty of very nice boys out there in Chicago. Go have a few dates!"

I nodded again, draining my mimosa in one gulp. I felt like the makeup kit was cutting off circulation in my legs.

"And you know, Caroline," she said, dropping her voice to a stage whisper, "it wouldn't hurt to find someone who makes a good living. Because honestly, I don't know how you expect to support yourself studying Greek gods."

"Norse, Mom," I muttered. "I study Norse mythology."

Mom threw her hands in the air, rolling her eyes.

My brother Geoff came to my rescue then, offering to get the two of us out of Mom's hair for an hour or so and promising to be back in time to help cook Christmas dinner. And we'd come here, to my favorite place in all of San Diego, the long, golden crescent of Coronado Beach.

He nodded at me, glancing out across the ocean. I

followed his gaze, shading my eyes as I looked over the waves. I could just see a freighter on the horizon, dwarfed by the vastness of the sunlit Pacific.

"Some pretty weird shit happened to me this fall," I said.

"Weirder than normal?"

I snorted a laugh. *Weirder than normal, indeed.* Weirder than me, the only person in my family with black hair and pale skin? The one who spent her sweet sixteen summer teaching herself to read German while everyone else snuck off to Mexico and had magical first kisses on the beach? The one who decided to move to Chicago and study ancient Viking gods while every other person in my family ran Capello's Landscaping & Tree Surgery?

"Yeah," I said. "Weirder than normal."

My brother nodded. "Weird shit happens to our family," he said. "You wanna talk about it?"

I looked over the Pacific. Seagulls whirled and dove into the waves, their lonely cries echoing off the beach. Beyond the breakers, the ocean was a pale, translucent blue. *Like his eyes,* I thought. *Just like his eyes.* My heart tightened painfully in my chest.

"Not just yet," I said.

I was in no rush to tell my brother about Loki.

* * * * * * * *

"Looks like the party's started," my brother said as he pulled his white Jetta into my parents' driveway.

I could see Aunt Adrianna's VW Bug parked on the street, and Uncle Tony and Aunt Michelle were already in the driveway, unloading several huge, covered bowls from the back of their blue Camry.

"Caroline!" Uncle Tony waved as soon as I stepped out of the car.

I walked over, kissing Aunt Michelle on both cheeks and grabbing the last enormous salad bowl from their trunk. I winced as Uncle Tony clapped me on the shoulder.

"You look good," he said, as we walked inside. "How's Chicago?"

"It's great," I mumbled.

I could hear Aunt Adrianna's thundering cheer from the front door as the entire family came out of the kitchen to hug and kiss each other. My dad has three sisters, and they all work for him. Their husbands all work for him. My mom, my brother, even my brother's fiancee Di; they all work for Capello's Landscaping & Tree Surgery. I imagine the family gets to spend enough time together, but every single time someone comes over to the house, it's like they've all just been reunited after decades of separation.

By the time Tony and Michelle finished kissing and

hugging everyone, and complimenting Adrianna on her new haircut, and telling my dad what a shame it was the Chargers wouldn't make the playoffs, and telling Di and Geoff yet again how happy they are about the engagement, the front door swung open for Uncle Donny, Aunt Julia, and their four screaming kids. And the entire process started up again.

Once the greetings finally settled down, my mom called me into the kitchen and put me in charge of drinks while Di finished the besciamella sauce.

She's not even Italian, I thought, *and she can make besciamella.* I can't even manage to cook spaghetti *al dente*, and I'm a Capello. That's why my mom told me to hand out the drinks; she wants me as far from the actual cooking as possible.

Di smiled at me as I walked very carefully around the two lemon chiffon cakes she made last night. I smiled back as I inched out of the kitchen.

It's not that I don't like Di. I don't even think it's possible for anyone to dislike Di - she's perfect. Perfectly charming, perfectly helpful, perfectly beautiful. If my brother hadn't proposed to her this summer, I think my mom would have gone out, bought the ring, and done it herself.

That much perfection can be a bit hard to handle. I was happy to wander into the backyard with my one job: taking drink orders.

"Carol!" Uncle Tony clapped me on the back again. "You know what you should be studying?"

I knew what was coming. Uncle Tony is the proudest half-Italian in all of southern California.

"Can I, uh, get you a drink?" I asked.

"The Romans!" Tony thundered. "The greatest civilization the world's ever known! Now that'd be a hell of a topic to study, right? And it's your blood!"

"I'd love a glass of white," said Aunt Michelle, maneuvering herself in front of her husband.

"Have you had any of that deep-dish abomination they call pizza?" Uncle Tony asked, with a wink.

"Uh, no," I said, "I haven't gotten out much. Been pretty busy."

Uncle Donny came over to join us.

"You started cheering for the Bears, then?" he asked me.

"Um, I'm still not much of a basketball fan," I told him. "Can I get you a drink?"

Donny and Tony seemed to find this hilarious.

"Okay," I said, "white wine for Michelle."

Aunt Michelle put her arms around my shoulders as we navigated the crowd back to the kitchen.

"We were so sorry to hear about Doug," she told me. "I just want you to know it's his loss. Really. I'm one hundred percent positive there's a nice, sweet boy out there in Chicago, just waiting for you."

"Thanks," I muttered, handing Michelle her wine before pouring myself a glass. A very full glass.

I'd had three glasses of wine when we sat down to Christmas dinner, and by then I was thoroughly enjoying my entire family. I even found it hilarious and charming when the three-year-old twins both took matching bites out of Di's cakes, and I was surprisingly convinced by Uncle Tony's rant about how the Greeks get too much credit when it was really the Romans who founded Western civilization. I was even starting to feel nostalgic for the summers I spent working in the office of Capello's Landscaping by the time the sun set and the aunts, uncles, nieces, and nephews started heading for the door.

* * * * * * *

It was late Christmas night before the house was quiet again. To apologize to my mom for my shortcomings as a chef, I finished the dishes, sipping coffee to sober up. Now I was sitting in the backyard, enjoying the soft, quiet night.

When I first stepped off the plane from Chicago, I was surprised to realize I could smell the ocean. But I must have become acclimatized, because now I could only smell the night-blooming jasmine, the small, hidden blossoms on the lemon tree, the soft, freshly-mown grass. Shadows shifted and danced across the backyard, radiating from the light pouring out the kitchen window.

My dad's backyard is his masterpiece. The Capellos have owned a landscaping business since my grandfather's time, and this yard is his biggest advertisement. He has a lot of parties here, hosting potential clients. And he begins every party with the same story: *When I started...*

I heard the sliding door opening behind me.

"You know, when I started..." my dad said from behind me.

"This was just a tree and a quarter acre of bare dirt?" I asked, smiling.

"Well, it may have had a rock or two," he said, sitting next to me and handing me a steaming mug. It smelled like chamomile tea.

"Thanks," I said.

We sat in silence for a moment, listening to the crickets. I watched the dark leaves of the California ash rustle against the stars. My brother Geoff likes to joke that our California ash belongs to another world, because its leaves swirl and dance, even when the air is still.

"Your mother means well," my dad said, delicately.

I rolled my eyes, hoping it was too dark for him to notice. "Are you sure I wasn't adopted?" I asked, hugging my steaming mug.

"Well, now that you mention it..." He smiled at me in the warm, yellow light coming through the kitchen window. "Of course, I seem to remember that your mother was in labor for -"

"Forty-eight hours!" I said. "And she'll never let me forget it!"

"And she is proud of you," he said. "We both are. Hell, I only made it through one year of college, and your mom didn't go at all. When you graduated from U.C. Davis, well, that might have been the proudest moment of her life."

Because I had a boyfriend, I thought. *Because there was still hope I might lead something vaguely resembling a normal life.*

"I don't know," I said. "It's just - I mean, Mom was prom queen."

"And you skipped prom to study," he said, chuckling. "That doesn't mean you're adopted."

I shrugged. My mom *sobbed* when I missed the prom. She bought me a dress and booked me a makeover, even after I'd told her I wasn't going. When I got a perfect score on all my AP exams, she sniffed and told me I'd have done just as well even if I had gone to prom.

"And I'm sorry about Doug," he said. "But to be honest, I always thought you could do better."

I laughed over my tea. "Dad, I thought you loved

Doug!"

My dad smiled at me in the yellow glow of the kitchen light. "Honey," he said, "I love you." Then he stood, stretched, and kissed the top of my head. I heard the sliding glass door open and close behind me.

I sat in the garden for a long time after my dad went inside, listening to the small, hidden animals rustle branches in the yard, trying to smell the ocean.

And hoping I wasn't losing my mind.

CHAPTER TWO

One month earlier, I'd been in Chicago. In November.

And November in Chicago was abysmal.

The sun rose late and set early and, even when it was shining, the light came at an odd angle, always directly in my eyes. I knew Chicago would be cold, but the wind off Lake Michigan was violently so, pulling my breath away when I opened the heavy, oak doors of Swift Hall, slicing through my clothes when I walked home in full darkness at six in the evening. Even the University itself, with its soaring gothic spires and gargoyles, its dark wood paneling and stained glass windows, the University that felt like such an adventure in sunny September, was now dark and foreboding.

I tried to focus on the life of the mind. I did. But the darkness bothered me, and the cold bothered me, and the curling, shriveling, brown leaves gusting and swirling around my feet bothered me. I felt like the entire world was dying.

I kicked a pile of dead leaves out of my way as I walked into the long shadow of the library. The University's library is an enormous, aggressively ugly concrete block, like a prison, built over what used to be the football field. It's horribly out of place among the spires and gargoyles, and lately I'd begun to resent the entire building. *I requested those books in September, for fuck's sake,* I thought, *and they still haven't arrived.*

A handful of shivering undergraduates stood around a card table outside the library doors, smelling of cigarette smoke and nominally selling a pile of sweatshirts that read, "The University of Chicago: Where Fun Comes to Die." *That's not even funny,* I thought. I pushed open the doors and walked to the Requests desk.

"Yes?" The librarian gave me a stern look, although I'd been here every day for the past two months.

"Any books for Caroline Capello?"

She walked back to the metal shelves. "Oh yes," she said, with brisk efficiency. "Three of them?"

I smiled. November was finally looking up.

* * * * * * *

When I was thirteen, I found a book of Norse mythology in the junior high library. I read it in one night, fascinated by stories of eight-legged horses and serpents circling the world, of Óðinn stealing the mead of poetry from the giants and Thor raining lighting on the trolls. When I returned the book to the library, I knew all the stories by heart.

I brought home the rest of the library's mythology books the next day and, in the weeks after that, I started going to the San Diego public library. Once I'd read everything I could find, I spent a summer teaching myself how to read German to open up a larger world of myths and legends.

My brother told me I'd never have a boyfriend.

"Geoff, don't say that," Mom would yell. It was one of the few things my older brother could do to irritate our mother. "Caroline is so beautiful, when she puts a little effort into it. She'll have plenty of boyfriends to choose from!"

As it turned out, neither of them were right. I never had a plethora of boys to choose from, but I did eventually manage to get one boyfriend before I graduated from UC Davis; Doug McInnes, the philosophy major from San Francisco.

And right now, he was the only part of my life that wasn't going according to my plans.

* * * * * * *

I reached my dull, gray apartment building and hiked

up five flights of stairs to my dull, gray studio apartment. The place was a disaster, as usual; dirty clothes on the floor, dishes stacked in the sink, a tangled ball of mildewing towels outside the door to my closet-sized bathroom. *Tomorrow,* I told myself, *I am totally going to clean this mess.* I shoveled a few dishes off the cheap, fiberboard square that served as both kitchen table and desk, and I pulled the books carefully from my bag.

The Vikings and Their Gods. Being a Recollection of the Pagan Beliefs of the Northmen. And the *Sem Guði Hátíð,* The God's Feast. This was an account of a celebration held for the Norse gods in Svartalfheim, and it had never been translated into English.

I was going to do it. I was going to be the first person to translate it.

All I had to do was teach myself to read Icelandic.

But first I pulled my phone out of my pocket. Doug answered on the fourth ring. "Hey, sweetie," I said.

"Oh, hi Carol," he answered, somewhat less enthusiastically than I might have hoped.

"So, my books came in today," I told him.

"Books?"

"My books. The ones I requested the first week of the quarter."

I could hear static crackling in my ear.

"The God's Feast," I said. "You know, the Icelandic

one."

"Oh, yeah. Well. That's great."

The line hummed and buzzed. I decided to try a different tact. "So," I said, dropping my voice to what I hoped was a low, sexy growl. "What are you wearing?"

"Oh," he said, and there was another pause. "Uh, this isn't a great time, actually. I've got a lot of stuff to get through."

"I see." Actually, it was a relief. Phone sex was not exactly working out for us.

"I'll call you in the morning, okay," he said.

"Yeah. Sounds good." I hung up and glanced over my shoulder at the framed picture of the two of us, smiling at Coronado Beach. Handsome Doug, with his dark, wavy hair and dimpled cheeks, his arm draped around my shoulder.

"The distance won't matter," I told him when I was packing for Chicago. "The important connection is here," I said, my hands on his shoulders, standing on my toes to kiss his forehead.

But it wasn't working out that way, and I couldn't understand what had gone wrong. Suddenly we had nothing to talk about; our conversations were filled with the hiss and buzz of static. When I could get him to answer his phone at all, that was. I sighed and turned away from the picture of Doug's smiling face, all the way in California.

I had work to do.

* * * * * * *

The *Sem Guði Hátíð* was slow going as my two windows rattled in their panes and cold rain streaked the glass. The lights flickered but stayed on; Chicago knew how to handle a storm. The only dictionary I'd managed to find translated Icelandic into French, so I had a second dictionary to translate the French into English. Some of the dictionary entries were supremely unhelpful, offering that the translation for the French preposition "de" could be "of, to, from, by, with, than, at, off," and, under some circumstances, "out of."

There were familiar characters in the *Sem Guði Hátíð*, like Óðinn, Thor, and Loki, but there was also plenty of ambiguity. Haf, for instance. According to my Icelandic-to-French dictionary, this meant "ocean," but was this the actual ocean? Was it the name of the god of the ocean? Or was it meant as a description, an attempt to evoke the vast size of the feast hall? Sometimes I was almost certain I'd understood a full sentence, but mostly it was like feeling my way through an unfamiliar room with the lights turned off.

It was fascinating.

I told myself I'd only work until midnight. When midnight came I made another cup of tea and said I would only work until one in the morning. Now the clock above my tiny half-oven blinked quarter to two, and I ignored it.

"Girnud," I muttered to myself, trying out the words. I rolled them on my tongue, imagining Viking ships and longhouses, imagining woodsmoke, the spray of salt from the ocean.

"Girnud, löngun."

And then I was no longer alone in my apartment.

CHAPTER THREE

There was, perhaps, a crackle of electricity in the air, a quick gust of cold on the back of my neck, like a melting snowflake.

I looked up from the table. There was a very tall man standing in the middle of my apartment. I stood and stumbled backward, bumping awkwardly against the wall. Our eyes met, and my breath caught in my throat. He was unreasonably attractive.

"Uh, hi?" I stammered, staring at his full lips and long, fiery red hair.

He smiled, and my heart surged. *Damn, what a smile.* I fought the insane urge to smile back and tore my eyes off him, glancing at the door to my apartment. It was still closed, bolted, with the chain drawn. *How did...?*

I turned back to him, and he moved a step closer. He wore strange clothes; they looked like leather, black with streaks of gold and red, with an enormous cloak rippling behind him. His fingers were delicate, and his ice-blue eyes seemed to be laughing. He bent toward me, so close our lips were almost touching. So close I could smell him. Woodsmoke. Salt spray. Cold, and leather.

"Hello," he whispered, his breath warm on my neck.

My skin prickled, and I trembled as my body flushed with heat. I swallowed and tried to think. *It's the middle of the night,* I told myself. *And there's a strange man in your apartment.* I turned to face him, my gaze lingering on the soft curves of his full lips, wondering how they would feel -

I shook my head to stop myself. *You should not be thinking about kissing him.*

"What are you - " The words died in my throat as a jolt of recognition surged through my body. *I know you,* I thought. *I've been reading about you since I was thirteen.*

"Loki?" I whispered, my voice sounding very small. "Loki... of the Æsir?"

His eyes danced. "Very good. I am Loki, son of Laufeyiar." He gave me another slow, incendiary smile. "And right now, I'm admiring you."

The room suddenly felt very warm. I took a deep breath. "That's not possible," I whispered.

He tilted his head to one side and raised an eyebrow. "What's not possible?"

Neither of those things are possible, I thought, but before I could say anything he stepped back and his eyes dropped, running slowly along the length of my body, lingering on the swell of my breasts, the curves of my hips. He was lean and muscular under his leather armor. And his armor was very tight, especially around his hips. There was a flush of heat between my legs and I bit my lip, trying to look somewhere else. Anywhere else.

His eyes caught mine, and I had to remind myself to breathe. "Very nice," he whispered.

"You too," I said, before I could stop myself.

Then my mouth went dry as he pulled a blade from somewhere in the depths of his cloak. It glowed blue under my yellow kitchen light. He reached for me with the knife.

I'm going to die, I thought. Then, *This can't possibly be happening.*

I closed my eyes. I heard a small *skritch* and felt another gust of cold air. It didn't hurt. Perhaps dying did not hurt, after all. I opened my eyes and looked down, expecting to see the hilt of the strange, blue blade buried in my abdomen.

I was topless. He'd cut open my shirt, and the tattered remnants hung from my arms. My skin was flushed, my nipples hard.

I looked up. Loki was standing close enough to touch, his head tilted, his eyes sparkling. I flushed with embarrassment and crossed my arms over my chest, trying to pull the shreds of my T-shirt back over my nipples.

Loki moved closer, the blade still in his hand. I closed my eyes again.

"Are you going to kill me?" I asked. My voice sounded small and distant, as if it were coming from far away.

He laughed, and then his mouth was next to my ear. His hair brushed gently against my neck. "Of course not," he whispered. "What fun would that be?"

I felt him cut the drawstring on my sweatpants, and they fell to the floor. Then he touched my wrists, his hands cool and gentle, and my entire body trembled. He pulled my arms away from my breasts, exposing my nipples, my skin flushed with heat. His smell surrounded me; woodsmoke, salt spray. My body hummed under his touch. Loki stepped back, again tilting his head to one side. And he stared at me, his eyes burning.

I've never been very happy with my body. I'm too tall and awkward, I hate my nose, and my breasts are so small my mom keeps buying me bras with an inch of extra padding. But as I stood naked in front of a Norse god, and his eyes traveled the length of my body, devouring me with a hunger I'd never seen before, not even from Doug, I flushed with heat and shivered with arousal, and I felt sexy.

I actually felt sexy.

I watched him as he stared at me. I could trace the lines of his muscles through his leather armor, and I wanted to touch them, wanted to run my hands up his arms, along his chest. I wanted to pull his face to mine, to sink my fingers into his hair, to again feel those cool hands on my skin.

"Yes, very nice," he said, his eyes once again meeting mine. His voice was thicker this time.

I nodded and swallowed, hard. "Thanks," I whispered, frantically trying to think of something clever I could say to him. *You're fucking hot as hell,* I thought, and then I bit my lip again. *Caroline, you cannot say that.*

He took a step closer to me, and I could feel his body, wrapped in leather, inches from my naked skin. I trembled; the inside of my thighs were wet. I hoped he couldn't tell. I hoped he couldn't hear the wild pounding of my heart.

His cool fingers wrapped around my upper arm, and he leaned close to me. I felt the whisper of his hair against my skin, the warmth of his breath on my neck.

"Mortal woman," he said, with a catch in his voice. "I desire you."

It was suddenly very difficult to breath. My head swam with his scent, my body buzzed with his nearness. His face fixed on mine, waiting. The earlier dancing amusement in his eyes vanished, replaced by hunger and need.

I was not a virgin. I'd had sex with Doug, many times, and enjoyed it. But my body had never ached like this for Doug's touch. I had never wanted anything as singularly, as fiercely, as I wanted this tall stranger. Now.

We were only half an inch apart; the space between us vibrated with energy.

I hesitated for another heartbeat before my hips rocked into his, my naked breasts pushed against his soft leather armor, my hands reached up, plunging into his hair. I pulled his face to mine.

Our lips touched and electricity surged through my body. His mouth parted slightly, and I could taste salt on his soft lips. Then his tongue entered me, and heat filled my body as he explored me, his cool hands running down my back, pressing my trembling body against his.

He laughed when we pulled apart, and his eyes sparkled. "I must warn you," he whispered in my ear, his voice now low and thick, "I'll ruin you for all mortal men."

"Oh, please," I gasped. "Please ruin me."

He laughed again, deep and wild, and his shirt disappeared. I pressed my body against his naked chest, my skin burning against him. I could feel the hard length of his cock inside the soft leather of his pants, throbbing against my inner thighs, and I moved my hips against his as he ran long, delicate fingers down my neck. He kissed and then gently bit my ear, and my entire body responded, trembling. *I need him,* I thought, my breath catching in my throat. *I need to feel him –*

He bit my neck, harder, and I cried out, aching for him. Then his pants vanished, and he grabbed me, lifting me by my thighs. He pushed my legs apart with his hips and my knee hit the chair, knocking it over. My head hit the wall, hard, as I arched my back, offering myself to him. He moaned softly as he entered me.

Relief and pleasure crashed through my body as I felt him inside me. I wrapped my legs around his hips. For a heartbeat we were still, my arms around his neck, my legs wrapped around his thighs, his breath fast and shallow on my neck.

Then he began to pull back and thrust against me, my hips banging into the wall, shaking the entire apartment. I clung to him, my body rocked with heat and ecstasy, moaning and gasping. He was inside me, fucking me, and still I wanted him, wanted more of him, wanted to destroy the distance between us, obliterate the distinction between our bodies. I arched my back against the wall, pushing him deeper as his slender hips crashed into me again and again.

My picture frames shattered as they fell from the trembling walls and hit the floor. I realized I was screaming his name, digging my nails into his back as our bodies came together, the space between us collapsing and exploding into fire. My entire body was aflame - it had never been like this before, never, it had *never* -

We came at the same time, like an explosion. The heat of my orgasm burned over me as his head arched back and he cried out, eyes shut, his pale face tilted to the ceiling. I felt his cock spasm inside me, and I pushed my hips into it, my entire body trembling and covered with sweat.

We pulled apart as my feet again found the floor. His scent was intoxicating; the room spun as I leaned against him, gasping for breath. He brought his face to mine and kissed me, a slow, gentle kiss, a kiss that felt like our bodies had known each other forever. Amazingly, I felt heat building between my legs again, although I'd sworn to Doug I could only come once in a day. I moaned into his lips, my nipples growing hard against his cool chest.

"Are you still hungry, mortal?" he growled, his eyes once again dancing with amusement.

I didn't trust myself to speak. He pushed his hips against mine once again, and I could feel him growing hard against the soft skin of my stomach. I gasped, wrapping my arms around his naked body, moving my hands down the smooth muscles of his back to cup the sweet curve of his ass.

He swept me into his arms and carried me across the room to the futon. *This cannot be happening*, whispered some small, still rational part of my mind.

And then Loki spread my legs, and the rational part of my mind disappeared.

* * * * * * *

My head rested on his shoulder as I watched the world grow lighter outside my window. *Now I wake up,* I thought, and my heart clenched.

But I didn't wake. Instead, I shifted onto my pillow as Loki lifted himself to his elbow and looked out the window, where I could just see the bare branches of the sycamore trees, black against the indigo pre-dawn sky. Then he brought my fingers to his mouth, kissing them gently.

"Still hungry?" he asked. His eyes were gentle, his body tired and relaxed. Our legs were intertwined; his skin was cool and smooth against mine.

How many times had we come together that night? Half a dozen? More? Yet my body still trembled when he touched me. "I don't think I can get enough," I said, my voice shaking, embarrassed by my own naked honesty.

He laughed and lay back down, his flaming hair spreading over the mattress, catching the growing light. I felt like he was about to pull me closer, perhaps on top of him again, when an odd, dark look passed over his face, like a cloud obscuring the sun. His brow furrowed, and for a moment he looked old. Very old.

Then he sat up, his body once again formal and rigid. "I apologize," he said. "I am needed elsewhere."

He bent and kissed the top of my head. "Thank you," he whispered. "That was *fun*."

And he was gone.

I fell back into my bed, exhausted.

* * * * * * *

I woke hours later, the bright sun of late morning painted across the ceiling. My phone was ringing, and I was alone in my futon. *It was a dream,* I thought. *Of course it was a dream.* But I lay still a moment longer, ignoring the phone's shrill demands. I'd never had a dream that intense, that real. I could almost conjure his smell; woodsmoke, salt spray, leather. I shook my head to wake myself up and stood, walking across the room. I grabbed my phone from the table and screamed as a red stab of pain went through my foot.

"Carol! Are you okay?" Doug's voice echoed through the phone..

My foot throbbed, and I hopped against the table. "Yeah," I said quickly. "Just stepped on something..."

I leaned against the table and pulled my foot up to find a wedge of broken glass, winking in the sunlight. Dumbly, I looked down. Shards of glass littered the floor, shimmering in the light. Broken glass from the picture frames that fell to the floor last night, as Loki pounded me against the wall.

"Carol?" Doug asked. "Hello?"

There was an uneven pile of clothes next to my upturned chair. I picked up my T-shirt. It was ripped down the middle, a clean, even cut. *Loki's blade*, I thought, my hands shaking. *Loki's blue blade.*

"Hello! Are you okay?"

Some part of my mind noticed a frantic edge creeping into Doug's voice. I put the phone down on the table, held the tattered shirt to my face, and breathed deeply. Then again. No, I wasn't imagining it - the smell of woodsmoke, faint but unmistakable.

I'm losing my mind, I thought.

Doug's voice was still coming from the phone on the table. I picked it up. "Hey," I said.

"What the hell, Carol!" he yelled.

"I can't quite hear you," I said. "I think I'm having some issues with my phone. Call you back, okay?"

I hung up without waiting for his response, picked my way carefully around the broken glass, and plugged in my phone. Then I stared at the pile of books in front of me. I flipped the pages of the largest, a beautifully illustrated version of the *Edda* based on tenth century illuminated manuscripts:

There is one also reckoned among the Æsir whom some call the Lie-smith, the originator of deceits. His name is Loki Laufeyiarson, son of Laufeyiar of Útgarðar. Loki is pleasing and handsome in appearance, very capricious in behavior.

And there was a picture, a woodcutting from the fifteenth century, showing the trickster god in his leather armor, his long, flaming hair, his high, regal cheekbones. His sparkling eyes. It was exactly how he'd looked last night, when he was growling in my ear. When he was thrusting his hips against mine.

I slammed the book closed with a shiver. *I'm losing my mind,* I thought again, and I felt a cold knot in the pit of my stomach.

I took a long shower and examined my body under the fluorescent bathroom light. My upper thighs both had dark bruises the shape of a man's hand with long, delicate fingers, where he'd held me as he pounded me against the wall. I had a large, red circle low on my neck, where he'd bitten me. I traced it gently with my fingertips, and my skin prickled as I flushed with the memory.

I dried off, swept the floor, cleaned up the glass, put the apartment back into some state of order. Then I picked up my ruined clothes, the T-shirt and sweatpants Loki cut from my body. *I should throw these out,* I thought.

But they smell like him.

I stuffed them under my bed, blushing.

CHAPTER FOUR

By Friday morning the bruises had all but disappeared. Only the handprints on my thighs remained. I traced them in the shower. *This is where his hands held me*, I thought, pressing my fingers against the ghosts of the bruises. *His hands -*

You cut your clothes yourself.

I froze in the shower, almost slipping against the wet porcelain. The idea was so sudden, so assured, it felt like it came from some other place, from some other person. I turned off the water and opened the shower curtain, feeling jumpy. I was alone in my bathroom.

I walked to my steamed-over bathroom mirror, putting a hand on the glass to wipe away the condensation. Then I froze. I wiggled my hand slightly, pulling down before I backed away. The handprint in the condensation on my mirror was slightly wider than my own. It had long, delicate fingers.

It matched the bruises.

This means nothing, I told myself, pulling on

sweatpants and lacing up my running shoes. *Nothing.*

Doug was an atheist. He was also a philosopher, so he loved to argue. One of his favorite activities back at UC Davis was finding a true believer and arguing with them. Usually this was my friend Bianca, who eventually stopped going out with us.

His favorite tact was called *What's More Likely?*

"What's more likely?" he'd ask, usually after a couple beers. "There's some huge, invisible, superhuman lurking in the clouds up there, who never gives us any concrete evidence he exists, but still really cares about each and every detail of our meaningless and insignificant lives? Or..." and he'd pause dramatically, sometimes even raising an eyebrow. "People tell stories to make themselves feel better?"

I tried not to get involved in these conversations. "I study the past," I told him. "I don't want to talk about what's really out there, or what isn't."

But as I ran along the Chicago lakeshore, the cold wind biting through my jacket, I couldn't stop playing *What's More Likely?*

What's More Likely: Loki Laufeyiarson, the trickster god of an ancient, pagan culture, somehow actually exists, and somehow actually appeared in my crappy studio apartment - mine! Not some supermodel or movie star! - and fucked me all night long.

Or: I'm lonely. I'm sad. I destroyed my own clothes. I

smacked my own ass hard enough to leave a bruise.

I made it all up.

My breathing fell into a rhythm as my feet hit the pavement, the wind hissing above the gentle susurrus of the waves against the concrete pylons. *What's. More. Likely? What's. More. Likely?*

I slowed to walk the final two blocks back to my apartment, wanting time for my muscles to cool down. And then another question occurred to me: Whom can I tell?

By the time I got back to my apartment I'd decided.

* * * * * * *

Doug answered the phone on the second ring. He sounded out of breath.

"Hey," I said, "I've got to talk. Something really weird happened the other night."

"Oh, hey," he said, and the phone made an odd rustling noise as he adjusted the receiver. I heard a voice in the background. "This is not a great time, actually."

I did the time change in my head. It was just barely seven in the morning in California. "Not a good time?" I asked.

I heard the voice in the background again. It sounded like a woman. It sounded like she said, "Doug..."

"Who the hell is that?" I demanded.

"Roommate," Doug said quickly. "Listen, I'll talk to you later. Soon."

The phone went dead as he hung up.

What's More Likely: My distant, long-distance boyfriend got a new, female roommate, and didn't mention her to me, and for some reason that roommate really wants to have a nice conversation at seven in the morning.

Or: He's cheating on me.

* * * * * * *

Laura turned to me as we filed out of the classroom that afternoon. "You up for dinner tonight?" she asked. "Or are you opening the coffee shop tomorrow?"

Laura was a cheerful Midwestern blonde obsessed with the Puritan witch trials, and my closest friend in Chicago. Actually, she was my only friend in Chicago. "Dinner sounds great," I said.

"You mind if Vance joins us? And I thought I'd invite Debra?"

"That'd be - " I paused, realizing I hadn't actually talked to anyone all week, aside from static-filled pauses on the phone with Doug. Well, that and a wild hallucination involving a Norse god.

"I'd love to see Vance and Debra," I said.

* * * * * * *

When I got back to my apartment I took a deep breath and dialed Doug. He actually answered. "Hey, Carol," he said. "Look, I'm sorry about this morning."

Embarrassingly, I felt tears starting to prick my eyelids. I tried to summon the anger I'd felt this morning. "So, are you going to tell me what the hell's going on?"

There was a long pause. The line hummed and buzzed.

"Are you sure you want to do this now?" he asked. "You'll be back in San Diego in, what, a month? We can do this face to face."

My heart clenched painfully; *What's More Likely* had won another round. He was cheating on me.

"Okay," he said, taking a deep breath. "I'm real sorry about this, Carol."

"Really," I said, automatically.

He took another deep breath. "Yeah. Really. Uh, the distance thing, it's just not -"

He paused. I knew he was waiting for me to say something. I pictured him wrinkling his forehead, running his fingers through his dark, wavy hair.

"You know it's not you, right?" he said. "I mean, you, you're great. Totally. I just-"

My stomach churned. "So you're breaking up with me?"

He said nothing. The line buzzed, softly.

"Uh, yeah, I guess this is - I mean, it's just not -" he stammered.

"Fine," I said. "That's just fine."

Silence.

"I've been seeing someone else, anyway," I said, surprising myself. *He's tall and he's handsome and he's a hallucination,* I thought. *And fuck you, Doug.*

"Oh!" Doug sounded surprised.

I pressed the red "END" button on my cell phone with as much force as I could muster, and I slammed the phone down on my table. Then I picked it up and slammed it down again, my shoulders trembling.

I turned to the wall, saw the picture of me and Doug on the beach, and grabbed it, bringing it down, hard, against my thigh. The cheap wooden frame snapped in half. I pulled out the picture and ripped it to shreds. I went to pull the battery out of my phone, hesitated, and called Laura instead.

"Hey Carol," she said. "Is there a problem with dinner?"

"I just broke up with Doug," I said, hating how thick and trembly my voice sounded.

"Oh! Oh, my gosh! Okay, let's meet at the pub. Right now. Heading there now."

I yanked the battery out of my phone and threw the phone across the apartment.

Fuck you, Doug.

* * * * * * *

The University of Chicago pub is a dive bar in the best sense of the word. It's hidden away in a basement, with no windows and black paint flaking off the concrete walls. It smells like cheap beer and fried food and is always dimly lit, with uncomfortable plastic chairs and peeling vinyl booths.

Laura was already there when I arrived; she gave me a beer first and a hug second. Laura's boyfriend Vance gave me an awkward half-hug, and then Debra arrived, shrugging off her black jacket and releasing an avalanche of blonde curls from her absurd pompom hat, ready to dominate the conversation. Debra is also in the Historical Religions program, but she's a few years ahead of Laura and me. She's studying for her qualifying exams and teaching undergraduates, which means she's got a plethora of hilarious stories about students who can't tell the difference between the ontological argument and the argument from design.

Vance is in the business school; his eyes glazed over pretty quickly, although Laura, Debra and I laughed and laughed. Eventually Vance abandoned any pretense of following our conversation and just stared into the distance, or headed to the bar to refill the beer pitcher whenever it was empty.

"Carol?"

I shook my head and tried to focus on my friends. Everyone was silent. They were all staring at me. My cheeks flushed. I realized I'd been thinking of Loki, remembering how his skin felt cool, even when it was covered with sweat. Even when it was pressed against mine.

"Uh, yeah?" I said.

"Carol," said Debra. "Pardon me for saying this, but I didn't think you'd be so... smiley. Happy. You know."

I waved my hand in the air as I finished my beer to give myself a minute.

"I mean," Debra said, "was this guy just a total asshole, or what?"

Laura gave a shocked laugh, her hand flying up to cover her mouth.

I shook my head. "Not a total asshole. Maybe, like, eighty-five percent an asshole."

Everyone laughed, even Vance, and I lifted the pitcher and refilled all our glasses. "To new beginnings," I said, raising my foaming pint glass with all the dignity I could manage.

"Damn right!" said Debra, and we all clinked pint glasses together over the table, spilling foam everywhere.

I looked at my friends, at Laura who'd only known me for a few months and was ready to drop everything to go out with me, at Vance who was politely putting up with our ridiculous in-jokes, and at Debra, who was patting me on the back and telling me I'm better off without him, even though she'd never even met Doug.

"I love you guys," I said.

"And you're officially drunk," said Vance, bopping my nose with his finger. "Come on, let's get you wild women home."

We walked home together, stopping at Debra's apartment first and then walking to my drab, gray building. I fumbled a bit with the key but got the door open, waving goodnight to my friends. And then I peeled off my clothes, tripped over my jeans, and collapsed on the futon, thinking about his cool, smooth skin, his laughing eyes, his hungry lips pressed against mine...

CHAPTER FIVE

I shook my head, trying to focus on what I was reading. It was the morning of New Year's Eve, my flight to Chicago was delayed, and I'd been in the San Diego airport for an extra three hours. Already. This should have been a great time to finish some of the work I'd ignored over Christmas, but I had trouble focusing. My eyes kept sliding off the page and into the clear, blue sky outside the windows.

I hadn't spoken with Doug since the night we broke up. He'd sent me one email, a faltering "have a nice life" message with a half-hearted offer to meet in Monterey over break, if I wanted. I didn't write back.

I supposed I missed Doug, in a way. I missed the easy excuse of having a boyfriend, the idea that there was someone who cared about me above all others, even if that hadn't actually been the case.

But I missed Loki more. And I hadn't seen him again, either.

Which is a good thing, I reminded myself.

I'd done my research. I spent enough time in the library as it was; it was no trouble to wander into the mental health section and pull out the latest *Diagnostic and Statistical Manual of Mental Disorders.* It's not that difficult to diagnose yourself.

I'd had a full blown hallucination. Auditory, visual. Sensory. I must have tried to convince myself it was real by destroying my clothing, my picture frames. By giving myself bruises. Subconsciously, I must've known Doug was cheating on me. I must have wanted to create... something. Another relationship, something to make myself feel a little better. So I picked a familiar image, probably an image I'd just looked at, and I -

Well, the technical term is "psychotic break." I had a psychotic break. With Loki. It was the only explanation that made any sense.

I didn't seem to be a danger to society or to myself, so I hadn't said anything to anyone, not even Geoff. There could be consequences. I didn't want to leave graduate school, to leave Chicago. I didn't want to end up back here, in San Diego, working for Capello's Landscaping & Tree Surgery, having to explain to my entire family why I wasn't still studying whatever the hell it was they thought I studied in Chicago.

I shivered and stood up, stretching as I stared out the wide airport windows at the pale blue sky. *Time for another cup of coffee,* I thought.

* * * * * * *

My flight touched down just as the sun was setting over Chicago. I sighed as I dragged my suitcase past the steaming lines of idling taxis, bitterly wishing I could afford one. The streets of Hyde Park were cold and dark when the El finally pulling into the station, and I shivered as I walked the six long blocks to my apartment building, my suitcase clattering over the icy sidewalk.

I took a quick shower to thaw out and decided to ring in the New Year catching up on my reading. When the letters on the pages began to blur together, I stood, stretched, and turned to the sink, filling my tea kettle. *Five minutes to midnight,* I thought, glancing at the clock above the oven. *Five minutes to the new year.*

And then I smiled, sat back down, and reached for the *Sem Guði Hátíð.*

Don't do it, I told myself.

"But why the hell not?" I muttered. "It's New Year's Eve. And nothing bad happened the last time."

I opened the book to the first page. "Girnud," I said. My voice wavered, and my skin prickled. I closed my eyes, picturing him. His flaming hair, his dancing eyes. His cool skin.

"Girnud, löngun." His lips pressed to mine. My legs

wrapped around his.

Nothing happened. I heard a distant, muted cheering from the apartment building across the street, and I opened my eyes. My oven's clock read 12:00 in luminescent green.

"Well, shit," I said, slamming the book shut.

It was a long time before I was able to fall asleep on New Year's Eve.

* * * * * * * *

"Caroline," Mom said, her voice wavering over the phone, "I just wanted to let you know Chicago is supposed to get some snow. Maybe even a lot of snow."

"Thanks," I muttered. "I've heard that, actually."

We were two weeks into winter quarter, and every single radio channel was warning Chicago about the impending storm. So was every single television station, and all the newspapers. Even the University was sending out emails announcing that, while they were not about to cancel Friday's classes, they did advise students to "exercise discretion" in their travel arrangements.

I saw my first snowflakes at four in the morning, walking the cold, dark sidewalks of Hyde Park on my way to my opening shift at the Higher Grounds Coffee Shop. They looked rather innocent, singular and crystalline in the faint glow of the streetlights, and they swirled and danced when I pulled open the coffee shop's front door. I stared out the windows as I ground coffee and wiped down the counters, waiting for this apocalyptic snow storm.

And then I saw him. Tall, pale, his orange hair down to his shoulders. His easy, muscular gait. Those long, delicate fingers.

I dropped my broom and ran for the door, pushing it open to a flurry of tiny, cold flakes. The sidewalk was empty.

"Are you okay?" asked Kara, the shift supervisor. We were the only two people in the coffee shop.

"Yeah," I said. "I just thought I saw...." I stopped, realizing how crazy I'd sound. *I just thought I saw a god.*

But my hands trembled, and I couldn't focus. I'd take an order, then stand at the gleaming metal of the espresso machine and completely forget what I was supposed to do. I forgot we charge $4.75 for a medium latte. I dropped a mocha, straight through my fingers, and had to get the mop under Kara's concerned eyes.

"Not my best day," I muttered, and she nodded slowly.

My shift ended at one. I hung up my apron and stared out the window, into the swirl of snowflakes. I thought about just going home. Back to my apartment. Where he might be waiting-

"You have class today?" Kara asked from behind me. I'd heard a rumor Kara was once in the PhD program, and she'd dropped out with a Master's degree to take over the coffee shop. I shuddered.

"Yeah," I said. "I've got Early Puritan Theology."

Kara laughed. "Better you than me," she said as I pulled on my jacket and shouldered my book bag.

* * * * * * * *

I pushed open the door and entered a blizzard.

I couldn't believe how quickly the snow had covered the landscape. I'd seen snow a handful of times since moving to Chicago, but it had always been a little dusting, like a sprinkle of powdered sugar on the sidewalks and cars and trees.

But this was snow, serious snow. The kind of snow we watched on the news in San Diego with horrified fascination. Already the world looked foreign, transformed. And already the snow was deep enough to swallow the tops of my shoes, soaking my feet.

I was shivering by the time I got to the classroom. I gave Laura a half-hearted wave, sat in the front row, and tried very hard to look like I was even the slightest bit interested in Early Puritan Theology with the world's foremost authority on the Puritans, Professor

Elizabeth Stuart. After twenty minutes, Professor Stuart had already filled two blackboards with names, dates, and words like *eschatology*, and I knew she was just getting started. I sighed and looked back at my notebook, trying to keep up.

And then I felt something, like a gust of wind on the back of my neck. Or a melting snowflake. I turned to the window, my heart suddenly hammering. Loki was standing in the quad, in the middle of the blizzard. He looked through the window, right at me. Smiling, he raised a finger.

Come.

"...you okay?" whispered Laura. She'd put her hand on my arm. The room suddenly seemed very hot.

"Fine," I whispered.

I looked out the window again. Loki was still there, wearing a long, black jacket over a charcoal gray suit, his red hair pulled back. A blonde in a red peacoat stumbled as she walked past him, then turned around to look at him again. I felt a hot stab of jealousy and shoved my notebook in my bag.

Professor Stuart stopped in mid-sentence when I stood. I mumbled an excuse, then I was running through the hall, running down the stairs. *He'll be gone, he'll be gone, he'll be gone,* I thought, my heart pounding in my mouth. I pushed through the heavy oak doors, down the steps to the sidewalk.

He was there.

He smiled at me, his eyes laughing. I slowed down, my breath catching in my throat, feeling suddenly hesitant. The snow swirled around his lean body, his pale face. He offered me his hand and I took it, feeling the warmth of his jacket as he pulled me into his arms, the cool of his fingers as he touched my chin.

"Hello, mortal woman," he said.

I opened my mouth and found I couldn't speak. Relief flooded my body, relief and the slow burn of arousal. *He's real,* I thought. *He's real, and he's here. In my arms.* I pulled his face to mine and kissed him, tasting salt and woodsmoke, the snow swirling around us. When I gasped and pulled away, his teeth closed around my bottom lip, delicately, pulling me back to him. I sighed and surrendered to him, his lips pressed hard against mine, my hands tight around his waist.

When I opened my eyes we were back in my apartment. There were snowflakes in Loki's hair, melting in the warmth.

"Nice to see you again, Loki of the Æsir," I said, breathless.

"Likewise," he said, and then his hands were in my hair, and his lips were on my neck.

He pushed open my jacket, running his hands along my waist and up my back. My body came alive under his touch. My nipples pushed against my bra, and my hips rocked into his. I moaned when we pulled apart and then yanked off my jacket, fumbling to pull my shirt and bra over my head. Then I wrapped my arms around his hips and stepped backward, pulling him to the futon.

He raised an eyebrow. "You're in quite a rush," he said.

I laughed. It was so damn good to see him again, to feel his body against mine, to taste the salt of his lips. "I thought - " I said, and then I stopped, not entirely certain what I was going to say. *I thought I'd never see you again.*

I thought I was psychotic.

"Just kiss me," I said, pulling him down to the futon.

He smiled as he climbed on top of me, straddling my hips, wrapping his hands around my wrists and pinning me to the mattress. He pushed his lips against mine and kissed me, deeply, for a long time, our mouths locked together, his body pressed on top of mine, my nipples hard against his cool leather armor. Then he started to move his hips above me, and I moaned, straining against him. He bent to run his cool tongue along my neck. I cried out, arching my back against his body. He did not release my wrists.

"What do you want?" he growled, his hips undulating on top of mine, his teeth tracing the curve of my collarbone.

"I want you," I gasped, lifting my hips to meet his.

He leaned back, releasing my wrists, and stood above me. My hands fumbled with the button on my jeans, ripped the zipper apart, pushed them down over my thighs and to the floor. Loki crawled over me again, laughing low in his throat.

"What do you want, mortal woman?" he whispered, his voice thick, his cool fingers tracing my inner thigh.

"You," I growled, reaching for his neck, pulling his lips to mine.

He kissed me, hard and deep, and then he laughed again, pulling my legs apart and thrusting inside me. It happened so quickly I cried out. And then he leaned over me again, grabbing my wrists, pinning me once more to the mattress. He lowered his head to my chest, his cool tongue circling my breasts, sucking on my nipples. I moaned, arching my back against him, pushing my hips against his, driving my head back into the mattress.

There was a crack like an explosion, and the mattress dropped from under my head. *We just broke the bed,* I thought, dimly.

Loki sat up, releasing my wrists. "Are you - "

I grabbed his hips. "Don't stop!" I cried.

He leaned over me again, his breath fast and shallow. His hips moved against mine, and I wrapped my legs around his, pulling him into me. I arched my back to meet his rhythm, my hands grasping at the sheets.

"Don't stop, don't stop," I moaned as the room began to spin.

He did not stop. I closed my eyes as my orgasm crashed over me, and I cried his name as ecstasy filled my body, obliterating thought.

I collapsed against the mattress as my orgasm ebbed, and I opened my eyes to see Loki above me, panting. He gave me a wicked smile, and then he started to move his hips against mine. I was so sensitive I flinched as he rubbed against me.

"Ohhhhh," I moaned and writhed under him, trying to turn my hips. "Loki, I just - I can't again - "

He stopped my words with his lips, kissing me hard, his hungry mouth pressed to mine as his hips circled, slowly and delicately, against me.

He pulled back and brought his lips to my neck. "I'm not done with you," he growled.

I gasped as his hips pushed into me, the pressure and movement somehow starting to feel... *good*. Really good. My body flushed with heat, again, as he moved inside me, his breath shallow. In the pale snow-filtered light I could see sweat beading on his forehead. My hips began to rock with his, my body rising and falling against him. I moaned again, reaching for him, grabbing his thighs.

"Don't - stop -" I panted, and then my body began to tremble and I could no longer speak.

He laughed as his body danced with mine, first slowly

and then faster and faster, until we were crashing together, and I moaned and trembled beneath him, beyond speaking, beyond thought, filled only with his smell, his touch, the heat and fire of woodsmoke and salt. My eyes closed and my head tilted back as I came again, flooding with pleasure, every muscle in my body firing. Above me, Loki stopped holding back; his hips slammed into mine, and I heard the sound of splintering wood as he cried out.

Then I felt the weight of his body on top of mine, heard his ragged breathing against my neck. I wrapped my arms around him, shaking, until the room stopped spinning.

"Mortal woman," he panted, slowly, "I believe we have destroyed your bed."

I blinked open my eyes, slowly becoming aware of my body again. My torso was on the ground, my legs raised, and something was stabbing me in the ribs.

"Oh, ouch," I said.

I tried sit up, slipped, and fell backwards. He caught me and helped me climb off the mattress. My legs trembled as I stood. The wooden slats of the futon frame were completely destroyed, and they'd been pushed apart as we'd forced the mattress to the floor. The sheets were a tangled mess above the crumpled mattress, the splintered wood.

I smiled, then laughed, and then he was laughing too,

his voice wild and ringing.

"Wow," I said. "I had no idea that was even possible."

Loki wrapped his arms around me, kissing the top of my head. "Allow me," he said, and he walked to the ruined mess of my futon, pulling the mattress to the middle of the floor. He gestured to the mattress, and I sat down, my legs still trembling. Then he piled the shattered frame against my bookcase. I watched him in the fading evening light. His naked, muscular body was so elegant, so graceful.

He is real, I thought. *I couldn't possibly imagine this.*

I watched as he bent to pick up the last broken shard of the frame and felt a rush of heat between my legs. *And I cannot possibly be horny again,* I thought, but then he turned to me and smiled, and my breath caught in my throat.

Without speaking, he sat down next to me and began to run his cool fingers along my arms, my shoulders. I reached for him, tracing the muscles in his arms, running my fingers along his chest. I felt his pulse quicken when my fingers reached his neck. Then he brought his lips to mine, his breath coming short and fast.

I couldn't possibly imagine this.

CHAPTER SIX

I woke to sunlight on my ceiling, and I rolled over to find I was on the futon mattress on the floor, staring at the broken wood of the frame piled against my bookcase. *Holy shit,* I thought. *Did that actually happen?*

"Good morning," Loki said from behind me.

I turned to see him sitting on the floor, leaning against my dresser, reading my copy of *Theorizing Myth.*

"You... spent the night?" I blushed as I looked around my grubby studio apartment in the morning light. It wasn't exactly fit for a god.

"Of course," he said, sounding amused.

"Can I, uh, make you some coffee?" I asked, running my fingers through my hair, wondering how I looked. I was painfully aware that my entire kitchen contained only coffee, half a box of Hot Pockets, and some instant oatmeal. Plain instant oatmeal. *No food to offer,* I thought. *I'm a failure as an Italian.*

"I'm fine," he said, with a smile. "The storm is over. Would you care to walk together?"

I stretched and rubbed my eyes. "I'd love to."

* * * * * * *

Loki offered me his arm as we left my apartment building, and I took it, savoring the warmth of his black jacket, the solid strength of his body against mine.

Hyde Park, Chicago was utterly transformed. The cars along the street were miniature uniform mountains, the sidewalk a frozen undulation of drifts, the trees shifting patterns of white and black. Some of the drifts came up to my knees, and I laughed as my feet broke through the surface crust and I sank deep into the snowbanks.

"No wonder snow is such a powerful symbol," I said, leaning against Loki's arm to pull myself out of a drift.

His eyes danced as he held my hand. "Is snow a symbol, then?"

"Well, of course. I mean, most commonly for death, but you've also got purity, aging, the dulling of youthful passions. And don't even get me started on James Joyce - " I brought my hand to my lips as I realized how impossibly nerdy I sounded. *And this is why you never have a boyfriend,* I thought, heat rushing to my cheeks.

"Sorry," I muttered. "Never mind."

"No, please," he said, smiling. "I happen to enjoy James Joyce."

I stared at him, unsure if he was joking. Doug used to joke like that; he called it *Being Ironic.*

Loki turned to me and raised an eyebrow. "Renewal," he said. "For snow, as a symbol. And memory, especially for Joyce."

I sighed and relaxed against his arm, smiling. "Yeah. Renewal. Look at it - the entire world is renewed."

We walked together, arm in arm, talking about symbols and literature, until we were almost to the lakeshore. The wind was growing stronger when he stopped, abruptly, and his eyes went dark.

"I must take my leave," he said. He bent to kiss me, and he whispered, "Thank you."

Then he disappeared.

One minute I was leaning against him, my arm wrapped around his; the next I was alone, watching snow swirl in the space where he'd been standing. I shivered and rubbed my eyes, looking back at our tracks in the snow. There were two sets, my smaller footsteps, his larger ones. I stared at them as the wind increased, bringing sharp, biting snowflakes to fill in the prints. *In an hour they'll be gone*, I thought.

I fumbled in my pocket for my cell phone. My hands trembled as I turned my phone to the footprints, snapping pictures. *Proof.*

By the time I made it back to my apartment, shivering in the growing wind, the sidewalk had been plowed; our footprints had disappeared. I took a long, hot shower, trying to thaw my frozen feet. And then I flipped through my cell phone's photographs, my hair wrapped in a towel.

The pictures were blurry, indistinct. I could see vague gray indentations in the white snow, but they could have been anyone's footprints. *These could be anything,* I thought, slamming the phone down on my desk. *Stupid.*

I took a deep breath and turned to my demolished futon frame.

It took me four trips down the service elevator to get rid of the frame, which looked like it had broken in at least three places. It should have been irritating, dragging the splintered wood through the building, but I couldn't help being just a bit proud of myself. Of us.

Still, my pathetic apartment looked even more pathetic when I was finished. Just a table with one lone chair, a dresser, a bookcase that was already jammed completely full, and a hand-me-down futon mattress on the floor.

Is this how you entertain Loki Laufeyiarson of the Æsir?

And then I decided my translation work could go fuck itself today. I was going to buy a proper bed.

* * * * * * * *

I Googled "mattress store Chicago" and got about ten thousand results. Then I tried to find one I could get to without a car, and without too much hassle. Finally I pulled on my jacket and headed out.

The wind was bitter, the gusting snowflakes abrasive against exposed skin. The freshly plowed sidewalks sparkled with salt crystals. Chicago is used to snow. The storm dumped about a foot, but that's hardly enough to shut down the city, and the El was still packed with people heading downtown.

The two blocks between the El station and the Mattress World outlet seemed like a long walk. I felt slightly ridiculous, trudging through the first snowstorm of the year to buy a mattress, and I started to wish I'd brought someone with me. Laura, perhaps.

A bell jingled above the glass doors of Mattress World as I entered. The place appeared to be abandoned. I stood for a minute, shifting my weight on my frozen toes, and then a woman in an aggressively pink business suit appeared from the back.

"How can I help you today?" she asked, walking toward me. She appeared to be about my age, although it was hard to tell with all the makeup. She had perfectly manicured hair and an intimidatingly bright smile. Her nametag read: JOELLE *How May I Help You?*

"I'm, um, here for a mattress," I said, looking around the store. It was pretty clear they only sold mattresses. I wasn't sure what she was expecting me to say.

"Oh, you've come to the right place," she said. "What are you looking for?"

I had no idea. "I'm just, uh, moving in with my boyfriend," I lied.

"Ohhhh!" Her eyes lit up, and she gave me a sly sort of wink. "Well, congratulations! So, is he a big guy? You looking for a king?"

I could feel my cheeks burning. "He's, uh -" *Possibly imaginary*, I thought. "Sort of... tall?"

"Well, usually it's best to have both partners come in to test out mattresses," she said, walking toward the front of the store. I followed her.

"You want to pick out some favorites and come back together to try them out?"

"No," I said, my cheeks still flushed. "He's, uh, out of town at the moment."

"Well," she said, gesturing expansively over the first mattress in the window, "try this. This model is really top of the line, over 900 coils in here with a gel memory foam core. And it's got patented Active Edge Technology, to keep it firm over years of use."

I looked at the mattress. It looked exactly like every

other mattresses I'd ever seen.

"Try it out," Joelle urged. "Lie down like you do at home."

I sat on the edge of the mattress, feeling uncomfortable. Then I slipped out of my shoes, noticed I was wearing one green Christmas sock and one white snowflake sock, and felt even more uncomfortable. "It's great," I said. "Springy."

"Lie down," Joelle said, tapping the mattress with her bright pink fingernails. "Get comfortable. Like with your boyfriend."

I kicked my legs onto the mattress and lay down, my hands on my chest. I imagined Loki pinning my wrists to the mattress, kneeling on top of me, biting my neck. *What do you want?*

"This one's great," I said, sitting up.

"Oh, no," said Joelle, shaking her head. I got the sense she was really enjoying this. "Get comfortable! Just like you do at home."

I rolled onto my side, bringing my arm under my head. Joelle sat down on the other side.

"So, how's your boyfriend sleep?" she asked. "Is he a side sleeper, a back sleeper?" Then she lowered her voice, and winked at me again. "A stomach sleeper?"

He doesn't sleep, I thought. *He just sits there and reads. Unless he vanishes into thin air.* I sat up, kicked my feet off the mattress, and slipped my shoes on. "I'll get this one."

Joelle's eyes lit up. "Well," she said, "are you sure about that? Because if you're sure, if this is really the one, I can offer you a special deal. Some special financing. Just for today."

By the time it dawned on me to ask how much a mattress and frame could possibly cost, it was too late.

* * * * * * *

I leaned against the clattering metal walls of the El's blue line, watching snowy Chicago flash past the windows, and trying to justify my insane decision to buy the world's most expensive king size bed.

I do need a bed, I thought. And it was a comfortable mattress. Plus I got a coupon for 20% off bedding from Bed, Bath & Beyond, and the sheets with the rosebud pattern were damn cute.

I sighed and rested my forehead against the cold glass at the El rattled toward Hyde Park. *I'm going to be paying this off for at least a decade.*

There was a liquor store halfway between the El stop and my apartment, a fancy liquor store decorated with sparkling white Christmas lights and advertisements for Cotes du Rhône wine and Bombay Sapphire gin. The sun was just setting as I walked past their windows with my Bed, Bath & Beyond bag of king-sized sheets, and I noticed something I'd missed before. In the bottom of the window was a sign pretending to be parchment, reading "Mead: Drink of the Gods!" I walked in, pulled two bottles off the shelf, and went to stand in the checkout line.

You broke the futon yourself.

I almost jumped. The voice was so confident, with such authority, that I turned to see if someone had spoken to me. There was no one else in the aisle.

You broke the futon yourself, and you're going to drink these bottles. By. Yourself.

"You need anything else?"

"Excuse me?" I said, startled.

The cashier had a shaved head and arms full of intricate tattoos. He looked bored. "The mead. Is that it?"

"Uh, yeah, please," I said, fumbling with my bags to get to my purse. "Is this a good, um, brand?" I asked. "Of mead?"

He shrugged, putting my two bottles in a paper bag. "Never tried it."

As I walked home, juggling bags of sheets and mead, my brain started up another round of *What's More Likely?*

What's More Likely: Loki the Trickster God of Asgard is real, he decided to swing by my apartment a second time, and then, after a night of amazing, bed-breaking sex, we had a romantic walk in the snow and a nice conversation about our favorite books?

Or: I just had another psychotic break.

* * * * * * *

The mattress was delivered four days later. The snowstorm messed up their same-day-delivery, Joelle explained apologetically over the course of several phone calls, and then the delivery van got lost in the streets of Hyde Park.

I was dreading the delivery, convinced it would be horribly embarrassing. But when the van finally arrived, I opened the door to the service elevator, and the two sturdy men carrying the mattress hardly said a word. They took my beaten-up futon mattress from the floor, assembled the bed frame with silent, bored efficiency, and brought up the box springs and mattress in under ten minutes.

"Thanks," I told them, fumbling as I handed them each a twenty dollar bill. I really hoped that was an appropriate amount to tip for a mattress delivery.

"You take care, now," the older, larger man told me, his eyes already focused on their van, which was blocking a lane of traffic, its blinker lights flashing in the gathering darkness.

I went back to my apartment and opened the door.

The new bed dominated the entire room. I put the rosebud sheets on slowly, feeling embarrassed. Then I took off my shoes and sat down in the middle of the bed.

It's a big bed for one person, I thought.

"But you are coming back?" I asked the empty room.

The room did not respond.

"You'd tell me if you weren't coming back, right?"

My voice echoed off the walls. I looked at the two bottles of mead on my kitchen counter, and my stomach sank. *I'll be drinking them alone,* I thought. *Or they'll sit on my kitchen counter for years, gathering dust next to my stupid new bed.* I stood up, grabbed my book bag, and headed to the library.

I had work to do.

CHAPTER SEVEN

My entire body shivered as I was falling asleep, as if I were pushing through a sheet of cold water. And then I blinked open my eyes, and I was in a forest.

Not a scrubby little stand of oak and elm, like the nature preserves outside Chicago. Not the sunny pine forests of the Laguna Mountains outside San Diego. No, I was in a true forest, a dark, misty, Germanic forest, dense with the looming pillars of trees. The air was cold; the ground was wet against my bare feet.

The forest was silent. I could hear my breathing, my heartbeat. There was a white fog rising from the earth, hovering around my knees and hips. *It smells like him*, I thought. Somewhere in the cold mist was a hint of woodsmoke, of salt spray. Of sex. I walked through the massive tree trunks, my legs making the white mist swirl and dance.

And I found Loki.

His back was turned toward me, his eyes fixed on

something in one of the trees. I followed his gaze and saw an enormous black squirrel nestled in the crook of a branch. The squirrel looked at me, blinked, and fled up the trunk.

Loki turned, his mouth opening as he saw me. "What are you doing here?" he asked, his eyes wide in the misty half-light.

"Kissing you," I said, and then I wrapped my arms around his neck, my fingers winding through his hair. His breath was warm against me; his hands moved along my back and thighs.

I pressed my lips to his, and his mouth opened to me. I ran my hands down the smooth leather on his chest as his tongue flickered against mine, tentatively at first, and then thrusting deeper, his lips hard against mine until we were sharing breaths. When his back straightened and he tried to pull away, I closed my teeth around his bottom lip, softly, and pulled him back to me.

His lips curved into a smile as we came together again. He wrapped his hands around my waist, pulling my body to his. I moaned as our hips connected, feeling the hard length of his cock pressing against my stomach.

"You're a dream," he whispered, his voice low and thick against my neck. "I'm dreaming."

"No, I'm dreaming," I said, smiling against his chest,

trailing my fingers along his hips, searching his pants for the zipper, or the clasp, or the... something. I felt nothing but smooth, unbroken leather. I pushed my hips against his, frustrated, wanting to feel his cool skin against mine.

"Um, I don't know how to take your clothes off," I said, feeling my cheeks flush.

He laughed and picked me up, then laid me down gently on the mossy forest floor. He brought his lips to mine, ran his hands along the length of my trembling body. And then he was naked. The skin of his legs felt so good against mine I gasped, grabbing for his hips. His fingers traced the inside of my thighs. I moaned against him, wrapping my legs around his hips as I brought my hand down to guide him into me.

"Yes," I gasped as I felt the head of his cock pushing against me. "Oh, I want you!"

"Do you now?" he panted.

I rocked my hips against his, but he moved his cock tantalizingly, so it was just outside of me. My body was trembling, aching for him. "Just fuck me," I growled, and he laughed above me.

"You're always in such a rush," he whispered, his fingers plunging through my hair.

He entered me slowly, holding his breath. Then he was moving inside me, moving with agonizingly sweet slowness, and then all that mattered, all that mattered in the world, was his mouth, his hands on my body, his hips rocking against mine.

Gradually the wet, cold moss of the forest floor faded away, became warm and dry. The misty gloom of the forest became darkness, became the distant sodium glow of streetlights through my windows. I shivered once, shivered with my entire body, and then I was in my own bed, my new bed, with my legs wrapped around Loki's thighs, his breath coming fast and shallow above me.

"Please don't be a dream," I whispered, and I could feel tears biting at the corners of my eyes.

He moaned above me, bending to take my nipple into his lips. I arched my back against his cool mouth, gasping as I ran my fingers over his shoulders, my hips moving with his, heat and pleasure rocking through me in waves. And then his hands wrapped around my hips, and he was crashing into me, hard, crying out. My eyes closed as the room fell away, my body and mind dissolving as ecstasy took me. He collapsed next to me, panting for breath, our bodies curled together, our sweat commingling. I moved my head to rest against his chest, listening to his heartbeat, my head swimming with his salt and woodsmoke scent.

And then I remembered the bottles of mead I'd hidden in the kitchen cabinet. I tried to think of something witty to say, some brilliant, clever way to offer a Norse god mead, but my mind went blank and my stomach twisted painfully.

Don't be so stupid, I chided myself. *You can fuck him but you can't offer him a drink?*

"Loki," I whispered, my voice wavering in the dim half-light of my apartment. "Would you, uh, like something? To drink?"

I felt his chest shudder as he laughed. "That would be lovely," he said.

"I'll, um, I'll have to turn on the light," I warned him, standing and feeling my way to the switch.

The overhead light was blinding.

"Sorry!" I cried, pulling out the mead and grabbing two empty jelly jars for glasses. I turned off the light, twisting off the bottle cap in the dark.

"I hope this is okay," I said, sitting next to him on the bed and handing him a glass. "It's mead."

Loki smiled and raised an eyebrow. He looked especially beautiful in the soft yellow glow of the streetlights outside my window.

"Thank you," he said, taking the glass.

He took a sip, coughed, and then laughed. "Oh," he said. "This is..."

I tried it myself and gagged. It tasted like sour rubbing alcohol with a hint of honey. "Ugh, that's terrible!" I said. "Is that what it's supposed to taste like?"

He laughed again, putting his glass down on the window sill. "Not quite," he said.

And then the space in front of me was empty. Loki was gone. *Well, shit,* I thought. *That was an unqualified disaster.* I felt my eyes prickle with tears, and I blinked furiously.

There was a momentary crackle of electricity and the air thickened somewhat as he re-appeared, sitting in front of me, his outstretched hand holding a goblet. "Here," he said. "This is what it's supposed to taste like."

I tried to wipe my eyes discreetly before I took the cup from his hand. It was made of smooth wood, thick and solid. Loki raised a second goblet in his own hand and brought it to his lips.

This mead was amazing, tingling like champagne, dry with a subtle sweetness. It was like drinking sunlight. "Wow," I said. "How did you...?"

Loki waved his hand dismissively in the half-light. "Oh, I have many talents."

I blushed, embarrassed by my sad little apartment, my stupid attempt to impress him. "I'm sorry," I said.

We both fell silent. It was not an entirely comfortable silence, and I was surprised that I could feel this shy in front of him, shy after sharing so much of my body.

"Woman," he said, abruptly, "may I ask you a question?"

"Of course."

"How did you find me tonight?"

I shrugged, taking another sip of mead. It lingered on my tongue, warm and sweet. "I don't know," I said. "It was a dream. It's not like I was -"

And then I stopped. It wouldn't be exactly true to say I *wasn't* looking for him. Ever since that first night, I was constantly looking for him.

"Maybe I was... looking for you," I whispered, glad the darkness hid my burning cheeks. "But it was a dream. You don't control what happens in dreams."

He was silent for a moment, and then he took my hand and brought it to his lips, kissing my fingers, sending a delicate shiver of electricity through my body. "Perhaps it was me," he said, his voice low. "Maybe I wanted to be found."

He turned to look out the windows, his eyes dark. The silence stretched between us, and I found myself remembering Doug, remembering the static that buzzed and hummed on my cell phone when we tried to talk.

"Loki," I said, my voice hesitant. "I have a question as well."

"Please."

"If this is. If you," I took a deep breath. "If you aren't coming back. I mean, if you don't want to do this. Again. Will you tell me?"

He turned to me and smiled. The smile didn't quite reach his eyes. "Yes," he said, his voice soft. "If I tire of you, I will tell you."

There, I thought, *you've negotiated with your own delusion.*

But at least he was smiling now. I smiled too, feeling the muscles in my shoulders relax. "So this is...Midgard," I said, running my fingers over the smooth, golden rim of my goblet, wanting to keep him smiling. "And you come from..." I hesitated. It just sounded so *crazy.*

"Asgard," he said, gently.

"So there really are Nine Realms? Are they... different planets?"

Loki laughed. "You mortals love to count things. You love to put names on them. As if that somehow led to understanding."

"So there aren't nine of them?" I asked. "Or they aren't planets?"

He smiled at me and shrugged his shoulders.

"Fine," I said, feeling slightly annoyed. "You don't have to tell me."

Loki took a sip of his mead and gestured out the window. "What do you see?" he asked.

I saw the darkened windows of the brick apartment building across the street. I saw the streetlight against the bare branches of the sycamore tree, their pale bark folding like skin. "The branches?" I asked.

He nodded. "Now, what are they? Is each branch one world, or are they all part of the same tree?"

I shook my head. "But Asgard isn't a part of this world. I mean, you can't walk there..." I trailed off, looking at Loki.

He laughed again. "Of course you can walk there," he said, his eyes sparkling. "If you know where to walk."

"But it's not on a map," I insisted.

"The realms overlap," he said. "Maybe not as much as they once did. But we're all part of the same World Tree."

"Yggdrasil," I said. "The World Tree. That's a... a metaphor for social structure."

Loki laughed again. "No, it's a *tree*," he said. "It's an ash tree."

I was absolutely lost.

"Here," he said, putting down his goblet and leaning close to me. "I'll show you."

His lips touched mine, soft and cool, and my mouth parted for him. I could taste the honey mead on his lips and tongue as he entered my mouth, lingering. I tilted my head and his tongue moved further into me, slowly and delicately. I felt the world around me dropping away, my entire being focused on his soft lips, his urgent tongue.

I gasped when he pulled away. Slowly, the world

came back into focus. He raised his hand to brush my cheek.

"There," he said, with a small catch in his voice. "We're two separate people, sharing the same space. And when I'm inside of you... well, where do you end and I begin?"

"We... overlap," I said, and he smiled.

"Show me again," I said, leaning toward him.

* * * * * * * *

I woke to bright sunlight. I was alone in my vast, new bed. It still smelled like him. I pulled the sheets to my face, burying my head in them. Woodsmoke. Salt. Leather. I sighed, hugging the sheets. And then I had the very distinct feeling I was being watched. I sat up in bed, the blankets falling off my shoulders, and looked out the window.

There was an enormous black squirrel staring at me from the sycamore branch just outside my window. *And is each branch one world, or are they all part of the tree?* I thought, smiling to myself. The squirrel tilted his head to one side.

"Shooo," I said, waving my hand at the window. I stood and walked to the shower, stretching my sore body. Smiling.

CHAPTER EIGHT

"Put some clothes on," Loki said, his eyes dancing.

We were well into our second bottle of wine, lying together on my bed, legs intertwined. The tea candles along my dresser had long ago sputtered and flickered out, and the radio was playing low, smoky jazz. The clock above my half-oven said it was just past one in the morning, but I didn't feel much like sleeping with Loki's body against mine, humming with electricity.

I am hallucinating, I thought. *I'm alone in my bed, and insane.*

"Excuse me?" I asked.

"Clothes," he said again. "Put some on."

"Something warm?" Chicago hadn't gotten above freezing in two weeks, and I could feel the cold seeping in through my windows.

"No," he said, running his fingers along the sensitive skin on the back of my neck. "Something sexy."

I don't even care, I thought, as a shiver of pleasure ran the length my body. *If this is what it means to be insane. I. Don't. Even. Care.*

"Sexy," I muttered, getting out of bed and opening my closet. I didn't have much in the way of sexy. I finally settled on a short, red cotton dress. It was meant for the beach, the kind of thing you pull on over a bikini, casual and comfortable, but it was very short, and I liked how it hugged my curves.

"What do you think?" I asked.

"Shoes," he said. He was now wearing a dark, expensive suit, cut to cling to his lean, muscular curves. Somehow, the suit screamed *sexy* even more than his naked body.

It took me a few minutes of digging to find my lone pair of heels. I pulled them on. Then I turned to Loki and raised an eyebrow.

He walked to me, wrapped an arm around my waist -

- and we were surrounded by a crush of people, in near darkness, engulfed by swirling cigarette smoke and the heavy thud of trance music. I could feel the beat in my bones. Lasers shot through the gloom overhead. Bodies shuddered and swirled and throbbed around us, and Loki pressed against me, his hands moving down my back.

"Where are we?" I shouted to be heard over the music.

"One of my favorites," he said, his mouth against my ear.

I tilted my head, looking around. In the darkness the room seemed to go on forever. "But where?" I said again.

"Does it matter?" he shouted over the music.

I thought for a minute, my body pressed against his, our hips swaying together. I could just barely smell him over the cigarettes and perfume and sweat and alcohol, just a hint of woodsmoke.

"No," I yelled to him, closing my eyes. "It doesn't matter."

He bent to kiss me, our bodies one small island in the enormous dance floor. "Berlin," he said when we pulled apart. "Willkommen."

I laughed, not sure if he was joking, not sure if I cared either way. And then there was a drink in my hand, something fizzing and sweet on my tongue that burned my throat. The music thudded and pounded, Loki's hands moved over my body, and we danced.

* * * * * * *

"You look rough," Kara said.

It was five in the morning, and the two of us were opening the coffee shop. The sky outside was an angry, bruised violet, the last of the stars just fading from view.

I nodded. "There is not enough caffeine in the world," I said, making myself another espresso.

By the time Loki and I re-appeared in my apartment the room was beginning to lighten with the rising sun. I still smelled like Berlin cigarette smoke, and my lips still tasted like him. I hadn't even had time to shower.

"Were you... studying last night?" she asked slowly.

Nope, I thought. *I was in a German nightclub with a Norse god.*

"Yeah, of course," I said, forcing a laugh. "What else would I be doing?"

I turned as the bell above the door jingled and our first customer, Dr. Elbert, walked in. But I didn't turn quickly enough to miss Kara giving me a very strange, measured look. I was pretty sure Kara thought I was insane.

Maybe she was right.

* * * * * * *

Laura came in the coffee shop around ten. By then I'd had so much espresso my fingertips were shaking, but exhaustion still pressed down on me like a weight. Five more hours stood between me and collapsing in my bed.

"Wow," Laura said, her Midwestern accent flat and friendly as the dawn. "Rough Saturday night?"

I laughed, waving to Kara that I was going to take a

few minutes off.

"You want a mocha, right?" I asked Laura. She nodded and I turned the knobs until the espresso machine shrieked into the silver carafe of skim milk.

Laura and I sat together at a table in the window. She waved her hand in a very strange way as she lifted her mocha. I blinked in the strong sunlight coming through the windows.

"Yeah, I was just working on my translation last night," I lied, running my fingers through my hair.

Laura waved her hand again and I squinted at her.

"What's with the...?" I fluttered my hand.

Laura's bright, happy laugh filled the shop. "Oh my gosh, Carol, look at the ring!"

"Oh!" Of course, there was a diamond ring sparkling on Laura's left hand. "Oh, congratulations! How did it? I mean, when?"

"At Charlie Trotter's," she said, leaning across the table conspiratorially, her smile beaming. "You know I've been wanting to go there for ages, and Vance kept putting it off, but we finally went last night. And he got down on his knees!"

An image appeared in my mind, unbidden. Loki of the Æsir in Charlie Trotter's, kneeling, a ring in his hand. I shook my head. *Now that's insanity.*

Then I squealed, because that's what she seemed to expect, and I hugged her. "I'm so happy for you," I said.

We spent the rest of my break talking about weddings, and then she waved goodbye, the diamond refracting the morning sunshine into a thousand rainbows.

* * * * * * *

It was still dark when my alarm clock started screeching at 4:30 in the morning. I sat up in the darkness, looking around my apartment to see if I was alone. I was. I sighed heavily, whacked the button to turn off my alarm clock, and contemplated falling back into bed. But then I shook my head and dragged myself to the shower. I had bills to pay.

When I got to Higher Grounds, the entire shop was dark. I checked my watch, surprised Kara was running late. But I had a key, so I shrugged, opened the door, and turned on the lights. I sighed again as I walked over to the counter. As usual, the closing crew had done a piss-poor job of shutting the place down. The stack of paper cups near the register was almost depleted, there was still a carafe of cold coffee in the brewer, and the countertop was downright disgusting.

I grabbed a rag and wiped the counter, then turned to empty and wash the carafe. The bell above the door jangled over the sound of running water, and I turned, expecting to see either Kara or Dr. Elbert.

I saw Loki.

I stared at him, stunned. He crossed the room, his long strides graceful, walking around the counter to meet me. He grabbed my arms, pulling my face to his, and he entered me with his tongue, harsh and urgent, his lips hard against mine. I closed my eyes as the rest of the world faded into a haze of woodsmoke and salt spray and the smell of leather, the feel of his cool hands on my shoulders. My body thrummed with electricity, my breath caught in my throat, and I already wanted him, wanted him -

"Now," he said, his voice low and rough in my ear, his breath warm on my skin.

"In here," I panted, pulling him past the counter and into the gloom of the supply closet. I shut and locked the door behind us, then pushed myself against him, pressing my lips to the cool saltiness of his, plunging my fingers through his hair. He was already hard inside his pants, throbbing against my thighs.

Loki ripped at my jeans, his hands fumbling with the button. I helped push them down over my hips, my breathing fast and uneven. I was so ready for him I moaned when he pulled away.

Then he grabbed my thighs and lifted me against the locked door. He hesitated for a heartbeat, rubbing his face along my neck, before he thrust me against the door and entered me, hard. I wrapped my legs around his slender, muscular hips, feeling him deep inside me. He brought his face to mine and our lips pressed together, sharing breaths.

His hips moved slowly at first, generating heat, and then faster as my body began to tremble. My hands grabbed at his back, clinging to his shoulders, my burning skin pressed against his cool body. He felt *so* damn good -

I buried my face in his neck to keep from crying out as my orgasm crashed over me, flooding my body. I clung to him, trembling, as he finished, deliciously sensitive to his final thrusts. I felt the muscles in his neck tighten as his head tilted back; I heard his cry as he came inside me.

My legs trembled as my feet found the ground. "That was... unexpected," I panted. "But wonderful!" I added quickly. "Very, very wonderful."

Loki pulled me into his arms and kissed the top of my head. "Thank you," he whispered.

I expected him to disappear. Instead, he rested his head on mine, and we leaned against each other, catching our breath. I listed to his heartbeat, his breathing. I tried to memorize the feel of his chest against my cheek.

Then he said, softly, "I'm off to magnificent battle."

I pulled back, tilting my head to look at him, but his eyes were clouded and distant. "Stay safe," I whispered, the words immediately sounding stupid, pointless.

He stepped away from me, and I staggered somewhat as I tried to pull on my pants. Then I saw his neck. "Oh, I'm so sorry!" I reached out to trace the red circle on his shoulder, the mark my teeth left on his pale skin.

He tilted his head, smiled, and took a deep breath. "No matter," he said. He brushed his shoulder with his fingers and the mark disappeared.

"Magnificent battle," he said again, his voice low and soft, almost a sigh. His eyes met mine as he vanished, a strange mixture of emotions swirling in their blue depths.

"Be careful," I whispered, but the room was already empty.

* * * * * * *

I finished pulling on my pants and unlocked the door to the supply closet, panting slightly, my mind racing. Magnificent battle? Was that fear or excitement in his eyes?

Kara stood behind the counter, watching me with wide eyes. "What's going on in there?" she asked, peering around me through the open door. "Did you, uh, drop something?"

I tried to act nonchalant, although my legs were still trembling. "Just getting more coffee cups," I said.

My arms were empty. Kara raised an eyebrow at me and then walked away. *Shit,* I thought. *I'm losing my mind at work now.*

But I shouldn't have worried. After that morning in the Higher Grounds stockroom, the hallucinations stopped.

CHAPTER NINE

Springtime. It was the end of the quarter, and the University's main quad was a riot of color: daffodils and tulips, the sticky, electric green of new leaves, the rich, heavy scent of lilacs.

At the end of every quarter, the University of Chicago plasters the campus with posters asking the students to please not kill themselves. This spring's poster featured an aggressively cheerful sunshine with a cartoon speech bubble reading "WE'LL SEE YOU TOMORROW!" The bottom half assured me "Your Life *IS* Worth Living," and it had tear-offs with the telephone number and email for Counseling Services. Almost all the tear-offs were missing, from almost every poster.

I briefly considered what I would say to Counseling Services as I pulled open the library doors and climbed the steps to the Requests desk. *I've been having these vivid hallucinations, psychotic breaks, actually, where I'm visited by a god...*

Really, the counselor would say. She'd probably be overweight, probably wearing glasses. *That's a serious problem.*

No, that's not the problem, I'd explain. *The hallucinations aren't the problem at all. The problem is he stopped showing up.*

I was trying not to keep track, but I hadn't seen Loki for months. Two months. And three days. I hadn't seen him since he surprised me at Higher Grounds during opening shift. Since he kissed me and told me he was off to magnificent battle.

And that's a good thing, I thought. *I'm no longer going psychotic.* But I didn't feel good. I felt like shit. Sleep was impossible. I tossed and turned, arguing with myself. *He did not say he was tired of me,* I'd tell myself. *He's coming back.*

He is literally the god of lies, I'd counter. *He is not coming back.*

Then the cold, distant voice in the back of my mind would speak up: *You invented Loki.*

I knew it was rationality speaking, but that voice made me feel truly insane. Sleeping medications didn't help, at least not the kind you could get over the counter. And for anything prescription strength, I'd have to tell someone what was going on. There was no possible explanation that would make me seem anything less than full-blown crazy.

A week ago I'd tried drinking wine. And wine was even worse than sleeping pills. I'd finished an entire bottle in under an hour, and then I pulled out the clothes he'd cut off my body. When I realized they no longer smelled like him, I'd sobbed and sobbed. Then I'd had to go into Higher Grounds at five in the morning with a pounding headache and a mouth like sandpaper.

Great idea, Caroline. Get drunk alone and cry yourself to sleep. Great. Fucking. Idea.

The only thing that helped was working on my translation of *The Gods' Feast*. I'd climb out of my enormous bed after hours of tossing and turning, watching the numbers flicker past on the clock above the oven, and I'd turn on the lights and open my books. Sometimes I'd even light the tea candles, turn on the radio. It felt like being close to him again, to study the old gods, to read the ancient prose aloud and imagine it coming from his soft, cool lips.

And now even that was over.

I'd been avoiding this for weeks; I couldn't bring myself to stall any longer. I finished my translation almost a month ago. I'd gone over every line, again and again. And then I hesitated for another week, wanting to show it to Loki.

"You mean, wanting another hallucination," I muttered.

"Excuse me?" The librarian raised a stern eyebrow at me.

I cleared my throat, hoping I wasn't blushing. "I'm returning this," I said, pulling the *Sem Guði Hátíð* from my bag. My fingers lingered over the red cloth cover as I placed it on the counter. *I was reading this the first time he appeared,* I thought. *The night we met.*

The librarian grabbed the *Sem Guði Hátíð* with brisk efficiency. "Anything else?" she asked.

"No," I said. "No, that's all." I walked out of the library, blinking in the bright spring sunshine.

* * * * * * *

"This is quite good," Professor Loncovic told me the following afternoon.

I'd just given her my completed translation of *The Gods' Feast.* It was a brutal day, with all the dreary cold of Chicago's winter and all the relentless rain of Chicago's spring.

Professor Loncovic and I sat together in her enormous office on the third floor as sleet pounded against the leaded windows. Her gray hair was piled in a messy bun, and she read my translation with bifocals, the glasses and the shifting, stormy light making her look severe and academic.

My gaze wandered to her soaring ceilings and

haphazardly stacked bookshelves as she leaned forward in her chair, flipping the pages of my translation and occasionally consulting my photocopy of the original. I hadn't realized Icelandic was one of the twenty or so languages she could read, but I wasn't exactly surprised. Professor Loncovic seemed to be an expert about pretty much everything.

"Your translation is so eloquent," she said, finally leaning back in her chair, taking off her bifocals, and meeting my eyes. "Especially for Loki. It makes him seem almost sympathetic."

I nodded, not trusting myself to say anything.

Two weeks later, my analysis of *The Gods' Feast* was accepted for publication by the *Midwestern Journal of Nordic Studies*. I read and re-read the acceptance letter. That night, for the first time since Loki disappeared, I fell asleep instantly.

* * * * * * *

"You're going to be published?" Laura sounded incredulous.

"Well," I said, "it's a pretty small journal, and it won't come out until October."

"Published?" she asked again, her mouth open.

I nodded, smiling. "Looks like I'm not going back to San Diego with my tail between my legs. At least, not yet."

"Well, we have to celebrate," she said. "Let me call Debra. What do you think, tonight or tomorrow?"

I hesitated. I'd spent every night for the past two months and three weeks in my apartment. Not because I was waiting for Loki, specifically, but just in case. Just in case he showed up.

"Oh, no you don't," Laura said, with a wide smile. "You don't get published as a first year graduate student and then go hole up like nothing happened. This is something you *have* to celebrate."

"Fine, fine," I said, waving my hand dismissively. "Tonight?"

* * * * * * * *

Laura, Vance, and Debra met me outside my apartment. It was a beautiful night, one of the first warm nights of the year, and all of Chicago smelled like flowers. We took a taxi downtown, which felt like an extravagant luxury, and everyone bought me drinks. The bars started to blur together, and then it seemed like a very good idea to go somewhere to dance. We found a blues club with no admission fee and stumbled in.

"What do you think?" Laura called to me over the music.

"It's nothing like Berlin," I said, before I could stop

myself.

"Him?" Laura said, giggling and gesturing at something behind me.

I turned to see what she was talking about. A tall blonde in a nice suit caught my eye and gave me an awkward wave. *Cute,* I thought. *But no Æsir.*

But it was too late; Laura was already walking toward him. *Shit,* I thought. My heart started to race as she grabbed his arm and pulled him over to our table.

"This is Mark," she said, rather too loudly, her flat Midwestern accent especially noticeable. "And this is Carol," she said, gesturing to me and spilling a fair amount of her beer on Mark's shoulder. "She's just been published!"

His brow wrinkled above his brown eyes. "Punished?" he asked. "For what?"

Debra and Laura collapsed in fits of laughter.

"Published," I repeated, at a loss for what to say next. Suddenly my translation of a thirteenth century Norse manuscript seemed like the most boring topic of conversation imaginable.

Luckily, the band picked that moment to start playing again, and no one could talk much over the silky, smoky blues swirling through the club. Mark offered to buy me a drink, and I asked for a whiskey, because I'd already had quite a few beers, and nobody drinks mead anymore, and I worried asking for wine would make me seem too high maintenance.

Mark handed me a drink a few minutes later, an oily, dark liquid in a squat, solid glass clinking with ice cubes. It was almost as bad as the mead I'd tried to serve Loki. But I choked it down, and then Mark invited me to the dance floor, and I accepted.

It was no Berlin, but it was dark and loud, and my head was swimming with whiskey, beer, and lonely, longing music. Mark wrapped his arms around my hips, and it felt good to have someone's hungry hands against my body again.

The band stopped at two in the morning. Laura and I were in the bathroom when the live music switched to a CD. "Totally cool if you want to stay," Laura said as we squatted above the filthy toilets to pee. "Cause he's totally hot."

She whistled and dissolved into drunken giggles, but I shook my head.

"Nah, I'll ride home with you," I said. Mark's hands felt good on my hips, and I supposed he was handsome, too. But no.

Mark walked outside with us and I gave him my number, watching as he punched it into his phone. He handed me a business card. Then, just as the taxi pulled up, he grabbed me and kissed me. It was a sloppy kiss; our teeth banged together.

"Damn!" said Debra, once I closed the door.

I saw Vance roll his eyes from the front seat as Laura tried to give me a high five.

"That was a terrible kiss," I said, wiping Mark's drool from my cheek.

"Carol, I will take that number from you," Debra said.

I laughed and waved them off.

* * * * * * * *

Mark called the next day. I ignored my phone, letting it go straight to voicemail.

"Hi Carol, this is Mark..." his message began. "I had a lot of fun dancing with you at Rosa's Lounge, and I'd, uh, really like to see you again."

I deleted it and went for a long run, my feet pounding along the shore of Lake Michigan. *I am not counting,* I thought. *Not counting.*

"Two months," I whispered, watching the waves crash against the concrete pylons. "Two months. Three weeks. Six days."

* * * * * * * *

"So," said Laura, handing me a beer, "did you call Mark back yet?"

Laura and Vance invited me over for a barbeque, and

we were standing around their tiny Weber grill on the concrete patio behind their fire escape. Vance was tending the hamburgers with a level of care bordering on obsessive, dressed, as always, in pressed slacks and a button-up shirt. I wondered idly if that was part of the business school uniform.

I shrugged and took a sip of the beer. Goose Island Summer Ale. It was good. "Nah," I said, trying to sound casual. "I don't think I'm going to."

"Oh my gosh, Carol," she sighed. "How many times has he called you?"

"Twice," I said. *Three, actually. But only two messages. Plus a couple of texts.*

"So why not? He seemed nice."

I shrugged again and started peeling the label off my Goose Island. "I don't know. I'm just not sure I'm ready."

"Ready? You broke up with Doug in, what, November? Seven months ago?"

Three months, I thought. *Three months, four days.* "Yeah, okay," I sighed. "But that kiss. It was really bad."

Laura laughed at me. "Did you have fun with him?" she asked.

"I guess," I shrugged.

"Did you like dancing with him?"

"Yeah," I said, petulantly.

"Call him back," she said. "He can learn how to kiss."

I sighed again and took another sip of my beer, watching the smoke from the grill drift into the sky. It wasn't just that Mark was a bad kisser. It wasn't just that I missed Loki, although I did miss him; I missed him so much I sometimes awoke with tears burning on my cheeks. But my hesitation to see Mark was about more than all that.

It was something Loki said, that first night.

I'll ruin you for all mortal men.

What if that was true?

"Fine," I said. "I *might* call him back. But I'm leaving for San Diego tomorrow morning, so it's not going to be tonight."

Laura laughed again. "Good enough," she said.

* * * * * * *

I stood in my apartment, my bag packed, as the early morning light began to spill across the walls. I had to catch the El soon to make it to O'Hare on time, but still. I walked to my desk, picked up a pen. Put it down again. Walked back to my suitcase.

"I'm going to California," I told the empty room. "For my brother's wedding."

My voice echoed off the walls. I sighed, walked back to my desk. Loki, I wrote. I'm in San Diego. I'll be back Tuesday. Then I grabbed the piece of paper, balled it up, threw it in the trash.

You invented Loki.

I picked up my suitcase again, put my hand on the door. "I'll be back Tuesday," I said. I locked the door behind me and headed down the stairs, out to the empty sidewalk.

CHAPTER TEN

The air in San Diego was warm and soft on my skin as I stepped off the airplane. It felt like I'd traveled to a different planet, a world where the air was always warm and smelled like the ocean. My dad met me in baggage claim, and we drove away from the airport just as the sun set over the Pacific.

"I should warn you," Dad said, patting my knee as he navigated the airport exit, "your mom is a bit... serious... about this wedding."

"I'm sure," I said. "But thanks for the warning."

When we walked in from the garage, my mom was sitting at the kitchen table, which was covered with hundreds of pink ribbons. "Oh, hello, Caroline," she said, standing to embrace me. "You've lost weight," she said, approvingly. "But, honey, you look like something the cat dragged in. I've got us both booked for the spa tomorrow morning, and no complaints. Now, have a seat, and help me tie the ribbons on these programs."

The wedding programs were printed on lush, ivory

paper. My mom was punching two holes in the top of the program and tying a pink bow between the holes. This seemed like an utterly useless thing to do, but I kept my mouth shut, rubbed my eyes, and sat down at the table to tie pink bows. My mom chatted amicably for almost an hour about catering and champagne and how they finally decided - finally! - that the calamari would have been just too much.

It was almost midnight by the time I made it to my room. My bridesmaid's dress was hanging on the back of the door, a strapless, silky, dusky rose evening gown with a slit up the side. *He'd like the dress*, I thought, before I could stop myself. And then I couldn't fall asleep.

I lay awake, staring at the ceiling, until I was ready to scream in frustration. Finally I left my room and walked quietly to the back yard, sliding open the door. I'd brought a copy of my reading for the wedding; Elizabeth Barrett Browning's *Sonnet 43*. Apparently that was Di's favorite. So it would be nice if I could manage to not screw it up in front of over one hundred people at the wedding.

I read the poem until the words started to swim together, and then I turned off the light and sat in the darkness, hugging my knees to my chest. It was a calm, warm night, but the dark leaves of the California ash danced against the indigo sky.

"Must be having a storm where you're from," I told the tree, yawning, as I grabbed the book and headed back to my bedroom.

* * * * * * *

Mom woke me early. "Rise and shine, sweetheart! You've got a full morning at the spa!"

I tried to stifle my groan. I absolutely hated going to the spa. Everything they did hurt - pulling out my eyebrows, pouring hot wax over my privates, sanding down my feet. Even the river stone massages were painful. Mom and I used to argue about this constantly. *Beauty isn't worth it,* I'd tell her. *I'd rather be comfortable.* My mother would look horrified and throw her hands in the air.

I pulled on some jeans and a T-shirt that read, *The University of Chicago: Where the Only Thing That Goes Down on You is Your GPA,* and I stumbled to the kitchen for a cup of coffee. Dad gave me a smile and a discreet thumbs-up from the kitchen table. I smiled back, feeling ragged.

"Now," Mom said, raising a manicured eyebrow in my direction. "Eat something quick, because we're leaving in ten minutes." She took a deep breath, expecting a protest.

"Sounds great," I muttered. Chances are good this

will be the only wedding my mom gets to plan. I'm not going to stand in her way.

Mom spent the drive telling me what she'd arranged at the spa. A full-body scrub of some sort (which would probably be painful), eyebrow threading (also probably painful), a haircut and highlights (that would smell bad, but at least it wouldn't hurt), and a wax. *Ouch.* Also, a full manicure and a pedicure, and she'd already picked the colors. I would match the ribbons on the wedding programs, down to my toenails.

"Great," I said, managing to suppress my groan.

Once we got to the spa I was whisked away to be plucked, waxed, highlighted, and painted. *This is what normal people do,* I thought, munching on dried apple slices and sipping a seltzer water in a fluffy terrycloth robe as I waited for my eyebrow-whatever. *Normal people go to the spa. They get waxed.*

They don't translate ancient books from Icelandic into English, or hallucinate Norse gods in their bedroom.

"Oh, honey, you look better already," Mom said, sitting down next to me. Her face was covered with some sort of shockingly blue goop, and her hair was in a big, white bag.

"Thanks," I said. "Uh, you look -"

She laughed. It was, I realized, the first time I'd heard her laugh since I arrived. And then a girl who looked barely old enough to be out of high school sat down in front of me to thread my eyebrows, and the trip to the spa became painful again.

* * * * * * *

I saw Di for the first time at the wedding rehearsal that afternoon. She was wearing jeans and a white BRIDE T-shirt, carrying a paper plate covered with bows. She looked radiant.

"Now, turn to the happy couple," the minister told us, "and smile!"

We practiced smiling. My brother held Di's hands under the paper plate. They looked into each other's eyes, and my heart gave a little twinge.

"All right, who's Caroline?" the minister asked.

I stepped forward.

"Do you want to practice your reading now?"

"No," I said, shaking my head. "I'm good."

Di hugged us all after the rehearsal, and then she pulled me aside and handed me a small, white jewelry box. "I'm your sister now," she said, putting her hands over mine. "You may call on me, if you have need."

I raised a sore, plucked eyebrow, not exactly sure what she meant by that. Di liked organic food and natural cleaning solutions; she could be a bit, well, *California* at times.

"Thanks," I said, and she hugged me again.

I opened the jewelry box as Dad drove us to the rehearsal dinner. Inside was a delicate chain bracelet with a dangling silver scallop shell. I put it on and walked into the restaurant.

* * * * * * *

My brother spent the night before the wedding at our parent's house, with me, instead of the house he shared with Di.

"Shouldn't you be out, you know, celebrating?" I asked.

We were drinking beer, watching TV, and ostensibly wrapping packages of flower seeds in white tulle. I was holding the cool beer bottle against my threaded eyebrows; they still hurt.

He laughed. "Already had the bachelor party," he said. "Besides, there's nowhere else I'd rather be."

I smiled at him, and he raised his beer toward me, and we clinked the necks of the bottles. "Thanks," I said. "It's good to see you, too."

Mom walked in the living room at that moment and screamed. "We have over *one hundred* guests coming tomorrow!" she yelled. "And it looks like you've made THREE favors!?"

My brother stood up, gave her a hug, and walked her

back to the kitchen while I bent over the seeds and tulle, getting to work.

It was nearly midnight when we finally finished the wedding favors, over a hundred little balls of flower seeds, wrapped in tulle, tied with a dusky rose ribbon, and labeled with cute little tags reading *"Geoff & Di - Watch Our Love Grow!"* I stacked them all in a box and moved the box to the kitchen counter, along with the other two dozen things we couldn't forget tomorrow morning.

"Look at the ash tree," my brother whispered.

I joined him at the kitchen window, and we watched the high branches tossing wildly in the calm night air.

"Something's going on," he muttered.

I stared at my brother, about to ask him what he meant, when I heard Mom's footsteps in the hallway. "Bedtime!" she called, clapping her hands together, just like she did when we were kids. "The groom needs to be well rested!"

I crawled into bed, closed my eyes, and tried not to think about Loki. His smooth, cool skin; his wild, dancing eyes. The curve of his neck as he bent to lick my breasts. *Three months,* I thought. *Three months. One week. Two days.*

I was awake for a long time, watching passing headlights trace the shadows of tree branches on my ceiling.

* * * * * * * *

Wedding day. My brother seemed, improbably, nervous. I wasn't sure I'd ever seen my brother nervous before. It was strangely touching.

I helped load the car, making sure we remembered our dresses, our heels, the wedding favors, the wedding programs. Geoff's tuxedo. Geoff's shoes. Then Mom and I left the house to go to the florist's and pick up the boutonnieres. On the way, she had me read from a handwritten list of things to remember.

"Carol, do you have your reading?" she finally asked.

"Of course, Mom," I said. *It's literally the one thing I need to do for the entire wedding, and it's right here in my -*

Shit.

We decided it was easier to stop at a bookstore for a new copy, instead of driving all the way back to the house.

"I'm so sorry," I said, cringing with embarrassment as I climbed back in the car, a new copy of *Sonnets from the Portuguese* in my hand. Mom said nothing, her hand thrumming on the steering wheel. I could tell she had a mental countdown going until the wedding, and we were now running behind.

We drove to the church and unloaded the programs,

the favors, the flowers. I saw Di and the other bridesmaids across the chapel, and I offered a little wave. Then we headed to the women's bathroom, where I helped my mom into her very stylish maroon mother-of-the-bride dress. I pulled on my bridesmaid's dress in the cramped stall and came out to let Mom do my hair and makeup.

"Oh, Carol," she said, her eyes teary. "You look so beautiful!"

I turned to look at myself in the bathroom mirror. "Wow," I whispered.

I did look good. More than good. I actually looked sexy. *He'd love it,* I thought, and my cheeks flushed. *He'd run his hand up the slit in the side, and he'd growl in my ear, and he'd say-*

"I just know there's someone out there for you, too," Mom said, patting me on the cheek.

And then it was over. The moment was officially ruined, and I was back to being skinny, clumsy Caroline Capello, with no boyfriend and her nose always in a book.

"Thanks, Mom," I muttered.

"Come on," she said, "the guests will be arriving soon."

* * * * * * *

I hugged Uncle Donny and Aunt Julia as they came in, and smiled and nodded when they both commented on how I'd really grown up, I sure wasn't a little girl anymore, and then I kissed each of their four kids and directed them to the groom. I hugged Aunt Michelle and told Uncle Tony I'd finally had deep dish pizza, and it really wasn't that good. Then I hugged Aunt Adrianna, who always looked a bit unhinged at weddings, and I walked her to her seat.

And then the music started, and it was time for me to take Geoff's friend Andy's arm, trying to balance my little bouquet and my new copy of *Sonnets from the Portuguese* as I walked down the aisle.

I took my place in the row of bridesmaids and turned to my brother, reminding myself to smile. He looked very handsome, and just slightly nervous, in his tuxedo. His boutonniere was a little crooked, and I grinned, knowing that was going to drive my mom nuts.

Then the music changed, and the entire chapel came to their feet.

If I thought Di looked radiant in her jeans and T-shirt, she was almost unearthly in her wedding dress. Her long, blonde hair tumbled down her shoulders, and her dress was a cloud of sea-foam billowing from the curves of her hips. A cascade of dusky pink roses fell from her arms.

I looked at Geoff and then turned away. The

expression on his face made my heart ache. Di reached us, and we all turned together to face the minister.

"Dearly beloved," he began.

And then he nodded at me, and it was my turn to read. I handed my bouquet to the girl next to me and walked to the podium, trying to ignore the people in the audience. The many, many people in the audience. My hands shook as I opened the new book to the dog-eared page. Sonnet 43.

"How do I love thee?" I read. "Let me count the ways."

Don't think about him, I told myself. And then he was all I could think about.

"I love thee to the depth and breadth and height,"

His cool skin against mine.

"My soul can reach..."

My head against his chest, my lips against his neck.

"I love thee to the level of everyday's..." My voice was trembling now.

Woodsmoke and salt spray and STOP IT!

"Most quiet need, by sun and candle-light."

His face in the candle-light, his smile, his wild, dancing eyes.

STOP IT!

"I love thee with a passion put to use," I read, and tears flooded my eyes, "in my old griefs, and -"

His lips pressed to mine, his hands on my wrists,

pinning me to the mattress.

What do you want, mortal woman?

I looked up. Everyone in the church was staring at me. Di looked especially concerned, her beautiful forehead wrinkled. I looked back at the page, my vision blurring with tears.

"And with my childhood faith," I said, taking a deep breath.

I want you.

"I love thee with the breath, smiles, tears, of all my life," I gasped, mumbling the words as quickly as I could. "And, if God choose, I shall but love thee better after death."

I stumbled away from the podium, my cheeks burning. I stared at the scallop-shell bracelet on my wrist for the rest of the ceremony, forgetting to smile at the happy couple.

* * * * * * * *

I stayed in the back, at the bar, during the reception. A few people awkwardly complimented me on my reading.

"It's always emotional," Uncle Donny told me, clapping me on the shoulder. "Always emotional."

I muttered a thanks and ordered another glass of red wine. I was planning on drinking wine until I either forgot about Loki or forgot about embarrassing myself in front of the entire wedding. The bartender handed me a new glass. I finished it in a few big gulps and sighed. The room was starting to spin a little around the edges... and nope, I still hadn't forgotten the fucking unreasonably sexy Trickster God of Asgard.

But he forgot me.

"I'mma need a refill," I said, waving at the bartender and then shoving my empty wine glass in his direction.

He nodded and handed me another glass as Mom walked over. She sniffed. I had to fight the impulse to down the entire glass in front of her. Instead, I took a deep breath and looked out across the reception hall, at Di and Geoff on the dance floor. The happy couple. *Do not mess up this wedding,* I told myself. *At least, not any more than you already have.*

"Hey, Mom," I said, putting down the wine glass and struggling to think of something that might make up for my disastrous reading. And my current state of almost embarrassingly drunk. "I met someone in Chicago."

Her face lit up.

"His name's Mark," I said, "and he does, uh, business. Things. Finance stuff. He's left a few messages. I'm, um, I'm gonna call him back."

My mom smiled with her entire body.

"You'd like him," I added, realizing it was true. Mom would *love* Mark.

She reached for me, squeezing my cheek. "I am so happy for you!" she said.

My stomach lurched violently, and I decided I might lay off the wine for a little while.

* * * * * * * *

I didn't drink enough to forget Loki or my horrible reading, but I did drink enough to have one hell of a pounding headache on the flight back to Chicago. The El broke down twenty minutes outside of O'Hare, and it was over an hour before I made it onto another train, dragging my suitcase behind me and feeling like I might kill someone to get a drink of water. It was dark by the time I unlocked the door to my apartment.

"Hello?" I said, tentatively, flipping on the lights.

It was empty; nothing had changed in my absence. I fished the balled-up note out of my trashcan, smoothing it out. Loki, it read. I'm in San Diego. I'll be back Tuesday.

I haven't seen him in three months, I thought. *Three months, one week, four days.*

If I tire of you, I will tell you, he said, sitting on my bed, drinking the mead of Val-Hall.

"You know what they call Loki?" I muttered to myself. "The Lie-smith. They call him the Lie-smith."

I grabbed my note and ripped it in half, balling up

the pieces and throwing them in the trash. I threw them so hard one of the pieces bounced out of the trashcan and rolled across the floor. I stomped on it. Then I pulled my cell phone out of my pocket and called Mark.

"Carol," he said, answering almost immediately. "Wow, it's great to hear from you."

"Yeah," I said. "Sorry about the delay. I was in San Diego for a wedding."

"No problem, no problem. Look, I'd love to take you out on a date." I imagined that was the voice he used at work, settling a big, important deal. He sounded very authoritative.

"Uh, sure," I squeaked.

"How about Friday?" he asked. "Would Friday work for you?"

"Yeah, Friday's great."

"Just tell me your address," he said, "and I'll pick you up at eight." It sounded like he was smiling.

My hands trembled as I plugged my phone back into the charger. *There,* I thought. *I'm going on a nice, normal date. With a nice, normal guy.*

Be happy about this.

CHAPTER ELEVEN

Friday night.

I hung the bridesmaid's dress from my brother's wedding next to the dress Mom bought me for the prom I'd skipped. The bridesmaid's dress was a wrinkled mess after traveling back from San Diego, and the prom dress had a scorch mark from where I left an iron on the back just a bit too long. My fingers brushed the soft cotton of the red dress, the one I'd worn to Berlin with Loki. I pulled back, leaving that one in the closet.

I sighed and decided to go with the prom dress, which was sleek and black with gold filigree along the chest. Hopefully it would be dark enough nobody would notice the iron burn. Besides, my only high heels were black, and they wouldn't match the dusty rose of the bridesmaid's dress.

I took a long shower, shaved my legs, and dried my hair in a towel. Then I pulled on the dress and dusted off the Mary Kay makeup kit Mom gave me for

Christmas. When I was done, I stood back in the mirror to check my work. I sighed. *You look fucking ridiculous*, I thought, and then I bit the inside of my cheek to stop myself.

It doesn't matter. Tonight we dine with the mortals.

* * * * * * *

Mark picked me up at eight. It was a beautiful early summer evening, the light just fading from the sky, moths beginning to swarm the streetlights.

"Wow," he said, "you look great."

"Thanks. Yeah, you too."

Mark did look good. He wore a dark suit with a white tie, and he wore them comfortably, with a relaxed confidence, like he'd stepped out of the pages of a magazine. *Oh, Mom would love you,* I thought. I took a deep breath, smiled at him, and got in his car.

"So," I asked, "where are we headed?"

Mark smiled as he guided his car to Lake Shore Drive. "Charlie Trotter's."

I tried not to gasp. Charlie Trotter's was the nicest restaurant in Chicago. I couldn't even afford to walk along the sidewalk outside Charlie Trotter's.

"Oh," I said. "Oh, wow."

Mark's smiled widened. "You're going to love it."

* * * * * * * *

An impeccably polite older man in a tuxedo showed us to our table. It was an ocean of white linen and flickering candles tucked next to the window. Mark ordered two martinis immediately.

"I figure a girl who likes whiskey will like a martini," he said, with a smile.

"Of course," I said, trying to remember if I'd ever had a martini before.

"So," he asked, as the drinks appeared, "you've just been... published?"

I waved my hand dismissively. "I'm a grad student," I said. "I just translated this old Norse text, *The Gods' Feast*. It's, um, not the most exciting - "

"Norse gods," he said. "Like Thor?"

My mouth dropped. "You know the Norse gods?"

He laughed. "Well, I read the comic books. When I was a kid."

"They have a comic book about Norse gods?"

Mark smiled at me. "Seriously? You didn't know they have comic books about Thor?"

I found myself smiling back. "I... I don't get out a whole lot," I admitted.

"Well then, you'd better enjoy this night to the fullest," he said, raising his glass. The elegant inverted triangles of our martini glasses clinked together, and I took a sip.

The martini burned my throat. I tried not to flinch.

"To your publication," he said, raising his drink again.

I touched my glass to his a second time and took another sip. *Gross.* I set my martini back down. It still seemed depressingly full. The waiter appeared with menus printed on thick, creamy paper. Mark ordered a bottle of wine while I stared at the menu, wondering if it actually was handwritten. The listings did not include prices. *Yikes.*

"What looks good?" Mark asked, staring at me over the candlelight.

"I don't know," I said, blushing as I turned from his intense eyes to stare at the menu. "I don't even know what some of these words mean."

Mark laughed and reached across the table, squeezing my hand. His palm felt clammy against mine, and I pulled away, discreetly. I hoped.

The waiter appeared with a bottle of wine. Mark inspected the label, which appeared to be entirely in French, and the waiter poured a sample into Mark's glass. He tried it, nodded, and the waiter poured us both full glasses, leaving the bottle on the table with a white napkin tied around the neck.

"This is one of my favorites," Mark said. "It's from Bordeaux."

"Great," I said, reaching for my glass.

The wine was excellent, rich and smooth on my tongue. I finished my glass before we agreed on an appetizer, and the room was beginning to soften and buzz pleasantly.

And then I felt something on the back of my neck, like a gust of wind. Or like a snowflake, melting against my skin. I spun around.

"Is something wrong?" Mark asked.

I waved my hand dismissively, but I stood slightly in my seat, looking toward the back of the restaurant.

He was there.

Standing in the shadows near the back of the room, wearing a black tuxedo, was Loki Laufeyiarson of the Æsir. He smiled as our eyes met and a rush of heat filled my body, fast as fire. He raised one finger, gesturing. *Come.*

I turned back to Mark. He was no longer smiling. *Shit*, I thought, my heart hammering against my ribcage. *Shitshitshitshit.*

"Are you all right?" Mark asked, glancing toward the back of the restaurant.

"Oh, I'm fine," I said, a little too quickly. "Listen, uh, I'll just be a minute. Just one minute."

I grabbed my purse and pushed back from the chair. Loki turned, and I followed him through the restaurant, through a heavy, red curtain, held back with yellow tassels. The restrooms. *Really, Loki?* I pushed open the door, and there he was, tall and handsome and smiling against the white marble walls. The room was lit by candles, and their soft, golden light made his face look like a sculpture. Perfect. Untouchable.

The door closed behind me, and I heard it lock.

"Loki...?" My voice trailed off as he grabbed my arms, and I could smell him. Woodsmoke, salt spray, and leather. He slammed his body into mine, pushing me against the door.

"This is not -" I said, but he pressed his lips to my mouth, his tongue urgent and forceful as he kissed me. My legs trembled when he pulled away.

"Hello, mortal woman," he whispered against my neck, his voice jagged.

"Three months," I said, catching my breath. "You've been gone - "

He stopped me with another hungry kiss, his hips hard against mine, pushing me into the door. I wrapped my arms around his waist, running my hands down the smooth fabric of his shirt.

"You missed me," he said.

"Of course," I gasped.

He stepped away, leaving me shivering against the bathroom door. "I have returned from magnificent battle," he said, his voice rough, his eyes wild and flashing. "I would celebrate with you."

Mark, I thought. *Mark is waiting for me.* Over the sound of my thudding heart, I could hear the soft murmur of conversation, the clink of crystal glasses. I could hear violins.

I stepped closer to Loki, so close we were almost touching. I could smell him, could feel his body trembling next to mine. I could see his pulse racing in his neck.

"Yes," I whispered.

Loki grabbed my dress in his fists and *ripped*, the fabric coming apart in one long tear down the front. Then he pressed his body against mine, rubbing his face along my neck. I could just feel the scrape of his teeth along the sensitive skin under my ear, and I shuddered, bringing my hands to his head and running them through his hair.

"Maybe you missed me, too," I whispered, my voice trembling as his hands pushed my ruined dress off my body.

I could feel him laugh against my collarbone. His face moved along mine, and he sighed into my hair. His cool hands pulled my body close, pressing my chest against his. For a heartbeat, I thought his arms trembled.

Then he grabbed my shoulders and spun me around, pushing me against the counter, hard. I could see his face reflected in the mirror, shifting in the dancing candlelight. His tuxedo jacket was still neatly buttoned as he leaned over me, tracing my backbone with his tongue, pushing his hips against mine.

I jammed my fist in my mouth to keep from crying out as his graceful fingers reached for my breasts, circling my nipples. I shoved my hips into him, feeling his aching stiffness through the smooth material of his tuxedo pants. He squeezed my nipple, and I moaned his name.

I tried to turn, to rip off those pants and finally feel him inside me, but he grabbed my shoulders and held me down, my stomach flat against the counter. He ran his long fingers through my hair, pulling my head back. I watched him in the mirror as he leaned down to trace the curve of my neck with his tongue. My body flushed with heat as he bit my neck.

"Loki..." I whispered. Somewhere on the other side of the door, people were drinking expensive glasses of wine and having pleasant, refined conversations.

The door handle shook, and I flinched.

Above me in the mirror, Loki grinned wickedly. "Shall I let her in?" he whispered in my ear. "I could just... disappear."

"Don't you dare," I growled.

And then I gasped as his hand trailed along my thighs, gently teasing my throbbing sex. He moved his fingers across me, pushing softly without entering. I shuddered as heat and pleasure coursed through me, building and building. I bit my hand again to keep from crying out.

Loki pulled his hand away from my shoulder as his clothes vanished, and I could feel his legs against mine, naked and cool. I moaned, pushing into him. He rubbed the head of his cock against me without entering me, and I the room spun. Then he pulled away, and my entire body trembled. My face collapsed on the white marble of the countertop.

I felt a cool flicker between my legs, and I looked up at the mirror. Loki was on his knees, his face buried between my legs. He circled my sex with his tongue, his hands around my hips. My body flushed with heat; my legs trembled as waves of pleasure crashed over me. His lips and tongue flickered against my clit. I moaned as his fingers slid inside me, moving in a slow circle. I could feel myself trembling on the verge of orgasm -

And then Loki's face was next to mine, whispering in my ear. I could smell my sex on his breath. Our eyes met in the mirror.

"Mortal woman," he panted, as his fingers moved inside me. "What do you want?"

I groaned, wondered if my voice even worked any longer. "You," I whispered, my mouth dry, "I want you. Oh, fuck, I want you!"

He sighed, his face against my neck, and then he stood and penetrated me. I wanted him so badly it almost hurt. Then he was inside me, his slender hips a perfect fit against mine, the full length of his glorious cock moving inside me, filling me, filling me with crashing ecstasy.

"Oh, Loki!" I cried out, forgetting where we were, forgetting why I should be quiet. My orgasm washed over me as every muscle in my body grew taut, my eyes rolled back in my head, and the room disappeared.

I opened my eyes as Loki came. His neck arched back above me and his eyes closed as he cried out, his cock shuddering inside me. Then he collapsed against my back, panting hard. I stood and turned, wrapped my hands around his body, rested my head against his smooth chest. Breathing in woodsmoke and salt spray and cold.

It took me a moment to realize his back was wet, soaking wet. I pulled my hand away and saw blood.

I gasped. He was covered in blood. Blood ran down his pale cheeks and neck. In the mirror I could see blood running in rivers down his arms. I brought my hands to his face. "Oh, Loki, are you..?"

He backed away from me and shook his head. In a second, the blood was gone, the immaculate tuxedo restored. *God of illusions,* I thought. I shivered.

"Are you all right?" I asked, realizing this was exactly what Mark asked me before I abandoned him at the most expensive restaurant in Chicago.

"Jötunn blood, not mine," he said. His voice was calm, although his sharp blue eyes were still wild.

I reached for his arm. He pulled away, and his eyes flashed cold and hard. The candlelight in the bathroom flared red. Suddenly the room was darker, and he was taller, and the shadows came together to form a great, black cloak behind him.

"Woman! I come here tonight to celebrate victory, not for your foolish ministrations!"

"But you're hurt..." I said, hating how small my voice sounded.

"No!" he thundered, backing away from me. His huge, dark frame seemed to fill the small room, his face wild and angry in the leaping candlelight.

And then he was gone, and I was alone in the bathroom.

* * * * * * *

I stared at myself in the mirror. My hair was a mess, my pink eyeshadow smeared across my cheek. There was an angry, red bite on my neck. One of my heels was broken. And my dress was ripped down the middle. If I crossed my arms over my chest, I could hold the dress together, covering everything that needed to be covered. Barely.

I sighed. I could tell Mark I'd... had an accident? In

the restroom? That involved a bite on my neck?

Or I could run like hell.

I cracked open the heavy door. The thick, red curtain blocked off the seating area. At the far end of the hallway was a swinging door with a round, portal window. The kitchens. *Now or never,* I thought. I crossed my arms over my chest to keep my dress from falling off, tucked my purse under my arm, held my head high, and pushed through the door to the kitchens, limping on my broken heel.

"Hey, ma'am," someone shouted at me, as soon as I entered. "Ma'am, you can't come in here!"

I ignored the voice and walked through the steam and clatter toward the shining red beacon of an EXIT sign. *I'm going to kill him,* I thought as shouts moved through the kitchen. *I am going to kill him.*

I pushed open the exit door, ditched my heels, and ran down the alley. I was certain the entire kitchen staff of Charlie Trotter's was on the phone to the police department, reporting a deranged, half-dressed woman running through the kitchens.

I ran for three blocks, and then crashed out of the alley into the lights of Fullerton Avenue. I briefly considered trying to ride the El home, barefoot, in my shredded dress, and decided I could afford a taxi this one time.

"You okay?" the driver asked as I tried not to flash all

of downtown Chicago climbing in the seat.

"Hyde Park," I mumbled. "If you take credit card."

* * * * * * *

My hands trembled as I unlocked my door. I had never been so happy to see my dingy, dark apartment.

"Hello, mortal woman," he said, from the darkness.

I turned on the lamp. Loki was sitting on the bed in his black tuxedo. My back stiffened as rage flooded my body.

"You fucking *asshole!*" I screamed. "Look at me!" I raised my arms, letting the shreds of my dress fall open.

Loki stood and walked to me. There was something off about his gait, something awkward. He wrapped his arms around me, and his body felt hot against mine. "Mortal woman," he mumbled against my neck. "My woman."

I pushed him away. "What the fuck is wrong with you?" I screamed. "You could have taken me home! You could have - You could have at least left me your fucking jacket!"

He sat down heavily on the bed, his cool eyes unfocused. I suddenly felt very tired. My arms hurt from holding my dress together. My feet throbbed from running barefoot down the alley.

"Fuck you," I said, although it sounded more like a

sigh. "I'm taking a shower."

* * * * * * *

The apartment was so silent, so still, when I opened the bathroom door I thought Loki had left. The lamp was still on, casting deep shadows around the room, and I heard him before I saw him. His breathing was slow, deep. He was on the bed, his eyes closed. Asleep.

I stared at him. For all the nights we'd spent together, this was the first time I'd seen him sleep. His face looked especially soft in the pale glow of the lamp, and the shadows were so dark...

I stepped closer to him. They weren't shadows.

They were blood.

CHAPTER TWELVE

Blood covered his face and arms, soaking into my sheets, into the pillows. His long, delicate fingers hung over the side of my bed, dripping blood, which pooled on the floor, dark and shiny. *No illusions when he sleeps,* I thought.

And then, *Don't you dare die.*

The Norse gods are mortal. It's one of their defining characteristics, one of the things setting them apart from almost every other pantheon. They can die. They will die. In fact, the Norse gods know exactly how they will die, in the final battle of Ragnarök.

I was suddenly very cold.

I'm off to magnificent battle, he said, his head resting against mine in the Higher Grounds stockroom.

Magnificent battle. The final battle of the Æsir, led by the All-Father Óðinn, against the Jötunn, led by the giant Hrym.

Had it happened? While I flirted with Mark and translated *The Gods' Feast* and fucked up my reading at

Geoff and Di's wedding, did Ragnarök begin somewhere along the World Tree? Were the Jötunn riding their monstrous ship across the waters between the worlds? Did Loki meet Heimdallr in the bloody and burning fields of Vígríðr?

"Oh, no," I whispered, dropping to my knees next to Loki's body. *Still breathing,* I thought, reaching for him. *He's still breathing.*

Did you have nowhere else to go, Loki of the Æsir?

Gently, I pulled up his sleeve and exposed his arm. I took the damp towel from my body and held it against his hand, against his wrist and forearm. When I pulled it back, I sighed in relief; most of the blood was not his, it seemed. But there was a long gash just below his elbow, and I held the towel against it, trying not to wake him.

I stared at him as I tried to stop the bleeding. Without illusions, his pale arm was a patchwork of old wounds, with especially thick, red scar tissue around his wrists. Even his handsome, angular face was covered with scars; pale, white lines radiated from his eyes.

And his mouth... My stomach churned as my eyes traced the thick, white scars crossing his lips. *Of course,* I thought. *They sewed his lips shut, in Níðavellir.* My hand trembled against his arm.

He stirred slightly in his sleep, and I tore my eyes away from his battered face, moving the towel away from his elbow. The bleeding seemed to have stopped, at least here, and my towel was now dark, soaked. I watched him, struggling to ignore the panicked thrumming of my heart; then I bent and began to unbutton his shirt.

I gasped as I pulled his shirt open. His chest was a bloody wreck, barely rising and falling with his shallow breathing. I went to the bathroom, dropped the bloody towel in the tub, and grabbed a clean one.

"Don't you dare die, Loki Laufeyiarson," I whispered as I began to gently wipe the blood from his chest.

Once again, it seemed as though most of the blood was not his, although he had a nasty gash just above his hipbone, and another across his left pectoral and around his side. I held my towel against both of them until it was entirely soaked, and then I threw it in the tub and grabbed the spare sheets. I pressed a pillow case against his side, as hard as I dared, and I tried to think. The cut across his chest looked bad, really bad, but I was also worried about his legs. The pool of dark red under his right leg was soaking the rosebud sheets. And getting bigger.

There was no way I could get his pants off without waking him up. I sighed, left the pillow case against his chest, and got a pair of scissors from the kitchen. *This is for my prom dress*, I thought as I began to cut open the soft fabric of his pants.

His right leg looked bad. He had a puncture wound bleeding on both sides of his calf, and a deep, jagged cut across his lower thigh. I started to cry as I finished peeling off his blood-soaked pants.

"Don't you *dare* die," I whispered, over and over. "Don't you *dare*."

I wiped the rest of the blood from his body, trying to move quietly and gently, and then I tied my sunflower-print beach towel around his right calf, covering both sides of the puncture. I held my spare sheets against his thigh. I lost count of the scars on his legs.

Still, there were two wounds that would not stop bleeding: the cut on his side, and the puncture wound in his calf. My bathtub was full of bloody towels and sheets, my bed a riot of stained blankets and tea towels. I lay down next to him, pressing my body against his side. He was very still, his breath barely stirring the quiet air. His skin felt cool against my cheek.

"Stay with me," I whispered, pressing the comforter against his side, feeling his blood seeping through my fingers.

* * * * * * *

I awoke to bright sunlight streaming through my windows. I was alone in my bed. The blood was gone. My rosebud sheets, my midnight blue comforter;

everything looked untouched.

"Loki..?" I sat up in bed, looking slowly around the room. *It happened again.*

The hallucinations happened again.

"Loki, are you... are you okay? Are you here?"

My cell phone was flashing three messages, so I put it on speaker and set it back down on the table.

And then I noticed a pool of blood under my bed, dark and shiny. *From his hand,* I thought. *It was dripping down his fingers.* I walked slowly to the bathroom and looked in the mirror. There, on my neck, was the red bruise from the bite he'd given me at Charlie Trotter's. I traced it lightly with my fingers.

How could I imagine this?

My hand trembled as I pulled open my blue plastic shower curtain. My bathtub was full of bloody towels, bloody sheets. Bloody pillowcases. *So much blood,* I thought. *He lost so much blood.* I braced myself against the sink, my heart hammering.

"LOKI!" I screamed. My voice echoed off the bathroom walls.

I walked back to the bed, arms and legs shaking. I heard a beep and realized my phone had stopped; I hadn't noticed who left the messages. I hit the play button again, realized I was walking in circles.

"Carol?" Mark's voice, of course.

I was back in the bathroom. *How much blood can a*

person lose?

" - you alright? I didn't even see - "

Three pints? Four? This looks like more than that.

"- Trotter's, wasn't sure what happened, they were very -"

But he's not a person. He's of the Æsir, how much blood...

" - going to contact the police -"

My head snapped up as "the police" echoed through my apartment. I walked back to my phone, took a deep breath, pressed play a third time, and forced myself to listen. Mark's first message sounded hurt. By the third message he was angry. And he said, very clearly, he would call the police if he hadn't heard from me within twenty four hours.

I walked back to the bathroom, looked at the bloody mess in my bathtub. I looked at the blood pooling under my bed. *No police*, I thought. My fingers trembled as I dialed Mark. He answered immediately.

"Hey, Mark, I'm so sorry," I said.

"Jesus Christ, Carol, are you all right? Are you home?"

"Yes," I said. "Yes, I'm home. I'm fine." *How much blood can an Æsir lose?*

"What the hell happened last night?"

"I...." I hesitated. I had no idea what to say. *I hallucinate? I'm psychotic? I've been ruined for all mortal men?* "I'm really sorry," I said.

There was a long pause on the line.

"Listen," he said. "Is there someone else?"

I don't know, I thought. *Maybe.* "It's not..." I hesitated again. "It's not what you think," I finally said.

Mark sighed. "Carol," he said. "I know we just met. But I like you. I really like you. I just - I just don't want to share you."

Share me. I wondered if this was the tone of voice he used when he was trying to close a big deal; friendly, with just a touch of pleading.

"I am really sorry about last night," I said. "And I like you too. But -" *You're a terrible kisser,* I thought, and I smiled in spite of myself.

"This is just a really bad time for me," I told him.

I hung up the phone and went for a run. It was a perfect day; the sun sparkled and danced along the tips of the waves, and the wind coming off the water was fresh and cool. My feet pounded a rhythm along the lakeshore: *of the Æsir, of the Æsir.* And beneath that: *Alive. Please. Be. Alive.*

When I got home I unplugged my phone and ran the apartment building's industrial laundry machines with bleach and hot water until the towels and sheets had only faint ghosts where they had absorbed the blood of an Æsir.

And then I went to the library. I couldn't stand the

silence of my empty apartment.

* * * * * * * *

After two hours in the darkest, dustiest, loneliest corner of the library I could find, my legs were starting to fall asleep, and I'd made no progress on my work. I sighed and stretched, leaning back, closing my eyes. Then I raised my hand to the back of my neck. I'd felt something there, like a melting snowflake.

"Mortal woman," he said from behind me, his voice resonant and formal in the small space.

I turned and saw Loki. He was wearing his leather armor, black and scarlet and golden, tight against his muscular body. His wide cloak flared behind him. His eyes were dark in his pale face.

Relief flooded my body. I pushed away from the desk and stood, throwing my arms around him. But I felt his back stiffen at my touch, and he stepped away. I dropped my arms, remembering the deep gash in his side.

"I'm so sorry," I whispered. "Did I hurt you?"

"No," he said, his eyes focused somewhere just above me. He took a deep breath before he spoke again, his voice low. "I should not have left you."

I stared at him. "Are you talking about last night?" I whispered. "Wait... are you *apologizing*?"

He turned away, absently gazing down the rows of bookshelves, his weight shifting slightly from side to side. I'd never seen him look uncomfortable before; it made him almost human. I smiled, and then covered my mouth with my hand.

"No, you shouldn't have left me," I said.

His back stiffened and, for a heartbeat, his illusions *flickered*; I could see the angry, white scars across his lips.

"Listen," I whispered, reaching for his hand. "Last night probably could have ended a little, uh, better. But you were - " I hesitated. *Compromised? Incapacitated? Dying?*

"You were in pretty rough shape," I whispered. "When you were gone this morning, I - I wasn't sure if you'd - " I could not quite bring myself to say it.

He shook his head, his brow furrowed. "You were... concerned? About me?"

"Loki," I said, and then I stopped as I heard a door on the far side of the library open. A second later I heard the door close again. "Of course I was concerned," I whispered. "You were-"

"I am a burden on you," he said, his voice low, his eyes distant.

"No." My voice was loud in the still, dusty air. "No, Loki, you aren't."

I wrapped my arms around him, resting my head on

his chest. His body stiffened in my embrace, his muscles tight. I closed my eyes and thought about Mark, sitting by himself at Charlie Trotter's. *I don't want to share you,* he'd said. I wondered how long he sat at that candle-lit table before he realized I wasn't coming back.

"Last night," I whispered. "I don't regret it. Any of it." I pulled back, meeting his distant, clouded eyes. "It was - " I hesitated, searching for the words. "It was good to see you again," I finally said, my voice thick.

He cupped my chin in his cool hand. "It was good to see you as well," he said, and he kissed me. It was soft and gentle, barely more than his lips brushing mine. Even so, it left me breathless.

"I would like to see you again. Tonight," he said, and he finally smiled. "To *apologize.*"

"I'd like that," I said.

"I'll be in the park."

Then he turned and walked away, dust swirling between the bookcases in his wake. I watched him go until my heart stopped racing.

* * * * * * *

I forced myself to stay in the library for another two hours, although I spent most of that time arguing with myself. *You're hallucinating again,* I thought, drumming my pen against the desk. *You're psychotic.*

You should not be happy about this.

When I finally allowed myself to push away from the desk, it was early evening. I met Laura as I walked down the steps of the library.

"Carol," she called. "Wow, must have been a good date!"

"Date?"

"You're all smiles," she said. "You must've had a good time with Mark."

"Oh, right," I stammered. Charlie Trotter's already felt like it happened years ago. "Uh, yeah, that didn't go over so well. With Mark."

"Oh, my gosh! I'm so sorry. Do you want to talk about it?"

I glanced at the sky. The clouds were already streaked with gold, the sun dipping below the spires of the University. *Tonight,* I thought. *The park.*

"Thanks," I said, "but not tonight. I've got, uh...." *I've got a date. With a psychotic hallucination.*

"That's okay," said Laura, and she leaned close to hug me. "Anytime you need, you just call."

"Thank you," I said. "Really."

CHAPTER THIRTEEN

The evening air was warm and still as I walked home. I could hear crickets through the open windows as I got the red dress out of my closet, ate a leftover pesto chicken salad from Higher Grounds for dinner, and took a long shower.

By the time I pulled on the dress, it was dark outside. I left my hair down and decided - what the hell - to put on some eyeliner. I added lipstick and smiled at myself in the mirror. *Totally unnecessary,* I thought, admiring the way the dress hugged my hips. *When you met Loki, you were wearing sweatpants. And not for long.* I smiled again, took a deep breath, and locked my door behind me. I let my hips roll as I walked, my hair swishing against my shoulders.

I reached the park at Promontory Point and walked to the water's edge. The water was calm, the waves lapping and murmuring against the shore. I gazed down the lake to the gleaming high rises of downtown Chicago. A couple walked ahead of me, holding hands, their heads bent together. Somewhere behind me, a dog barked.

A flash of light caught the corner of my eye, and I turned away from the water, toward the towering cottonwood trees. The air was thick with the rich, honey scent of their sticky buds. I saw the light flash again, a shimmer of yellow green alighting from the branches of a rose bush. Then it was joined by another flash, and another, and another, rising from the grass.

I gasped. There are no fireflies in San Diego. I had not realized what I was missing.

The fireflies spun and circled further into the trees. I followed them, stepping carefully around the rose bushes. And there, in the middle of the flashing glow of the dancing fireflies, was Loki. He was wearing jeans, perfectly fitted to his slender hips, and a dark, tight shirt. The fireflies shimmered, luminescent in the night air above him.

I smiled, my heart thudding wildly. "You do know how to make an entrance," I said.

He took my hand and brought it to his lips, kissing it gently. "My darling," he said, giving me an elaborate bow.

"The fireflies," I said. "Don't they call them Loki's Lights in Norway?"

"I've no idea," he said, but his smile seemed pleased, his eyes drifting up to follow the flickering spots of light.

My eyes followed his, watching fireflies rise in the warm night air, so I didn't notice when he moved to embrace me from behind, one arm around my waist, one hand moving down the red dress.

"Your dress," he whispered, with a hint of a growl, "is as sexy as spring in Midgard."

"Thank you," I said, feeling heat rush to my cheeks.

Loki ran his fingers along the dress, circling my breasts. My hips rocked into him, and I sighed with pleasure, watching the fireflies dance above us.

Then I heard voices, and I jumped. The couple I'd noticed earlier was walking through the trees. They were laughing together, hands held, heads tilted toward each other. Lost in their own world. They looked like they were going to walk into us. I moved, but Loki wrapped his arm around me.

"They can't see us," he whispered.

The couple passed us. They came so close I could smell the faint trace of cigarette smoke on his jacket, and I could feel the air swirl behind them.

Loki watched them go, his hand still tracing the curves of my breast. "Shall I invite them to join us?" he whispered.

I hesitated, unsure if he was joking.

"He certainly looked like fun," he said, squeezing my nipple through the fabric of my dress.

I leaned against his shoulder, showing him the full stretch of my neck, closing my eyes as I felt his lips, soft and delicate on my skin. I smiled as I remembered Mark's terrible kiss. "Loki, you've ruined me for all mortal men. So, no, I'm afraid adding mortals would do nothing for me."

I felt him laugh into my hair. "As you wish," he said, and his hands lifted my skirt, hooking his fingers into my underwear and pushing them down to my knees. I turned to face him. Our lips met as I ran my hands over his dark shirt.

I heard a voice behind me and jumped again. Just over Loki's shoulder, I could see a tall brunette walking her dog, talking on a cell phone.

"Don't be shy," Loki whispered. "They still can't see us." He smiled as he pulled away from my arms and lay down, waving his hand over his dark cloak, which was spread across the grass.

I sat next to him, and he ran his cool fingers along my arm. My body shivered in response to his touch. "Are you sure you're... okay?" I asked, thinking of my towels, of his blood.

He laughed, and his eyes sparkled with hunger. "Yes, I am recovered. Here."

Loki kissed my fingers and then ran my hand down his chest, to his hips, and then under his shirt. Gently, I touched his waist, the spot that had not stopped bleeding last night. His skin felt cool, smooth and even under my touch. *Illusions,* I thought. I pulled my hand away.

"I don't want to hurt you," I said.

He grabbed my arms and pulled me on top of him. "Mortal woman," he growled, "you cannot hurt me."

And then he kissed me, pushing my dress up and over my waist. I wrapped my legs around his hips, closing my eyes, losing myself in his smell and his taste. Woodsmoke and sea salt. When we pulled apart my eyes swam with tears.

"I thought - " I said, my voice hardly more than a whisper. "I thought you were - "

"I'm here," he said, soft and low in the warm air. "I'm here with you."

And then he was naked, naked under my arms and legs, and he kissed me again, his mouth pressed against mine, his tongue urgent, insistent. I moved slightly, straddling him, easing myself onto him.

I gasped as he entered me, and I threw my head back. There were fireflies, hundreds of fireflies, dancing and flickering above our heads. His hands grabbed my hips as I rocked against him. The fireflies came down, circling around us on the grass, their flickering matching our movements as our hips came together faster and faster, the heat building between our bodies.

"Ah, woman," Loki moaned, wrapping his fingers in

my hair and pulling my face to his. "Don't be in such a rush."

I sighed and tried to force my hips to slow down, savoring the feeling of his chest against mine, my legs wrapped around his. His skin was still cool under my hands, although I could see a sheen of sweat on his face, his high cheekbones and smooth brow. His hands moved under my dress to cup my breasts, squeezing my nipples.

"Oh, that's not fair," I cried, pushing my hips against his, waves of pleasure crashing over me.

"Don't," he growled, grabbing my thighs, forcing me to hold still. The world spun around us, an ocean of flickering, burning lights.

I sighed and buried my face in his hair, licking the sweat off his neck. He gasped and arched his back under me, filling me so quickly I cried out. I bent down again, licking his collarbone, his nipples. His hands moved up my back as his hips rocked and swayed against mine. His breath came fast and shallow, and his eyes rolled back in his head.

"Don't be in... such a... rush," I growled, and he laughed, his head back, his neck taut.

Then he grabbed my arms and pushed me over so quickly the world spun. I opened my eyes and felt his soft cloak against my back, saw fireflies burning above his head. His hair and eyes were wild as he pinned me to the ground by my wrists, his hips thrusting between my legs.

"Oh, don't stop," I cried, and he laughed again, a wild sound, a sound that had no place in the mortal realm.

And then the fireflies were spinning above us, the entire world was spinning, and I tried to fight it but I was drowning, drowning in him. The world fell away as my body surrendered to his, my legs clinging to him as my voice cried his name over and over.

Above me, Loki cried out as his hips crashed desperately into mine. And then his weight collapsed against me, his head resting on my neck, panting. I wrapped my arms around him, my entire body spent.

"You're always in such a rush," I whispered in his ear, and he laughed again, rolling off me.

"Woman, you are impossible," he said, smiling as he ran one finger along my cheek.

I heard another voice behind us, and I jumped again, pulling Loki's cloak over me.

"Shall we go somewhere more private?" he asked, taking my hand.

I nodded, blinked -

- and together we left the mortal realm.

* * * * * * *

I stood naked in the center of a round, white room.

Walls of windows opened to a sparkling expanse of water, the surface gently ruffled with waves. The windows curved behind me to meet walls, walls lined with bookcases. In the center of the room was a enormous, round bed, covered with white pillows.

"Do you like it?" Loki stood behind me, whispering in my ear.

"It's incredible," I said, walking to the windows. They were open, and I could smell salt in the air. The ocean, then. I could not see the shore in any direction. *If I fell from those windows,* I thought, *where would I be?*

"Is this... Asgard?" I asked, not really expecting an answer.

Loki laughed and shook his head. "This is Nowhere," he said. "It's a hole in the bark of the World Tree."

I walked to the bookcases, staring at the volumes. They were bound in soft, supple leather of different colors, with gleaming golden inscriptions.

"What language is this?" I asked. "It looks like Norse, but the runes are curved..." I ran my fingers across the spine of one of the books, a thick, green volume with a leather cover soft as flannel sheets, and the runes on the spine seemed to flicker. I jumped, pulling my hand back.

"I don't make a habit of bringing mortals here," Loki said, and then he was behind me again, wrapping an arm around my waist.

"Did you like him?" he asked, suddenly.

"Like who?" I was still staring at the thick green book, waiting to see if the golden runes would flicker again. I could have sworn I could almost read them...

"The man in the restaurant," he said.

"The who...?"

I turned, and I jumped again. Mark stood behind me. Mark, wearing the same white tie he'd worn to Charlie Trotter's. The same handsome face and brown eyes.

Mark's figure spoke with Loki's voice. "I can be anyone you want me to be."

"Oh, no, no," I said, waving my hand in front of my face. "Oh, yuck, not Mark!"

Mark's handsome face rippled, changed. And then I was staring at Doug McInnes, his curly dark hair and full lips. Doug, the philosopher. My first lover.

"You had several pictures of him in your apartment..." Doug said, with Loki's voice.

"No," I said, with a shudder. "No, please."

With a slight shimmer, Doug disappeared, became Loki again. He was wearing the same dark jeans he'd worn, briefly, in the park.

"Thank you," I said, uncrossing my arms. I hadn't realized I'd crossed them over my breasts.

Loki raised an eyebrow at me.

"Really," I said. I stepped closer to him, putting a hand against his bare chest. "You're... you're perfect. I don't want someone else."

Loki reached up, put his hand over mine. And then he put his lips against mine, and the rest of the world fell away.

* * * * * * *

"You stare at the books," Loki said.

We were lying together on the circular bed, our legs intertwined, my head resting on his arm.

"Well, of course," I said. "I could probably write my entire doctoral dissertation on just one of these books. If I could read it."

"Ah, yes, the dissertation," he said, lifting himself to his elbow and smiling at me. "And what is your focus?"

"I study..." I trailed off. *I study you? Is there any way to say it that doesn't sound totally creepy?* "Pre-Christian Norse mythology," I said, finally.

Loki's eyes sparkled. "Is that what I am, then? A myth?"

I sighed. "I don't know what you are," I said. "Everything in my world says you don't exist, and yet..." I sat up in the bed, looking out the open windows to the sunlit sea. In the silence of the white room I could hear the waves beneath us, falling over each other, forming and reforming.

"Most of the time I just think I'm going insane," I whispered, and I was surprised by my own honesty.

"It's the language of the Æsir," Loki said, sitting up behind me. "The books. They are in no mortal tongue." He bent to kiss my neck. "And you're not insane," he whispered.

I felt something around my neck, and I looked down to see a small silver and gold pendant sparkling between my breasts, smooth and cool.

"What is this?" I asked.

Loki shrugged, his eyes drifting to the books. "Proof," he said.

* * * * * * *

I awoke in my own bed, in my own apartment,, on a beautiful Chicago morning. The silver and gold pendant hung between my breasts, cool against my skin.

Proof.

CHAPTER FOURTEEN

The steps to getting your doctorate at the University of Chicago are pretty straightforward: all the required coursework, followed by your qualifying exams, followed by writing and then defending your dissertation. And if you pass, you get to put a Ph.D. behind your name.

Simple, right?

By the beginning of my second fall in Chicago I'd finished my coursework, and I scheduled my exams for May. Debra took her exams last year, so I invited her out for beer and a few questions as the quarter started.

"Any advice about exams?" I asked. We were sitting in a dark, wooden booth in the University pub with a pitcher of Goose Island between us.

"Well," she said, pouring a glass, "they test you over sixty books. I assume you've read them already?"

I nodded. I did have the list of books, and I'd read the entire list. Close enough.

"You'll want to take really careful notes," she said.

"Starting, like, yesterday. And get some supplemental readings from Professor Loncovic. Plus, it really helped me to work with someone. You should get in touch with Steve."

Steve was the only other person taking the Historical Religions qualifying exams this year. I thought I'd probably recognize him in a crowd.

"He'll be at the Halloween party," she said. "You can network there."

"Great," I said, trying not to roll my eyes.

"Oh, come on, Carol. It's a party. It'll be fun."

"I'm sure," I said. "I know Laura and Vance will throw, uh, you know. A great party."

Now Debra rolled her eyes. "Really? Carol, when was the last time you went out?"

Two nights ago I went to Nowhere, I thought, and my cheeks burned as I remembered Loki leaning me against the bookcases. The leather-bound books were soft on my naked skin...

"Last spring?" Debra asked. "When you met Mr. Sexy... what's-his-name? Guy in a suit?"

"Mark," I said, distractedly.

"Hmmmm," she said, managing to look disapproving as she finished her beer. "You are seriously due for a party."

I sighed, refilling our glasses. "Yeah. I'm sure Vance's business school buddies will be a raging good time."

Debra ignored my irony. "Oh, one more thing," she said, reaching for her glass. "Everyone ends up in the ER at some point."

"Excuse me?"

"With the exams," she said. "Like, the week before. I had tension headaches so bad I couldn't walk. And Rahul had back spasms and needed prescription muscle relaxants."

I nodded. Suddenly my beer didn't seem so appealing.

"I think Liang even had a full psychotic break..." Debra said, staring off in the distance.

"Liang?" I asked. It's a small department, and I thought I knew everyone, but that name didn't sound familiar.

"Before your time," she said. "He didn't pass."

He didn't pass. So it's true; some students don't pass. Some of us end up in the ER, take the exams, and then leave with nothing but a pat on the back and a, "Thanks for the memories!" Suddenly, devoting my life to studying Norse mythology felt like a hell of a gamble. The first cold tendrils of panic settled deep in my stomach.

"Don't worry," said Debra, taking another sip of her beer. "You'll probably be fine."

"Probably," I muttered.

As far as advice goes, it could have been a tad more optimistic.

* * * * * * *

My classroom was painfully hot. It was late October, and it was one of those gorgeous Midwestern Indian summer days, the sun warm as July in the brilliant turquoise sky. But the ancient radiator clanged and hissed as it relentlessly pumped out heat. And the windows did not open. *Maybe that's to keep the students from jumping out,* I thought, although none of my students looked like they would be up for that much physical activity. I suspected at least two of them were asleep, and the pretty blonde in the front row smelled like a distillery.

My first quarter of teaching was off to a glamorous start.

"So, one of the reasons Christianity took root in the Germanic regions," I said, "is because it adopted so many of the local traditions. You like your gods and goddesses? Boom! Now they're saints! You want to keep your holy well? Sure! We'll slap a cross on..."

I felt something on the back of my neck, a whisper of cold air.

I raised my hand to my neck, turned my head. There was a shadow on the linoleum floor outside my classroom. "Excuse me a minute," I told my students, and they shifted a bit in their seats, glancing at each other.

Loki stood in the hallway, dressed in an expensive, tight black suit. He tilted his head and smiled at me, his eyes slowly traveling along my body. My cheeks burned, although I was just wearing black yoga pants pants and a crew top.

"Mortal woman," he growled, leaning close to my ear.

"Loki, I'm in the middle of teaching a class," I whispered. My heart surged, and it was suddenly very difficult to keep from throwing myself into his arms.

"I would see you tonight, then," he said, his breath warm on my neck.

"Of course," I whispered. *Although* - "Shit. It's Laura's party tonight." I brushed his hand. "Just come by a little later."

He pulled back, raised an eyebrow. "Party?"

"Yeah, it's a Halloween thing. Look, I won't be there long. I'd rather be with you, but if I don't go, Laura might   be   upset."

"Woman," said Loki, his eyes sparkling, "do you still think yourself insane?"

I hesitated.

The pendant he'd given me was cool and smooth against my skin. My flower-print beach towel still had faint stains from his blood, and I'd kept the clothes he destroyed the first night he appeared in my apartment, even though they no longer smelled of woodsmoke and salt spray. *Still...*

If my students looked out the door right now, would they see Loki Laufeyiarson of the Æsir? Or would they just see Caroline Capello, talking to herself?

"Sometimes," I muttered.

Loki kissed the top of my head. "Tonight, then," he said, and he walked past me down the corridor.

I took a few deep breaths and returned to the classroom. *Did anyone see a man walk past this door? Anyone at all?*

"Any questions?" I asked, embarrassed to sound breathless.

The blonde in the front row raised her hand. "Have you finished grading our essays yet?" she asked.

* * * * * * * *

The Halloween party. *Sigh.*

I wore a black turtleneck and a pair of plastic cat ears. As I walked to the liquor store, I tried to calculate the absolute minimum amount of time I could spend there without offending anyone. *Forty-five minutes*, I decided. Forty-five minutes should be long enough to chat with Laura and Vance, network with Steve, drop off a six pack of beer, and sneak out. Then I could come home, open a bottle of wine, light the candles. Put on some music, something soft and sexy in the background. Maybe I'd wear the red dress. Maybe I'd wear nothing at all.

I smiled as I pushed open the door to the liquor store and grabbed a six pack of pumpkin ale. *Please have a different cashier,* I thought.

No luck. It was the same burly, bald, tattooed guy who'd sold me two bottles of zinfandel an hour ago. And then, just as I was headed out the door, I'd grabbed a bottle of cheap champagne and had him ring me up a second time.

"Beer this time, huh?" He smiled as he scanned the six pack. My cheeks burned.

"I'm going to a party," I muttered.

"Meow!" he said as he handed me my bag.

What the fuck?

I was almost to Laura and Vance's apartment when I remembered I was still wearing the cat ears. *I swear I'm going to find a different liquor store,* I thought.

* * * * * * *

"Hey, the place looks great," I told Laura as I gave her an awkward one-handed hug, trying not to drop the pumpkin beer.

Their apartment did look great. They'd draped all

the furniture in white sheets, and covered the lights with red cloth. There were dozens of candles and mirrors reflecting the flickering light; the punch bowl gurgled and steamed with dry ice.

Laura and Vance were dressed as a king and queen. She looked fabulous in long burgundy and scarlet robes, with an enormous plastic crown that probably weighed about ten pounds.

"Vance refused to wear the tights," she whispered to me. I glanced in the living room and saw Vance wearing a crown that matched Laura's, and the same pressed khaki pants and button up shirt he always wore.

"He still looks... regal," I said, and she laughed.

I eyed the knot of Vance's business school friends standing around the couch. They all looked stiffly formal. The two girls were both dressed as angels, and the men were all wearing the exact same thing as Vance, minus the crown: pressed slacks, button up shirts. I wasn't sure if it was a costume or a uniform.

I found my people when I dropped the beer off in the kitchen. Debra wore a gray hoodie sweatshirt with flippers and a shark fin hat. She waved her fin at me and shoved me toward a tall, skinny blonde wearing a fireman's jacket. He moved like he'd played sports in the past, like he was ready at any moment to catch something.

"This is Steve," she said.

"Hey," I said, "we should get together."

Steve stared at me.

Right. Introductions.

"I'm Carol," I said. "I'm taking the Historical Religions exams this year too."

"Ah," he said, shaking his head. "Get together -"

" - to study," I finished. "Yeah. Sorry. I wasn't being very clear."

I gave Steve one of my pumpkin beers as we exchanged emails and made plans to get together for coffee next week. I checked my cell phone. *Twenty more minutes.*

"Hey guys!" Laura came in the kitchen, suddenly very cheerful. She sounded suspiciously like she was trying to draw us into the rest of the party. "So, cute costumes."

Debra grabbed my arm, hard.

"What the..?"

"Stop," she said, dropping her voice to a whisper. "Check it out."

I followed her eyes to the front door. Someone had just walked in, someone tall, in a tight, expensive dark suit. His long, red hair was pulled back. His eyes were laughing.

Loki.

"Oh, my gosh," said Laura. "Who is that?"

It's him, I thought, but I couldn't quite force my

mouth to work. *It's Loki.*

And they can see him.

I froze in the kitchen as Loki walked across the living room. He shook Vance's hand. He murmured something to the business school guys around the couch, and they all laughed. And then he was standing in the kitchen doorway, smiling at me.

"Hello," said Laura, stretching out the *oh* as she held out her hand. "I don't think we've met?"

Loki took her hand in his and brought it to his lips. "I'm Lucas," he said. "It is my immense pleasure to meet you, Laura."

She giggled. I'd never heard that kind of giggle from Laura before.

"And what are you supposed to be?" Debra asked, tilting her shark-fin hat at his suit.

"I'm real," he said, his sparkling eyes meeting mine.

* * * * * * *

Loki and I walked back to my apartment early the next morning, as the sky faded from black to gray and the party finally started to wind down.

"Thank you," I said. "Thank you. Thank you."

My feet stumbled on the sidewalk, and I fell against him. He turned to catch me, and his eyes sparkled wildly in the momentary illumination of a passing car, the headlights flashing against his pale face.

"It was a fun party?" he asked.

I laughed. It felt good to be in his arms. "It was -" I paused. "It was *The Party*. The party by which all other parties shall be judged, and found wanting."

He laughed and pulled me to his lips. His mouth still tasted like the single malt scotch we'd been drinking, smoky and thick.

"Really," I said, "I don't know how you got everyone to play *strip* beer pong. On the roof. And then Debra and that guy, locking themselves in the closet -"

"You enjoyed yourself, mortal woman?"

I smiled at him, his face soft in the yellow glow of the streetlights. "Yes," I said. "But that's not -"

He pulled me close and kissed me again, and I lost the words. *That's not what I'm thanking you for,* I thought. *Thank you for showing me I'm not insane.*

Thank you for being real.

* * * * * * *

Laura surprised me at Higher Grounds Sunday morning.

"How are you, um, feeling?" I asked as I brought her mocha to the table. She looked terrible, with dark circles like bruises under her eyes. But she was smiling.

She laughed as she leaned across the table toward

me. "We made breakfast," she whispered. "How crazy is that? A Halloween party, and people stayed long enough to make *breakfast.*"

I glanced at Kara behind the counter. She waved her hand at me. *Go ahead.* I sat down opposite Laura, next to the wide front window. "Yeah," I said, smiling. "That was an amazing party."

"So," Laura said, wrapping her hands around her wide, white coffee mug. "Lucas."

And that's why you're here, I thought. My cheeks flushed, and Laura raised an eyebrow.

"You two were pretty close. At the party. And you left together."

"Yeah," I stammered. "I actually, uh, I knew... Lucas. Before the party."

"You invited him!" Laura's face lit up.

"Well, I mentioned it to him. I think he kind of invited himself. He just sort of... shows up."

"Carol! You're dating someone and you didn't even mention it?"

"It's kind of..." I hesitated, blushing furiously. "Complicated."

"Oh, my gosh," Laura said. She looked like she was enjoying this immensely. "Tell me everything."

I paused. "He doesn't... I mean, he's not... He doesn't exactly... live... in Chicago," I stammered, awkwardly.

Laura dropped her voice to a conspiratorial whisper.

"Don't tell me he's *married!*"

I opened my mouth, and then I closed it again. The legends are very clear. All of them have wives. Óðinn is married to Frija. Thor is married to Sif.

And Loki is married to Sigyn.

I opened my mouth again, but nothing came out.

Laura laughed and covered her mouth with her hand.

"Carol! I had no idea you were so wicked!"

CHAPTER FIFTEEN

"I love it here," I said.

Loki and I sprawled together on the circular bed in Nowhere. The sun was sparkled across the distant waves; the windows were open to the soft breeze. My eyes traced the room again, from the open windows to the curving bookshelves. The soft, leather bindings on the books were made to be held, the golden runes on their spines beckoning. Loki turned to me, kissed the top of my head. His hands began to trace the curve of my hip.

"Wait a minute," I said.

I got to my feet and walked to the bookcase. I could have sworn I'd seen it again; the golden runes on the back of a huge, scarlet tome *flickered*. I brushed the soft leather with my fingertips. There! The golden letters flowed together, almost forming something I could recognize.

"They changed," I said, turning to Loki. "The letters. I swear they just changed."

Loki smiled. "The books like you," he said. "I imagine if you were here long enough, you'd be able to read them all."

"But..." I turned back to the red book, stroking its spine gently. The letters flickered again, flowing gently under my fingertips. It wasn't Cyrillic... it wasn't Norse...

Then the letters stiffened, and I could read them.

RAGNARÖK

"Oh!"

I pulled my hand away. I could read the books next to it as well: DEATHS OF THE ÆSIR FORETOLD. TWILIGHT OF THE GODS.

I turned to Loki, my hand trembling. "Are they all about... Ragnarök?"

"Oh, no," Loki said, still smiling. "Most of them are recipes for custard."

I swallowed and tried to smile. *I think I preferred it when I couldn't read the books,* I thought, stepping away from the shelf.

"So Ragnarök hasn't happened yet?" I asked.

"No," Loki said, his voice suddenly serious. "It has not yet happened. It is the destruction of all Nine Realms, your world as well as mine."

"But if you know how it happens..."

"Yes!" Loki said, coming to his feet. "Yes, exactly! If a thing is foretold, can't it be prevented?"

"But how?"

Loki spun on his heels to face me, and he smiled, bringing his fingers together in front of his lips. "Yes, how?" he asked me. "How would you prevent Ragnarök, mortal woman?"

I thought for a moment, walking to the open windows. "Well, a peace treaty would be the most obvious option."

Loki shook his head, his fingers still resting on his lips. "The enmity between the Jötunn and the Æsir is older than civilizations," he said. "The only thing that has ever united them is a common enemy."

"But if it means the destruction of the entire world... of all the worlds..."

Loki waved his hand dismissively. "They're idiots," he spat. "Do you know what they do for fun in Óðinn's Val-Hall? To entertain themselves?"

"They feast all night," I said, trying to remember the exact wording. "And..." I closed my eyes. I could picture the passage from the *Edda*, and I recited it exactly:

Each day after they have got dressed they put on wargear and go out into the courtyard and fight each other. And when dinner-time approaches they ride back to Val-Hall and sit down to drink.

"Ugh," said Loki, making a face. "Close enough. Can

you imagine a more idiotic way to spend the centuries?"

I was silent as the full weight of what he'd said began to sink in.

Somewhere out there, Val-Hall was real. The Nine Realms were real. Óðinn was real, presiding over those who fall in battle and join him for an afterlife of feasting and fighting. Ever since Laura and Vance's Halloween party I'd been trying to wrap my mind around the idea that Loki was real, but somehow I hadn't thought...

"Out of ideas?" Loki asked, raising an eyebrow.

"Isn't there someone who could broker a peace treaty?" I asked.

Loki laughed, a sharp, bitter laugh.

"Fine," I said, waving my hand. "Let me think. The legends talk about what happens during Ragnarök, but not when it happens, right? So you don't know what causes it?"

"Right. We don't know the trigger."

"Let's see. It starts with three long winters. And then Hrym's ship sails, the ship of the Jötunn."

Loki nodded. "The ship Naglfar."

"Can it be stopped?" I asked, turning to face him. "The Naglfar? Can it be destroyed?"

He smiled at me. "The last battle I fought was on the decks of that wretched vessel," he said. "We've been destroying it for a thousand years."

"I remember the last battle you fought," I said,

thinking of bloody towels in my bathtub.

Loki turned away from me. For a heartbeat, he seemed uncomfortable. Then the floor shook beneath me, and the room went dark. There was a great crashing rumble across the ocean outside the wide windows.

"Damn," whispered Loki, now standing beside me. "You'll have to excuse me."

I turned to him. He was now wearing his full leather armor, his cape flared behind him, and I was suddenly afraid.

"Be careful," I whispered, reaching for his hand. "Come back to me."

"Your concern is - " His brow furrowed, and then he turned to me and smiled.

"Touching, actually," he said. He raised my fingers to his lips, kissing them gently. "I shall be... careful."

Then he turned to the windows, his expression fierce

-

- and I was back in my empty apartment.

* * * * * * * *

Sunday dawned gray and cold, a haze of freezing rain obscuring the street outside my windows. I watched ice build on the smooth branches of the sycamore trees as I spent the morning hunched over my desk. Researching

Sigyn. Wife of Loki.

She was beautiful. *Great.*

And she was the goddess of fidelity. *Good for her.*

I kept reading, although I knew the story by heart. After Loki tricked Höðr into killing Baldr with a mistletoe spear, he and Sigyn were both imprisoned in the earth. Loki was bound under a great snake who dripped poison into his mouth and eyes, and Sigyn caught the poison in a bowl. That was the end of Sigyn's story. And the end of Loki's story too, until he escapes his imprisonment for the final battle. For Ragnarök.

But Loki is no longer bound under the earth, I thought, and I shivered, remembering the delicate white scars radiating from his eyes. *So where is Sigyn?*

I slammed the book shut in frustration.

"Why don't you just ask him?" I muttered to the empty room.

I ran my fingers through my hair and whispered, "Hey, Loki, I was just reading the *Edda* and I noticed you're... married."

I groaned and put my hands over my face.

"Come on, Carol," I said. "You talked about your mom for hours the last time you saw him. Just say, hey, Loki, you'd tell me if you were, uh, married, right?"

Ugh. Fuck. This.

I swept up my books and notes and turned to something moderately less depressing: my finances. My part-time job at Higher Grounds and my graduate student stipend covered the bills, barely, but I was beyond ready to move out of my shitty studio apartment and into something that could fit more than my bed, my dresser, and one sad little bookcase; I was already stacking books on the floor. The extra money I earned teaching freshman classes should make a difference...

After an hour with a calculator, graph paper, and six months worth of receipts, I had to admit the extra money from teaching made zero difference. I was still paying off the goddamn bed and my goddamn credit card, and I would be forever. Even if I cancelled my internet and my cell phone, there was no way I could afford a higher rent.

And I'd managed to put myself in one hell of a bad mood. Reading about Loki's beautiful, faithful wife and then determining exactly how screwed I was, financially speaking, probably was not the best way to spend my Sunday. I laced up my running shoes, determined to do something productive with what was left of the day.

It was a horrible day for running. The paths along the lakeshore were gritty with a layer of ice; the freezing rain soaked through my jacket in seconds. I watched dark clouds skating across the lake, gray rain coming down in sheets above the churning water.

As I followed the curve of Promontory Point, I noticed a lone figure standing on the path. No, not quite on the path - next to the path, leaning against a tree. In the rain. Almost as if he were waiting for someone.

My heart leapt as recognition dawned on me, and I ran to him.

"Hello, mortal woman," Loki said, smiling at me as rain poured down his face.

I smiled and slowed down, catching my breath.

"I've come back," he said. "As you requested." He pulled me into his arms and pressed his lips to mine. He tasted like the rain, cold and wild.

* * * * * * *

I awoke to the screech of my alarm clock, rolling over to slam it off. I sat up in bed, rubbed my eyes. My apartment smelled... *good.* Disturbingly good.

"Breakfast?" Loki asked.

I blinked open my eyes and saw two plates on the table, filled with fruit and thick slices of bread, and two steaming mugs of coffee. "You made breakfast?" I asked.

"I did not make breakfast," he said. "I stole breakfast. From Val-Hall."

I laughed. "I don't think I deserve you," I said.

"Absolutely true," he said. "You deserve the very best."

I felt my cheeks flush and I reached for him, but he

moved to the table and sat down. I pulled on my robe and joined him.

"What's all this?" he asked, sliding my calculator off the pad of graph paper where I'd written *apartment* and then crossed it out about fifty times.

I was intensely grateful I'd moved my notes about Sigyn. "It's nothing."

"Apartment," he muttered, running his fingers down the list of potential rent costs I'd written and then crossed out, one by one.

"Really, ignore it," I said, feeling my cheeks flush as I pulled the pad of paper out of his hand. "Mortal problems. Incredibly boring."

Loki raised an eyebrow at me. "If you need money..." he said, but I cut him off, waving my hand.

"I don't," I said. "Seriously. I've got a plan."

And I did have a plan. Sort of. If I really wanted an apartment with a wall between the kitchen sink and the bed, I'd go to the Financial Aid office and beg, on my knees, if necessary, for more student loans. There. My plan was brilliant in its simplicity.

Loki reached across the table to grab a strawberry from my plate. "So," he said, his fingers delicately tracing the length of my arm. "How much time do we have this morning?"

I shivered at his touch. "Damn," I muttered. "Not much. I'm due at the coffee shop in an hour. And I teach after that."

Loki sighed dramatically. He looked impossibly attractive with the pale light of early morning winking off his hair.

"You know what," I said, putting down my coffee and grabbing his hand. "Forget breakfast."

His eyes danced as he brought my wrist to his mouth. "An hour," he said, his breath warm against my skin. "What can we do with an hour?"

I shivered again as he kissed the inside of my wrist, his tongue flickering against my skin. My breath caught in my throat. *He should not be able to turn me on this much kissing my arm,* I thought. Then he stood and began kissing my neck, his cool lips sending shivers through my body.

"Do you want to move to the - " I asked, but my question turned into a low moan as he pushed my robe open and ran his hands along the curve of my waist.

"Absolutely not," he whispered against my neck.

He dropped to his knees in front of me, kissing my breasts, his tongue flickering over my nipples. I gasped and leaned back, hitting the table, dislodging a stack of papers. He glanced up, smiling at me.

"Ah, you are so hot," I gasped.

I bent toward him and he kissed me, his lips pressed against mine, his tongue inside me as his fingers traced the inside of my thighs, pressing gently against my clit, sending waves of pleasure through my body. My hips rocked into his hand. My breath was fast and shallow when he pulled away.

"Let's go to bed," I panted, reaching for him.

"Oh, let's not," he said, smiling wickedly.

And then his head was between my legs. There was a flood of heat as his tongue entered me, flickering against my clit, kissing and sucking until the room was spinning. I ran my hands through his hair, my hips rocking against him as he moved inside me, my body trembling. I closed my eyes. He felt so good, he always felt so good, so goddamned amazingly *good* -

I cried his name as I came, hard, against his lips, my entire body shaking under him.

I slowly opened my eyes as my mind staggered back to reality. Loki was sitting on his knees in front of me, and I stared at him; he looked so fucking gorgeous in the sunlight. "Wow," I panted.

He stood and started kissing my neck, running his hands gently along my breasts. I turned toward his mouth, opening to him. I could taste myself as our lips met.

"Mortal woman," he whispered, his hand cupping my breast, "I still desire you."

I glanced at the clock above my half-oven. "Yeah," I said. "Yeah, we've got time."

He grabbed me by my waist and picked me up,

carrying me to the bed. I spread my legs under him, and then he was inside me, filling me, fucking me, feeling so good, so unbelievably good, and I moaned and whimpered, low, animal noises of pleasure and longing. I braced myself against the wall and arched my back, driving him deeper as his thrusts became less rhythmic, more frantic.

And then his body shuddered against mine as he cried out, his hands tight around my hips. He collapsed next to me and we lay together, panting, our legs intertwined. I reached for his hand, laced my fingers with his.

"Woman," he said, sitting up to look at me. "You're going to be late."

I smiled. The sun was shining through his hair, making it look almost like it was on fire, like it was made of flames, casting delicate, dancing shadows across his full lips, his pale cheeks. *I could stare at him all day,* I thought.

"I don't even think my legs work anymore," I sighed.

He smiled and kissed my hand. I tore my eyes away from him and forced myself to stand up, pulling on my jeans with trembling hands. I glanced at the clock -

"Shit," I muttered. "It's a fifteen minute walk. I really am going to be late." I yanked the first shirt in my closet over my head and grabbed my jacket. "Thanks -"

Loki cut me off, wrapping his arms around me and

pressing his lips against mine -

- and it was suddenly very cold. I opened my eyes. We were outside. I blinked and turned to see the windows of Higher Grounds Coffee Shop. The lights were blazing inside, and I could just hear K.D. Lang singing about northern Ontario while Kara stocked pastries in the display case.

"Thank you," I said, somewhat breathlessly. "That was... nice. Of you."

Loki shrugged and kissed me again, softly, before he turned and walked away, down the cold Chicago sidewalk. I took a deep breath and pushed open the door to Higher Grounds, the bell above the door jangling as I entered. Kara was staring out the window, staring at the spot where Loki and I had been kissing.

"Uh, good morning," I said, my cheeks flushing.

"I didn't know you had a boyfriend," she said.

I laughed, shrugging off my jacket. "Oh, I don't. I mean, he's not. We just - " I caught the look on Kara's face, the one that said she was pretty damn sure I was totally insane, and I shut up.

It was two hours before I realized my shirt was on inside out.

* * * * * * *

It was dark by the time I made it home. I unlocked my

door and blinked in the gentle, gray light. It looked like my table was covered with a stack of... bricks? I rubbed my eyes. The bricks didn't move. I turned on the light and walked to the table.

It was money.

My table was covered with piles of hundred-dollar bills, neatly stacked and banded. The pad of graph paper sat casually atop the stacks, open to the sheet where I'd written *apartment*.

I covered my face with my hands and cried.

CHAPTER SIXTEEN

The money changed everything.

I counted it and re-counted it, and then went through my bills with shaking hands. It was enough to pay everything: The bed. The credit card. My student loans. It was enough to pay everything and more. I could quit my job at Higher Grounds. I could finally get a laptop. And a smart phone.

And a new apartment.

I walked to the bank that morning and handed the teller a small fortune in cash. "I just sold my car," I said, with a relaxed ease I'd been practicing for hours.

The cashier didn't even respond. She just counted the bills, handed me a receipt, and said, "Next."

And then I went apartment hunting.

I toured the Hyde Park Towers first, but the apartments felt cold and sterile. Then I toured the Mayfair Apartments, but the rent seemed outrageous, even for someone who'd just found stacks of hundred dollar bills on her desk. Finally I walked to the

Flamingo, an elegant, if somewhat crumbing, pink-brick high rise along the lakeshore.

"Well, we've got a one-bedroom just opened up," the Albanian superintendent told me as we rode the elevator to the fourteenth floor.

We walked down the narrow hallway together and he unlocked the door. The apartment was filled with sunshine. The floor had dusky pink carpeting, and there was a wall of windows facing the lake. I could see the bare branches of the trees along Promontory Point, where Loki had first shown me fireflies. White-capped waves tossed and churned the surface of Lake Michigan. *He'd like it here*, I thought.

"I'll take it," I said.

The superintendent stared at me. "You wanna see the rest of the apartment, lady?"

"Sure," I said, smiling.

The bedroom was dark and small, although it looked like it would fit my enormous bed, and the bathroom had a claw-foot tub that could probably fit two. *We'll have to test it*, I thought, running my fingers along its cool porcelain rim. The kitchen was so small I could stand in the middle, spread my arms, and touch both walls, but my culinary skills were pretty much limited to Ramen noodles, so I didn't mind.

I followed the superintendent back downstairs and signed the papers, handing him a huge stack of hundred dollar bills as a security deposit and first month's rent.

"We're going to love it," I said.

He stared at me.

"I," I stammered. "I'm going to love it."

"You at the University?" he asked.

I nodded.

"Thought so," he said, as he handed me a set of keys. "Welcome to the Flamingo."

* * * * * * * *

I spent the weekend unpacking and decorating my new home in the Flamingo building. I stuffed the rest of the money into a box and hid it in the bottom cabinet in the kitchen, behind the untouched mixing bowl set Mom sent me for my birthday. And then I went shopping.

I bought a huge wrought-iron wine rack that covered almost the entire kitchen counter, and I filled it with zinfandels and pinots, the wines I knew Loki liked. I bought a full set of crystal wine glasses, long and delicate and sensuous, and I left two of them out on the counter.

Ready.

I bought an elegant cherry-wood dining table with curving legs, and a full set of china plates etched with small, silver fireflies. The table could seat four people, maybe even five or six if we squeezed together. *I could have dinner parties,* I told myself. *In fact, I will. I will have dinner parties.*

I bought a proper roll-top desk for my new laptop, with a comfortable, black office chair, a printer, and a wooden filing cabinet. I wrote "DISSERTATION" on the top drawer and "EXAMS" on the bottom drawer, and then I spent an entire afternoon organizing my notes.

For the living room I bought a soft, cream colored couch with curving arms and an ice-blue rug, and I lined the walls with white bookcases. It wasn't until I'd finished unpacking my books that I realized I was trying to recreate Nowhere: the wall of windows, opening to the water, curving to meet the wall of books behind.

Later that week I walked home past the undergraduate art show. I went in before I could stop myself and bought a huge, abstract painting, a wild swirling chaos of black and scarlet and vermillion which reminded me of Loki's armor. I hung it above the bed and lined the top of my dresser with tea candles.

"It's ready," I said, stepping back. The painting looked amazing in the flickering candlelight.

"Ready when you are," I said, my voice echoing in the empty room.

I walked through the apartment again, running my hands across the soft couch, staring out the windows at the headlights flickering along Lake Shore Drive. I lit the candles in the living room and on the dining table. Their light danced and shimmered across the silver fireflies in the china on the table. I could see the candlelight reflected in the dark windows and, above that, I could see the dim outline of my own reflection. Standing alone in my new living room.

With a sigh, I blew out the candles and headed to the shower. It was getting late.

* * * * * * *

The apartment seemed very dark when I stepped out of the shower. I fumbled along the bedroom wall for the light switch.

"Hello, mortal woman," Loki said.

I smiled and gave up looking for the light switch, letting my towel fall in a heap at my feet. "You found me," I said, with a slight tremble in my voice.

"Were you trying to hide?" he asked, sounding amused.

The tea candles flared to life, and I could see his smile. I sighed and reached for him, my arms around his chest, breathing him in. We stood together in silence, the sounds of traffic and the waves of Lake Michigan barely audible through the living room windows.

"I like this place," he said, leaning down to brush my

cheeks with his soft lips.

I wanted to thank him. I wanted to explain how I'd arranged every part of the apartment with him in mind, wondering if the couch would feel soft on his naked skin, imaging him smiling at the fireflies in the china.

I opened my mouth and kissed him.

CHAPTER SEVENTEEN

I ignored my grumbling stomach until it became painful, and then I ignored it just a bit longer. My exams were in one week, the date circled in red on the Historical Chicago calendar thumb-tacked over my desk. One. Week. And I still didn't understand Immanuel Kant, the seventeenth-century German philosopher whose ideas would assuredly be a huge part of the exam.

I had all his books spread out before me, from the *Groundwork for the Metaphysics of Morals* to the *Critique of Pure Reason*, including a copy of the *Prolegomena* in the original German. Plus an enormous stack of notes. But my vision was starting to blur, and ideas that made sense hours ago were falling apart. *One week,* I thought, biting my lip. *Seven. Days.* I pushed back from the desk and stood up. Maybe it was time to take a break.

The world suddenly got dim around the edges. I had enough time to wonder why my kitchen was getting so small before I passed out.

I woke up face-down on my living room floor. There was a hand on my shoulder, turning me onto my back. "Hey, you," I said, smiling as Loki's blue eyes and high cheekbones came into focus. He looked upset.

"Mortal woman," he frowned, "when was the last time you had something to eat?"

"Just, uh," I tried to remember, pushing myself to sitting, "this morning? I think I had... some almonds?"

Loki shook his head. "Come on," he said, reaching for me.

"Oh, no," I said, pushing his arm away. "I'm not done here. I've only got seven days, and I don't understand Kant!"

"Oh, shut up," he said, wrapping his arms around my shoulders -

-and then we were in Nowhere, and there was a table waiting for us.

I was too hungry and tired to protest any further, so I sat down at the table and helped myself to a cucumber sandwich and then a bagel with smoked salmon. Loki poured me a glass of something dark and red. It was sweet and sparkling, and it tasted amazing.

"Thanks," I said, grudgingly, as my stomach stopped growling and my blood sugar levels slowly returned to something resembling normalcy.

"Do you want me to intervene?" he asked. "I could

make it so the examiners believe your answers are the most brilliant exposition they've ever heard."

"Oh, God, no," I said, almost choking on my juice. "No, no, don't you dare. It won't mean a thing if I don't do it myself."

Loki smiled at me. "Suit yourself."

I stared out the windows to the gentle sun-lit sea. I suddenly felt very tired.

"So," Loki said, "what is it about Kant you don't understand."

I raised an eyebrow at him. "You've read Kant?"

He laughed. "My darling, what do you take me for?"

Fine, I thought. *I'm calling your stupid bluff.* "The categorical imperative," I said.

"Which formulation?" he asked, smiling. "You are aware of the fact that Kant offered three separate versions?"

He's not bluffing, I thought, and I tried to hide my smile behind another cucumber sandwich. "All of them," I said. "Tell me everything."

By the time Loki walked around the table, picked me up, and carried me to the bed, I finally understood Kant.

* * * * * * *

I woke in the middle of the night, sitting up in the darkness. "My exams!" I gasped.

"Four days away," muttered Loki, without moving. "Go back to sleep, woman."

I sat in the darkness until my frantic heartbeat calmed, listening to the lap and murmur of waves outside the windows. It was very dark in Nowhere, the darkness of a place with no streetlights, no cars, no gleaming or beeping electronics. Outside the wide, open windows, the sky shimmered with unfamiliar stars. The delicate white curtains filled and luffed in the breeze off the ocean.

Everyone ends up in the ER before exams, Debra told me. I sighed. *I guess this beats the ER.* The sense of panic that had been tightening in my chest since September slowly began to drain out of my body. Four days until the exams that would determine the course of my entire life. I should have been terrified. I should have been studying.

I lay down next to Loki, savoring his woodsmoke scent, listening to his soft, rhythmic breathing. And I fell asleep.

* * * * * * *

My exams took place on Thursday and Friday; two written exams on Thursday, the final written exam and the verbal exam on Friday. I had four hours for each exam, with a thirty minute break in between.

I woke at four in the morning on Thursday, alone in my bed. For one disorienting moment I thought I was back in Nowhere, but the blue glow of my bedside clock was nothing like the stars outside those windows, and the sound of cars along Lake Shore Drive was nothing like the gentle muttering waves of that alien ocean.

I went for a run along Promontory Point as the sun rose, trying not to think. And then it was time to eat something, shower, get dressed. Walk to campus. Face the music.

My hands trembled as I opened my laptop in the exam room. Steve sat two desks away, looking very pale, and I smiled at him. He gave me a gladiator salute, thumping his chest and raising his hand.

"Those who are about to die, salute you," he said.

"Very encouraging," I said. "Thanks."

Then we were given our questions, and the room filled with the sound of tapping keyboards.

* * * * * * *

Steve and I left Swift Hall together after our final exam, late Friday afternoon. He put an arm around my shoulder at the foot of the staircase.

"Carol," he said, "we are going directly to the pub. Do not pass go, do not collect two hundred dollars."

"Yes, please," I said.

Laura was already at the University pub with Vance. She looked exhausted and shell-shocked, and I realized that's how Steve and I must look too. Debra sat at the table with her business school boyfriend, and she welcomed us with hugs and a fresh pitcher of Blue Moon. Then she came back to the table with tequila shots.

"Now, this is the tradition," she said. "One shot for every exam. Here's for Thursday morning."

We grabbed the shot glasses, clinked them together, and knocked them down, wincing as the cheap tequila burned our throats.

"Yay!" Debra said, clapping. "Finish your beers and I'll get a shot for Thursday afternoon!"

I shook my head, my throat still burning from the tequila. "Ugh," I said, "Not just -"

"Oh, my gosh!" Laura squeaked, hitting me on the arm. "Is that Lucas?"

I turned and saw Loki. He looked impeccable, and absurdly out of place, in an expensive dark green three-piece suit. He walked across the the dingy basement pub as if he owned it, oblivious to the stares following him.

He stopped at our table. "May I join you?" he asked.

Debra jumped up and actually hugged him, and I saw a look of concern flit across her boyfriend's face.

"Lucas!" said Laura. "I had no idea you were in town!"

"Wouldn't miss it for the world," said Loki, pulling a chair to the table and then sitting in it backwards. His eyes met mine; I smiled and felt blood rush to my cheeks.

"Now," he said, his eyes dancing wickedly as he pulled out a bottle of champagne, "I believe we are celebrating tonight."

* * * * * * *

We finished three bottles of champagne in the pub, and then Loki reached in his pocket and pulled out a silver iPhone. I stared at it.

"Our ride has arrived," he announced.

"You have an iPhone?" I said.

He ignored the question and stood, offering me his arm. I took it, and we all walked out of the dark basement. A gleaming black limousine waited on the street. Loki walked to it and swung open the door.

Debra shrieked as she pulled her boyfriend into the limo. Laura stared at me, her mouth open. "Is this for real?" she asked.

"I don't know," I told her, honestly, and I followed Debra into the dim interior of the limo.

I sat next to Loki, my body pressed against his. There were several more bottles of champagne waiting in a silver ice bucket.

"Now," said Loki, popping the champagne cork out the open window as the limo purred into motion, "we have to finish this before the next stop."

The champagne spilled and bubbled and frothed as he filled our glasses, and we all laughed.

"Lucas," said Steve, raising his glass, "you're all right."

"Why thank you, Steve," said Loki, raising an eyebrow. "Drink fast."

* * * * * * *

The limo stopped downtown, next to a neon sign of dancing flames, arching and spinning against the sky. Low, loud music throbbed out of the building. The entrance was blocked with red velvet ropes and several large, black-suited men, and the line behind the ropes stretched around the corner.

I turned to find the end of the line, but Loki grabbed my hand and murmured something to one of the bouncers. They unhooked the red ropes and stood aside to let us pass.

"Oh, my gosh," said Laura, shaking her head as we walked into the nightclub.

Vance leaned over to me. "How exactly did you meet Lucas?" he asked.

But I didn't have time to answer, because Loki was

pulling me through the club, across the dance floor, into a large, red paneled room marked VIP. A row of shots stood waiting on one of the low, dark, candle-lit tables.

"One for every exam, right?" Loki said over the music.

"Thursday afternoon," said Debra, delighted. She handed shots to Steve, Laura and me. "Go ahead," she said. "It's a tradition."

We smiled at each other and clinked our shot glasses together. This time it was not cheap University pub tequila, and it didn't burn. I felt the heat of the shot travel down my throat, spreading through my body. And then the world began to tilt.

* * * * * * *

"Ugh, I can't handle this song," Debra yelled to me.

I stopped, trying to listen to the music. The guy next to me had dropped to a squat, thrusting his hips, his arms stretched in front of him with his wrists crossed.

Right. Gangnam Style. I held out my hands and crossed my wrists. Debra stuck out her tongue at me.

"I'mma get another drink," Debra yelled. "You want one?"

I gave her a double thumbs up, and then I turned around, searching the crowd. *Where is-*

Loki was standing in a dark corner. Not alone.

The two women talking to him were stupidly attractive. The blonde wore a short, tight silver dress. Even from here, I could tell her face was absolutely perfect. Next to her was a redhead in tight jeans with sexy black heels and what looked like a bikini top.

I stopped dancing and looked at my own outfit. Black yoga pants and a green sweater. *I'm wearing a sweater,* I thought. *In a nightclub.*

I am the least sexy person alive.

I froze as the blonde laughed and put her hand on Loki's chest. *He could have them,* I thought, my heart clenching painfully in my chest. *He could have anyone in here.* I watched as Loki's suit *flickered,* and then he was wearing his leather armor, his black cape sweeping the floor behind him. He reached for her hand, pulled it off his chest, placed it at her side. Then he bent low, said something that made them both laugh, and walked away.

By the time he found me he was wearing his suit again. "My darling," he said, kissing my neck.

Tears bit at the corners of my eyes. "What are you doing with me?" I asked.

He pressed his lips to mine and kissed me. His mouth tasted like champagne. We kissed for a long time, trading breaths while the dancers twirled and gyrated around us. I sighed when he pulled away.

"I'm celebrating with you," he said, his voice rough,

his mouth close to my ear. "And later tonight I'll be fucking you."

I shivered. Maybe I wasn't the *least* sexy person alive, after all.

"You're irresistible," I said, twining my hands around his neck. "You realize you could have anyone?" I waved my arm to encompass the entire dance floor, the nightclub. The blonde in the silver dress. The redhead in the tight jeans.

Loki grabbed me by my hips, pulled me to his body. "Ah, but I don't want anyone," he growled.

I felt like my heart would explode. I pressed my body against his, our lips touching, and we kissed and kissed as the world spun around us.

* * * * * * *

The limo was waiting for us when the club closed, and we all staggered into the warm, dim interior. Loki handed us glasses of champagne as the limo took off. He was talking to Vance, something about industrial finance that I found hilarious, and I could not stop staring at him. *Real,* I thought, giggling. *He's really, really real.*

"Hey, this isn't going to Hyde Park," said Steve, staring out the window.

"No," said Loki, as the limo slowed to a stop. "It's

not."

I climbed out and blinked. We were on the North Avenue Beach. The city lights blazed behind us, and a few stars danced and spun over the vast, black lake.

I smiled at Loki as my friends stumbled out of the limo. "What are you up to?"

He grinned as he shrugged off his suit jacket. "Swimming," he said. He started to unbutton his shirt. "Who's with me?"

"Why the hell not?" Vance said.

I turned and my mouth dropped open. Vance was sitting in the sand, carefully putting his socks inside his shoes. Laura looked as surprised as I felt.

"Well, fuck, I'm in," said Steve, peeling off his shirt.

Loki slipped out of his pants and then turned to the dark water, revealing the gorgeous curves of his amazing ass. I felt my cheeks burn.

"Come on, ladies," Steve yelled, running after Loki. "You're not going to let us do something this stupid alone, are you?"

"Oh, it's on," said Laura, kicking off her shoes.

And then I pulled off my sweater and slipped out of my pants, almost tripping over myself as I kicked off my shoes, and I ran into the water, laughing and shrieking.

I remembered North Avenue Beach as long and shallow, but the shore fell away quickly where we were, and soon we were floating in the cool lake, the streetlights reflecting off the water. We laughed and shared stories, and after a while it felt like there was no distinction between the black water and the black sky, like we were all floating, suspended, among the stars of the night sky.

"Oh, my gosh, Carol, I can see you!" Laura suddenly shrieked.

"So?"

"It's the sun," said Debra, and we all turned to look across the water. The sky was lighter in the East; the clouds were beginning to blush pink.

"Shit," said Steve, "it's getting light!"

"We've got to get out of here," yelled Laura, and then we were all headed for the shore, laughing and splashing in the water.

I tried to dress quickly, tried not to look at my naked friends as I pulled on my crumpled green sweater and brushed the sand off my feet. And then we were all sitting on the beach, hair dripping, watching the sky above the lake turn from gray to pale, shimmering blue.

"Here," said Loki, handing me a red, plastic cup. "Pass it down."

"What is it?"

Loki sat next to me, shirtless, his pale chest still dripping with lake water. I noticed Laura sitting next to him, holding a red cup. Not exactly watching the sunrise. "Trust me," he said, his eyes sparkling.

I handed the cup to Debra, who passed it to Vance.

"Oh, my God," said Vance. "This is amazing. Lucas, what the hell is this?"

I knew before I brought my cup to my lips. I sat with my friends on the shores of Lake Michigan, watching the sunrise, drinking the mead of Val-Hall.

* * * * * * *

My phone rang around noon the next day. I reached a hand out of the covers and fumbled on my nightstand, pulling the phone back under my pillow.

"Hello?" I muttered without opening my eyes.

"Hi, it's Laura," she said, her voice sounding groggy. "I just wanted to check. Did last night actually happen?"

I laughed and rolled onto my back. "You mean the club?"

"I mean all of it," she said. "Lucas showed up with a... a limo?"

"And about a hundred bottles of champagne," I said.

"Ugh, don't mention the champagne," she groaned.

"Well, I'm pretty sure the VIP room really happened, too," I said.

"Yeah, I remember the VIP room. And, uh," her voice dropped to a whisper, "did we really go skinny dipping?"

I laughed. "Yes," I said. "Yes, we really did."

"I remember the beach," she said. "I remember riding the limo there, and swimming. But I don't even know how we got home."

Loki got you home, I thought. *Loki got you all home after we shared the mead of Val-Hall so we could make love in the crashing waves and watch the sun rise.*

"Yeah, I think it all really happened," I said.

Laura let out a loud sigh. "Lucas should really come out with us more often," she said. "He is *amazing.*"

I hung up the phone and turned to smile at Loki, who was sitting in my bed reading *The Myth of the Eternal Return.*

"I think she'd like to fuck you," I said.

"Not a chance," he said.

CHAPTER EIGHTEEN

Exactly one week after exams concluded, the results were posted in the lobby. I passed. Laura passed. Steve passed. We all passed. I ducked in the women's bathroom until I could stop crying.

Loki was sitting on my couch when I got home.

"Congratulations," he said, before I'd even stepped through the door. "And, for the record, I played no part in this."

"Thank you," I said, smiling.

It was a strange feeling; I wasn't sure if I wanted to scream, or dance, or just curl up and sleep. My body was exhausted and I was trembling from too much coffee but, for the first time in months, I felt like I could relax. I actually felt relaxed.

"I've brought you something," Loki said, pulling a small bottle from his coat pocket.

It was an odd container, with a long neck and a round bottom. The golden liquid inside was phosphorescing in the spring sunlight.

"What...?"

"It's mead," he said. "Óðinn's mead."

"*Óðinn's* mead?" I asked, shaking my head as I sat next to him. "You mean, the mead that inspires all poetry?"

He smiled wickedly.

"I thought only Óðinn could drink that mead."

Loki's face dropped into an expression of shock. "Oh, no, I think you're right," he said. "I'd better return it!"

Then he bent toward me, his face next to mine as he whispered in my ear, "Of course, how boring the world would be if we all did what we were supposed to..."

There were only a few sips of mead in the bottle, and we drank them together. Then Loki put his arms around me -

-and we were standing, hand in hand, before a tree.

The grass beneath us was green, an aggressive, neon, electric green. And the tree in the middle of the grass was unimaginably tall, taller than the Chicago skyscrapers, with twisting branches sweeping up and over our head in all directions.

Plato was right, I thought. *This is The Tree, the very Form of Tree.*

"Is this...?" I asked, turning to Loki.

"Yggdrasil," he said. "Yes, it is."

I stared at Loki in the strange, shifting light filtering

through the leaves of the World Tree. His hair was not just red, here; his hair was flame, leaping and dancing in the space above his head. He looked very wild, and very ancient, and not even remotely human.

I love him, I thought, and the realization surged through my body, forcing the air from my chest. *I love the God of Lies.*

Like loving the wind.

"Don't waste your time staring at me," he said, although not unkindly. "Look at Yggdrasil. Few mortals have ever seen the World Tree."

It was very difficult to tear my eyes from Loki's dancing, shifting, beautiful face, and I don't think I could have done it if he hadn't also put his arms around my waist, turning me to face the tree.

It is an ash tree, I thought, stepping closer, staring at the bark. *It's a California ash tree. Just like the tree in my parents' yard.* I moved toward the deeply lined bark of the World Tree and realized it was shifting. The lines became runes, became words, became figures.

And then it was not bark, but the face of my brother Geoff. His hair dripped salt water, and he wiped his eyes with the back of his hand. Then his hand returned to the ocean, and he paddled his surfboard into the waves. I could see the California sunshine sparkling off the waves, like the very gold Coronado was seeking.

"All is well in Midgard," Loki whispered, his body

pressed tightly against mine.

"Unbelievable," I said. "What else can I - " And I put my hands on the warm, living bark of Yggdrasil.

A shiver ran the length of my body. Then I was walking through my parents' house, empty now in the middle of the day, and Loki walked beside me, his hand in mine. I opened the sliding glass door to the backyard, and we entered a forest, a light and scrubby California oak forest that grew deeper and darker as I walked. The ground became rough, rocky and broken beneath my feet, the light faded, and it grew cold. At some point I realized I was walking alone. I could not remember the exact path Loki had taken, and my heart clenched.

I kept walking, now climbing a hill. The hill became a mountain, and the trees dropped away. I picked my way around huge boulders, climbing through a scree field of shattered granite. As I neared the top, I had to scramble on my hands and knees, slipping once and banging my kneecap hard on a stone.

Then I stood on top of the mountain, and I looked out across a battlefield.

There was no battle. But it was a battlefield, it had always been a battlefield; it was a battlefield the same way Yggdrasil was a tree. *The Battlefield.*

I heard the beating of heavy wings, felt a gust of wind on my cheek, and I turned to find a raven perched next to me. He was tall enough to look me in the eye.

"Shouldn't be here, mortal girl," he said, his black eyes glinting in the pale sunlight.

"I'm not here," I said. "I'm on my couch. In Chicago."

"No," said the raven. "No. You're not."

I shivered. The wind above the battlefield was cold.

"He's in Chicago," said the raven, tilting his head. "He tried to impress you. Now he thinks he's killed you."

Killed you. I felt the first cold spike of fear travel my spine.

"You could pick a better boyfriend," the raven said, conversationally. "How often is he around when you need him, anyway?"

I felt my cheeks flush, and I ignored him. "What is this place?" I asked.

"Vígríðr," said the raven, lifting his wing to nip at something underneath. "But you already knew that. Try asking something else."

I stared across the empty battlefield. The wind picked up, whipping my hair back from my face. I could almost hear the armies marching, marching to Vígríðr for the final battle, the battle that ends everything.

For Ragnarök.

"When is the battle?" I asked.

"Not today," said the raven. "Soon. But you already knew that, too." His black eye glinted at me.

"How do you prevent Ragnarök?" I muttered, half to

myself.

CAW! I jumped back. The crow was laughing at me.

"You can't, stupid girl." The crow shook his head and spread his wings. The next gust of wind carried him off the mountain ledge.

"But you already knew that..." he cried as he left.

"Well, thanks for nothing!" I yelled after him, leaning to see which way he'd gone.

I leaned too far, and I stepped to catch my balance. My foot found nothing but air, and I pitched forward, toward the eternal battlefield. Toward Vígríðr.

* * * * * * *

"Caroline!"

Somewhere, someone was calling my name.

It sounded like Loki. It couldn't be Loki. He'd never called me by my name. And his voice was always level and cool. This voice was frantic, desperate.

"Caroline!"

Perhaps it was my father. Yes, that must be it. Had I done something wrong?

"CAROLINE!"

Something had happened. Someone must be in trouble, someone must need me...

With tremendous effort, I managed to open my eyes.

* * * * * * *

Someone's died.

Loki's face floated in front of mine, tears running down his cheeks, the scars across his lips livid against his pale skin.

Who is it? Who's died?

I tried to ask, but I was still very far away. I could not reach my mouth, could not move my tongue. If only I could reach him - if only I could touch him. I painfully, desperately did not want Loki to be unhappy.

I *pushed* toward him.

And then I felt the floor beneath me, and Loki's arms around my shoulders. I gasped, opening my eyes. His face was smooth, his eyes the cool, translucent blue of the Pacific. *Funny,* I thought, *to imagine he'd been crying.*

Loki grabbed my face. "Where did you go?" he demanded. "Where did you go?" I shook my head. My tongue felt heavy and useless.

"You went somewhere - somewhere I couldn't follow," he said. "I couldn't bring you back."

I realized the arms holding me were trembling. I closed my eyes, trying to remember where I'd been. It was like grasping a dream.

"I talked... to... a bird," I said, my voice a rasping whisper.

"What bird?" said Loki. "What did it say?"

He insulted you, I thought. *He said you're not a good boyfriend.* "I...can't remember," I lied. I did not want him to be unhappy. I leaned against his chest, but his back stiffened as my head touched him.

"You need rest," he said, picking me up and carrying me across the living room, setting me down on the bed. He brushed my cheek, so lightly I may have only imagined it, and then he stepped away. *He's wearing his armor,* I thought, dimly.

"You need rest," he said again, his expression formal and unreadable.

No, I thought. *Stay with me. Please.* But my tongue was still leaden, and I couldn't force my lips to work.

Loki dissolved in front of me. The smell of woodsmoke and sea salt and cold lingered for a moment more, before it too dissipated and was gone.

CHAPTER NINETEEN

That summer I could finally travel to Iceland.

For years, I'd wanted to travel to Reykjavik and visit the libraries. There are some manuscripts that have never left that island, and I was certain I'd find something there, where the stories about Óðinn, Thor, and Loki were first recorded.

I'd applied for travel grants, but Iceland was expensive, and I could all but hear the application committees laughing at me. And I'd never been able to afford a trip to Iceland working part-time at a coffee shop.

But now - now the world was open to me.

I set my alarm for three in the morning to call the National Library of Iceland and plan my visit around their special collections.

"Ja, very good," said a cheerful woman on the far end of the phone. I imagined her sitting behind a big, wooden desk, wearing a sweater, with bright, chill sunlight coming through the windows.

"Oh, and if you study the myths, you want I should put you in touch with Professor Jŏrn?" she asked in a Nordic sing-song.

"Yes, please," I said. I had no idea who Professor Jŏrn was, but I could use all the help I could get.

Professor Hæmir Jŏrn called the next morning. He spoke perfect English with a slight, clipped accent, and he introduced himself as a professor of pre-Christian antiquities at the University of Reykjavik. He was *very* interested in the Norse gods, he told me. In fact, he was leading an archaeological expedition north of Reykjavik in June, and would I be interesting in joining them for a day or so?

"I'd love to," I said, scribbling down the dates.

I booked my plane tickets that afternoon.

* * * * * * *

It was slow, coming out of my dream.

I'd been in a forest, some dark, misty forest. I was by myself, but not exactly alone. Something followed in the trees above me, scurrying on branches just out of sight. Then I shivered, just once, with my whole body, as though I were pushing through a sheet of cold water, coming through the layers of my dream, through the mist and the dark, silent branches. To my own bedroom.

And I could smell... *coffee?*

My bedside alarm clock said it was just past six in the morning. And my apartment smelled like coffee. I walked out of the bedroom, not bothering to pull on my robe. There was, after all, only one other person in the Nine Realms who could have started the coffee pot in my apartment.

Loki stood in the living room, watching the low, gray clouds over the lake, his full, black cape flaring behind him. *Battle armor,* I thought, and my heart twisted with a strange little pang.

"Hey, handsome," I said, softly.

He turned to me with a smile that didn't quite reach his dark eyes. "Mortal woman," he said. "I would speak with you."

Oh, shit.

I felt cold. I hadn't seen him in almost a week, since I found out I passed my exams, since our bizarre night drinking Óðinn's mead. Five nights wasn't such a long time between visits, but I missed him, especially since I'd planned to spend the week after exams fucking him into oblivion. I assumed he was giving me time to recover, from the exams, from the trip to Yggdrasil. But now I wondered if something else had happened between us, something I'd missed, and my stomach clenched painfully. *It's me,* I thought, my heart hammering jaggedly. *I've been too crazy, too neurotic about the exams. About everything.*

He's tired of me.

I walked to him, wrapping my arms around his waist. His back stiffened at my touch. I realized I was afraid of what he might say, so I pressed my lips to his before he could speak. His tongue filled my mouth and his hands ran over my naked body, cool and smooth.

We pulled apart and his eyes closed. I reached for him, tracing his cheek with my finger. His face turned toward my touch. He sighed, and I ran my fingers along the gentle curve of his neck, along his shoulders and down his chest. I kissed him again, harder this time, pulling him close to me.

"Woman," he whispered, his voice rough.

"Shhhhh," I said, pushing him backward.

He stepped to the couch, and I pulled on his shoulders, forcing him to sit. Then I kneeled on top of him, straddling him. His eyes widened and he grabbed my hips, holding me still.

"This is not why I'm here," he growled.

"Hmmm, that's too bad," I said, leaning to run my tongue along the taut lines of his neck. "Because you're *very* good at this."

I arched my back, burying his face in the swell of my breasts, and he moaned. His hands tightened around my hips.

"You are quite distracting," he said, his voice thick.

I smiled. "Just imagine how distracting I could be if you were naked," I said, running my finger down the front of his leather armor.

He gave me an odd half smile, leaned back, closed his eyes. And then he was naked, sweat glistening off his lean, muscular chest.

"Much better," I whispered, pressing my lips against his as I reached down, rubbing the head of his cock, guiding him inside me. His hips strained against mine and we both gasped as he entered me.

I missed this, I thought, sighing as I kissed him. *I missed him. Only a week, and fuck, I missed him.* I grabbed the back of the couch and moved my hips against his until we were both panting, our bodies sparking electricity as the light of the rising sun danced across the wall behind the couch.

The heat between us rippled through my body, swelling and building until all I could feel, all I could smell, all I could taste was him, his sweet body beneath mine, his woodsmoke and salt on my lips and tongue. I gasped inside his mouth as my orgasm crashed over me, leaving me trembling, clinging to his chest.

His breath was rough and jagged against my neck. For a moment neither of us moved, and he wrapped his arms around me, breathing deeply into my hair. Then he grabbed me, holding my hips hard enough to leave bruises, and he thrust inside me, so deep and so fast that

I gasped, leaning back, offering my body to him as he filled me.

His fingers tightened around my waist and I felt his body shake as he came violently inside me. He cried out, his eyes closed, his voice thick; strange, guttural words I didn't know in a language I didn't recognize.

What the hell was that? I thought as he buried his head against my neck, his shoulders shaking. I closed my eyes, resting against him, feeling his wild, jagged pulse. I held him, my arms around his chest, my legs around his waist, until his trembling subsided, until his breathing was deep and even again.

"Coffee?" I asked.

"Please," he said, his voice thick against my neck.

I smiled at him when I stood, but he turned away from me, toward the window.

When I walked back to the living room, he was wearing jeans and a soft, dark shirt. *At least it's not armor,* I thought, handing him a coffee mug from Higher Grounds as I sat down next to him, my head on his shoulder.

"Thank you," I said. "For making coffee."

He did not respond, and I took a deep breath. "You wanted to talk?" I asked, my voice low, my hands curled around my mug.

He sighed and bent toward me, burying his head in my hair, breathing deeply. He was silent for a long time, our chests rising and falling against each other, my heart shuddering wildly.

"It can wait," he said, finally, his voice soft and low against my neck.

My shoulders relaxed somewhat. I opened my mouth to ask what he'd said, those harsh words in a strange language, but the moment seemed somehow fragile, and I changed my mind, saying something entirely different.

"So, I'm going to Iceland."

He did not respond.

"You know, Iceland," I said again. "Home of the Vikings?"

His lips formed a faint smile. "Yes, I am familiar with Iceland."

"Well, I'll be there for three weeks. In Reykjavik. You can show me the sights." I ran my fingers along his neck, pulling gently on his earlobe.

Loki said nothing. The rising sun was a bright, burnished disk, obscured and then revealed by the swiftly moving scrum of clouds. I stopped playing with his earlobe and put my hand on his chest, feeling the faint thudding vibrations of his heartbeat. He pulled my hand to his mouth, kissing my fingers gently.

"Thank you," he murmured. "Enjoy Iceland."

"See you there," I said as he vanished from my arms.

* * * * * * * *

My flight left O'Hare ten days later. I did not see Loki again in those ten days, and I tried not to think about it. Even though I usually saw him at least once a week, and there was a stretch in early April when it had been almost every night. When I'd just had to wrap my fingers around the pendant and think of him for him to appear.

I sat up in bed and wrapped my fingers around the pendant. "I leave tomorrow," I whispered to the empty room. "I'd like to see you."

Nothing. I sighed and rested my head against the wall, staring at the painting that reminded me so much of his armor. *Maybe if I lit some candles?* I got out of bed, lit the candles, took off my pajamas. Sat back down in the center of the bed and wrapped both hands around the pendant.

"I miss you," I said.

My words echoed off the walls. Nothing. *I would speak with you,* he said. But why? What happened? What had I done wrong? I shook my head. *He is a god,* I told myself. *He's got shit to do. Political intrigue. Battles.*

His wife.

I punched my pillow in frustration and got out of bed to see if I had any of those sleeping pills left.

* * * * * * * *

My heart soared as I stepped off the plane in Reykjavik. This was my first international flight, my first trip outside the country. Really, my first trip anywhere, aside from California and Chicago. And perhaps one night in Berlin.

Once I stepped into the bright, gleaming Reykjavik airport, I felt like I might as well be carrying a big, shiny badge: OFFICIAL ADULT. I found Baggage Claim, hailed a taxi, and checked into my hotel room by myself, carrying my brand new, red shoulder bag and matching suitcase.

My hotel room was clean and bright, with a view of the sparkling Reykjavik harbor. It was also tiny. Very, very tiny. The narrow, white twin bed filled the entire room; there wasn't even a desk. *Maybe I'll just spend the nights in Nowhere,* I thought, taking my shoes off and sitting on the bed, my laptop propped against my knees. There was an email from Professor Jörn saying he'd meet me in the hotel lobby on Sunday, and an email from the National Library confirming my appointment tomorrow morning to access the Special Archives.

I showered in the tiny bathroom, banging my elbows against the stall, and then I set out to wander the streets of Reykjavik in search of dinner, breathing the wind coming off the ocean, watching the sunlight cast shadows on the mountains across the sound, which were still snow-capped, even in June. The air smelled strange, with a low, sulfur tang behind the salt and diesel of the harbor. *Volcanic,* I thought. The entire island is volcanic; the geography, the electricity. All of Reykjavik hummed with strange energy. It felt like a place that would fit Loki, the volcanic energy, the potential and the chaos of fire and ocean.

I ate a dinner of fish and chips, sitting at an outdoor table on the sidewalk as the streets began to fill with young people, laughing and leaning on each other, speaking Icelandic much too quickly for me to follow their conversations. The sun was still high in the sky when I finished, although my watch said it was past ten at night. I almost wanted to keep walking, to wander into a club, drink beer, and dance in the long, golden light.

If Loki were here... I thought. But Loki wasn't here, and I was beginning to feel tired. I yawned, returned my red plastic fish and chips basket to the restaurant's take-out window, and walked the streets of Reykjavik back to my hotel room.

The hotel's blinds didn't do much to block out the light. I knew at this time of year the sun dipped below the horizon for a mere hour before re-emerging in an extended violet twilight. But I'd somehow missed the fact that I'd be trying to fall asleep in bright sunlight. I tossed and turned for a long time in the narrow bed, finally falling into fitful, uncomfortable sleep.

I jolted awake as I heard heavy footsteps in the hallway. Someone stopped outside my door, rattling the knob. I sat up in the bed, pulling the covers to my chest, my heart hammering madly.

"Loki?" I whispered.

The doorknob rattled again, and a voice muttered thickly in Icelandic. The footsteps thudded away. I got out of bed and pulled my suitcase to the door, trying to jam it under the knob. *This isn't going to stop anyone,* I thought, my hands trembling as I backed away. I sighed and lay down, pulling the comforter over my head and turning away from the window, away from the constant, blinding light.

* * * * * * *

I woke early the next day, thanks to the sunlight. My room was fully illuminated by four in the morning, the white vertical blinds reflecting and amplifying the light like some interior designer's bad joke.

"Ugh, these are just making the room *brighter,*" I muttered, squinting in the light and running my hands through my hair.

The National Library opened at eight. I wanted to give myself at least a half hour to get there; still, that left plenty of time to go for a run. I pulled on my shoes and left the hotel, headed away from the harbor, checking my watch.

After thirty minutes I decided it was time to go back to the hotel, so I turned around. Then I turned around again. I'd crossed under the highway, gone through some sort of a park, and then started jogging through a residential neighborhood. But now this street didn't look familiar.

I ran a bit faster, glancing down side streets and alleys. Nothing but houses. Cute, colorful houses. Hundreds of cute, colorful houses. I couldn't read the street signs, and honestly, I hadn't really been paying attention. I checked my watch again; ten minutes to get back to the hotel.

I stopped, forcing myself to take a deep breath and look around. Reykjavik is surrounded by mountains. *If I just head away from the mountains, downhill, toward the harbor,* I thought, *I will find my hotel.* I turned away from the mountains and ran. Quickly.

By the time I finally found the harbor, limping and wincing from the stitch in my side, it was 7:45. I was due at the National Library in fifteen minutes. I stared at the chain-link fence between me and the brooding cranes and shipping containers of the harbor, wondering which direction to go.

"Shit," I muttered, my fingers wrapping around the

pendant. "I could really use some help here."

I decided to turn left, because the big, yellow crane in that direction looked vaguely familiar. I walked for a few blocks before I caught a glimpse of him, disappearing behind a low-slung cinder block office building. Tall. Red hair. Dark suit.

Oh, thank you, thank you, I thought, jogging to catch up. "Loki!" I called.

He turned to face me. He was not Loki; he was a middle aged man, carrying a briefcase, wondering why a sweaty American tourist was yelling at him. I stammered an apology, the blood rushing to my face. *I'm going to keep my mouth shut for the next three weeks,* I told myself.

The man smiled and gestured, giving me directions in slow, sympathetic English. I was too mortified to listen properly, but I nodded and smiled as I backed away. When I finally rounded the corner, I checked my watch. I was due at the National Library in five minutes.

I felt like crying.

And then I finally saw something I recognized. It was the sidewalk cafe where I'd eaten fish and chips the night before. I limped toward it, recognizing the street that led back to my hotel.

* * * * * * *

"Ah, Caroline Capello, yes," said the imposingly large woman at the National Library's front desk. "I have you down for eight this morning, no?"

"I'm so sorry," I said, feeling my cheeks burn as I attempted to sound like a competent professional. "I got lost."

"Ah, is no problem," she said, with a wide smile. "Welcome to Reykjavik."

I returned her smile as I felt my shoulders finally relax, and I followed her past the front desk, ready to get some work done.

CHAPTER TWENTY

Sunday morning. Time to meet Professor Hæmir Jőrn in the hotel lobby.

I came downstairs a few minutes early to grab a cup of coffee, and I scanned the lobby for someone who looked like a professor of pre-Christian antiquities. I was picturing an older man in a tweed jacket, maybe even wearing a little cap.

It looked like Professor Jőrn wasn't here yet. There was only one other person in the lobby and, even by the admittedly high Icelandic standards, he was unusually attractive. He was tall, blonde, and muscular, wearing worn jeans and a dark green sweater with easy confidence. He glanced around the room and his eyes met mine. He smiled.

I smiled back, and I felt my cheeks flush. Then I immediately turned away, feeling embarrassed; only Loki could get that sort of reaction from me. When I looked up, he was walking toward me.

"Carol?" he asked. His English was nearly perfect,

with only a hint of a clipped accent.

"Hæmir?" I asked, unbelieving.

"It's me," he said, spreading his hands wide.

"I didn't think you'd be so-" *gorgeous*, I thought. "Young!" I stammered.

"And I wasn't sure you'd be a woman," he said, smiling. "Come on, I'm parked outside."

Hæmir drove a small, white Fiat. He handed me a travel mug of strong coffee, and we set off through the orderly streets of Reykjavik.

"I like your Loki," he said, after a moment's comfortable silence.

I stared at him, not sure I'd heard him correctly.

"The necklace," he said, gesturing to his chest. "It is his symbol, no?"

"Oh!" My hands went to the gleaming pendant between my breasts. *Proof.* "Yes, it is," I said.

"It's funny you should be wearing that," Hæmir said, smiling. "We've just found something you'll find very interesting."

The urban sophistication of Reykjavik dropped away quickly, and we were soon driving past stony outcrops and bright green grass, cropped low by wandering flocks of sheep, their muddy white flanks marked by orange, red, and green spray paint. Hæmir was a perfect traveling companion, chatting amicably about the countryside, allowing the conversation to fall silent when appropriate. I noticed he wore no wedding band. Of course, neither did I.

Hæmir gave me no hints as to what he'd found at the excavation, but he knew a tremendous amount about the National Library, and he answered all my questions enthusiastically. We even had a bit of a debate about the origins of Óðinn, although that quieted once Hæmir pulled off the highway and had to focus his attention on a narrow, bumpy road winding toward the ocean.

"Here we are," he said as we approached a small town huddled against the rocky coast. "Lokisfen."

It was a beautiful little town. White houses surrounded an orderly green town square and colorful fishing boats bobbed in the harbor, which was a brilliant, almost Caribbean, blue in the full light of the Nordic midday. A squat, stone church sat above the town, facing the water. Black stony cliffs extended to the ocean on either side of the harbor, sheltering the village.

"Our site is just beyond the church," Hæmir said, navigating smoothly around a slow-moving herd of indignant, bleating sheep. "There's a good pub in town. Would you like lunch before or after?"

"Oh, after," I said. "Unless you promise to tell me what you've found!"

Hæmir laughed and we continued toward the church as the road grew rougher. "It was a pagan site before it was a church, of course," he said. "We believe it was a sacred grove. They built the church right on top of it. Last year there was a small earthquake that revealed... Well, that's when they called us."

A handful of cars were parked behind the church, and shimmering plastic sheeting lay flat over a small rise beyond the parking lot. I got out of the car and shaded my eyes against the bright light.

"Come," said Hæmir, holding out his hand.

We cleared the rise and I could see the equipment of an archeological dig: picks and brushes, survey stakes, a handful of carefully labeled artifacts spread on white plastic sheeting. The dig itself was mostly covered with clear plastic, although two people were working on the far side.

"Hello!" yelled Hæmir, and the students stood to wave. They were both young and, as seemed to be the case with everyone in Iceland, they were unusually attractive.

Hæmir stepped carefully around the plastic sheeting, and I followed him. He exchanged a few words of Icelandic with each of the students before turning to me with a smile.

"Here," he said, kneeling before the plastic sheeting. "Tell me, what do you think?"

He pulled the sheeting back to reveal three large, rectangular rocks covered with intricate carvings.

I stepped into the excavation pit to approach the stones, aware that the two students had stopped working to watch me. I held my hand to the stones but glanced at Hæmir before touching them. He nodded, and I traced the delicate carvings gently with my fingertips. Although the day was warm, the stone was cool and smooth under my fingers. *Like his skin*, I thought with a shiver.

"It's snakes," I said. "Intertwined, two snakes..."

Hæmir nodded at me, smiling.

"But that's one of Loki's symbols," I said, turning to Hæmir. "And the size of these, the shape, it suggests a sacred grove."

Hæmir nodded again, his handsome face beaming at me.

"But there were no Loki groves," I said slowly, turning around in the excavation pit as the full implication dawned on me. "There are no records..."

"There are no records of anything," Hæmir said. "The Vikings were anti-literate. Nothing important was ever written down."

"But this is *huge*," I said, my voice rising in excitement. "This is amazing! Historical evidence of a sacred grove dedicated to Loki - this changes everything!"

"I know," Hæmir said, smiling as he stood and brushed the dirt from his knees. "Although why anyone would build a sacred grove for that slippery bastard is beyond me."

I felt a hot stab of anger. "He's not a bastard," I said. "He's funny, charming...." My voice trailed off as I realized what I was saying, and I turned toward the ocean, my cheeks burning.

"I mean," I said in an even voice, touching the smooth, cool stones, "the myths paint a complex picture."

"Perhaps," said Hæmir, sounding amused. "Now, how about lunch?"

* * * * * * *

Hæmir and I outlined our first collaborative paper in the pub, on the back of our paper napkins. We shared two orders of smoked lamb with dark, sweet rye bread, and we talked for the entire drive back to Reykjavik, sharing ideas and theories about the Lokisfen grove. We were still discussing the grove when his Fiat pulled in front of my hotel.

"Tomorrow you visit the library, no?" he asked as he opened the car door for me, a gesture I found strangely charming.

I stood and found myself suddenly very close to him, almost touching his thick, green sweater. I looked up to apologize and met his hazel eyes. My heartbeat quickened, and my breath caught in my throat. *Ridiculous,* I thought. *We've been talking for hours. Keep it professional.* I forced myself to step away from the car. And his handsome smile.

"Yes, tomorrow at the library," I said.

"Do you perhaps have plans for dinner?" he asked. His smile was a bit lopsided, I realized, his lips full and soft. My cheeks burned as I tried to look away.

"Dinner would be lovely," I said.

* * * * * * * *

Friday night.

I'd been in Reykjavik for almost two full weeks, spending my days in the National Library, my notebook in hand, examining manuscripts so delicate I had to wear gloves to turn their brittle pages. When the library closed, I'd walk to the hotel to shower and change before meeting Hæmir for dinner. And, if I could just keep my eyes from lingering on Hæmir's smile, or watching the way the light fell across his face, or wondering what those strong arms would feel like around my waist, I could have a great time.

Hæmir was waiting for me in the lobby after I showered and pulled on the nicest outfit I'd brought to Iceland, which meant black yoga pants instead of ragged, old jeans. We walked together through the thick, golden evening light until we were at the Reykjavik port. Hæmir led me up a creaky wooden staircase to a tiny restaurant tucked under the eaves of a pink stone building.

The waitress led us to a candlelit table on the porch overlooking the harbor, and Hæmir ordered in Icelandic. We ate tiny, smoked fish and drank white wine that sparkled in the long evening light. Hæmir looked especially handsome in that gentle light, the blue flecks in his hazel eyes reflecting the blue evening skies. He kept making me laugh, telling me stories about strange Icelandic foods he'd had to endure as a child. When the waiter asked if we'd like a second bottle of wine, I said yes.

His hand brushed mine reaching for the bottle, and my body shivered with electricity. He apologized, giving me a lopsided grin. My skin flushed with heat and my nipples pressed against my shirt. I crossed my arms to cover them. *What the hell is going on?* I thought as I struggled to bring the conversation back to our work. *Only Loki can do this to me.*

"So," Hæmir said as the waiter cleared our dishes, "I am afraid tomorrow you must dine alone."

My hand knocked my glass, and I felt blood rush to my cheeks. "Oh?" I said, trying to act normal.

"I've got to visit my dig in the north. Apparently they found something."

I risked a glance at his handsome face and was relieved to see he wasn't staring directly at me with those brilliant eyes. *Good*, I thought to myself, *a break from all of this sexy nonsense.*

"Well, I'll miss our conversations," I said, and then I took a deep breath as I realized how true that was. In just two weeks, Hæmir had become a friend, and spending time with him was almost as satisfying as reading the ancient books in the library.

More satisfying, if I was being honest.

After dinner Hæmir and I walked together through the streets of Reykjavik, now throbbing with youth and energy. Every third building seemed to be hosting a party, and the streets were filled with beautiful people in tight clothing. But no one, no one, was as handsome as Hæmir.

When we reached the hotel's lobby, Hæmir said goodnight with a European air-kiss on both of my cheeks. I could feel his heat on my cheeks even after he pulled away, and my body responded, aching for his touch.

"Enjoy the library. I'll stop by to say hello when I return," he said, and he made a little bowing flourish as he walked out of the lobby.

I turned for the stairs, walking slowly, my pants suddenly uncomfortably tight. I let myself in to my hotel room, turned to fasten the deadbolt, and then leaned back against the door, sliding my hands into my pants, my entire body aching with need and flush with embarrassment.

Loki, I thought, *where are you?*

I closed my eyes, trying to remember how Loki touched me, how he made my body tremble. I tried to picture his flashing eyes, the curve of his mouth, the smell of his skin against mine. Yet when I finally managed to bring myself to orgasm, I wasn't sure whose arms, whose eyes, whose lips I was imagining: Loki or Hæmir.

CHAPTER TWENTY-ONE

I'd planned to stay in Reykjavik for three weeks, flying out on a Saturday morning. My last day in Iceland was rainy and cool, the library nearly deserted. I'd managed to look at almost everything, although I was disappointed to find no reference to sacred Loki groves in any of the books. The paper I was writing with Hæmir would be much stronger if I had some textual evidence to support what he'd found on the stones, and some part of me felt like I hadn't yet found what I was seeking, what I'd come to Iceland to find.

I heard footsteps across the climate-controlled Special Collections room and ignored them. Then I heard the scraping of a chair across the floor and glanced up, annoyed.

It was Hæmir. My heart thudded madly in my chest. It was very nice to see his lopsided smile again.

"I found something," he whispered with a conspiratorial smile.

"No way! What?"

The librarian gave us both a stern look, and I dropped my voice to a whisper. "Tell me!"

"You should see it instead," he whispered. "If you can possibly delay your return?"

I realized I was smiling like an idiot. "I'd love to," I whispered, slipping my notebook into my book bag.

I spent that afternoon on the phone with the airline, rescheduling my flight while I packed my suitcase and trying to tell myself my excitement about traveling to the far northern edge of Iceland with Hæmir was purely academic.

The next morning dawned gray and wet, with a windy storm streaking through the streets of Reykjavik. *Horrible weather for a flight anyway*, I thought as I packed my matching bags and headed to the lobby. Hæmir met me there, handing me a gleaming metal travel mug of strong coffee as I climbed in his Fiat.

"It's a long drive," he told me. "I've already booked you a room for the night, but I warn you, the town is a bit...rough."

"Rough is fine," I said with a shrug.

Hæmir laughed and sipped his coffee as he guided the car out of Reykjavik, heading north. The highway was all but deserted this early in the morning, and the rain came down in sheets, making it impossible for me to get a sense of where we were going. Hæmir refused to tell me anything about the dig. Instead, he talked about his family.

His small, warm car, dry and quiet despite the crashing storm outside, seemed like the most comfortable place in the world. I found it easier to talk to him when we were driving, when I could look out the window at the gray, rain-streaked fields and cliffs, instead of being distracted by his muscular arms or lopsided smile.

Our conversation fell into an easy rhythm. Like me, his parents owned a small business and thought he was a bit insane for choosing a career in academia. As I watched the road through the steady swoop-swoop of the windshield wipers, I found myself telling him things I hadn't told anyone, save Loki. How I envied my brother for his normal life. How I worried my mother might have been right about me all along.

"I also worry," he said, his voice low and serious as he focused on the windswept road. "I'd like a family, like everyone, no? But it's hard to meet women in a job like this."

I hoped the car was dark enough that Hæmir could not see me blush.

The rain began to clear as Hæmir's car climbed a steep volcanic ridge, Iceland's vibrant green grass giving way to jagged black rocks. The sun broke through the clouds as we crested the hill, revealing the shifting steely gray and aquamarine of the North Sea before us. Storm clouds piled against the horizon, and I could see three faint rainbows dancing across the heaving, white-capped water. I gasped.

"Beautiful, no?" said Hæmir. "You almost expect to see Thor walking out of the clouds."

No, I thought. *Not Thor.*

Hæmir's excavation nestled against the volcanic ridge, not far from the small town of Slyndennär, which seemed decidedly less cozy than Lokisfen. Hæmir explained the economic prospects this far north were pretty grim as he tried delicately to warn me about the "hotel" where we'd be staying.

But I loved the place.

The Slyndennär Inn was built of huge, white stones, and felt like it had been standing for a thousand years, resisting change. The innkeeper, a mountain of a woman named Bryndís who was almost as tall as Hæmir, had to stoop as she showed me up two flights of stairs to my room.

The room was tucked under the sloping eaves, a short walk from the shared bathroom. A small washbasin and a threadbare towel sat on a wooden chest of drawers, the only furniture in the room apart from a rickety bed with a looming brass frame. I was unpacking my suitcase when I heard a knock on my door.

"I apologize," said Hæmir. "I have a message from Reykjavik, and I've got to make a few calls. But I think the weather will hold. We should be able to get the the site tomorrow morning."

"Oh," I said, disappointed.

"This is a good place for hiking," Hæmir suggested. "Bryndís can pack you a lunch. There's a trail that takes you all the way to the top of the ridge."

* * * * * * * *

Bryndís had my lunch ready when I came downstairs. I was a bit worried about following her Icelandic directions through town, but the trail was easy to find. There was a small break in the volcanic cliffs surrounding Slyndennär, and a footpath led through them. It was a steep climb up the cliffs and the wind was strong, tugging against my flimsy summer jacket. The scudding clouds created rapidly alternating patterns of light and shadow, transforming the cliffs with every step. But the rain held off, and the air seemed fresh, scrubbed clean by the morning's storm.

I reached the top of the ridge, panting, and turned to face the vast, empty expanse of the North Sea. The ridge was in shadow, but sunlight sparkled across the dancing waves. The ocean was the exact color of Loki's eyes. My heart twisted painfully in my chest.

Loki, I thought. *I miss you.*

I sat down on the wet grass, my back against a rough stone. I imagined taking off my clothes, lying down on that wet grass. I imagined the wind whipping across our naked bodies as he filled me, twisting my fingers in the grass and dirt as I climaxed.

I heard a stone scrape behind me and whipped my head around. A small herd of sheep stared at me with little interest, chewing their cud.

I was suddenly cold and uncomfortable on the ground, bored with the shifting patterns of light and darkness across the ocean. As I picked my way down the steep trail, the lonely wind made my eyes fill with tears, which I wiped away and dashed on the rocks.

* * * * * * *

Hæmir's graduate students joined us for dinner at the Slyndennär Inn, and most of the conversation was in Icelandic. I could read Icelandic, and I could understand someone who spoke slowly and used lots of hand gestures, but I was totally lost for most of the meal, especially after the second bottle of wine. Eventually I gave up even trying to guess what they were saying, and instead I listened to the flow and rhythm of the conversation.

Everyone in Iceland must be beautiful, I decided.

Hæmir's two students, a woman named Annajär and a man named Marri, could have been models. They both had high, chiseled cheekbones, blonde hair, and piercing eyes. At first I assumed they were a couple, but even after several glasses of wine they made no attempt to move closer, to touch each other.

Instead, they both seemed to vie for Hæmir's attention. Of course, even in a country filled with beautiful people, Hæmir stood out. There was something about his eyes, some magnetism in the controlled strength of his body. Something that made you wonder what those strong hands would feel like wrapped around your waist, how his lips would feel on your neck.

My body flushed with heat, and I felt the thick seam in the middle of my jeans growing wet. Embarrassed, I decided it was probably time to go back to my room. Hæmir reached for my hand as I stood, and the room started to swim. *Whoa. Maybe I had more wine than I thought.*

"... you okay?" he asked, fixing me with his lopsided smile.

My nipples were hard under my bra, my legs beginning to tremble. I felt another rush of heat between my legs. *I can't believe I'm this turned on,* I thought. *For fuck's sake, we've just been sitting around a table, having dinner.*

"Fine," I said, trying to force myself to sound cheerful and upbeat. "I'm fine, just a little tired."

I stepped away from the table. Annajär gave me a distracted smile, and Marri gave me a small wave.

"Can you find your way?" Hæmir asked.

That's absurd, I thought. *There's only one staircase.* "Thanks, yeah," I said. I forced myself to yawn, trying to cross my arms subtly to cover my erect nipples.

"See you in the morning," Hæmir said as I turned to walk out of the room, my cheeks and face burning.

* * * * * * *

I locked my room's door behind me, my entire body aching. "Loki," I whispered through gritted teeth, my fingers a tight fist around his pendant. "Loki, Loki, please...."

The storm had picked back up, and the wind off the ocean threw sheets of rain against the windows, filling the room with diffuse, gray light. *This would be perfect,* I thought, imagining Loki bending me over the bed, imagining grabbing the brass railings of the headboard as he fucked me from behind, imagining screaming his name over the howling storm.

Dimly I became aware of a knocking sound. I looked to the window and saw nothing but empty, rain-streaked sky.

"Carol?" Hæmir's voice said from behind me.

He knocked again. I realized I was sitting on the floor, my back against the thin door. I stood and unlocked the door, the light from the hallway falling in a square across the wood floor.

"Are you... feeling well?" Hæmir asked.

"I'm fine."

"I thought I heard you crying," Hæmir said.

I blushed furiously. "No," I stammered. "No. I'm fine."

He shifted uncomfortably on the floor. "You left your purse on the table," he said, holding out my black book bag.

My cheeks flushed again. "Thanks," I mumbled, taking the bag and closing the door.

It took me a long time to fall asleep on that narrow bed, alone.

CHAPTER TWENTY-TWO

Hæmir was all smiles the next morning. He poured me a cup of strong coffee and talked cheerfully about the site's history over a breakfast of smoked fish, pumpernickel bread, and lingonberry jam, although he did not go so far as to tell me what I might expect to see there. Annajär joined us after several minutes, followed shortly by Marri, and we set off together.

It was a brilliant morning. The sunlight made the ocean gleam until it was almost painful to watch, and the water tumbling down the cliffs in dozens of small waterfalls was so blue it seemed unreal.

"Is it always so beautiful here?" I asked, and the three Icelanders in the car laughed.

"Always," said Marri from the front seat. "But in the winter, it's too dark to see any of it!"

Hæmir drove the car slowly along the ocean, threading his way carefully past enormous potholes and insolent sheep who watched our progress with complete indifference. We turned away from the ocean to climb a steep ridge and, as the hood of the car began to tip downward, Hæmir took his hand from the wheel and pointed.

"There it is," he said.

"Are those... trees?" I asked, squinting in the bright light. I hadn't seen more than a dozen trees since I'd arrived in Reykjavik.

"Rowan trees," said Hæmir. "Very rare." He seemed pleased I'd noticed.

The car buzzed with excitement. As we drove closer to the grove of twisted, bony trees, I could see the excavation on the hillside. It looked like a semicircle of granite slabs, half buried in the black, volcanic soil.

Hæmir parked the car and the four of us approached the stones. There were five slabs, all about as tall as Hæmir's broad shoulders and deeply weathered, covered with lichen and moss.

"What do you see?" Hæmir asked.

I followed Hæmir, stepping gently into the excavation pit. The stones were all covered with intricate carvings. I traced the images with my fingers; they were an odd mixture of artistic elegance and Viking brutality.

A man with a raven on his shoulder stood locked in eternal battle with an enormous wolf on the first stone. The man's spear pierced the wolf's side while the wolf's jaws closed around his chest. On the next stone a huge, handsome man held a two-sided hammer above a snake which crushed him in its coils, its fangs piercing his chest.

"Ragnarök," I whispered, my hands tracing the mortal struggle of Thor and the serpent Jörmungandr. "They're pictures of Ragnarök."

The third stone depicted a man blowing a great, curving horn as flames lept and soared behind him.

"That's Heimdallr," I said, "blowing the Gjallarhorn to start the battle."

"To begin Ragnarök," Hæmir said from behind me.

"So the other two stones must have... what?"

"See for yourself," he said, smiling.

The fourth stone had a great, horrible ship, frozen in a torrential storm, the waves sharp and angry.

"Naglfar," I said. "The ship of the dead."

"The ship of the Jötunn," Hæmir corrected.

I ran my fingers over the stone. The sharp lines of the ship felt cold.

"And your favorite," said Hæmir, gesturing to the final stone.

It was him, of course. Loki escaping his bonds. His angular face was triumphant, his eyes and hair wild. *Guess that part's already happened*, I thought. I did not touch the Loki stone.

"These are amazingly detailed," I said, turning from

the carving to Hæmir. "To have this kind of physical evidence to back up the texts - Have you dated them?"

Hæmir, Annajär and Marri were all smiling at me.

"That's not it," Hæmir said. He walked beyond the first stone and pulled up a clear plastic tarp. Beneath it were two more stones. "Go ahead," he said.

I knelt in the mud, running my fingers across the stone. "What the hell?" I muttered.

The stone's carving was four men seated at a table. One was clearly Óðinn; he had only one eye, and a raven sat on each shoulder. And Thor, with his hammer Mjölnir, and Týr, the one-handed god. The last figure I couldn't recognize, but I could tell he was huge, crouching to fit in the stone, ferocious tusks thrusting from his mouth.

"It could be...." I paused. "It could be the conference of the gods, before Ragnarök begins. But who's that tall guy?"

"You think that's odd," said Hæmir. "Look at this."

The final stone was still half-buried, but the carving had been painstakingly uncovered.

It was a woman.

She stood with her legs apart and her arms upraised. To her right was a line of men, including one with a raven on his shoulder. To her left was a figure on his knees, naked, bound and gagged.

I knelt in the mud a long time, feeling the sun on my

shoulders, the wind through my hair. "Are these..." I said finally, not quite believing it, "*new* images of Ragnarök?"

Hæmir laughed, his eyes dancing with excitement. "Well, I wouldn't exactly call them new. These stones are probably pre-Christian."

I waved my hand impatiently. "But, the carvings - I've never heard of anything like that. This is an entirely new perspective on Ragnarök."

Hæmir nodded, and I let out a long whistle as the implications sunk in. We know so little about the pre-Christian cultures of the North; a find like this could change our entire field. I stood and stared at the ocean while Hæmir moved around the site, chatting in Icelandic with Annajär and Marri. I felt very lonely, suddenly, there at the edge of the world.

"Carol," said Hæmir from behind me. "We have some work to finish here this afternoon. Would you wish to see the library in Slyndennär? It has a few unusual texts."

I nodded and followed Hæmir back to the car. Annajär and Marri were already hunched over the stones.

"It is amazing, no?" Hæmir asked as we drove back to Slyndennär. Dark clouds were building over the North Sea, and it looked like we might be in for another storm.

I shook my head in disbelief. "This could be the most

important find of our generation," I said. "This will change the way everyone thinks about Ragnarök. I mean, I'm going to start searching the literature - who is that woman? And that huge figure with the tusks?"

Hæmir laughed again. I let the questions swirl in my mind, knowing eventually they'd settle into a coherent plan. And then a paper. Hell, maybe a dozen papers.

Maybe my doctoral thesis.

"How do you prevent Ragnarök?" I muttered, remembering Loki asking me that same question.

"Prevent Ragnarök?" Hæmir asked, sounding amused.

I flushed, embarrassed.

"You cannot prevent Ragnarök," Hæmir said, his deep voice resonant in the small space. "That is the entire point, no? It is the destruction of the old world, but also the creation of the new."

I nodded, and he continued.

"One man, one woman, they survive," Hæmir said. "And then they get to live in the new world, the better world, once all the mess is finished."

We rounded a final turn along the volcanic ridge and saw the dingy, weathered buildings of Slyndennär spread before us.

"Ah, here it is," Hæmir said, pulling into a parking space in front of a dull, gray building that looked abandoned.

"This is the library?"

Hæmir shrugged. "Not much, I know," he said. "If you don't find anything interesting, there's always hiking!"

After a brief chat with Hæmir in Icelandic, the severe-looking librarian led me into a room in the back. She unlocked a metal filing cabinet and put several cardboard boxes on a folding table.

"The lights," she said, in a thick, clipped accent, "they are on timer. Every so often, you must - " she flapped her arms. "Then they come back on."

"Thank you," I said, pulling out my notebook and an Icelandic dictionary.

She gave me a curt nod and left the room.

I turned to the boxes, not expecting anything especially noteworthy. The first box held a copy of the prose *Edda*, complete with lovely illustrations but otherwise unremarkable. The second held a Bible with a complete record of the town's population from 1717 to 1892, which would be a treasure trove to a historian but was only of mild interest to me.

In the third and final box I found the reason I'd come to Iceland.

The Book of the Gods' Mortal Lovers.

CHAPTER TWENTY-THREE

It was a small volume, copied by hand and bound in crumbling leather. I put on the cotton gloves the librarian gave me and lifted it from the box, my heart in my throat.

The first pages were too badly damaged by mold and moisture to read. By the fifth page I was able to tell I was in the middle of a story. Ēostre, goddess of spring, had gotten herself into some sort of trouble and was standing before a collection of the Æsir, waiting for her punishment. And then her mortal lover Safír appeared to request a Trial of Æsìlynd. My Icelandic dictionary did not offer a translation for "Æsìlynd," so I assumed it was a name, copying it carefully in my notebook so I could ask Hæmir about it later. The next three pages were also damaged; I wasn't certain what happened with Ēostre and Safír and the Trial of Æsìlynd.

The lights turned out. I waved my arms and they flickered back to life.

The next section began with the heading Óðinn.

My hands trembled as I turned the page. Names. It was a long list of names. The handwriting changed with every couple of names, as if the entries had been written by different people over a long period of time. Most did not have happy endings.

Salína: Visited by All-Father at Sammhein. Driven mad.

Rūna: Visited by All-Father. Cast self into the ocean.

Kamí: Visited by All-Father. Filled with child. Died in travail.

I turned the pages with shaking hands. There were no dates, but from the handwriting alone it looked like at least twenty different people had recorded entries in the book. I saw the occasional, "Bore child," but nowhere did I read, "Lived a long and happy life."

Óðinn was followed by several blank pages. Then Thor and then Týr. I skimmed the pages, my heart thudding. The lights went off again. I flapped my arms.

Loki

My heart clenched painfully. I looked up at the particle board ceiling, holding my breath. *I can walk away*, I told myself. *I can put it down and walk away.*

I turned the page.

* * * * * * *

Gefjun: Visited by trickster god. Driven mad. Cast out.

Eggrún: Visited by trickster god. Driven mad. Leapt from cliffs.

Sigrún: Visited by trickster god. Guilty of witchcraft.

Rakel: Visited by trickster god. Filled with child. Driven mad. Drowned with child.

There were many names. So many names.

I took advantage of the next time the lights turned off to wipe the tears from my cheeks before they could fall on the book.

This doesn't mean anything, I thought. *Those societies were looking for any excuse to discredit a woman. One wrong move, and you'd be accused of fucking a god, and thrown into the ocean.*

But my heart was cold.

* * * * * * *

I jumped when the librarian opened the door. I'd been counting the names in *The Book of the Gods' Mortal Lovers.* Óðinn was in the lead, with nearly fifty accounts, but Loki was a close second with thirty-two.

Thirty-two, I thought. *Thirty. Two.*

"Is late," the librarian said. "We are closing."

"Thank you," I said, carefully putting *The Book of the Gods' Mortal Lovers* back in the cardboard box.

"Is interesting, no?" she asked, giving me a sideways look.

I busied myself with removing the gloves and packing my notebook to avoid meeting her eyes.

* * * * * * *

Caroline Capello, I thought as I wandered out of the library and into the narrow streets of Slyndennär. *Visited by the trickster god.*

The sun was still shining madly in the sky. I walked to the harbor and watched the rise and fall of the waves. A few rusty fishing boats bobbed on the water. The storm clouds had grown darker and moved closer to the shore, shading the distant waters in inky sheets of rain.

"So," said a familiar voice behind me. "Back to reality?"

I turned to see Hæmir walking toward me.

"What?"

"Your flight is tomorrow evening, no?" Hæmir raised one of his hands in the air, pantomiming a plane taking off. "Back to reality," he said.

I shook my head at his lopsided smile. "Nothing about today feels much like reality."

"Come," he said, offering me his arm. "Let's have dinner."

* * * * * * *

We were the only two people dining in the Slyndennär Inn. Hæmir explained that Annajär and Marri had to run an errand and would be back late. Bryndís served us poached salmon with scalloped potatoes, beet greens sauted in butter, and a basket of flaky biscuits still warm from the oven. Hæmir insisted I absolutely could not leave Iceland without trying brennivín, the national, very alcoholic drink, and Bryndís poured me a healthy glass of the clear, anise-flavored liquor.

It tasted so bad I coughed. Hæmir laughed.

"Ah, it burns," I said.

"At least I'm not making you eat fermented shark," he said, handing me a glass of wine to wash down the brennivín. "And look, you don't have that much left to go." He gestured to the thick, clear liquor in my glass.

It still looked like a lot to me. I raised an eyebrow at his handsome face.

"It is my duty," he said, his cheeks flushed with heat, "as an Icelander, to help you fully experience my culture. I would be remiss in my duties if you did not experience the full pleasure of brennivín."

I took another slug of the drink and managed not to cough, although it brought tears to my eyes. "I can see why the Vikings were in such a hurry to get out of here," I said, gasping for air.

Hæmir laughed again and put his hand on top of mine. I suddenly flushed with a different kind of heat.

Oh, not again, I thought, but I had a hard time taking my eyes off his face. It seemed to be the only part of the room that wasn't swaying.

Bryndís appeared with slices of a light and airy four-layer lemon cake for dessert, paired with strong coffee. Hæmir took his hand from mine, and the conversation moved back to fermented shark and the Vikings. By the time I finished my cake and two cups of coffee, the room was no longer spinning. But I was still struggling to avoid staring at Hæmir.

"Can you find your way to your room?" he asked when I set down my empty coffee cup. I met his eyes and shivered to see the hungry way he stared at me.

He glanced away quickly, embarrassed.

Oh, fuck it, I thought. "No," I muttered, my cheeks flushing bright red.

Hæmir stood and offered me his arm. I held it tightly as we walked together to the staircase.

* * * * * * *

My hands trembled as I unlocked the door to my room. I stepped inside; Hæmir followed. I turned to him, and he wrapped his strong arms around me.

"So, here we are," I said, my voice shaking.

"Yes, lovely Carol," he said. He brushed my cheek with the back of his hand.

He bent toward me, and a flood of heat filled my body as pressed his warm, gentle lips against mine. His kiss was soft, slow. He waited for me to yield to him, to open my mouth and allow him to enter me. His lips tasted like coffee and lemon cake, and his arms wrapped around my waist, pressing me against his strong body. I gasped when we pulled apart. He reached for my face, brushed my hair out of my eyes.

"Carol," he said. "Do you want this?"

I looked up at his hazel eyes, his strong jaw, and I shivered. His eyes were so serious, so hungry. I reached for his neck and pulled his lips to mine again, running my hand down his chest to his waist. I pushed his shirt up, feeling the tingle of his hair against my palms. He felt so solid, so *warm*. We parted as he pulled his shirt over his head, and then his hands pushed my shirt aside. I gasped against his mouth as his rough fingers traced the skin of my waist and electricity danced through my body, surging between my legs.

"Are you sure you want this?" There was a catch in his voice as he spoke.

"Hæmir," I muttered against his neck, "I've wanted this for weeks."

His chest rose as he sighed against me. "Oh, God, Carol. Me too." He bent to kiss my neck, his stubble rough against my cheek, and I moaned.

I ran my fingers through the hair on his chest,

enjoying his warmth, his solid strength, and then my hands dropped to his waistband, unbuttoning his fly. He gasped as I pushed my hands into his jeans, slipping them over his waist.

I grabbed the hem of my shirt and pulled it over my head, then fumbled with the catch on my bra. Hæmir sighed against my neck, his breath warm as his lips traced my collarbone, making me shiver. His rough hands slipped my bra over my shoulders and to the floor. He reached to cup my breast, my nipple growing hard against his palm. I moaned again as he squeezed gently, his lips meeting mine for another slow kiss.

I stepped back when we pulled apart, smiling at him as I lay down on the bed. He followed me, the mattress springs squealing as he kneeled above me. He stared at my bare chest with such open admiration and lust that I shivered. Then he bent over me and kissed me for a long time, gently and slowly, against the soft, white cotton sheets and feather pillows. His hands traced the length of my thighs, the swell of my hips; the heat of his cock pushed against my leg while he pressed his lips to mine, warm and hungry.

He slid his hand across my hips, running his fingers along the zipper of my jeans until I was wet and trembling, so ready for him I moaned and rocked my hips against his hand. He smiled as he bent to kiss my neck, softly and slowly, while I fumbled to pull off my pants.

And then my legs were finally naked against his, and his body felt so warm, so strong, above mine. I grabbed his hips to pull him into me, but he hesitated.

"Just a second," he whispered, climbing off the bed and reaching for his jeans. He unfolded his wallet and pulled out a foil-wrapped square.

I laughed, then covered my mouth with my hand. "You have a condom in your wallet?"

Hæmir's cheeks flushed a bright red. "I - I didn't want to presume -" he stammered.

"Oh, no, that's great," I said, smiling. "You're very... prepared. Come here. I'll help you put it on."

I slid to the edge of the bed and he handed me the condom. I ran my hands along his strong legs, loving the way my touch made him gasp. I tore open the condom and unrolled it over his impressive cock. His legs started to shake against my arms.

"Carol," he said, his voice thick. "Lovely Carol."

"Come on," I growled, pulling him toward me.

He grinned and climbed back on the bed, kissing me, hard, until I was trembling. Then he lay back and I rolled on top of him, running my fingers along his broad chest, wrapping my legs around his hips. He gasped as I guided him inside of me; I closed my eyes as he entered me.

"Oh, fuck," I moaned. "Oh, fuck, that feels good."

Hæmir bit off a cry as he grabbed my thighs, his neck taut and his head tilted back. He started moving his hips against mine, slowly, and my body flushed with waves of pleasure.

"Oh, that's amazing," I gasped, and he smiled and brought his hips to mine, slowly, again and again, until the room was spinning and I was gasping for air. I closed my eyes, my body rising and falling against him, every time we came together feeling better and better, making me want him more and more and *more -*

I cried out as my entire body trembled and then flooded with a crashing orgasm. Hæmir grabbed my hips and moaned, thrusting wildly inside me. Then his legs stiffened against mine as he came, his head sinking into the pillows as he groaned with pleasure.

I collapsed against Hæmir's massive chest, trembling and trying to catch my breath.

"That was... incredible," I panted.

I felt him chuckle. "Oh, Carol," he said, running his fingers through my hair. "You have no idea how irresistibly sexy you are."

I smiled, feeling sexy. "I once had a lover who told me - " But I bit off my words as I realized what I was about to say. *I'll ruin you for all mortal men,* Loki told me.

"Told you what?" Hæmir looked at me, his lopsided grin interested.

"Never mind," I said. "Clearly it wasn't true."

And then I was crying. No, not just crying; my body shook as I tried to choke back huge, racking sobs. I covered my face with my hands, burning with embarrassment. Hæmir held me in his powerful arms, kissing the top of my head. My tears ran down his forearms.

"Hæmir, I'm so sorry," I said, when I finally regained control of myself. "I'm so sorry."

"It's okay," he said, still holding me tightly in his strong arms. "It's okay, Carol."

"It's just," I said, hiccuping. "It's just been a lonely - " I bit my tongue again. *Life*, I was about to say. *It's been a lonely life.*

"Lovely Carol," Hæmir said, smoothing my hair, kissing my cheeks. "Lovely Carol. You are not alone now."

* * * * * * * *

When I woke in the morning, Hæmir had gone. I took a long shower in the shared bathroom down the hall and dressed slowly, packing my few things. When I had done absolutely everything I could conceivably do to avoid going downstairs, I sighed and left the room.

Hæmir was downstairs, sharing a table with Annajär.

"Carol!" he said brightly, rising to meet me and giving me two air kisses on my cheeks. "Annajär will join us on the drive to Reykjavik," he said, "but there is still plenty of time for breakfast."

I smiled at him. *Thank you*, I thought. *Thank you for not making this weird.*

Breakfast was flat Icelandic pancakes served with bowls of whipped cream and lingonberry jam. The black coffee was strong and good, and two cups of coffee with a pile of pancakes almost cured my lingering headache. I still felt awkward, but Hæmir was charming and funny and friendly, just like he'd been before I broke down, sobbing, in his strong, naked arms.

It helped to have Annajär in the car. The drive back to Reykjavik passed quickly and amicably as the three of us discussed our research. I offered textual support and analysis while Annajär took notes, and the windswept, dramatic countryside unfolded before us.

I could not believe how quickly we arrived at the Reykjavik airport. Hæmir offered to join me for lunch, but I turned him down gently, explaining I'd better get through customs.

And then I was horrified to feel the hot prick of tears in my eyes. *He's going to think I'm completely insane,* I thought, wiping my eyes furiously on my sleeve.

"Thank you," I said, blinking at Hæmir's lopsided smile and trying to force the tremble from my voice. "For everything."

Hæmir hugged me, and then cupped my chin in his

strong, warm hand. "I look forward to your return," he said, leaning to kiss my forehead.

And then I was walking through the sliding glass doors of the Reykjavik airport, wiping my eyes again.

CHAPTER TWENTY-FOUR

The flight home was smooth and uneventful. I tried not to think about any of it. The sacred grove. The carvings. *The Book of the Gods' Mortal Lovers*, with its horrible list of names.

Hæmir.

I tried to bury myself in the *Cosmopolitan* magazine I found in the seat back pocket. I read every single article, all the latest about eyebrow waxing and celebrity divorces and pleasing your man. It read like dispatches from another world.

When I got home, I crawled into bed and slept for twelve hours.

* * * * * * *

I'd just gotten out of bed, showered, and was beginning to think about making coffee when the room dissolved around me. I turned and found myself in Nowhere.

"Welcome back," Loki said. He was sitting on a

bench, holding a book, watching me.

I blushed at the flood of emotions his voice unleashed; anger, relief, desire. I wanted to run into his arms, and I wanted to smack him across his perfect face. I pulled my towel tighter around my body.

"Where were you?" I said.

Loki turned his head to the side and raised an eyebrow.

"Where were you?" I asked again. "In Iceland. Where the hell were you?" I was suddenly angry. No, not just angry - I was suddenly *furious.* All those lonely, desperate nights; all those tears. All that *Hœmir.* And here he was, sitting in Nowhere. Reading. A. Fucking. Book.

"I wasn't aware I had to report my movements to you," he said, his voice level and cold.

"I told you I was going," I said, my voice rising. "I was there for an entire goddamn month!"

"I cannot travel to Iceland," Loki said, spitting out the word *Iceland* like it was something extremely unpleasant. "The entire island is warded."

I snorted. "Well, was that hard?"

He raised an eyebrow at me.

"That - right there. Telling me you can't travel to Iceland. Was it that hard?"

He was silent.

"Was there a reason you didn't tell me a fucking

month ago?"

"Mortal woman," Loki said in that cold, even tone. "Do you tire of me?"

He was still sitting down. He was still holding his book. In fact, he looked exactly like he had when I arrived. He probably looked exactly like this the entire time I was gone.

It was as if I wasn't even here.

I spun on my heels, wanting to scream. "Goddammit, Loki," I said, walking to the open windows, to the sunlit, eternal sea. My shoulders sagged and I put the heels of my hands to my eyes. *I am not going to cry,* I told myself.

"I am tired," I said, hating the waver in my voice. "I'm tired of -" I waved my hand, unable to finish. *I'm tired of being lonely,* I thought. *I'm tired of needing someone I can't find.*

I turned. Loki set down his book and came to his feet. He looked totally composed. Anger surged through me again, that he should be so calm, so distant, when I was standing in a goddamn bath towel.

"Did you tire of Gefjun?" I yelled at him. "Did you tire of Eggrún, before she threw herself off the cliffs?"

I had not realized before that moment I'd memorized all thirty-two names.

Loki took a step backward, and when he turned to me his cool composition had vanished. His eyes flashed with anger.

"Do you even remember them?" I screamed, clutching my towel to my chest.

"Yes!" Loki yelled, and the room grew darker. And colder. "Mortal woman, I am over two thousand years old! And yes! I remember them!"

Loki raised his arms above his head and then spun around, his back to me. He *pushed* his hands in the air and all the bookshelves shuddered, the soft leather-bound volumes pouring onto the floor.

"I REMEMBER THEM ALL!"

The room was silent, cold, and growing darker. Loki's books lay in a jumbled heap across the floor. Outside the windows I could hear the waves crashing against each other, forming and reforming.

"You could have told me," I said, hating how small my voice sounded. "You could have just *told me* you can't travel to Iceland."

Loki turned to me, and I could see the white scars radiating along his cheeks, the thick bands across his lips. *No illusions now*, I thought. My chest felt tight.

"And am I your dog," Loki said, his voice low and hard, "for you to call whenever you wish?"

"Oh, no. No, you don't," I said, my back stiffening. "You don't get to show up in my apartment, whenever the *fuck* you feel like it, and then accuse *me* of mistreating *you*!"

I grabbed the cool, smooth pendant of silver and gold from between my breasts, the pendant I had not removed since Loki gave it to me last summer.

"I'm a dog to *you*!" I yelled, holding the pendant in my fist. "Look, here's my fucking collar! Here's my fucking leash!" I pulled my arm back and threw the pendant into the pile of books, as hard as I could. My vision was so blurred with hot, angry tears I didn't even see where it landed.

Loki turned his back to me and walked across the heap of books to his empty bookcases. He leaned against them, his head low.

"I have not been... good for you," he said. He took a deep breath. I could hear the gentle murmur of the waves outside the windows. "Goodbye, mortal woman," he whispered.

"Goddammit, Loki, don't do this to me!" I screamed as the room dissolved.

* * * * * * *

But I was already back in my apartment, my shoulders shaking.

"LOKI!"

I spun on my heels, furious. I saw the huge, abstract painting over the bed, swirling black and red and gold, the one that reminded me of Loki's armor.

I slammed my fist through the painting, the canvas ripping with a satisfying finality. My fingers stung as they hit the wall. I pulled back and slammed the wall again, and again, and again, until my knuckles were wet with blood.

I put my fist to my lips, my blood hot and salty against my tongue.

There was a delicate china serving platter on my dining room table, the one with the firefly pattern. I picked it up and brought it down, hard, on my naked thigh. It broke cleanly into two almost even pieces. I threw them against the wall and opened the pantry, pulling out the rest of the firefly plates, remembering buying them, remembering tracing my fingers across the silver inlay, remembering walking past all the *Wedding Registry* signs and the pictures of smiling, laughing brides and grooms and ignoring them, ignoring them fiercely, because I knew, I just knew, they would never apply to me.

I smashed the first plate against the table and it shattered into a dozen winking shards. I threw the second against the wall, the third against the window. Then I ripped off my screen, and I sent all the salad plates hurtling out, one after another, into the darkness over Lake Shore Drive.

I finished, panting, and looked around my apartment, feeling trapped. *I can't stay here*, I thought. *I can't. I can't.* My hands trembled as I pulled on clothes, laced up my running shoes.

I ran in the darkness along Lake Michigan until I had to bend over with exhaustion, the cramps in my abdomen and legs lancing me with hot, red pain. And then I forced myself to stand, to keep running, my head a maelstrom.

I have to go - have to go - I have to go somewhere.

California? Back to San Diego? Back to admit my mother was right all along, that I couldn't hack it at the University of Chicago, that I couldn't ever, ever, ever find a husband?

Iceland? Back to Hæmir? Where I had no job, where I could barely speak the language, where I would find another man who'd call me whenever he wanted to fuck?

I limped back to the Flamingo as the stars were fading, the sky turning from black to a deep, bruised violet. Numbly, I keyed the code on the entrance and headed for the stairs. I lived on the fourteenth floor, but I kept climbing, past my floor, up and up. The door at the top of the staircase was unlocked. There was a small gate at the very top to keep idiots like me off the roof, but it was easy enough to climb.

I walked slowly across the black asphalt of the Flamingo's roof, past the hulking air conditioner units and ventilation intakes. I walked until my throbbing feet were at the very edge of the building.

And then I looked down.

The Flamingo is eighteen stories tall. I could see cars streaming along Lake Shore Drive, their headlights leaving gleaming tracks through the night. They seemed very small, and very far away.

Caroline Capello, I thought. *Visited by the trickster god. Threw herself from the Flamingo.*

I looked out, over Lake Michigan. There was a narrow band of gold on the horizon, where the rising sun lit the waters of the lake.

And then I took a deep breath, shook my head, and stepped away from the edge. *No. I don't want to be another name on that goddamn list.* I limped back to the stairs, back to my apartment. My shoes crunched fragments of expensive bone china as I walked to the bathroom, peeled off my clothes, and took a very long, very hot shower.

Caroline Capello, I thought. *Visited by the trickster god. Lived a happy and normal life.*

I crawled into bed and pulled the covers over my eyes.

* * * * * * *

I woke in the morning to an email from Hæmir. It was long and strictly professional, a detailed write up of all the ideas we'd discussed over our dinners or in the car.

There was one short, personal note at the bottom:

I hope your return trip went well, and I'm looking forward to seeing you again in Iceland. Sooner rather than later! :) -Hæmir

I read the email three times. My fingers hesitated over the keyboard, not quite ready to write him back.

When I stepped out of the shower later that morning, I noticed Loki's pendant on the bathroom sink, gleaming silver and gold. I didn't remember bringing it back with me. I didn't remember putting it on the sink. In fact, I clearly remembered throwing it to the floor in Nowhere, into the piles of crumpled books.

I ignored the necklace and slammed the bathroom door shut.

Then I dressed and headed to the University. I walked past Lake Shore Drive on my way to campus. I could see the fragments of my firefly china on the asphalt. They had been ground to powder by the passing cars.

CHAPTER TWENTY-FIVE

By the time I made it to campus it was early afternoon. I only had a few errands to do - deliver a copy of my syllabus, check my mailbox - and I was determined to act like a normal person and finish them without falling apart.

As I was leaving the building, Laura caught me. She looked radiant. "Oh, my gosh, welcome back from Iceland," she said. "I can't wait to hear all about it! Is this a good time?"

"Sure," I said, with a shrug. I had no reason to hurry back to my echoing, empty apartment.

We headed to Higher Grounds, where Kara smiled and gave us each a free mocha cappuccino. Then we sat down together as the first heavy drops of a late August thunderstorm drummed against the windows. I told her a very edited version of my trip to Iceland, heavy on the archeological artifacts and light on Hæmir's strong arms and ready smile.

"I have some news, too," she said, fingering the top of

her white mug. "Vance got a job in Manhattan! We're moving at the end of the month."

I opened my mouth and then closed it again. "Wow," I said, blinking.

"And since I passed the exams," she continued, smiling, "I can basically write my dissertation from anywhere."

"Well, congratulations," I said. "That's great!"

And then I started sobbing.

Laura's face dropped, and her pink lips formed a perfect "O" as she reached for me. I covered my eyes with my hands, my shoulders heaving, the tears streaming down my cheeks. I tried to turn to the window, knowing the entire coffee shop was probably staring at me.

"I'm so sorry," I whispered, once I could breath again. "It's Lo - Lucas. We..."

Laura hugged me, her arms warm around my trembling shoulders.

"You come right over for dinner," she said, in a tone that made it clear I did not have much of a choice.

Debra was waiting on the steps to Laura and Vance's ground-floor apartment, huddled under an umbrella. Laura must have texted her the entire situation, because she had a bottle of red wine in her hands and an enormous bag slung over her shoulder. When I saw her I started crying all over again, and soon I was sobbing

SAMANTHA MACLEOD | 271

on the sidewalk, in the rain. Debra and Laura put their arms around my shoulders and led me into the apartment. By the time I could breath again, I was sitting on Laura's couch with my shaking hands wrapped around a very full glass of red wine.

"Do you want to talk about it?" Debra asked as I sniffed into my glass and wiped my cheeks with my sleeves.

"No," I said. "No. I really do *not* want to talk about him."

"Okay then," said Debra, reaching into her bag. She handed me a pint of Ben & Jerry's ice cream.

"And," said Laura, "we have movies! What do you think? *Bridesmaids? Pitch Perfect? The Dictator?*"

I smiled, blinking my swollen eyes. "Thank you," I said, my voice raw from tears.

* * * * * * * *

We'd finished the first bottle of wine and all the ice cream by the time Vance came home. Laura walked over to him and whispered in his ear; they smiled at each other and shared a brief hug that was exquisitely painful to watch.

"I'll be back with more wine," Vance said, nodding to me. "And a pizza."

"Thanks," I muttered, feeling embarrassed.

Eventually, sometime after we'd opened the second bottle of wine, I told Debra and Laura about Hæmir. At least, I told them he was young. And single. And gorgeous.

"I don't know, Carol, he sounds perfect for you," Laura giggled. "I mean, he studies Norse mythology! What are the chances?"

"He does live in Iceland," I pointed out.

"So what?" said Debra. "You'll defend in, what, two years? Three years? Then you're Dr. Capello, Viking expert, and you've gotta believe some Icelandic university would just snatch you up."

"Maybe you can try long distance," Laura suggested, pouring me another glass of wine.

I nodded but didn't trust myself to speak. *I don't have such a great track record with long distance relationships,* I thought.

Or any relationships, for that matter.

I walked home from Laura and Vance's late that night, after pizza and a few stupid movies. I unlocked the door to my apartment and ignored the shards of my firefly china covering the floor like glittering, broken constellations. Loki's pendant was still gleaming on my bathroom sink. I ignored it. *Tomorrow,* I told myself, *I will totally clean this up.*

* * * * * * * *

The next morning I called my parents. As I listened to Mom recount all the exciting details of Capello's Landscaping & Tree Surgery's thrilling summer, I wrote and re-wrote an email to Hæmir.

Hi Hæmir,

Thanks for the email! I promise I'll give a more thorough response tomorrow, once I've got my notes in front of me. For now, I just wanted to let you know that I got in just fine, no complications.

Thanks again for everything - really! - and I look forward to seeing you, too.

I drummed my fingers on the desktop, hesitating. Then I typed: Perhaps I'll join your dig next summer!

Hopefully that struck the right tone. If he didn't want me to join him, it could come off as a joke. If he did want me to join him...

"Carol, are you listening to me?" Mom asked.

"Of course!" I said.

"I thought I heard the keyboard in the background," she said.

"Nope." I hit the *Send* button and the email to Hæmir vanished.

"Well then, what do you think?"

I had no idea what she was talking about. The last

thing I remembered was a discussion about a new golf course and a bidding war for the landscaping.

"Oh, I agree with you," I said, hoping I didn't just sign up for something.

Mom sighed in exasperation. "Caroline," she said, "you have no idea what I just said, do you?"

I mumbled something noncommittal into my phone.

"Would you please just call your brother?"

"Okay, okay," I said. "I'll call Geoff later. I promise."

I hung up the phone and stared at my email, waiting to hear back from Hæmir.

* * * * * * *

I was still staring at my computer when my phone rang two hours later. It was Geoff.

"Hey," I said. "I was about to call you."

"Yeah," he said. "You talk to Mom?"

"Kind of."

"Well." He took a deep breath. "We wanted to keep this under wraps for a few months, but it's just killing Mom. So, here's the news."

He paused. *You're selling Capello's Landscaping,* I thought, and I felt strangely cold.

"You're going to be an aunt," he said.

"A what?"

"An aunt," he said again. "An auntie. You know,

crazy aunt Carol."

"I - what?"

Geoff laughed. Even over the phone, his laugh made me smile. "Di's pregnant," he said. "We're going to have a baby."

My heart clenched, painfully and inexplicably, at the word *baby*. "Oh, wow," I said. "I mean, wow. A baby. Uh, congratulations."

"Yup, get the world ready for the next generation of Capellos," he said, and I could tell he was beaming.

"Well, I'm glad one of us is giving Mom some grandkids," I said, and he laughed again.

We hung up and I plugged my phone back into the charger. Then I stood and wrapped my arms around my aching, empty chest.

* * * * * * *

Laura and Vance left Chicago two weeks later, the same day classes began. Vance's new job paid for movers, so they didn't exactly need help. I came over to help anyway. Their cozy little apartment was stripped bare, with nothing but a few plastic crates of alarm clocks, shampoo bottles, and towels. There was an air mattress in their bedroom. The sheets had been stuffed in a plastic shopping bag, the blanket folded quickly and jammed on top. For some reason that made me cry, the tangled sheets, the blanket they had shared.

I ducked into the bathroom and rubbed my eyes with my sleeves, wishing I'd brought a pair of sunglasses. Then I walked out, my back stiff, and I helped Laura fold the air mattress and shove it into the trunk of their car.

"If we leave now," Vance was saying, "we should be able to make Newark by midnight. The Manhattan apartment'll be ready for us by nine tomorrow morning."

Laura turned to me, and this time she had tears in her eyes.

"You take care of yourself," she said, hugging me.

"You too," I muttered.

Vance shook my hand and then pulled me in for a hug. And then they climbed into their car, the doors slamming shut. They waved out the windows as Vance pulled away, headed for the highway.

* * * * * * *

When I got back to my apartment there was an email waiting from Hæmir.

Hi Carol,

Love to have you on the dig next summer! Funding might even be possible - I'll investigate. Any chance you're free this weekend? Would love to chat about Lokisfen - it could be a strong collaboration.

I smiled. Professional, polite, thoughtful; exactly like Hæmir. I imagined him at his desk, his strong arms reaching for his keyboard, maybe pushing his blonde hair out of his eyes as he typed.

I wrote back immediately: How about Saturday night?

His response dinged in my inbox less than five minutes later: It's a date!

I wondered if the double entendre was intentional. Then I wondered why I cared.

CHAPTER TWENTY-SIX

I shivered once, with my entire body, just as I was falling asleep that night. Then I was cold, violently cold, as though I were pushing through a sheet of ice.

I opened my eyes in a forest.

The trees towered above me, and a low, white mist clung to the damp ground. It was freezing, and I wrapped my arms around my shoulders. *I found Loki here, once,* I thought, and I tip-toed around the nearest tree, holding my breath, looking -

Nothing. Nothing save dark trees, white fog. Cold emptiness. I moved a little faster, my hands outstretched, trying to find him. I felt something low and tight in the small of my back, and the hairs on my neck prickled. *Something is wrong.*

And then I ran, bolting through the spaces between the trees, the cold air tearing at my lungs. *He needs me,* I thought. *There's something wrong, and he. Needs. Me.*

The dark branches whipped my arms and legs. The

fog barely stirred with my frantic footsteps.

I sat up in bed, gulping for breath, my heart pounding, my hand grasping at the empty space between my breasts where Loki's pendant used to hang. I was alone; my chest felt raw and hollow. I pulled my legs up to my chin and sobbed until the rising sun began to tremble across the walls of my empty bedroom.

* * * * * * * *

I was up late that Saturday night, talking with Hæmir. And then again the next Saturday, and the next Saturday, until it became a part of our routine. We worked well together, Hæmir and I, professionally. The Lokisfen paper was done in under a month. It was good work, and I was proud of it, even if it had hurt, just a bit, every time I typed the name "Loki." Our paper was accepted for publication almost instantly, and the same journal even expressed an interest in our analysis of the Ragnarök carvings in Slyndennär.

"We'd better come up with an analysis," Hæmir said, and I laughed.

"I'm sure we can throw something together," I said, yawning. It was almost one in the morning in Chicago; almost seven in Reykjavik. *The sun must be rising,* I thought, suddenly remembering exactly how Hæmir's blonde hair looked in the pale early morning light.

"Tired?" he asked

I shook my head and then laughed at myself, realizing he couldn't see me. "Nah, I'm fine. What about you?"

"Also fine." I could tell he was smiling, which made me smile too.

"Hey, listen," I said, glancing at my Google calendar. *Call Hæmir* was written on every single Saturday night. "I've been totally monopolizing your Saturday nights. Or, you know, your Sunday mornings."

Hæmir laughed.

"No, really," I said. "If you've got something, uh, more interesting to do with your Saturdays..."

"And what could possibly be more interesting than talking with you about the Ragnarök carvings?"

"I don't know," I stammered. *A party*, I thought. *A date. With someone who lives in your country.*

"You know, to be honest," he said, "I don't ever have plans for Saturday night. I guess I don't get out much."

"Yeah, me neither." I smiled, stretching out on the couch. "I mean, obviously."

We both laughed, and it occurred to me that I laughed a lot when I was on the phone with Hæmir. More than I laughed anywhere else.

* * * * * * *

It was mid-November before I could bring myself to touch Loki's pendant.

I left this in Nowhere, I thought, staring at it warily. *I ripped this off my neck and threw it on the floor.*

I bit my lip and held my hand above the gleaming metal, contemplating sweeping it into the trashcan. Or throwing it out the window. My heart clenched and I sighed in frustration. *It's been months,* I told myself. *And the bathroom sink is a stupid place to keep jewelry.*

I picked it up, the smooth metal cool against my palm. I walked to the bedroom, opened my top dresser drawer, reconsidered, closed the drawer, and lay the shimmering pendant on top of my dresser, next to the tea candles. I stared at it for another minute, wondering if there would ever be a time when it wouldn't hurt to look at it. Then I wiped my eyes and walked back to my desk.

* * * * * * * *

"So, uh, Baldr was, like, the son of Óðinn," stammered a pale, sickly-looking freshman in front of a sleek PowerPoint slide that had probably taken him hours to perfect.

It was the last week of classes, student presentation week, and I was trying to look plausibly alert and engaged. In actuality I was staring out the window at the swirling, fat snowflakes and the abnormally still, black squirrel perched on the window ledge. And I was trying to forget my dream. The same dream I'd been having for months, night after night after night.

I swear this squirrel is registered for my class, I thought. I'd seen the fat little bastard every day this month, sitting at the window.

I realized the freshman was staring at me.

"Yes, go on." I hesitated while I tried to remember his name. "Steve."

The PowerPoint flashed to a painting by Christoffer Eckersberg. An absurdly solemn crowd in pastel robes looked on, horrified, at a prone figure, one arm dramatically flung over his head, a bloodless spear wound in his stomach. *The Death of Baldur.*

And there he was, his proud face held high, in the far left corner of the painting. It wasn't a very good picture of Loki, but I would recognize him anywhere.

"So, uh, Baldur was, uh, he was invulnerable. Like, nothing could hurt him. So one day Loki starts asking around, like, is it really true nothing will hurt Baldur?"

I turned my attention back to the squirrel. It was focusing on me quite intently. I winked at it, wishing I could say the weirdest thing in my life was being given the stare-down by a black squirrel while teaching my Myths and Legends of Norse Mythology class.

"So then Loki makes a spear out of this mistletoe,

'cause it's the only thing that'll hurt Baldr, and then he gives it to this blind guy, uh, 'cause all the gods think it's funny, like, to throw things at Baldr."

I looked back to the PowerPoint.

"And as, um, as punishment," Steve said, his hand trembling as he changed the slide, "Loki was bound."

I hated this painting: *The Punishment of Loki*, by James Penrose. There he was, tied to the rock, helpless, naked, his lean, muscular body and handsome, arrogant face exactly as I remembered him. *And that's how he got the scars on his wrists and ankles*, I thought, swallowing hard as I turned away from the screen.

I scowled at the squirrel in the window, who was still staring at me. *Fuck off*, I thought.

"And the, uh, the snake, I mean the serpent, it, like, drips poison in his face. And his, uh, his wife, um, Sigyn, catches it."

"Thank you, Steve," I said once he finally stopped stammering. "Any questions from the class?"

Jen raised her hand, and I nodded at her.

"But I don't understand," she said.

Steve looked like he was about to pass out, so I walked to the front of the room and let him sit down.

"What don't you understand?" I asked.

"Why would Loki want to kill Baldr? Wasn't Loki one of the Æsir too?"

My classroom was silent. The radiator hissed and

clanked in the corner.

"I mean," Jen continued, "I guess I just really don't understand Loki at all."

"Well, you can't apply Western, Judeo-Christian morality to these stories," I began, but my voice trailed off as I looked out the window. Snowflakes were swirling and dancing in the fading light of late afternoon, and I was reminded of another snowstorm. When the trickster god of the Æsir met me in the quad.

I sighed. "You know what?" I said. "I don't understand him either."

There was a flash of motion as the squirrel disappear from the windowsill. *See you Tuesday,* I thought.

* * * * * * *

"Is something on your mind?" Hæmir asked, that Saturday night.

I was sprawled on my couch, my notes spread over the living room table, my phone next to me, set to speaker. I could almost close my eyes and believe Hæmir was sitting next to me.

"Nah, it's nothing." It was almost two in the morning in Chicago, so past breakfast time for Hæmir. We'd talked for longer than I'd intended. Again.

Hæmir was silent.

"Okay, fine," I said. "It's this... squirrel." I laughed,

hoping that would make me sound less insane. "I swear it's the same squirrel, and sits just outside my classroom window every single week. I mean, it's not a problem," I added, trying to keep my voice cheerful. "It's just... funny."

"Is it Ratatoskr?" said Hæmir. "Isn't he the squirrel who runs up and down the World Tree?"

I smiled at my phone.

"I doubt it," I said, although that sounded strangely plausible. *There really is a World Tree,* I thought. *Perhaps there's also a Squirrel.*

There was a moment of comfortable silence. Then I added, without thinking, "And I've been having the same weird dream for, ugh, forever."

"What dream?" asked Hæmir, his voice suddenly concerned. And serious.

"Oh, it's nothing," I said, waving my hand even though he couldn't see me. I really did not want him to think I was crazy, and it was crazy to have the same dream every night. For months.

"We can talk about the dream," he said. It sounded like he was forcing his voice to stay calm and friendly.

"No!" I snapped. "Nope, nope -" I staged a yawn. "It's getting pretty late."

It wasn't even a bad dream. It was just me, running through a forest. Actually, if that had been all there was to the dream, I might have even told Hæmir.

But I wasn't just running.

And, even though Hæmir and I were strictly professional, I still hesitated to tell him that I spent every night, every dream, searching for Loki.

* * * * * * * *

I got Hæmir's email on New Year's Day. The subject line was "Important News!!" and my heart skipped a beat.

Carol, great news!

Funding was approved for the summer - and you're in the budget! Of course I'd love to have you, and now the really good news is I can afford to hire you. That is, if you still want to come.

I booked my plane tickets that day: departing from Chicago on June 1st; leaving Reykjavik on August 15th.

I was going to spend an entire summer with Hæmir.

CHAPTER TWENTY-SEVEN

Springtime, and warmth finally returned to Chicago. All my windows were wide open, and the entire apartment smelled like the sun-warmed waters of Lake Michigan. I was trying to pack for Iceland; my bed was covered with clothes, and my open suitcase waited on the floor. So far I'd managed to pack my running shoes, two pairs of socks, and a sports bra.

I picked up a pair of jeans. *Jeans are good.* I folded them and reached for my suitcase. Then I hesitated. The jeans looked a little, well, frumpy. I sighed and put them back on the bed. *But frumpy is fine,* I told myself. *You just don't want to be sexy.*

Right?

I ignored the jeans and picked up a sweater. The green sweater, the one I'd worn during my exams. And then after, in the nightclub. The sweater I'd ripped off my body and left on the beach as we went skinny dipping, following Loki's naked, graceful body into the waves.

I balled up the sweater in frustration and shoved it back in my dresser. *I never used to worry about what I wore with Loki,* I thought. And then I smiled at myself. *That's because you usually didn't wear anything with Loki.*

Something sparkled and glimmered on my dresser. I looked up and his pendant caught my eyes, reflecting the spring sunshine.

"Stop it," I said. "I'm not taking you."

I turned back to my closet and saw the red dress, pressed against the far wall. I pulled it out and held it to my body, smoothing the fabric. *Maybe we'll go out,* I thought. *Maybe Hœmir likes to dance.*

I swayed against the dress, moving my hips. And then I caught a glimpse of myself in the mirror. Blood rushed to my cheeks. *Sexy as spring in Midgard,* Loki said, once. My heart gave a funny little pang. I sighed and hung the dress back in the closet.

"This is not going well," I muttered, looking at my nearly-empty suitcase.

There was a small crash in the living room, followed by the sound of rustling papers, and I darted out of the bedroom. The wind had knocked over the stack of essays I needed to grade and strewn them across the living room floor. I picked them up, trying to put them back in order, and I decided the packing would have to wait.

* * * * * * * *

I lay in bed until I felt the shiver, the bracing rush of cold through my entire body that meant I was once again falling into the dream world.

And then I opened my eyes in a forest.

No, not just a forest. *The* forest. The same forest I found myself in every single night. The same dark, towering trees. The same cold, damp earth. The same sense of urgency, desperate and growing stronger.

Loki needs me.

I took a deep breath and started running. Running across the wet ground, branches whipping my face. Running past trees, trees like huge stone pillars. Running into the darkness.

The forest was absolutely silent. No birds chatting in the trees above, no rustling noises from small, hidden creatures. I could smell water, moss, decay as I sprinted through the trees, not sure I was making any progress. Not sure I was even moving. And I could sense... *something.* Some vast, searching presence.

I was not the only one looking for Loki among those dark dream trees.

And then a phone began to ring, and I was running to that, too, running to answer the phone. I looked around and around, thinking *phone, phone..?*

I shivered and blinked in the darkness of my own room. There was still a phone ringing. *Di's baby girl,* I thought. *I must be an aunt.* I fumbled for my cell phone and pushed "ANSWER."

Someone was sobbing on the other end. It took me a minute to realize it was my mom.

"Caroline," she said, "it's your father."

* * * * * * *

I was at O'Hare International Airport two hours after Mom's phone call, standing in line to go through security, my cell phone propped under my chin, apologizing over and over to Hæmir.

"I might be able to make it in a week or two," I said, blinking furiously as I tried to keep my voice level. "It's his heart. He's in the hospital now, but if he can come home soon..."

Hæmir sounded very calm, although I'd woken him in the middle of the night. "You take care of your family," he said. "The dig isn't going anywhere."

For some reason, his strong, understanding voice just made me cry harder.

* * * * * * *

Because I was flying last minute, my route took me

through Denver and then Phoenix. I had to sprint through the Phoenix airport, barely making the flight to San Diego. They held the doors for me, and I found my seat just as the severe, overweight flight attendant was demonstrating proper seat belt buckling procedures. I finally caught my breath as the plane taxied down the runway. *I am going to make it home,* I thought, closing my eyes as my heart finally stopped racing.

Then I shivered violently in the seat, my entire body suddenly freezing, gasping for breath -

And I opened my eyes in the forest.

It was darker now, under the looming, silent trees. My heart hammered frantically in my chest; the cold, damp air stung my lungs. I heard the sound of flowing water and followed it until I came to a stream. Fireflies danced above the ripples, swirling and shimmering. I stepped into the water; it was so cold it hurt my feet.

The fireflies moved upstream, and I followed them, slipping on the rocks, plunging my hands into the water. Finally the stream slowed, and I was in a deep pool, soaking wet and freezing, shivering violently.

Loki stood on the far bank, facing a tree. In the tree was a squirrel.

No, not *a* squirrel - it was *the* squirrel, the exact same black squirrel that had been sitting outside my Myths and Legends of Norse Mythology class all quarter.

"- doing fine, all things considered," the squirrel said. "She still mourns you. There's no one else."

"There was," said Loki, his voice low and dangerous. "There was someone else. In -"

His voice dropped, and his words were swallowed by the hiss and gurgle of the river. But I didn't need to hear him to know what he said.

Iceland.

"Look, I'm not sure why you're doing this to yourself," the squirrel said. "If you want my advice - "

"I don't," Loki growled.

"You've got to move on," said the squirrel. "Forget about - "

I woke, shivering. Someone was shaking my shoulder.

"Ma'am, you need to put your seat back in the upright position," the flight attendant insisted. "We're landing."

I nodded, not trusting myself to speak. I wiped my cheeks with my sleeve, realizing they were wet. *I must have cried*, I thought.

When I bent to shove my carry on bag under the seat in front of me, I realized my shoes were also wet. Cold and wet.

* * * * * * * *

I took a taxi from the airport to the hospital. My sister-in-law Di met me in the lobby, hugely pregnant. She looked tired and scared. I was dimly aware of my wet socks in my wet sneakers squashing over the hospital floor as I walked to meet her.

"He's in surgery," she said, taking my hands. "It's a, um, coronary artery bypass graft."

She pushed the button on the elevator.

"They're basically taking one of the veins from his arm and putting it in his heart," Di told me, as the elevator rose smoothly and silently.

My legs felt frozen. *Open heart surgery*, I thought. *Dad. Open heart surgery.* The elevator doors opened and Di guided me around a few corners to a small, windowless waiting room. Geoff sat on the couch, holding my mom's hand.

She's old, I thought, with a shock. My mother, with her fiery temper and her stylish clothing and her platinum blonde hair, looked so small, sitting there on the hospital couch. So vulnerable.

Mom and Geoff stood and rushed over to me, and then suddenly we were all crying, clinging to each other. Like the survivors of some tragedy, shipwrecked together in the waiting room of Scripps Mercy Hospital.

Dad's surgery seemed to take a very long time. Perhaps it was a few hours; perhaps an entire lifetime. I walked the halls, I sat with Mom, and I watched the seconds tick by on the huge, round clocks without actually noting the time.

Finally a doctor in green surgical scrubs came into the waiting room to tell us Frank Capello was in recovery.

"He'll be in the hospital for a minimum of seven days," the doctor told us. "Most patients are able to drive again in four to six weeks, but honestly - " and here he gave us a serious, level stare " - he won't be fully recovered for at least two full months."

We were all very silent. I could see my brother's eyes growing wide, wild.

It was late May. The very beginning of the busiest season for Capello's Landscaping & Tree Surgery. There would be graduation parties, weddings, family reunions, hundreds of reasons for someone to hire a professional to spruce up their backyard. My dad ran the business; Mom, Geoff, and Di all worked there.

And Di was nine months pregnant.

I caught my brother's eye. "You don't have to," he said, knowing what I was thinking before I spoke.

"I'll stay," I said. "I'll stay."

* * * * * * * *

A polite, older nurse led us to the recovery room half an hour later. I held Mom's hand as we walked through the hall, as if I were a child. When we opened the door to his room, my dad looked very small against the white hospital bed. Strange, when my entire life he'd seemed so tall, so strong.

His chest was covered with a warren of wires and tubes. He had tubes coming in and out of his nose, an IV in his arm, a monitor strapped to his leg. *Are you in there, Dad?* I thought, and my heart clenched painfully.

"Hey, pumpkin," he said, giving me a weak smile. "You didn't have to come all the way out here."

"Wouldn't miss it for the world," I said. I gave his hand a quick, gentle squeeze, and then I moved out of the way so Mom could sit next to him.

Geoff put his arm around my shoulder, and I leaned against him. Together we watched our parents under the fluorescent glare of the hospital lights.

"Thanks," he whispered.

I just nodded.

Mom and I drove home together, hours later, once the nurses finally forced us to leave, insisting Dad really needed rest. We were both silent on the drive, the darkened streets of San Diego rolling past us. The house was still and silent when we walked in from the garage.

Mom cleared her throat. "I haven't had the time to put sheets on your bed," she said. "And your room may be a bit dusty."

"Mom, it's okay. I didn't come for the sheets." I turned to hug her in the living room. She felt small and fragile in my arms.

"Thank you," she said, patting my cheek.

I nodded. "Get some rest," I said. Then I picked up the suitcase I'd so carefully packed for Iceland and headed to my room.

* * * * * * *

I called the airline first thing in the morning. Changing my plane ticket wasn't a problem: ten minutes on the phone, and I was now leaving San Diego in two months instead of two days. Yes, the woman in the customer service department assured me, I would have an outstanding credit with United Airlines for the flight to Reykjavik I would no longer be taking. Yes, I could use that credit to purchase another flight to Reykjavik, sometime in the future.

And then all I had to do was call Hæmir.

I pressed his name on my phone. It was very early in the morning, and I was sitting in my parents' garden, my knees pulled up to my chest.

"Carol? How is your father?"

I started to cry. His concerned, compassionate voice sounded so damn far away, an entire planet standing between his body and mine.

"He's going to be fine," I sobbed. "I'm so sorry, but I can't - I mean, I need to - "

"Oh, Carol, Carol," he said. "Carol, it's okay! Please, I promise you, I will make no breakthrough discoveries until next summer. When you can join me."

And then I was both laughing and crying.

"Okay," I said, wiping my eyes on my sleeve. "Next summer. I can do next summer."

* * * * * * * *

Someone shook my shoulder, and the cold, white mists of the dream forest swirled, evaporating as I awoke. I opened my eyes and stared, not certain of my surroundings. The bed was small, the room dark. I couldn't smell him, his woodsmoke, his -

"Caroline?" Mom's voice was low and urgent in the darkness.

I sat up in bed and glanced at the clock. It was just past three in the morning. "Oh no," I said, the knot of fear from my dream still tight in the pit of my stomach. "Is it Dad?"

"No, it's the baby! Geoff and Di are headed to the hospital. Start getting dressed, we're going to meet them."

Scripps Mercy Hospital was strangely peaceful at three in the morning. We were the only people in the waiting room of the Maternity Ward.

"Come on," Mom said, checking her phone. "Geoff said they're in room 234."

I shook my head. "I'll just wait here," I stammered.

My mother arched her eyebrow at me. I waved my hands in defeat and followed her down the quiet hallways until we reached room 234. The door was slightly ajar, and the lights were turned off. Di had, of course, wanted a natural childbirth. Soothing flute music drifted through the open door, and I could see the flicker of candles. There was a sharp, unpleasant animal smell under the waxy lavender scent of the candles, and I could hear someone panting. I shuddered and took a step backward.

Geoff came to the door and smiled at us. Mom hugged him and walked into room 234. I backed away from the room and almost stumbled over a metal cart in the hallway.

"Good luck," I whispered to Geoff. And then I fled.

I sat in the waiting room for what felt like a very long time. Mom walked past me every thirty minutes or so, asking bizarre questions like whether or not I'd noticed an ice machine. I could not imagine why she wanted ice.

Eventually I pulled my phone out of my pocket and stared at it. *Hæmir.* I did the time zone calculation. It was almost noon in Reykjavik. I wondered if Hæmir was already at the dig. I wondered if he'd be ready to break for lunch, maybe head back to the Slyndennär Inn. My finger hovered over his name. Then I sighed, shoved my phone back in my pocket, and got up to look for an ice machine.

Almost two hours later I heard screaming from the direction of room 234, and a cold stab of fear bolted down my spine. *There can't be a problem,* I thought. *Not after Dad. There can't be—*

And then Mom walked down the hallway, beaming.

"Carol," she said, with tears in her eyes. "You're an aunt."

She took my arm and pulled me down the hallway to room 234.

The room was heavy with the scent of lavender and orange, and the thick, low tang of blood. Di reclined in the hospital bed, beaming. She looked exhausted, and somehow still radiant.

In the bassinet next to her was the most beautiful child in the world.

Geoff lifted her gently and then turned to me. I shook my head. I've never been comfortable around babies, let alone newborns. I don't know how to hold an infant or change a diaper, and I'm terrified about flopping their little heads around or touching the wrong spot on their skull.

Geoff ignored my silent protests and placed my sleeping niece in my arms. I took a deep breath and the fear evaporated as she nestled against the curve of my breast. She was so delicate and tiny, and so warm, and so solid. I kissed her soft head and took in her smell, baby powder and sweet milk and just a hint of woodsmoke.

You're imagining, I told myself. *No, you're remembering.*

I looked at Geoff and Di in amazement. "I love her," I said, my voice trembling. "I love her already."

"I know," Geoff said. "Crazy, isn't it?"

CHAPTER TWENTY-EIGHT

"Caroline, do you have your notebook?" Mom waited for me at the kitchen table, her manicured eyebrow arched with impatience.

"Yeah, almost," I said, grabbing for a cup of coffee. "I've only been up for, like, two minutes."

She tapped her bright pink fingernails on the table.

"Okay, okay," I said, pulling the cap off a pen with my teeth. "Fire when ready."

"I'll be in the hospital all morning with your father," she said. "And then I'm going to help Geoff and Di take baby Devi home this afternoon. So." She took a deep breath. "The Rodriguez project finishes today. You'll need to email them a Customer Satisfaction Survey and a copy of the invoice. Invoice first. Then survey. And please call the Chen family to check on their eucalyptus tree. We should be finished taking it down by tomorrow."

I scribbled my notes while she talked.

"Luis will probably ask you for an advance on his paycheck. His daughter's Quinceañera is coming up. Give him the advance, but not more than five hundred dollars. No interest."

She paused to let me catch up.

"The Kingsleys," she said, and took another deep breath. "We are not going to begin work on their backyard until we have our advance payment. In cash. You'll need to drive over there. And Caroline." She paused until I looked up at her. "Do not leave their front steps until you have the payment. Cash only. And for God's sake, do not send Aunt Adrianna over there."

I nodded, scribbling frantically.

"Now, we're re-doing the koi pond for the -"

"Hold on," I said, trying to massage my cramping hand. I looked up at my mother, sitting across the table from me. She'd been at the hospital until almost one in the morning, but she looked perfectly composed. Her makeup was flawless. Well, maybe not totally flawless; the eyeliner on her right side was a bit smudged.

"How do you remember all this?" I muttered. She didn't even have a calendar open.

"Caroline. This is my job." She smiled, a brief, professional smile, and then got back to work. "Now, the koi pond -"

* * * * * * *

I didn't see Mom again until late that night, when we met for dinner in the hospital cafeteria after visiting Dad.

"Geoff and Di got the baby home all right?" I asked.

She nodded, brisk and efficient. "The Rodriguez account?" she asked, peeling the top off her Weight Watchers stir-fry chicken dinner.

I checked my notes. "Yes, I sent them the invoice. And the survey. In that order."

"And Luis?"

"Got an advance of three hundred dollars, and said he's very grateful," I flipped the page. "Also, we got an invitation to the Quinceañera next month. For all of us."

She nodded. "And did you get the advance payment from the Kingsleys?"

I didn't need to check my notes for that one. "Yes, I did," I said. "And it may have been the most awkward twenty minutes of my life. Which is saying something."

She laughed at that, her voice ringing through the hospital like sunshine.

"And, uh, Stan Kingsley asked me out," I said, hesitantly. I almost didn't tell her, and now I was very quiet, waiting for her reaction. Waiting for her to declare I'd better snatch up that pretty rich boy before someone else did.

Mom looked at me over the rims of her reading

glasses. "Honey," she said, "you can do better."

* * * * * * * *

Dad came home after a week in the hospital, and Mom created an elaborate spreadsheet to track his new schedule. I stayed home with him in the mornings until noon, when Aunt Adrianna came over until three, or until Mom returned from the office. Except for Tuesdays, when Aunt Julie came over, and Fridays, when Uncle Tony alternated with Aunt Michelle. And she'd color coded his many doctor's appointments. Mom left two copies of the spreadsheet when she headed to the office; one in the living room, and one on the fridge.

"And I've emailed you a copy," she said, hesitating at the door to the garage.

"Yeah, thanks. I think I've got it," I said.

"Evelyn," Dad called from the bedroom, "I think we can handle it."

My mom looked at me as if she doubted very much that we could handle it.

"Mom," I said, "I promise I'll call the office if there's any trouble."

She sighed and I saw her shoulders sag. I walked over and gave her a hug. "Seriously," I said. "You'll be home by three."

She took a deep breath, reminded me again about the

copy of the schedule on the fridge, and then finally opened the door to the garage. I smiled and waved to her, trying to look confident. Then I turned back to the kitchen. *I am going to make breakfast,* I thought. *Damn it.*

* * * * * * *

"Hey, pumpkin," Dad said. He was propped up on pillows in the bedroom. He still looked pale, but he was smiling.

"Hey, Dad," I said. "I'm making French toast."

He raised his eyebrows. I shrugged. The recipe I found online seemed simple enough. I should be able to handle cooking one straightforward breakfast item; my Italian cooking genes had to kick in at some point, right?

He patted the side of his bed, and I sat down next to him. "I wanted to thank you," he said, clearing his throat. "You didn't need to stay here."

"Oh, Dad, stop it. It's really not a big deal."

"That's not what your mother tells me. She said Capello's Landscaping would've gone under without you."

I laughed. "It's only been a week, Dad."

He shrugged, smiling, and I wrapped my fingers around my coffee mug. "Hey, can I ask you something?"

"Anything," he said.

I hesitated, took a deep breath. "Have you ever, um. I mean, did you ever - did you ever love anyone? Other than mom, I mean? And, uh, get over it?"

Dad leaned back on his pillows and sighed, and I instantly regretted the question. "Never mind," I said, standing up.

"No, no, it's no problem," he said. "I mean, I dated some other girls. Nothing as serious as you and Doug, of course."

"Doug and I weren't serious," I muttered.

He gave me an inscrutable smile. "I'll tell you when I knew," he said. "Oh, we were just kids. One day, we went to Mission Beach, got some hot dogs, splashed in the water. And then she turned to me, right around sunset, and she smiled at me. I don't even remember what she was smiling about. But boom - that's when it hit me. I love her." He leaned back on the pillows, smiling.

Great, I thought, remembering Yggdrasil. Remembering the shifting, dancing light playing across Loki's face. *That happened to me. With the God of Lies.* I shivered, then tried to turn it into a stretch.

"So that was it, huh?" I asked, staring at my empty coffee mug. "First comes love, then comes marriage?"

"Oh, God, no," he said, chuckling. "We broke up that night."

"What? Dad, I've never heard that!"

"Your mother doesn't like to talk about it," he said, shifting position on the pillows. "But hell - I was only nineteen years old. I was scared to death. And I came crawling back a month or so later."

I shook my head. "What the hell, Dad?"

"People get scared," he said. "We do dumb things. That's why it's so important to forgive - Do I smell smoke?"

"Oh, shit!" I ran to the kitchen.

I walked back to the bedroom twenty minutes later, holding a tray.

"French toast?" Dad asked, cautiously.

"Corn flakes," I said, putting the tray across his lap. "And, uh, I may need to get you a new pan."

My dad did an admirable job of turning his laugh into a cough.

"So," he said, giving me a sideways glance, "any particular reason you're asking about love?"

I waved my hand dismissively. "Nope. Totally irrelevant. And I can't believe you dumped Mom."

Dad shrugged over his corn flakes. "I was surprised to hear you cancelled your trip to Iceland. I hope it's not going to set you back too far?"

Thank you for changing the subject, I thought, with a smile. "It won't. Don't you worry about me."

The phone next to the bed rang, loudly.

"That'll be your mom," said Dad, reaching for the receiver. "Hello, Evelyn," he said, and then he paused. "Yes, I'm just fine. Carol made breakfast and then we had a nice conversation about love."

I rolled my eyes and grabbed the tray.

"No, I'm not joking," he said, waving to me.

I closed the door softly behind me.

* * * * * * *

The phone rang. I was sitting at my mom's desk at Capello's Landscaping & Tree Surgery, and the phone had been ringing non-stop for the past six hours.

"Capello's Landscaping," I said into the receiver. "This is Caroline. How may I help you?"

"Ah, hello, Carol." It was Hæmir.

I frowned and looked at my hand. I was holding my cell phone.

"Oh! Oh, no, Hæmir, I'm so sorry."

I glanced up to see Aunt Michelle smiling at me. "Go ahead, honey," she whispered, waving her hand at me. "Take your call."

I waved back at her, pushing away from the desk and heading for the parking lot. "Hey, Hæmir, it's nice to, uh -"

I cut off to nod and smile at Tony and Donny as they carried pizza and three bottles of Coke into the office.

"Hey, Carol," Uncle Tony boomed. "How's your father today?"

"Did you get the Kingsleys' payment?" Donny asked, simultaneously.

"Yeah, hey, I'm on the phone," I said, waving at my cell as I walked out the doors.

"Sounds busy," Hæmir said, gently.

I groaned. "I've been here since six in the morning. And I'm only halfway through the reconciling -"

Geoff pulled into the parking lot and waved at me. I waved back as he walked inside. "How's the dig?" I asked. "Where are you? Uh, what time is it?"

Hæmir laughed. "Slyndennär," he said. "It's going well, and it's not too late." I did the time zone difference in my head. "Hæmir, isn't it past midnight?"

He laughed. "That's not so late. The sun is still up! Besides, I haven't heard from you in weeks."

"Uh, yeah, I'm sorry about that. I got your email, it's just -"

"Carol?" Aunt Michelle came to the doorway and waved to me. "You want some pizza? It's not very good, you know, but I can bring some out, if you'd like."

I covered my cell with my hand. "Not now," I said. "I'm on the phone!"

"Listen," said Hæmir, "you sound busy."

"Yeah," I said. "I mean, no. Yes, busy. But it's nice to

hear from you." I paused, shifting my weight on the sidewalk. I could hear the office phone ringing inside. "I miss talking to you," I said, finally.

"Me, too," he said.

"Hey, sis," Geoff said, pushing open the door. "I've got some messages from Mom. Stuff she wants you to have a look at."

I sighed. "Hæmir, I'm really sorry. Can I call you back?"

"Of course," he said. "Take care of yourself, Carol."

"You too." I slid my cell phone back in my pocket and followed Geoff into the offices of Capello's Landscaping.

CHAPTER TWENTY-NINE

"You look tired," Di said, with a sympathetic smile.

"I'm all right." I shrugged, not wanting to complain about sleep to a woman with a newborn baby.

"Is something troubling you?"

We were sitting on the back patio of their house, watching baby Devi sleep in her swing. It was early Sunday morning. The sky was a vivid blue overhead, and Geoff was making breakfast in the kitchen.

"Everything's fine," I said.

Everything should be fine. Dad is home; the paperwork for Capello's Landscaping is now only a month behind schedule. Hæmir's last email had even started to outline plans for next summer. *So why do I feel so shitty?*

"Bad dreams," I said, shaking my head with a little laugh to show it wasn't a big deal. "Nothing serious."

But it felt serious. And they were getting worse.

Last night I'd seen Loki. Just a glimpse, but enough to frighten me. He stood at an odd angle in the gloom of the dream forest, supporting himself against a rock. He looked weak, hurt. I called to him, and he disappeared. When I forced myself to walk over to the rock, I found blood pooling next to it.

This morning I'd woken with his blood on my hands.

"Tell me about it," said Di.

Birds sang in the lemon tree. I could smell bacon and coffee from the kitchen, could hear my brother humming to himself as he cooked. Geoff and Di's backyard seemed very far removed from the dark cold of the dream forest, from blood on the cool moss.

I took a deep breath. "Well. I keep having dreams where I'm looking for my... friend. Boyfriend, sort of. I mean, ex-boyfriend, I guess."

Di looked very serious, and very interested. I felt slightly unsettled.

"I'm running through a forest, of some sort. Usually I can't find him. But sometimes I do see him, and then he just vanishes." I tried to laugh again, but it came out a strangled sort of cough.

Di nodded, then closed her eyes. "It sounds like you two still have a strong connection."

I snorted into my coffee. "Well, that's the most California thing I've heard all day," I said. Then I looked up to make sure I hadn't offended her.

But Di's clear eyes were unfocused, gazing across the morning sky. "I wonder if he - " she muttered. Then she stopped and smiled at me, reaching across the table for my hand. "Carol, the next time you see him, grab him. Hold him and don't let go."

* * * * * * *

With much fanfare, Frank Capello returned to the offices of Capello's Landscaping & Tree Surgery, exactly one month and one week after his heart attack. He walked slowly to his desk, leaning heavily on my mom's arm. Then he picked up his phone and spent the rest of the morning calling his clients. He remembered every single "Get Well Soon" card, I noticed, and every bouquet of flowers delivered to the hospital.

He was exhausted by lunch and went home with Mom while I stayed behind, promising to reconcile the payroll for June. *I'll be going back to Chicago soon*, I thought, slightly alarmed at how quickly the small, crowded offices of Capello's Landscaping & Tree Surgery had become almost comfortingly familiar.

I pressed my palms against my eyes, trying to ward off the headache that usually followed hours of staring at Excel spreadsheets. I hated payroll, hated it even more fiercely because I knew it was probably the most important thing I did. The offices were dismally empty by six that evening, and I had at least another two hours before I'd be finished. Aunt Michelle brought me a Subway sandwich for dinner and offered to stay, but I waved her away. Payroll reconciliation is a one-woman job, sadly.

Just another fun-filled Friday night for Caroline, I thought. I tossed my sandwich wrapper in the trash, stood, and stretched as a shiver ran the length of my body.

My next step was in the forest.

What the hell?

I didn't remember falling asleep. I was in the middle of payroll, for fuck's sake, in the middle of the office. I held very still, listening. *He's here,* I thought, taking a deep breath.

I started walking, slowly, carefully. I tried to think of nothing but him, his cool fingers on my skin, my thighs wrapped around his slender, muscular hips. The smell of woodsmoke and salt spray. His lips against mine, his tongue, his face at the moment of orgasm, eyes closed, head tilted back.

And then he was in front of me. Loki leaned against a tree, gripping his side. He looked up, and our eyes met. My heart shuddered in my chest. *Oh, damn,* I thought, *was he always so beautiful?*

"Hi," I said, my voice sounding strange and flat in the dream forest.

He smiled, and I reached for him. He took my hand, and then I was in his arms, my head swimming with his scent, with the feel of his body against mine.

"I miss you," I whispered, and he sighed, his head resting on mine, his arms tight around my waist.

Then his body stiffened, and he cupped my chin in his hands, tilting my head to meet his eyes. "Caroline," he said, and I shivered. *My name. He's never said my name before.*

"You have to stop. It's not safe here. You can't keep - " His head jerked up.

I heard it too, or rather, I sensed it. Some electric spark in the air, perhaps the snap of a tree branch. We were no longer alone. Something was searching for Loki in the darkness of the dream forest. And something found him.

He raised his arms, his palms facing out.

Grab him, Di said. *Hold him and don't let go.*

The ground trembled under my feet. The wind roared in my ears, tore at my hair, my clothing. I did not let go.

"Caroline!" he yelled, and I opened my eyes.

It was dark and howling rain. The windows were open, and the tumult of the storm was pouring in, streaming across the smooth, white floor. *The windows are always open here,* I thought, and I realized with horror where we were. I was standing in Nowhere, my arms tight around Loki's chest.

The room was being torn apart.

The ocean outside was a nightmare of waves tall as mountains with looming chasms between their crests. The sky ripped open in rain and lightning. The floor, the walls, were falling apart, crumbling everywhere I looked.

Loki grabbed my arms, pulling them away from his chest. "You can't follow!" he screamed, his scars livid against his pale face. "You have to let me go!"

I realized he was disappearing, fading in front of me. And then the floor split beneath my feet, and I fell toward that apocalyptic sea.

* * * * * * *

I woke, shivering, on the concrete floor of Capello's Landscaping. My entire body ached, and I rolled to my side, coughing up seawater. I was soaking wet; I could feel the water running off my body and pooling beneath me.

It was dark in the office. I pulled myself up on Aunt Adrianna's desk, looking out the window at the empty parking lot in the sodium glow of the street lights. I must have been gone for hours. Long enough for the sun to set; not long enough for anyone to miss me, or to come by the office to check on me.

Or perhaps they did come, and I was gone, I thought, hugging my wet clothes as I shivered in the darkness. I gazed slowly around the echoing emptiness of the office, my heart racing, wondering what the hell had just happened. *Loki's gone,* I thought, panic welling in my stomach. *Loki's gone.* I took a deep breath, forcing myself to calm down and think. I'd seen Nowhere destroyed; I'd seen Loki vanish.

But that's not all you saw.

No. I saw one final thing as I fell. There was a man next to Loki, pulling him back. A man holding a giant, double-headed hammer. *Mjölnir,* I thought. *Thor.*

I rubbed my hands over my shivering arms, then grabbed my purse and walked out the office doors. The warm, humid air of the parking lot felt good on my damp skin. I stood in the parking lot, watching the moths cluster and swarm around the streetlights. *Thor must have taken Loki to Asgard,* I thought. *What do I know about the Æsir being taken to Asgard?*

I closed my eyes and leaned against the brick wall of Capello's Landscaping. An image floated into my mind. A crumbling book, in a cardboard box, in a dingy library in Iceland. I shuddered. *The Book of the Gods' Mortal Lovers.*

But it wasn't just a list of names, was it? The book opened with a trial. With one of the Æsir, taken to Asgard. And with her mortal lover, coming to save her by demanding...

I opened my eyes. "The Trial of Æsìlynd," I whispered to the darkness. "Her mortal lover demanded the Trial of Æsìlynd."

* * * * * * *

The car's radio said it was just past two in the morning as I navigated the quiet streets to my parents' house. My parents had left the porch light on for me. I saw dinner sitting on the table, thoughtfully covered with plastic wrap, but I didn't stop. I didn't know how much time I had. I suspected it wasn't much.

I went to the bathroom, tip-toeing past my parents' bedroom, and stripped off my wet clothes, putting them in the bathtub. I grabbed the first thing I found in my suitcase: old, black jeans and my University of Chicago T-shirt reading *If I Wanted an 'A' I Would Have Gone to Harvard.* Then I hesitated and grabbed a hoodie sweatshirt, too. My sneakers were still full of salt water from some alien ocean, so I put on flip flops.

It hardly seemed like the best outfit for leaving the mortal realm.

I kept thinking of things I should probably bring: matches, a compass, a jacket... But I didn't have matches, or a compass, or a jacket, and I didn't want to waste my time tearing through San Diego looking for them, so I just grabbed my book bag and added a few bottled waters from the fridge.

I stopped on my way out the front door and looked back at the kitchen, one light still on, my dinner still waiting for me on the table. Tomorrow morning Mom would find that dinner on the table, my wet clothes in the bathtub, my wet sneakers on the front porch. Tomorrow morning there might still be a pool of saltwater on the floor of the office.

I went back in the kitchen, grabbed the notepad by the phone, and hesitated.

Dear Mom & Dad, I wrote, my ex-lover Loki - he's the Trickster God, maybe you've heard of him - well, he's been taken by Thor against his will, probably to Asgard. I'm off to see if I can help by doing something I read about in a book. Well, sort of - not much of the book was left. Anyway, cheers, and I'll try to be back soon!

"Nope," I whispered, crumpling up the piece of paper and shoving it deep in my pocket. I glanced at the door, then grabbed a fresh sheet.

Dear Mom & Dad, I wrote again, my pen rasping against the white page. Something's come up. I have to leave. I'll be -

I hesitated. "I'll be what?" I whispered, chewing the end of the pen. "I'll be back? I'll be fine?" I shook my head, then crossed out I'll be.

Please don't worry about me, I wrote. I love you. ~Caroline.

I was halfway to the front door when I remembered something else. I crept back to the kitchen and wrote PS. I didn't finish the payroll. I'm sorry.

"Shit," I muttered, staring at the note. "If I survive this, Mom's going to kill me."

* * * * * * *

Of course you can walk there, Loki told me, years ago. *If you know where to walk.*

In the stories, the ancient stories, the gods of Asgard traveled to and from the human realm on the Bifröst, the Rainbow Bridge.

So, I just needed a rainbow. And I needed to know where to walk.

I pulled into the empty parking lot of the Rainbow Lanes Bowling Alley. Their neon rainbow sign lit the night, the colors so bright they reflected off the hood of my dad's dark blue Toyota Camry. The night was almost over, the sky above turning a velvety gray. *Get going,* I thought, feeling like this would probably work better in the darkness. I got out of the car, locked it behind me, and then hid the keys over the driver's side wheel. God knows if I'd need those again.

I took a deep breath and turned to face the neon

rainbow.

I seek Loki Laufeyiarson, I thought.

And I stepped off the human world.

CHAPTER THIRTY

The bridge between worlds was cold.

I pulled my sweatshirt's hoodie over my head and silently berated myself for wearing flip flops. *Stupid mortal.*

Cold, white mist swirled around the bridge, making it impossible to see anything, even my own freezing feet. Sounds were dampened and distorted in the thick fog; sometimes I could hear my own footsteps echoing, and sometimes I heard nothing at all. The path wandered, split, and diverged. Sometimes the mist felt colder against my face, sometimes warmer. Once I heard a woman singing, clear and cold, the patterns and intonations of her language unfamiliar. Later, I heard a man's voice call my full name, just once, somewhere in the distance behind my right shoulder.

I reached between my breasts and was not surprised to feel the weight of Loki's pendant around my neck. *I seek Loki Laufeyiarson,* I thought, gripping it tightly in both hands.

And I let my feet find the path.

* * * * * * *

I walked for a long time without stopping. I was hungry and thirsty, but I was also afraid to stop in that swirling white mist, afraid I might not find the path again. My feet ached with the cold and then became numb. I shivered for a while, and then my arms and legs also became heavy and numb. Finally the fog began to grow a bit lighter, like the edge of the sky in the early morning. I strained, listening, and could hear the distant crash of waves, the cries of seagulls.

And then I saw a figure standing in the fog ahead of me. He grew larger as I moved closer, until he was impossibly huge, towering over me. His armor was golden, and he held a sword.

Heimdallr, I thought. *Watching the Bifröst.* And I began shivering again.

As I shivered, Heimdallr smiled, showing a formidable row of golden teeth. "You're a long way from home, mortal woman," he said, his voice a deep thunder.

I tried to stop shivering long enough to draw myself up tall. I still had to tilt my head to look in his face. "I am Caroline Capello," I said, "of Midgard. And I have come to demand the Trial of Æsilynd for Loki

Laufeyiarson."

Heimdallr chuckled. "Have you now?" he asked. "Well then, welcome to Asgard, whore of Loki."

My cheeks burned. I held my back stiff as I walked past Heimdallr, not looking at him.

My next step was on a rocky beach.

I spun around and saw Heimdallr standing behind me, his attention already focused elsewhere. The sun burned low against the horizon, huge, rolling breakers crashed along the shore, and seagulls dipped and dove in the surf. A distant rainbow hung suspended in the sky over the ocean. I suddenly felt very small, and very far from home.

I turned to face the shore. Past the rocky beach, the grass was a vivid, electric green. Rolling hills led to a forest, and towering mountains disappeared in the clouds beyond.

Between the forest and the beach was a Viking longhouse. It was half-buried in the hillside, its roof covered with the electric green grass and small trees, so it was difficult to tell where the longhouse ended and the hill began. Sheep and goats grazed on the roof.

I heard the distant clang of metal on metal, and the air held just a hint of smoke. With the smoke came the smell of food. My stomach groaned in protest, and I started to shiver again, my arms and legs aching as they began to thaw in the sunlight. I forced my feet to move across the rocky beach, walking toward the longhouse. There were people clustered around the house, I realized. Some of them seemed to be performing an elaborate dance on the rolling hills, coming together, then falling apart. *No, they aren't dancing,* I realized. *They're sparring.* I saw a flash of light off a sword as two men jumped at each other, and the beach echoed with the resounding clash of metal on metal.

"My warriors," said a gruff voice, and I jumped.

There was a man standing next to me. At first I thought he was an old man, but when I looked again I realized I'd made a mistake; he was young, barely older than me, with a tall, athletic build. *The hat makes him look old,* I thought, glancing at his dark blue, broad brimmed hat. When he turned to me, I saw his right eye was a black, empty socket. *Of course.* I would have recognized him anywhere.

"Óðinn," I said, sinking to a curtsey. "The All-Father."

"Loki's whore," he said, nodding toward me.

I felt blood rush to my cheeks. "I am not a whore," I said, my voice icy.

Óðinn turned to me, his cold blue eye dancing. "Really?" he said. "And do you fuck Loki?"

I said nothing.

"And does he pay you?" Óðinn continued.

My heart hammered against my ribs. I watched the

warriors in the grass, and I thought of the money, the piles and piles of hundred dollar bills now hidden in the bottom of my kitchen cabinet.

"You're..." I struggled with the words. "You're misrepresenting my relationship with Loki," I finally said, stiffly formal.

Óðinn laughed. "Perhaps. Come, walk with me."

He offered me his arm, and I took it.

"I've come to demand the Trial of Æsìlynd," I said as we stepped from the rocky beach to the thick, springy mat of the meadows. The grass was dotted with small, white flowers.

"Mortal girl," Óðinn said, with a trace of cold steel in his voice, "do you even know what those words mean?"

"Of course," I lied, holding my back stiff. "I'm an expert in pre-Christian Norse culture. I probably know more than any other person in Midgard."

Almost any other person, I thought, remembering Hæmir with a momentary pang.

Óðinn sighed and turned to face me. "You know, you're not the first mortal Loki's fucked."

"I know," I said, quietly, remembering *The Book of the Gods' Mortal Lovers.*

"I can send you home right now," he continued. "And I can guarantee fortune will favor you for the rest of your days. Just let this one go."

I glanced out, over the ocean, to the rainbow. It

looked very small, and very far away.

"I can guarantee you'll get your doctorate," Óðinn said, his voice low and conspiratorial.

A wave of anger rose in my chest. "I don't need your help!" I said. "And I will not leave. I demand the Trial of Æsilynd."

Óðinn sighed again, and for a moment he looked very much like an old man. "I am not pleased with this. I will not make this easy for you."

"I didn't ask for it to be easy," I said.

"Fine," said Óðinn. "I'll send someone over to help you get settled."

And then he was gone, and I was alone in the fields, shivering again. My feet ached. I waited, and I stared at the warriors sparring, and I tried to determine the size of the longhouse. It was difficult, because the house seemed to slip every time I tried to count the windows.

The wind shifted, and I could once again smell food, a hint of smoke and roasting meat above the tang of the ocean. The shadows began to grow long under my feet. I finally decided I was done waiting, and I climbed the rolling hills to the hall.

A flight of grand, swooping wooden stairs leading to enormous oaken doors in the center of the longhouse. The doors were flung open, light and laughter and the smell of food spilling out of them and into the twilight. I climbed the stairs slowly. A tall woman stood just inside the doorway, watching me. She was inhumanly beautiful, her high cheekbones and golden hair gleaming in the light pouring through the wide doors.

"Welcome to Val-Hall," she said, once I'd crossed the threshold and entered the longhouse. "I am Sif, the wife of Thor."

"I'm Caroline," I said, offering my hand. "The, uh, friend of Loki."

She did not take my hand, and I awkwardly dropped it to my side. Her perfect face was composed and completely unreadable.

"Óðinn asked me to show you to your quarters," she said, turning and walking inside.

I followed her through a massive hall lined with stone fireplaces and long, wooden tables. Torches flared on the walls. The peak of the ceiling was so high I couldn't make it out through the thick wood smoke swirling up the rafters.

Sif turned down a hallway without looking back, and I scrambled to catch up with her. She stopped abruptly in front of a rough wooden door that looked exactly like all the other rough wooden doors we'd walked past. She pushed the door open and walked in.

"Fourth door to the left," she said, her voice cool and even. "This room is yours, now."

The room was warm and comfortable. A fire smoldered in a stone fireplace between two windows.

There was a sturdy four-post bed and a small dresser. I was immensely relieved to see what looked like a bathtub behind a thick, red curtain. I put my book bag down on the dresser and turned to Sif.

"Any questions?" she asked.

"Where's Loki?"

"In Asgard," she said, her voice colder and more distant, her expression unchanged.

"And can I talk to him?"

"No. He does not wish to talk with you."

My heart clenched painfully. I squeezed my fingernails into my hand, trying to keep my face impassive. "But he's... okay?"

"He lives," she said.

We stared at each other in silence.

"And his wife? Sigyn?" I knew I was pushing my luck, but I couldn't help it. I had to know.

Sif's frozen expression finally shifted. She raised an eyebrow at me. "Sigyn has been dead for an age, mortal woman," she said.

"Oh." I tried not to look relieved.

"Loki killed her," Sif said.

CHAPTER THIRTY-ONE

There was indeed a bathtub behind the red curtain. I'd never been so happy to see a bathtub in my entire life. I spent a long time in the copper tub, thawing in the hot water. When I finally pulled myself out of the tub, I found a covered meal sitting on the dresser, although I hadn't heard anyone enter the room. It looked like pot roast, with buttermilk biscuits and a spicy green salad. The plate gleamed golden and the fork and knife were heavy in my hands. The napkin ran through my fingers like silk. I took a sip from the graceful, fluting wine glass, and my breath caught in my throat. It was the same mead Loki brought to my apartment, sweet and sparkling like summer sunshine. It was the mead we drank on the North Avenue Beach, with my friends, watching the sunrise. A lifetime ago.

I sat on the bed as I ate, staring out the windows and across the ocean, where unfamiliar stars sparkled across the gently rolling waves. When I'd finished eating, I put the empty dishes back on the dresser and stretched across the wide bed, wishing I'd thought to bring pajamas.

* * * * * * *

I woke to sunlight painting the ceiling above my bed. It was my fourth day in Val-Hall, and I'd made zero progress. *In fact,* I thought, as I sighed and pulled myself out of bed, *I'm bored out of my fucking mind.*

I walked to the dresser and opened the top drawer. Every morning I had two options: black with gold accents, and green with gold accents. The dresses were comfortable, falling to around my knees. They were low-cut, which made me feel a little awkward at first, but I got used to flashing the tops of my breasts. Besides, it's not like I talked to anyone. And the boots were magnificent. They laced up the sides, coming almost to my knees, and they were easily the most comfortable shoes I'd ever worn. No matter how long I spent circling around Val-Hall or tramping around the forest, my feet stayed warm and dry, and the boots were clean the next morning.

Breakfast appeared without fanfare. Scrambled eggs, bacon, and two thick slices of toast. A second later a steaming mug of black coffee appeared, and a slender glass of dark burgundy juice. I wondered idly how Val-

Hall knew I liked my coffee black. Then I ate my breakfast on the floor and tried to think of something to do with myself.

Val-Hall remained stubbornly closed to me. On my first day I'd managed to find what looked like a library, with sweeping ceilings and towering bookshelves. But the damn books were all incomprehensible. I'd opened a slender, green volume whose writing looked almost familiar, like Norse runes, but after a few pages I was staring at cuneiform. When I continued for a few more pages, the words shifted and molded themselves into hieroglyphics. *These books do not like me,* I'd thought, fighting the urge to throw one of them into the fireplace. After that first morning I couldn't even find the library again; every passage in Val-Hall led either to the great dining room, or curved back to my room. The fourth door on the left.

I sighed in frustration and put my breakfast dishes on the dresser, where they promptly vanished. Then I grabbed my book bag and emptied it onto the bed. Three plastic water bottles tumbled out, followed by a battered Icelandic dictionary and an unopened copy of *The Nature and Destiny of Man.* One spiral-bound notebook, a couple of pens. And my cell phone. I flicked my cell phone on and thumbed through my contacts. *Dad. Geoff. Laura. Mom.*

Hœmir.

I sighed and looked out the windows, where the morning sun danced off the tops of the waves. I had to admit, I could really use Hæmir's help. I pressed his name. My phone blinked and then read *Calling... Calling... Calling...*

Call Failed. Try Again?

I snorted a laugh. *Caroline, you're an idiot,* I thought, turning off my phone and shoving it back in my book bag.

I had no idea what I was supposed to do next. Did I have to say something, or do something, to start the Trial of Æsìlynd? Did I have to find Loki? Did I have to ask for help?

But I'd already told Óðinn I knew what I was doing, and I was terrified of losing that advantage. If they knew I was completely and utterly clueless, what would stop them chucking me out on the Bifröst?

Or off of the Bifröst?

I shivered and pulled my book bag over my shoulder, grabbing the water bottles. I wasn't going to find any answers in this tiny room.

* * * * * * * *

I wasted most of the day stomping around the forest behind Val-Hall, getting mad at myself. *What the hell good is it devoting my life to studying Norse mythology if I can't remember one damn thing about the Trial of Æsilynd?* I thought, over and over. I finally gave up and stumbled downhill, emerging from the trees near Val-Hall's long, curving porch.

It smelled like barbecue when I entered Val-Hall, and my stomach rumbled in protest. I'd missed lunch. The long, wooden tables were filled with food, stacks of ribs and bowls of small, new potatoes, smoked fish, and gleaming platters piled high with steamed greens. The benches were almost full, mostly with young men who cheered and called to each other from across the room.

I felt horribly out of place. *It's like high school all over again*, I thought, remembering the lunches I spent sitting alone, reading. I ignored the welcoming fire, the near-irresistible smell of dinner, and I turned down the hallway. Within seconds my feet brought me to the fourth door on the left, which opened as soon as I touched the handle.

My room looked very small and dark in the fading light. I sighed and glanced down the hallway, toward the long tables. *Maybe it's time to put high school behind me*, I thought. I took a deep breath, squared my shoulders, and turned around.

"I'm going to go out there, sit down, and eat with other people," I said. "Damn it."

I hesitated in the hallway for a few minutes, watching the men as my heart thudded in my throat. It didn't look like there were any seating arrangements; the warriors just wandered in, greeted each other, and sat down. I finally spotted another woman, took a deep breath, and headed toward her. She waved when she saw me, and I looked over my shoulder, figuring she must be waving to someone else.

"It's great to see another girl," she said as I sat down.

"Yeah," I said, with a smile. "Yeah, it is."

"I'm Hidy," she said, offering me her hand. "Hidy Merrill."

I took it, and we shook hands across the table. "Carol Capello. It's really nice to meet you."

"So how did you get here?" she asked, reaching for the potatoes.

I wasn't sure how to answer. "I, uh, took the Bifröst."

"Oh, must be after my time," she said. She gave me a fleeting, sympathetic look. Then her smile returned. "It was Iraq for me," she said. "Roadside bomb. IED, you know. Not the best way to go, but far from the worst."

My arms and legs suddenly felt very cold. It took me a minute to realize Hidy was still talking.

"When we got a choice," she said, "I figured I'd come here for a while. Seems like a good place."

I looked around the room, slowly. Hundreds of people, mostly young, mostly men. Hundreds of people who spend their days fighting together, and their nights feasting together. *My warriors*, Óðinn called them. And who gets to live in Val-Hall? Who gets to become one of Óðinn's warriors?

They are all dead, I thought. *I am surrounded by dead people.*

I stood suddenly.

"You okay?" asked Hidy.

"Excuse me a minute," I said. My voice was very calm, and it sounded like it was coming from very far away.

I turned and walked back to my room. I did not run.

My door had no lock. I thought about pushing the dresser against the entrance, but I realized that was a stupid, useless gesture, like hiding under the covers as a child. If someone wanted me, all they had to do was walk in this room. I had no way of keeping them out; I had no way of protecting myself. I was alone and defenseless, in Val-Hall, with the army of the dead.

I curled up in the bed, pulled the covers over my head, and cried.

I thought I would never fall asleep, but I woke to bright sunshine and the lonely cries of seagulls. I heard the distant crashing of the waves against the stone beach. I closed my eyes. I could almost pretend I was in Nowhere again, in Loki's bed, watching sunlight play across the water, staring at the rows and rows of books.

I ate breakfast in my room and headed to the great hall. The tables were already almost empty. I watched the dead warriors from the hallway. They certainly didn't act dead. In fact, they acted completely normal; they greeted their friends, they waved to each other, they sipped coffee in silence. I even saw two men reading books, and I felt a stab of intense jealousy. *They managed to befriend the library,* I thought.

I saw Hidy as I walked down the stairs. "Hi, Carol," she waved, coming toward me. "You feeling better?"

I took a deep breath. *She's dead,* I thought. *But how long are you planning on holing up in your room, by yourself? Crying?*

"Yeah," I said, taking a deep breath. "Yeah, I am. Thanks for asking."

"Good, good. Hey, I understand, it can be a rough transition."

"So," I asked, "what do you do all day?"

Hidy laughed. "Come on, I'll show you."

* * * * * * * *

I've tried a lot of things in my life, and I've been very, very bad at some of them. Cooking, for one. Field hockey, for another. In high school I joined the swim team and came in last at every single meet. My coach told me to keep studying. As in, stay out of the pool.

But I was a swimming legend compared to my fighting prowess.

Hidy tried to show me the basic stance: feet wide for balance, body turned to the side to offer a smaller target, hands up to protect your face, or to hold a shield, or a sword. *Warrior position*, she called it. When Hidy pushed my shoulder to show me how stable the stance was, I fell over backward.

There was a small group of warriors watching us by that point. They were polite enough not to laugh out loud, although there were a few coughs. A huge, burly black soldier with a shaved head and a full beard leaned over me, offering me his hand. I took it and climbed to my feet.

"Frank," he said. "Frank Washington."

"I'm Carol," I said, dusting myself off.

"Oh, I know," he said, flashing his teeth in a wide smile.

My cheeks burned. *Infamous already.*

"Here," he said, "try it like this."

Frank spread his legs wide and bent his knees. Then he held his arms out in front of him, crossing his wrists. "Gangnam style!" he said, thrusting his hips. "Come on!"

"I hate that song," I said, gingerly rubbing a new, angry bruise on my thigh.

"Oh, me too," Frank said. "Still, don't you kind of miss it?"

I shook my head, spread my feet, and tried the

warrior position again. *Gangnam style.* This time I managed not to fall over when Hidy pushed my shoulders. And Frank was very understanding when I spun around too quickly and accidentally drove my elbow into his stomach.

"Well," I said, as we finally headed back to Val-Hall in the fading light, "I think I'm the worst warrior in Asgard."

Hidy shook her head and patted my arm. "You'll get better."

I laughed, running my fingers over the spreading bruise on my forearm, where I'd tripped over my own feet and crashed into a rock. "It's okay," I said. "It feels good to be doing something."

"And don't worry," said Hidy, giving my bruised arm a sympathetic look. "You'll be fine by dinner."

I wasn't sure if this was tough soldier talk, so I just nodded and limped through the doors of Val-Hall. *At least I have someone to sit with,* I thought.

Once I took the first sip of mead at dinner, I understood what Hidy meant. My bruises vanished as I drank the mead. They didn't fade gradually, becoming less and less sensitive until they finally healed. They were just gone, and so was the swelling on my lip and the stiffness in my arms.

"Whoa," I said, turning to Hidy. "So that's how you do it? That's how you fight all day, every day?"

"Yup," she said with a wide smile. "Cool, huh?"

* * * * * * * *

I'd just loaded up my plate a second time when Frank leaned across the table toward me. "So," he said, "if you don't mind me asking, how did you get here? Because - and no offense here - you don't exactly seem like a soldier."

I laughed. I'd lost count of how many glasses of mead I'd had, or how long we'd been sitting around the table. I was fully recovered from my warrior misadventures, the great dining hall was warm and pleasantly fuzzy, and I felt fantastic.

"No," I said, shaking my head, "not a soldier. I'm a grad student."

Frank, Hidy, and the other warriors stared at me blankly.

"I took the Bifröst," I said. "The bridge between the Realms. I'm, um, I'm a friend of... someone here."

"One of us?" asked Hidy, her eyes shimmering in the torchlight.

"Uh, no," I said, feeling slightly uncomfortable. "Not a - not a human. Not a warrior."

"You mean one of *them*?" asked Frank, with a vague gesture toward the far end of the hall.

"Well..." I hesitated, reaching for another glass of

mead as I tried to think of how to answer.

"You came here for one of them?" Frank spread his arms, his hands up. "That's the most goddamn romantic thing I've ever heard."

I felt my cheeks flush. "It's not exactly romantic," I muttered. "We broke up."

Hidy stared at me. "Then what are you doing here?"

I shrugged. "I think - I mean, there's been some... trouble. And I thought he could use - "

Frank laughed. He had a booming voice, and his laugh filled the hall. "That is absolutely the most goddamn romantic thing I've ever heard," he said, standing to clap me on the shoulders. Then he tilted his glass of mead toward me. "You're insane, you know that?"

"I know," I said, rubbing the sore spot on my shoulder where he'd whacked me.

"Wait a minute," said Hidy, grabbing my wrist. "Does this mean you can go back? Back to Earth?"

"I hope so," I said. "I mean, that's the plan."

"Can you take a message?"

* * * * * * * *

I went back to my room for my notebook and spent the rest of the night recording messages.

"I'm not absolutely certain I can get back," I told

Hidy for about the hundredth time.

"That's ok," she said, tossing her curly strawberry-blonde hair over her shoulder. "I feel better just saying this stuff."

Hidy had given me her parents' phone number and address. She wanted them to know she was safe, and happy, and that she'd crashed the car into the garage when she tried to sneak out her senior year of high school. The hole in the garage door was her fault. It wasn't because her mom forgot to put the parking brake on.

I'd written similar messages for dozens of the dead. The most heart-breaking was from Phil, who wanted me to contact his wife and let her know he wanted her to re-marry.

"I'm pretty sure she was cheating on me, anyway," he told me, his voice low and heavy with emotion. "But please don't tell her that." He sniffed and wiped his eyes. "At this point, I just want her to be happy."

My hands trembled as I recorded her phone number and address, and her parents' names too, just in case. By this point the wide hall was almost deserted. The fires burned low, and the sky outside the open doors was beginning to lighten. Hidy and I were the last ones at the table.

"So, who is he?" asked Hidy, covering a yawn.

I stretched my arms above my head, flexing my

aching hand. I wasn't used to writing longhand anymore. "Do you know Loki?" I asked, not sure what to expect.

Hidy shrugged. "I've seen him. I haven't spoken to him. We don't usually cross paths with them."

"Have you seen him lately?" I asked, now feeling fully awake.

"I don't know," she said, shaking her head. "Time is funny here. But no, I think it's been a while. At least since the last big battle." Hidy yawned and shrugged again.

"Tell me about it. Please."

"Óðinn led an offensive against the Jötunn," she said, as if this were the most painfully obvious news in Asgard. Perhaps it was. "We attacked their ship. My team was to destroy one of the moorings and, well, mission accomplished."

The first rays of the rising sun began to hit the rafters of Val-Hall's soaring ceilings. Hidy looked very pale in that cold, golden light, her freckles like bruises on her skin. "I saw Loki leading one of the teams." She frowned. "But I didn't see him afterward, here. During the celebration."

Charlie Trotter's, I thought, remembering Loki in my bed, his blood pooling on my floor. "Do you see them often?" I asked. "Óðinn and Thor and...them?"

"They eat here every night," she said, with another

yawn. "At the other end of the hall."

I stood to look down the length of the empty room. I couldn't even see the far side, just an endless line of torches flickering faintly against the growing dawn.

"I'm sorry," Hidy said, coming to her feet, "but I have got to get some sleep."

"Of course. Thank you."

CHAPTER THIRTY-TWO

I walked back to my room, undressed, lay down in the bed. But my room was already bright with sunlight, and I couldn't keep my eyes shut. I finally stood, put my clothes back on, and walked into the dawn.

It was a bright, windy day, the air carrying a hint of frost. I wondered if Asgard had seasons, if this was the very end of summer here, just like it was in Chicago. The thought of Chicago made me sharply and unexpectedly homesick. I thought of my bright apartment, my windows open to the lake, my bookshelves and desk. I sighed and let my feet carry me toward the forest, wondering again if there was something I needed to do, something I needed to say. Was I supposed to approach Óðinn in the great hall, demanding the trial? Did I need to find Loki first? Were we supposed to be working together? I shivered as I entered the cool shade of the forest, wishing I'd brought a jacket.

I'd been walking for perhaps an hour when I heard footsteps, very clearly, coming from behind me. I froze. The footsteps stopped as well. I tried to bring my hands to my face. Warrior position.

"Fancy meeting you here," said a familiar voice.

I turned. Hæmir Jőrn stood behind me in the dappled light of Asgard's forest. I screamed.

"Hey, hey, it's okay," he said, taking a step toward me.

I stepped back reflexively, hitting a jutting stump hard with my upper thigh. I winced. "Hæmir," I said, and my eyes stung as they filled with tears. "No, no - are you dead?"

"Oh, right," he said with his painfully charming lopsided smile. "No, I'm not one of Óðinn's warriors. I'm not dead."

My shoulders sagged with relief. I moved closer to him, and then I was in his arms, leaning against his strong chest. "Oh, damn, Hæmir, I'm so glad to see you," I said.

His arms tightened around my chest. "I'm glad to see you as well."

"I tried to call you," I said, and then I laughed. "I actually tried to call you. From fucking Asgard."

We stood in silence, his strong arms wrapped around my body, my head resting on his broad chest. And then a creeping, uncomfortable fear began to spread through my body; I felt cold despite the sunshine filtering through the trees. *I am in Asgard,* I thought. *What is Professor Hœmir Jőrn doing in Asgard?*

I pulled out of his arms and met his eyes, swallowing hard. "Uh, if you're not dead, then..?" My voice wavered in the dappled sunlight.

Hæmir's brow furrowed, and he took a deep breath. "Listen, I probably should have explained this earlier," he said. "My name's not actually Hæmir."

I stepped away from his arms, a hot bolt of panic rising in my chest.

"My name is Hyrm," he said. "I'm of the Jötunn."

I shook my head and backed away, my vision blurring with tears. *No,* I thought. *No, you're Hœmir. My friend Hœmir.* Then he was beside me again, his strong arms wrapped around my waist, his hands closed over my wrists.

"Carol, I'm trying to help you."

"Let me go!" I screamed, my chest a hard knot of fear.

"Fine!" he yelled, and I felt him release my wrists, my waist.

I stumbled forward and fell to my knees.

"Listen, Carol, what are you doing here?" He knelt next to me, offering me his hand.

I ignored him. I stood up and ran like hell, and I didn't stop until I was on the steps of Val-Hall, gasping, my sides burning. *It's not possible,* I told myself. *Not. Possible.*

I pulled myself up the stairs, staggered down the hallway to the fourth door on the left. This time I shoved my dresser against the door. I tried to shove the bed against the door, but it was too heavy for me to move. Not that it would stop a Jötunn, anyway. Whatever the hell a Jötunn really was.

I thought he was Hæmir. I unlaced my boots with trembling hands and crawled into the bed. *I thought he was my friend. My normal, human friend.*

I thought I had a normal, human friend.

* * * * * * *

I awoke hours later. The shadows were long in my room, and the light outside my window was the rich golden of late afternoon. There was a sharp knock on my door. I glanced down and saw I'd fallen asleep in my dress.

"Just a minute," I said, stretching and pulling the dresser away from the door.

I opened the door just wide enough to see Hæmir's lopsided smile. I slammed it closed again.

"Can we talk?" he said through the doorframe.

"No!" I yelled, shoving the dresser back in front of the door.

I went to the bathroom and filled the tub. Then I climbed in and sat there for a long time, ignoring the door. Eventually the water turned cold, and I started to get hungry. I pulled on a clean dress and moved the dresser as quietly as I could. Then I cracked the door.

Hæmir was sitting in the hallway across from my door. He smiled up at me. *Goddamnit*, I thought, slamming the door shut again. He had to be so infuriatingly handsome. I leaned against the door, weighing my options. Then I opened it again.

"I'm going to scream," I said, "until someone shows up. And then all the Æsir will know you're here."

He was still sitting on the ground, his hands hanging between his knees, looking uncomfortable and slightly embarrassed. He did not, I had to admit, look especially threatening.

"Oh, Carol," he said. "They already know I'm here."

I sighed in frustration. Slamming the door a third time seemed a bit ridiculous, and I was getting tired of my room.

"I'm going to stand up," he said. "Would you care to walk with me?"

I said nothing as he clambered to his feet. He ran his hand over his neck and smiled at me again. "When I heard you were here," he said, "I asked the Æsir if I could come, and they granted my request. I'd like to help."

"I don't need help."

Hæmir shrugged and turned to leave, walking down the hallway. I followed him, matching his stride.

"Where's Loki?" I asked.

He laughed. "Still stuck on him, are you?"

I felt a wave of embarrassment that hardened into anger. "At least Loki never lied to me about what he is," I muttered.

Hæmir spread his hands wide, looking embarrassed. "My dear," he said, "if you'll join me for dinner, I will attempt to answer all your questions."

I tilted my head at him. "Are you even really a professor?"

Hæmir laughed again, that clear, ringing laugh I'd heard a hundred times over the phone. "Yes," he said, "as a matter of fact, I am. Of course, it's a bit easier to make groundbreaking discoveries when you remember where all the artifacts were buried in the first place."

"Fine," I said. "One dinner. And you answer all my questions."

"As well as I possibly can," he said, holding out his arm.

I ignored it.

We walked further into the great hall than I'd been before, until we reached booths carved into the walls between the fireplaces. Hæmir gestured at one of the booths, and I sat down, painfully aware of all the meals we'd shared in Iceland. Especially the last one.

The table was lit with candles and set with two platters. Dinner looked like soup and smoked fish with rich, dark rolls and a side of steamed greens. There were two glasses of mead and a pitcher of sparkling water.

"So..." he began, raising an eyebrow at me.

"What is this place?" I asked, waving my hand at the dim booths.

"It's Val-Hall," said Hæmir.

I stared at him. "Really. Thank you. That's very helpful."

He laughed again, his eyes sparkling above his lopsided smile. "It is very nice to see you again, Carol," he said.

I said nothing, and I turned away from his radiant smile. *You were supposed to be Hæmir,* I thought. *My normal, human friend.*

The one part of my life that was actually somewhat normal.

"I apologize," he said, clearing his throat. "It's just another part of Val-Hall, somewhere private. Slightly more... intimate." He smiled again, his face soft and achingly familiar in the flicker of the candles. "So," he said. "Questions?"

"Where's Loki?" I asked.

Hæmir sighed, shaking his head. "I don't actually

know. I'm told he's here, in Val-Hall."

"How can I see him?"

Hæmir sliced open a roll and began to butter it. "I'm told he does not wish to see you."

I sighed in frustration, wanting to bury my face in my hands. "Yeah, I'm told that too."

"Well, you can't see him unless he agrees," said Hæmir, taking a bite of his roll. "Rules."

"But is there some way I can reach him? Get a message to him?"

Hæmir shook his head. "I'm afraid not."

I took a long drink from my glass of mead, wishing it could help the dull ache spreading across my chest. "Speaking of rules," I said, "what are you doing here? Didn't the Jötunn and the Æsir just have a big battle?"

Hæmir smiled, his eyes sparkling once again. "The Jötunn and the Æsir are always having battles," he said. "It's what we do."

"That - that doesn't make any sense," I said.

"Look at it this way," he said. "What if you knew, with absolute certainty, how and where you would die?"

"I suppose I'd avoid that place," I said.

He laughed. "We all avoid Vígríðr," he said. "In fact, we cannot visit the final battlefield until we're pulled there. Until Ragnarök."

I nodded, thinking of Loki. *You went somewhere I couldn't follow,* he'd said, the night we drank Óðinn's mead. The night I saw Vígríðr.

"But if you knew, say, that you could never die in a car crash," Hæmir continued. "Wouldn't you want to crash a car? Just to see how it feels?"

I shook my head. "I think - if I knew how I would die - I'd try to prevent it."

Hæmir chuckled. "Well, you are very young," he said.

I pulled the napkin into my lap, fiddling with the smooth fabric as I looked around the hall. There was a couple in the booth across from us. They must have been Æsir; they were too beautiful to be mortal. They laughed together, and then he reached up and brushed her cheek. She caught his hand and held it, smiling.

I turned away. *We never went out to dinner,* I thought. *Not even once.*

Hæmir reached across the table and took my hand. "Carol," he said, his voice gentle in the candlelight. "Don't you want to go home?"

Yes. Yes, I do.

"I'm not going to leave him," I said, hating the waver in my voice.

Hæmir leaned back abruptly, releasing my hand. "He doesn't deserve this -" he waved his hands. "This absurd level of commitment. Not from you. Not from anyone."

My cheeks flushed as I remembered the feel of Hæmir's lips against mine, the stubble on his cheeks rough against my neck. "You lied to me about who you are," I said, hoping he'd think the heat spreading across my face was due to anger. "You don't get to have a say in my - my commitments."

Hæmir smiled and spread his arms wide, his palms up. "I do apologize. But really, what was I to do? Shake your hand in the airport and introduce myself as Hyrm of the Jötunn?" His voice softened, and he reached for my hand again. "You would have thought I was insane," he said.

His skin was warm against mine. I met his eyes in the flickering candlelight. *He could take me home,* I thought, and my breath caught in my throat. *He could come with me to Chicago, and wrap me in his strong arms, and tell me again that I am no longer alone.*

I sighed. *And what would happen to Loki then?*

"Look," I said, pulling my hand back and getting to my feet, "I think this was a mistake."

"No," he said, standing and reaching for my arm. "Carol, wait."

I blinked away the feeling of tears, remembering how I'd stared at my cell phone, at his number. Remembering how desperately I'd wished I could talk to him. *If I stay here much longer,* I thought, *I'm going to take him up on his offer.*

"I don't think I have any further questions," I said, trying to stop the waver in my voice.

"I can walk you back to your room," he said, looking

concerned. Looking exactly like he had in Reykjavik, when he kissed my forehead at the airport. The last time I'd seen him in the mortal realm.

"No. No, thank you." I turned, took a deep breath, and walked away without looking back.

CHAPTER THIRTY-THREE

There was another knock on my door the following evening. I'd spent the day embarrassing myself with Hidy and the warriors, up to and including hitting myself square in the face with a wooden sword and splitting my lip. I was staring at my dresser, waiting for the goblet of mead to appear so I could drink it and get rid of the bruises on my face. And I was not feeling especially patient.

"Goddamn it, Hæmir, I said I don't have any more questions," I yelled, throwing the door open.

It was Sif. Her beautiful face regarded me coolly. "Óðinn requests your presence," she said. "At your earliest convenience."

I thought about apologizing for yelling at her and then changed my mind. Instead, I straightened my back. "Lovely," I said, my words somewhat distorted by my swollen lower lip.

"Are you ready now?" she asked. "Or do you need a... minute?"

I brushed my lips with my fingers. They felt huge and angry, and I thought I might have a black eye as well. *Just perfect.* "I'm ready when you are," I said with a slight bow.

"Very well," she said, turning down the corridor.

The hallways lengthened in front of Sif, revealing curves and passages I'd never found. *I bet she can read the books,* I thought bitterly. *I bet she can visit Loki.* And then I clenched my fist tight, driving my nails into my palm to keep the tears away. I did not want to face Óðinn with a black eye, a swollen lip, and tears.

Sif swept into a large room. There were three men seated around an enormous round table, and two empty chairs.

The men turned toward me, and I recognized them immediately. One-eyed Óðinn, his staff resting against the table. Týr the brave, his dark hair falling over his shoulders, his right arm ending in a stump where the monster-wolf Fenris bit off his hand.

And Thor.

Thor was shockingly beautiful, towering over the other warriors, his body all but radiating light and raw male sexuality. He stood as I entered the room, and he laughed. It was such a wild, joyful laugh, I couldn't help but smile.

"So, you're the mortal who's been bumping uglies with Loki!" he boomed. "Come on in!"

My jaw actually dropped. *I just met Thor,* I thought. *And he said "bumping uglies"..?*

"Hello, Carol."

I heard a voice from the doorway and turned to see Hæmir. Not trusting myself to speak, I gave him a stiff nod.

"Carol," he said, "I apologize, but once I enter that room, I will be Jötunn."

My eyes darted to the table, and to Óðinn. Óðinn did not look entirely pleased to see Hæmir.

"I'm sorry you have to see this," Hæmir whispered. He entered the room.

The transformation was instantaneous. One minute he was handsome, muscular Hæmir from Reykjavik. The next, he was a monster.

Hrym the Jötunn towered over everyone, even Thor, whose hand was now on his hammer Mjölnir. His hair and beard were an avalanche of dark curls. Tusks thrust from his mouth.

"Holy shit," I breathed, and the monster turned to me.

"Don't be afraid," Hrym said in Hæmir's gentle, familiar voice. "It's still me." He tapped his chest, gesturing to his heart.

Óðinn pushed his chair back and stood. "Hrym, whore of Loki, please, come to the table."

Hrym sat down, and I was hit with a bizarre sense of

deja vu, as though I'd seen this all before, perhaps in a dream. I realized the men were staring at me.

"I'm not a whore," I said, still standing, my back stiff.

Thor laughed at this, but he was the only one.

"What would you like to be called?" Týr asked me, his voice soft.

"I'm Loki's... friend."

"That bastard doesn't have friends," said Thor, his voice booming and echoing around the room.

I ignored him. I put my hands on the back of the chair, very aware of my swollen lip and black eye.

Óðinn sighed, rolling his one eye dramatically. "Fine. *Friend* of Loki, please, come to the table." He gestured to the one remaining empty chair.

I sat. The table seemed very large. The four men stared at me in silence.

I cleared my throat. "I've come to demand the Trial of Æsìlynd for my...friend," I said, hoping my voice sounded confident.

Óðinn coughed. "And of course you know all about that," he said. "You're, what, a third year graduate student?"

Fuck. You. All. I thought, anger rising in my chest.

"I walked the Bifröst," I said. "I came to Val-Hall. I'm here to demand the Trial of Æsìlynd for Loki Laufeyiarson, and you are honor-bound to give it to me."

I had no idea if they were honor-bound to give me anything, but I wasn't getting anywhere sitting in my room or stomping around the damn forest or hitting myself in the face with wooden swords.

The room fell silent. The men stared at me: Thor. Óðinn. Týr. And the Jötunn Hrym, formerly my friend Hæmir. I held my chin high. This time I would not be the first to break the silence.

Finally Óðinn cleared his throat. "Caroline Capello of Midgard," he said, his voice friendly and understanding. "We'd like to ask you to reconsider. We're prepared to make you an offer."

I held my breath.

"First," said Óðinn, "we can give you money. Basically, unlimited money."

I said nothing.

"Second," he said, "you'll complete your doctorate. With distinction. With or without our help, of course, as you see fit. And finally -" Óðinn shifted a bit in his seat, looking somewhat uncomfortable.

"A husband," said Thor, in his deep, echoing voice. "A husband, kids, whatever you want."

I narrowed my eyes, not sure I'd heard him correctly. "Excuse me?"

"Thor is correct," said Óðinn. "The final part of the bargain is a partner, a husband."

"But how is that even...? Loki - "

"Not Loki," said the achingly familiar voice next to me.

I turned to face the monster who had been Hæmir, and I realized his eyes were unchanged. Above the curving tusks and riot of hair were Hæmir's laughing hazel eyes.

"Me," he said, his voice disconcertingly gentle coming from that fierce face. "I would marry you, if you would have me."

"I'm sorry, what?"

"He's a better partner than Loki," said Thor. "It's a solid deal."

I wanted very badly to push away from the table, to walk, to run, to wander into the forest and process what I'd just heard. I wanted at least to cover my face, my black eye, my swollen lip. To hide behind my hands.

Money. My degree. A husband. A family. Well, that did cover all the bases, didn't it? I hadn't dared to hope for a husband, not since I was a kid and my brother first teased me, saying I'd never find a boyfriend with my nose in so many books. And a family... I remembered holding my infant niece Devi for the first time, her soft weight curling into my arms, shaping herself against my breast.

I looked around the table. Týr smiled at me, his dark eyes cheerful. Thor's eyes danced, although his face was still stern, and Óðinn's shoulders relaxed. I could not quite bring myself to look at Hrym.

They think they've got me, I realized. *Give the woman some money, tell her she can have babies.*

They think that's all there is to me.

I remembered something else, then. I remembered passing out on the floor of my apartment and waking to see Loki above me. I remembered Loki in the dappled light of the World Tree, his hair aflame above the strange angles of his inhuman face. I remembered the first time he appeared in my apartment, his pale blue blade flashing as he cut the clothes from my body.

And I remembered Nowhere, torn apart. And Loki ripped from my arms.

"No."

I watched their faces drop. It was almost funny.

"Woman, this is unwise." Óðinn's voice was hard.

"I don't want your money, and I don't need your help."

"And the husband?" Thor asked.

"Oh, fuck you!" I spat. "Is that really the best you four could come up with? Just put a ring on it, and she'll shut the hell up?"

I took a deep breath. I still could not bring myself to look at Hrym.

"There is one thing you could offer me," I said. The four men leaned in to follow my words. "Let Loki go. Let me watch you release him, and swear to me you will not pursue him further."

"Technically two requests," said Týr in his soft voice.

"Oh, for fuck's sake," said Óðinn, now looking very old and very annoyed. "The Trial of Æsìlynd starts tomorrow."

He grabbed the staff resting against the table and banged it on the floor -

- and I was back in my room, my entire body trembling..

As I climbed into bed, the image of the huge, round table flashed through my mind. Thor. Óðinn. Týr. Hrym's hulking Jötunn form. The image again struck me as somehow familiar, and I was suddenly very certain I'd missed something, something important. Sleep took me before I could figure out what it was.

CHAPTER THIRTY-FOUR

I awoke before dawn, my heart racing, unable to fall back asleep. Whatever was going to happen would happen today.

I tried to take a bath, but adrenaline made my body jittery, like I'd had too much espresso, and I drained the tub before it filled. I paced my room and stared at the unfamiliar stars over the unfamiliar ocean, trying to guess what time it was. Trying to guess where Loki was.

Finally I opened the door.

Hæmir was standing in the hallway outside my door. I jumped and then hoped he hadn't noticed. *Has he been standing here all night?*

"Good morning," I said, folding my arms across my chest.

"Why, Carol?" he asked. "Why would you choose -"

"I could ask the same of you," I said, cutting him off. "Why me?"

Hæmir shrugged. The corridor was lit only by torches, and it was difficult to read his face in their flickering light.

"Walk with me," he said. "You have hours before the trial."

I sniffed and fell in beside him.

Hæmir led me to the wide doors of Val-Hall, and together we walked down the wide staircase into the gloaming. The air was still and cold; the waves seemed loud against the rocks.

"Mostly it was to fuck with Loki," Hæmir said as we started across the grass. "I can't stand him, and it was obvious he'd marked you for himself."

"Oh." My voice sounded small in the vast darkness.

"In the beginning, that is," he continued, sounding apologetic and somehow hurt. "It... it became more than that. Truly, Carol."

I said nothing as I followed him across the damp grass. Hæmir wove a path along the fields, heading toward the cliffs. He spoke without turning to face me. "I'd make a good husband."

"Stop it," I said. "Really. I'll turn around."

Hæmir fell silent. We climbed together until we reached the top of the cliffs. The sky was growing lighter over the ocean. In the far distance I could see a gleaming sliver of moon suspended over the woods.

"Shhhhh," said Hæmir, although we hadn't been speaking. "Here she is."

Dawn came to Asgard. Light poured over the water

and the clouds turned golden and pink and finally red, the tips of the waves gleaming in the light. I stared at the sun until my eyes watered.

"What's going to happen today?" I whispered.

"I have no idea," Hæmir said. "In fact, I believe my invitation to Asgard is about to expire."

He took my hand, casually, and I did not pull away. We walked in silence back to Val-Hall, the wind picking up with the sunrise, tugging at my dress and hair. Gulls wheeled and dove across the water, their lonely cries echoing off the empty beach.

* * * * * * *

Hæmir and I shared breakfast, and we tried to resume the conversation we'd had all year, over the phone. But it felt halting and strange to talk about life in Chicago or journal articles in the echoing vastness of Val-Hall, and it was too painful to talk of anything else. We finished our meal in resigned silence.

I had just set down my coffee to wave at Hidy when I felt a hand on my shoulder. I turned and saw Sif, tall and beautiful behind me.

"It's time," she said.

Then she nodded to Hæmir. "The Bifröst is open for you now. You may leave." It did not sound like a suggestion.

Hæmir and I stood. I wasn't sure how to say goodbye to someone whose marriage proposal I'd just rejected. He reached for my hands, took them in his own, and squeezed them gently.

"Good luck," he said, his hazel eyes dark above his lopsided smile.

I found I could not think of one word to say; I dropped his hands and turned to follow Sif. She gave me an odd expression as we left, almost a smile, although it was probably just a trick of the shifting, uncertain light. After a few steps we were in a new part of Val-Hall, an enormous, circular room. There were no windows; torches flickered and danced along the walls.

Under the torches sat the gods.

I recognized Óðinn, sitting on a raised platform directly opposite the door, holding his staff. Beside him sat Thor and Týr and Heimdallr, and behind them were rows of men and women, tall, proud, and stern. Some of them I recognized, but most were strangers. Sif walked past me to an empty seat along the wall. She did not turn to look at me.

In the middle of the room were two empty chairs. I took a deep breath, then walked to the one on the right. I looked directly at Óðinn as I sat.

"Last chance, mortal woman," Óðinn said. "Money, prestige, a family. All this I can give to you."

"I'll have all that anyway," I said, hoping my voice

sounded reasonably confident. "I am here for the Trial of Æsìlynd."

Óðinn sighed. He seemed deeply disappointed and, for a second, I felt ashamed. Ashamed to have disappointed the All-Father.

"Fine," said Óðinn. And then the air changed, grew colder, and the other chair was no longer empty.

Loki was naked and gagged with a golden cloth, his body tightly bound with stiff black rope. His arms were pulled back, his wrists and ankles tied to the chair. He was covered with raw scrapes and old bruises, and his left eye was swollen shut. He turned his face down, away from me.

"What have you done to him?" I screamed. I tried to stand, but I was yanked backward. I looked down. There were thick ropes around my own wrists and ankles, holding me to the chair. My heart started to race and I tried to remember to breathe.

"Clever thing, isn't it?" Óðinn said. "The bonds prevent him from using his magic. No illusions. And no lies."

"It's horrible!" I screamed.

Óðinn raised his staff and brought it down on the dais. The room echoed with the sound. "Mortal woman," Óðinn said, his voice reverberating through the room. "You have requested the Trial of Æsìlynd. Let the combat begin!"

He waved his hand, and the binds around my wrists and ankles let go. There were angry red burns where the ropes had been. I took a deep breath, raising my head. The gods shifted in their seats, looking at each other. I wondered whom I would be fighting. Every single person in the room looked like they would be able to kill me without breaking a sweat.

Then I turned to Loki. He was still facing away from me, his head down, his breathing shallow. I could see the curve of his neck, the hair that had fallen across his cheek. Suddenly I wanted nothing more than to brush the hair out of his bruised face.

I stood and slowly walked to the center of the room. I looked at Óðinn as I turned sideways, spreading my legs and bending my knees for better balance. *Warrior position*, Hidy called it. I raised my hands to protect my face.

Thor erupted in laughter. Then Óðinn started laughing, and Týr, and soon the entire room was rocking with laughter. I trembled, and my cheeks burned. I did not want to die to the sound of laughter.

Finally Óðinn stopped laughing long enough to wave his hand dismissively. "Oh, we're just fucking with you," he said.

I dropped my arms and stood up tall, my back stiff.

"But she really would have done it," Thor said, wheezing to catch his breath, and the room again erupted with laughter.

I walked back to my chair, my head held high, trying to ignore all of them. "Lovely group of friends you have," I muttered to Loki, although I wasn't sure he could hear me.

I sat down and the ropes closed back over my wrists and ankles. I became very interested in a spot on the ceiling until the laughter died back down.

"All right, all right," Óðinn said, wiping tears from his eye. "Let's begin. Caroline Capello, you first."

I opened my mouth to ask what to do next, and left it open. The ravens appeared on Óðinn's shoulders, Hugin and Munin. Thought and Memory. Their heads tilted as they looked at me. And then both ravens took flight, spreading their enormous wings and soaring across the room. Toward me.

I felt myself *pushed* as both ravens flew at my chest. Into my chest.

* * * * * * *

I was thirteen years old again, a skinny, awkward kid with braces standing in the junior high library, the only place in the entire school where I felt comfortable. There was a book in my hands with a picture of a Viking longboat on the cover. Golden, looping letters spelled *Norse Myths & Legends.*

I turned and looked over my shoulder. Two enormous ravens stood on the houndstooth blue and gray library carpeting, tilting their heads to watch me. And behind the ravens was a vast, circular room, a room filled with the gods, sitting. Watching.

Slowly, I turned back around.

I opened the book and read the words Loki Laufeyiarson.

CHAPTER THIRTY-FIVE

E very kiss.
Every touch.
Every word, every moan, every cry.

The ravens stood behind me, and the gods watched, every single time Loki and I came together.

Loki pulled his blade out in my apartment and cut my clothes off, and the ravens stood behind me, and the gods watched. Loki and I danced in a nightclub in Berlin, our bodies tight against each other, and the ravens stood behind me, and the gods watched. They watched as I convinced myself I was losing my mind. They watched Loki fucking me against the wall in the Higher Grounds stockroom. They watched us in the bathroom of Charlie Trotter's, watched me making my way home afterward, holding the shreds of my dress around my body.

Sometimes I could hear them, could hear Thor laughing, could hear a long, low whistle as Loki and I kissed and bit and clung to each other, our bodies arching in ecstasy, our sweat running together.

It was worse than their laughter, worse than being naked.

It was worse than combat.

They watched as I read the books in Nowhere, as we rolled over each other in the crashing surf of Lake Michigan. As we drank Óðinn's mead together and stood beneath Yggdrasil, his hair flaming, and -

"I love him."

My voice, my words, rang out across the room. I'd never spoken those words out loud, but they filled the room nonetheless. I remembered how the thought surprised me, in the shifting, dancing light beneath Yggdrasil. *Like loving the wind.*

"I love him."

"I think we've seen enough." An unfamiliar woman's voice spoke from behind me, and I sobbed. *Yes, please, please. Enough.*

"No," said Óðinn. "She asked for this."

Iceland. Reykjavik. Hæmir and the dinners, masturbating frantically in my lonely hotel room, waiting and pleading for Loki. My last night, kissing Hæmir. Pulling off his pants. Crying in his arms.

Confronting Loki in Nowhere. Throwing the firefly china out my window. Standing on the roof of the Flamingo, cold wind in my hair, dawn painting golden streaks across the lake.

The dreams. Waking shivering with the cold of another world, Loki's blood on my hands.

Falling to the distant sea as Nowhere ripped apart beneath me.

Walking the Bifröst.

* * * * * * *

"And we're done," said Óðinn, slamming his staff on the stage.

I sagged forward against the ropes tying me to the chair, and I sobbed. For a long time there was no sound in the room save my wracking cries. Finally I caught my breath, and I tried to wipe my face on my shoulder.

Then I opened my eyes and turned to Loki.

He turned away from me. I could only see the side of his face, the arc of his neck, his body pulled tight against the ropes. I tried to blink away a fresh round of tears as I looked at the Æsir, facing some expressions that might have been pity, some that might have been scorn. Thor regarded me warily. Sif held a delicate hand over her beautiful mouth.

Finally I took a deep breath and turned to Óðinn. The ravens sat again on his shoulders. His face was as impassive as their black eyes.

"Is that all?" I said, my voice rasping and broken.

"Not quite," said Óðinn. He turned to Loki. "Your

turn, son of Laufeyiar."

Hugin and Munin flew into Loki and he was knocked back in his chair, his head to the ceiling, his eyes closed. The room grew very quiet. *They're watching him,* I thought. *Watching him like they watched me.* I shuddered.

Loki moaned as he thrashed against the ropes. He threw his head back, tears streaking his cheeks. When he turned to me, his eyes were blank and empty. I wondered where he was, if it was just our history he was re-living, or if he would have to again face Gefjun and Eggrún and all thirty-two names from *The Book of the Gods' Mortal Lovers.*

I wondered if he would see his wife Sigyn.

Loki moaned again, shaking his head violently, straining against the ropes that held him to the chair. Blood trickled down his arms and torso where the binds cut against his pale, muscular body.

I'm sorry, I thought. *I am so sorry.*

I turned to the gods, wondering if there was something I could say to make it stop, but my tongue froze in my mouth. I wasn't sure if Óðinn would even hear me. The gods were watching closely, but they weren't watching me.

Finally I turned away from Loki, although I could still hear his gasping cries, muffled by the gag. I wished my hands were free so I could wipe the tears from my face. So I could hold him in my arms.

"I love her."

Loki's voice, cool and confident, filled the room.

I turned back to him, blinking through swollen eyes. His body slumped against the chair, the gag still over his mouth, his eyes closed, his breathing ragged and uneven. He hadn't spoken.

"I love her."

It was his voice, Loki Laufeyiarson, unmistakable. He had never said those words to me, as I had never said them to him, and yet –

"Oh, for fuck's sake," said Óðinn, slamming his staff on the dais.

Next to him, Thor spat on the ground, his expression thoroughly disgusted. Heimdallr stared at me as if he'd never seen me before. Sif's eyes sparkled with tears.

Óðinn cleared his throat. "Fine," he said, waving a hand at Loki. "You're free to go."

The ropes around his body vanished, and Loki exploded from the chair, fully dressed in his battle armor, his scars and bruises gone. His cape flared behind him as he made a slow, predatory circle of the room, staring at the Æsir.

He did not turn to me before he disappeared.

"You won't see him again," Thor said, shrugging at me. "Loki hates to be in somebody's debt."

The ropes burned against my hands and feet. I stared

numbly at the empty chair where Loki had been. *I've missed something,* I thought. *I've missed something important.*

"Right then," said Óðinn. "You both passed the Trial of Æsìlynd. Congratulations. Caroline Capello, of Midgard, you will suffer the punishment for Loki's crimes."

So that's what the Trial of Æsilynd means, I thought. And then the world went black.

* * * * * * *

I heard voices, men's voices. They seemed to be very far away, like a cell phone with bad reception. *Doug?* I thought, struggling to remember. But no, we broke up, didn't we? And there had been someone else. Someone *important.* But then we had broken up as well...

" - just bind her under the earth, like last time," someone said, his voice deep and resonant.

"No, no, no," said another voice, a softer voice. "She'll just die. That's not much of a punishment."

"It would be a punishment for *him*," said the deeper voice.

"No." A third voice spoke, heavy with authority. "He is beyond the range of our punishments. This idiot here protected him."

In the silence that followed I struggled to open my

eyes. My head was pounding, and my wrists and ankles burned. I opened my eyes and saw wooden rafters, blacked with centuries of soot. Cautiously, I turned my throbbing head. Óðinn the All-Father stood next to me, frowning. His disapproval felt like a weight on my chest.

I'm sorry, I thought. *I'm sorry I let you down.*

"No, you're not," Óðinn said. "In fact, I think you're quite pleased with yourself."

I tried to push myself up to sitting, but I couldn't get my arms to work. I fell back, whacking my head against something hard. White stars exploded across my vision.

"You're quite a stubborn little bitch," Óðinn said. "I respect that. But you've got terrible taste."

"Loki," I whispered. This time I managed to push myself up to sitting. Thor and Týr stood at my feet.

"Gone," said Óðinn. "I wouldn't follow him even if I could. And you, my dear, cannot. So," Óðinn clapped his hands and turned to Thor and Týr, "what shall we do with her?"

Thor shrugged. "Banishment, I suppose."

"It's closest to what we'd do to him," Týr said.

"Very well," said Óðinn, sounding bored. He grabbed his staff and hit the ground, and the room disappeared.

CHAPTER THIRTY-SIX

The world was light and pain.

Somewhere I could hear a dull thundering roar, the crash of breakers against the beach. My head throbbed, my arms and legs were leaden, and I could hear the harsh, lonely cries of seagulls.

My cheek pressed against something soft and warm. I tried to open my eyes, failed, tried again. It was too bright to make out much of anything; light, everywhere. Light flashing off waves, light burning off the sand. And maybe - I squinted - people?

"It was a brave thing you did in Val-Hall," a woman's voice said, above me.

Val-Hall. I should know that name. I squeezed my eyes shut, trying to think. *Val-Hall.*

"Loki," I said, my voice hardly more than a whisper.

"He lives," said the woman. Her voice was strangely flat, devoid of emotion. "He lives and he is free, thanks to you."

I sighed, let my body relax against the warm sand.

The waves crashed and rumbled, the gulls cried, and I heard voices, human voices. Happy human voices. *I've missed something. Something important.*

"What did I miss?" I rasped, trying to get my arms to move. I pushed myself onto my hands and opened my eyes, staring across the endless, shimmering sand to...

The Hotel del Coronado?

"Here," said the woman's voice, "take my hand. Easy now."

I turned to see Di. My sister-in-law, Di.

I closed my eyes and fell back on the sand.

* * * * * * *

When I opened my eyes again, I was staring at a rainbow beach umbrella. *Rainbows,* I thought. *The Bifröst.*

"Let's try this again," Di said from behind me. "Sit up. Slowly."

I felt her hands on my shoulders, pushing me up to face the ocean. There were kids playing in the surf, running and screaming in the crashing foam.

"Here," said Di, "have some water."

I turned to see my sister-in-law sitting under the umbrella. My infant niece Devi slept in her carseat on a beach towel. I took a gleaming, silver water bottle from Di's outstretched hand and sipped carefully. It was still

SAMANTHA MACLEOD | 381

cold.

After a few seconds I noticed Geoff standing beside us, watching the ocean.

"Are you back?" he asked, the breeze ruffling his platinum blonde hair.

"I... I think so," I whispered. It hurt to talk.

Di took my hand in hers, examining the angry, red rope burns on my wrists. She made a loud, disapproving noise deep in her throat. "Those Northern gods," she said. "So barbaric."

Geoff laughed. "I know," he said. "All I had to do was get you a golden apple."

My brother and his wife exchanged a smile.

"I'm sorry," I said, the words scraping out of my throat, "but who are you?"

Di smiled at me, radiant. "I'm your sister," she said. "Aphrodite."

"Mom always said you should have studied the Greeks," Geoff said, laughing.

"What? How?" I stuttered, and then the edges of the world began to grow dim again, and I put my head between my legs.

"Shhhhh," Di whispered. "Another time, sweetheart."

Di's gentle hand rubbed my back until the world stopped spinning, and I could choke down a few more sips of water.

"When you're ready," said Aphrodite, the Greek goddess of love, "we'll need to face the music."

* * * * * * *

Facing the music involved going to the police.

I'd been gone for over a month. My parents filed a missing person's report, and I was only a few weeks away from being declared legally dead. And then I washed up on Coronado Beach, dressed like I'd come from a Renaissance festival, with deep, angry rope burns on my wrists and ankles.

"Tell them you broke up with your boyfriend," said Di as she handed me a sweatshirt. It was the kind with loops in the sleeves for my thumbs, and it covered the burns on my wrists. "Tell them you just had to get away," she continued, adjusting the sweatshirt's sleeves as we walked to the parking lot. "The interviewer will be sympathetic, I promise."

Geoff eased baby Devi's car seat into the back and then got in the driver's seat. "Try to strike a balance between quirky and emotionally unstable," he said.

"That won't be too hard," I whispered, and Geoff and Di both laughed. "But what the hell am I going to tell Mom and Dad?" A hard knot of panic rose in the pit of my stomach, and I clenched my hands into fists, digging my nails into my palms and trying to remember to breathe.

"I'll deal with them," Geoff said, pulling into the police station. "Don't worry about it. We'll meet you here in a few hours."

A small, blonde policewoman took me to a back room, where I sat on a folding chair at a folding table. I cleared my throat, and then started my official statement by telling her I'd been seeing Lucas, Lucas Laufey, but I kept it a secret because he was married. Then he just... disappeared from my life.

The crying part came naturally.

After an entire box of tissues and a stern admonition to seek professional counseling, the blonde policewoman recorded my statement and let me go.

* * * * * * *

I walked out of the back room, limping somewhat on my sore ankles, and saw my family standing in the lobby. Mom hugged me first, and then my dad joined her, and then we stood together in silence in the concrete lobby of the San Diego police department.

"I'm..." I whispered. After all the crying, my voice sounded raw and scratchy.

"Oh, honey, your brother explained everything," Mom said, holding both my hands. "You don't have to say a word."

I raised an eyebrow at Geoff, wondering what the hell he'd told them. He just smiled.

As we drove home, Mom talked nonstop about how she'd just called Chicago, she made sure everything was fine with my apartment, and the University was expecting me, if I was still prepared to teach my classes, because the quarter started in just under a week...

Then we pulled into the driveway of my parents' house, and I limped into my room, peeled off my Asgardian dress and boots, and collapsed on the bed. *I missed something,* I thought as my head hit the pillow, and then I was asleep.

I dreamt of the stones.

The sky was a dull, heavy, leaden gray, the sun flat and low on the horizon. I stood among the stones in Slyndennär, the images of Ragnarök. Óðinn and the Fenris-Wolf. Thor and the serpent Jörmungandr. Heimdallr blowing the Gjallarhorn, Loki escaping...

I turned back to the stones, but the images faded before me, the stones filling with dirt. I tried to brush the dirt away, but the more I moved, the thicker the earth became, until it was covering my legs, covering my hands, covering my mouth -

I woke, gasping for air. My room seemed very loud after a month in Asgard. I heard the clock ticking, the refrigerator humming down the hall. I could hear the trickle of water through the plumbing. I looked out my window, through the leaves of the California ash, but the lights of San Diego drown out the stars.

I reached for Loki's pendant, but the space between my breasts was empty.

That's because it's in Chicago, I told myself, but my hand trembled.

* * * * * * *

My parents were exceedingly gentle with me during the three days before I flew back to Chicago. I offered to help out in the office, but Mom waved my suggestion aside.

"Your dad's back, sweetie," she said, "And Di's coming in during the mornings, now. We're doing just fine."

Her eyes seemed to suggest this was not entirely the case, but I didn't push the issue. I was the one who'd disappeared for weeks without a trace; I supposed she had a right to treat me a bit delicately. Besides, once she'd left for work, I was glad to be alone.

I had phone calls to make.

I took my book bag and left the house, following the path I'd driven the night I walked off Midgard. I hadn't dared ask to borrow Dad's car, not after I left it abandoned in the parking lot of a run-down bowling alley. Besides, I was looking forward to the walk. I'd done a lot of walking in Asgard, and it felt good to stretch my muscles again.

I made it to the parking lot of the Rainbow Lanes Bowling Alley in just under an hour. The place looked worse in the daylight; the "b" and "o" lights were burned out, and the two cars parked on the cracked asphalt looked like they may or may not be operational. I stared at the glowing neon rainbow for a heartbeat, feeling for Loki, but it was no use. It was just a sign, now; the Bifröst was closed to me.

The payphone booth under the neon sign stank of cigarette smoke, and the heavy, yellow phone book dangling beneath the receiver had been shredded. I opened my bag and pulled out my notebook, flipping to the page where I'd written *Hidy Merrill.* Then I fed the first of several dozen quarters into the payphone and dialed.

"Hello?" A woman's voice rattled over the line.

"Hi, Mrs. Merrill?" I said. "I've got a message for you. Uh, you might want to sit down first..."

* * * * * * *

I was back at my parents' house by early afternoon. I felt exhausted, worn thin by the long distance telephone calls. Everyone had been home. Some of them had yelled at me, some had cursed me, some had sobbed. But they had all listened.

Phil's wife was the worst. She didn't even ask my name, or where I was calling from, or who the hell I thought I was. She just cried. I thought I heard a child in the background, but I told myself it was the TV.

I was staring out the kitchen window, trying not to think about those phone calls and wondering if 4:37 was too early to crack open a beer, when I heard the garage door rumble open. Mom walked in with a little white Verizon bag, and slid it across the round table to me. Inside was a new cell phone.

"The next time," she said. "If there is a next time. Just call."

"Thanks," I mumbled.

I didn't have the heart to tell her my cell phone had been in my bag all along, and it would probably still work, if I just plugged it in to recharge.

* * * * * * * *

Di and Geoff offered to drive me to the airport the morning of my flight back to Chicago. Dad loaded my suitcase in the trunk.

"You can always come home," he whispered as he hugged me.

"Thanks," I said, suddenly unsure where I would even find home. *San Diego? Chicago? Val-Hall?*

Geoff, Di, and I were silent in the car, watching the picture-perfect blue California skies, the occasional glimpse of the sun sparkling off the Pacific. Geoff pulled the car into Departures, parked, and climbed out, putting my suitcase onto the sidewalk and accidentally triggering the sliding automatic doors.

I hesitated, my hand on the door handle. "Do you know where Loki is?" I whispered to Di.

"I do not," she said.

"Am I going to see him again?"

Di said nothing, so I repeated the question, although I could see Geoff staring at me, his hand tapping my suitcase.

Di turned to me and patted my hand. "I'm so sorry," she said. "I don't prophesize."

CHAPTER THIRTY-SEVEN

My apartment in Chicago was exactly as I'd left it. I didn't have pets to feed; I didn't even have a single houseplant to die of neglect. *I've been ready to drop everything and go to Asgard since I moved in,* I thought, and the realization did not feel good. The air in the apartment was musty after an entire unoccupied summer. I opened the windows, put my suitcase down on the bed, ran the vacuum.

Loki's pendant winked at me from the top of my dresser. I walked over to it, ran my fingers across its shimmerescent surface. Then I fastened the chain around my neck, feeling the cool weight between my breasts.

"I'm wearing your sign," I told the empty room. "I think I've earned it."

The room did not respond.

When I finally made myself turn on my computer, I had about a million emails. Most of them were useless: invitations to graduate student nights in the pub that I would have ignored anyway, visiting speakers who had already arrived and departed. There was an email from my advisor, Professor Loncovic, asking me to contact her as soon as I returned to Chicago in order to discuss the progress I'd made on my dissertation over the summer.

Not much, I thought. I spent the first half of my summer trying to keep Capello's Landscaping & Tree Surgery afloat, and the last half of my summer in Val-Hall with the dead and the Æsir, so no, not a lot of progress made on my dissertation.

And there was a single email from Hæmir. My heart hammered wildly as I clicked the message open.

It was perfectly normal. He'd attached a copy of the latest article we'd written together, about the sacred grove in Lokisfen. This was our second article about that grove, and I knew it was going to be controversial. Before my dad's heart attack, before walking the Bifröst to Asgard and completing the Trial of Æsìlynd, I'd been excited about that paper.

Now I didn't know what to feel. The real world seemed hopelessly boring, and I felt a sudden wave of homesickness for Val-Hall, for my warrior friends Hidy, Frank, and Phil, for my room with the cozy fireplace and the view of the rocky strand.

And, when I was in Val-Hall, at least I had some small hope of seeing Loki again.

I shook my head, sighed, and reached for my books. I was teaching two classes this quarter, and I had an entire summer's worth of work on my dissertation to complete.

* * * * * * * *

It took me two weeks to find the courage to respond to Hæmir's email.

I was strictly professional, saying only that the summer had been "crazy," which was a bit of an understatement. I had several recommendations for the article, and I promised to write more later, once I was settled.

I felt a flicker of hope about Hæmir. After all, there was a chance it had all been an illusion. Óðinn and the Jötunn Hrym might have struck some sort of deal to trick me by projecting an image of someone I cared about, someone I trusted. Trying to offer me something I'd want.

I sighed and turned off my computer. It was getting late. I pulled off my clothes and climbed into bed, trying not to think about Hæmir. Or Hrym. Just as I was falling asleep, my entire body shivered, violently, like I was pushing through a sheet of icy water.

And then I was back in Slyndennär, in the rowan grove outside the city, looking across the North Sea.

The air was biting cold, and the wind coming off the ocean smelled of snow. *There's a storm coming,* I thought.

I turned to the stones; they were almost completely submerged in the dark, volcanic soil. I scraped and shoveled with my hands, pebbles abrading my knuckles, the cold sinking deep into my fingers, but the more I shoveled, the more earth fell against the stones. I could only see the very tops, the heads of Óðinn and the Fenris-Wolf, of Thor and Jörmungandr. *I've missed it,* I thought.

"Too late," cawed a voice above me.

I looked up to see a huge raven, black against the gray sky. The raven's wings ruffled in the wind as it landed on the ground in front of me.

"What is it?" I screamed, and the wind ripped the words from my mouth. "What did I miss?"

"Let it go," the raven said. "You're too late. And it can't be stopped."

I punched the cold, black ground in frustration and screamed.

"You should leave them buried." I turned to see Hæmir standing behind me, his face strange and distorted in the flat, gray light.

"I missed something," I said, my voice frantic. "I missed something important!"

"Forget them," he said, his eyes flashing, and

suddenly he was no longer my friend Hæmir, with the strong arms and the lopsided smile; he was Hrym the Jötunn, his massive form blocking the weak sun, his tusks reaching to the sky. "Leave this place!"

I shivered and jumped at the anger in his voice, and I found myself back in my bed. There was dirt under my nails.

I have to go back to Iceland, I thought, scrubbing black, volcanic soil from my hands into my bathroom sink. *But that's insane.* It was the middle of the quarter, I had classes to teach, I had a dissertation to write, and the only person I knew in Iceland, the only person who could take me to the stones, might be a monster. A Jötunn. Whose marriage proposal I had just recently declined.

Whatever I missed, whatever I'd been dreaming about, I had to find it here. In Chicago.

* * * * * * * *

That night I started searching.

I had literally hundreds of pictures of the stones on my computer. I made myself a mug of herbal tea and opened my laptop, flipping through picture after picture: Close-ups of the carvings, overviews of the site I'd taken while I stood on the hood of Hæmir's car. The conference of the gods. The woman with outstretched arms. Óðinn, his face lined with effort, stabbing the Fenris-Wolf as its monstrous jaws closed around his chest. Thor bringing Mjölnir down on the head of the serpent. Heimdallr holding the Gjallarhorn, blowing the first notes to begin the battle. To begin Ragnarök.

I could hear their voices as I clicked through the carvings.

A husband, kids, whatever you want.

I can guarantee you'll get your doctorate.

The pictures of Loki's carving were in their own separate folder. Even before I went to Asgard, I found it difficult to look at them. They looked so much like *him* - the soft curve of his full lips, his proud nose, the flash in his eyes. I realized I'd put my fingers to the computer screen, tracing the arc of Loki's neck in the stone carving, a low, hungry ache in my chest.

Okay, it's definitely time to quit for the night.

* * * * * * * *

In the morning I had to admit I hadn't seen anything. The carvings were exactly as I remembered: detailed, passionate, a disconcerting combination of stylized human figures and graphic violence. But I still couldn't shake that feeling, the absolute conviction I was staring right at something and still missing it entirely. *There's only one way I'm ever going to know,* I thought.

I took a deep breath, picked up my cell phone, and pressed a name I'd ignored since I woke up on Coronado Beach, wearing the dress and boots from Asgard.

"Carol?"

"Hæmir," I said. "Listen, I need to see the Slyndennär stones. Again."

There was a long pause on his end of the line. I realized too late I probably should have made some attempt at small talk, especially if he truly wasn't in Asgard this summer, if the whole marriage proposal really had been an illusion created by Óðinn.

"Okay," he said, slowly.

"I don't need to go with you," I said. "But I don't think... I mean, I wasn't sure if I could even access the dig without -"

"Carol, it's fine," he said. "It would be nice to see you again, too."

I hung up the phone and bought plane tickets to Reykjavik before I could change my mind. The earliest flight available was Saturday, two days away. I emailed my itinerary to Hæmir, and he wrote back saying he'd be happy to meet me at the airport.

I sent messages to my students, cancelling classes for the week. And then there was nothing to do but wait.

I spent the afternoon running along the lake. It was dark, with heavy storm clouds low over the water. The wind blew dead leaves and spray from the waves in my face and, eventually, hard, heavy raindrops. I ran and ran and ran, thinking about Hæmir.

He hadn't mentioned Asgard. There was still a chance, a remote chance, he was an ordinary, normal human. An ordinary, unreasonably attractive human. The only person since Loki I'd found attractive. The only person since Loki I'd -

I stopped, bending over. A lancing, red pain worked itself up my side and I gasped in the cold rain. I could hear a siren on Lake Shore Drive, could see the bifurcated reflections of headlights on the wet asphalt.

I pulled myself up to standing and forced myself to keep running.

CHAPTER THIRTY-EIGHT

I brought my laptop and a heavy stack of books and notes on the flight to Reykjavik. *I am going to keep busy,* I told myself. But I couldn't even get through the introduction to *Myth, Cosmos, and Society.* My eyes kept drifting to the airplane window. The setting sun winked off Lake Michigan, turning the water a brilliant ice-blue. *Just like his eyes,* I thought, my fingers drifting up to wrap around his pendant. I sighed.

Caroline Capello. Visited by the trickster god. Spent the rest of her life alone. I pressed the button to recline my seat a full inch, and I fell into an uneasy, dreamless sleep.

It was still dark when the plane touched down in Reykjavik. I'd managed a few hours of fitful sleep, but it was about three in the morning Chicago time, and I felt like hell. Not ideal circumstances to meet someone, let alone someone who might also be a Jötunn who'd proposed to me in Asgard.

Or just a friend. A friend who knew I'd vanished

from the face of the earth for over a month with no explanation.

Hæmir was waiting just outside the baggage claim doors, holding two cups of coffee. I smiled and waved to him. *I am not going to mention Asgard,* I told myself, *and it will turn out he's an ordinary human.*

Hæmir took my bag and gave me a warm hug, then handed me a coffee. "Carol," he said. "It's good to see you again."

I sighed as I climbed in his car. "You too."

"You want breakfast first?" he asked, navigating the car out of the airport and onto the darkened streets of Reykjavik. The sky was just beginning to lighten in the east.

"Nah, I ate in the airport," I lied. "Let's just head to Slyndennär. It'll be light by the time we get there, right?"

Hæmir laughed casually. "Yes, the sun still rises in November."

The city fell away quickly, a transition that felt more dramatic in the fading darkness. Then we were on the highway, watching as the growing light gradually revealed steep crags and distant mountains. The radio played electronic dance music, making the landscape feel a bit surreal.

"You know," Hæmir finally said, "I wasn't sure I'd see you again, after Asgard."

Damn. My shoulders sagged as I abandoned my "normal human being" theory about Hæmir. I rested my head on the cool glass of the window. "So, I guess that really happened," I said.

Hæmir laughed. He looked very attractive in the orange light of early morning, and I remembered standing with him, watching another sun rise over another ocean. "You know," he said, "I've never had a mortal resist me for so long."

"Excuse me?"

"It's true. I was sleeping with Annajär two hours after I met her."

"Great. Good for you. This conversation officially can't get any weirder."

We were silent again as sunlight filled the car. The empty space vibrated with unasked questions.

"Hæmir," I said, suddenly feeling timid, "or do you prefer Hyrm?"

"Hæmir's fine."

I took a deep breath, gripping my empty coffee cup tightly. Outside frost was melting in the first light, turning the fields from white to green.

"What is it?" he asked, turning to me. His hazel eyes were gentle.

"What did Loki do?" I asked, hating the waver in my voice. "I mean, when I stood trial for him. When I got punished for his crimes. What did I get punished for?"

Hæmir snorted. "He hasn't told you?"

I said nothing. I could feel the heat of tears building behind my eyelids, and I turned to look out the window.

"You haven't seen him, have you?" Hæmir's voice was hard.

I didn't respond. The landscape outside the car window seemed much colder.

"Your boyfriend," he spat the word, "tried to destroy my ship."

"The Naglfar?" I asked. "The ship that carries the armies to Ragnarök?"

Hæmir nodded. "My ship," he said.

We fell silent.

"He blew a hole in it," Hæmir said, his eyes fixed on the highway, "and then he cast an illusion over the whole thing, so we wouldn't notice it was sinking. That much power - and he took a lot of damage in the fight, too. It must have damn near killed him."

"Almost," I whispered, remembering the bloody towels. *He came to me,* I thought. *He was dying and he came to me.* I realized my fingers were curled around his pendant, and I dropped my hand back to my lap. "But...Ragnarök is the destruction of everything. Of everyone. Wouldn't you want that ship destroyed?"

"Oh, you mortals," Hæmir sighed. In the shifting, golden light he suddenly looked older. Much older. "Listen, I've been alive for over two thousand years. I've seen plenty. Hell, I've done plenty. And Ragnarök - it's not just destruction, you know. It's rebirth. There's a new world coming. It's a better world, and we need the Naglfar to start it."

"No," I said, shaking my head. "No, that's insane. You just fought over the Naglfar. In Val-Hall, Hidy told me you just fought over the Naglfar."

Hæmir's smile didn't reach his eyes. "Right. Did your friend tell you what they were doing?"

"They were targeting..." I closed my eyes, trying to remember.

Shit.

"They were targeting the moorings," I said. *Mission accomplished,* Hidy said.

"Exactly," said Hæmir. "Not the ship. Just the moorings."

"But why fight at all?" I said. "Why not just, I don't know, cut the thing loose?"

Hæmir laughed. "Why fight? Come now, you've been to Asgard. What do they do all day, those warrior friends of yours? Do they read philosophy?"

My cheeks burned as I turned to the window.

"Carol," Hæmir said, his voice gentler now. "We all know exactly how we're going to die, the Jötunn and the Æsir alike. And we know it won't be fighting over the Naglfar."

"So it was... practice?"

"Sort of," said Hæmir, with that charming smile.

"And Loki?"

"That bastard is a shitty warrior," Hæmir said. "Ever since he was freed from the serpent, he's been obsessed with Ragnarök. The rest of us are ready to accept our fate - to accept the *world's* fate - but that idiot is always trying to prevent the inevitable."

"Why was he freed from the serpent?"

Hæmir turned to me with cold eyes. "That you can ask him. This is our exit."

The car's tires crunched on cold gravel as we pulled off the highway and onto the rough road along the ocean. I saw the solid, white stones of the Slyndennär Inn in the distance. I felt like it had been a thousand years since I stayed there, in the little room under the eves, waiting and waiting for Loki. And then embracing Hæmir. Clouds raced across the North Sea and, in the shifting light, I saw the dank warehouse of Slyndennär's library.

"The Book of the Gods' Mortal Lovers," I said, remembering the room in the back, the motion detector lights. The list of thirty-two names.

Hæmir said nothing.

"You did that on purpose, didn't you?" I asked, watching the library shrink in my rearview mirror. "You took me to the library. You wanted me to read that book."

"Of course," he said, with a shrug. "I wanted you to realize you weren't the only mortal Loki's taken."

I fell silent, remembering the names. Remembering confronting Loki in Nowhere, throwing the names of his dead lovers back at him. Trying to hurt him.

"The Trial of Æsìlynd," I said. "That was in the book, too."

Hæmir laughed, but his voice was bitter. "That was not my intention."

"I suppose I should thank you."

"I thought those pages had been destroyed," he growled. "Trust me, they have been now."

We drove the last stretch in silence, a taut, stalemate silence, until I saw the dark branches of the rowan trees against the sky. Hæmir parked the car and turned to me.

"Are you sure you want to do this to yourself?" he asked.

I suddenly felt uneasy. "Why? Do you know what I'm going to find?"

Hæmir shrugged. The muscles in his arm rippled as he ran his fingers through his hair, and I thought about telling him to start the car, to go back to the Slyndennär Inn, book a room, and we could fall into each other's arms.

"I have to know," I said, opening the door.

Hæmir got out of the car but remained in the parking

lot. I walked to the stones, hugging my jacket against the biting wind off the ocean. It was fully light now, and the light had that odd Northern quality, the ability to shine directly in your eyes no matter which direction you faced.

The first three stones were exactly as I remembered, exactly as they had looked on my computer screen: Óðinn and the Fenris-Wolf. Thor and the serpent Jörmungandr. The ship Naglfar.

And Loki was on the fourth stone. I couldn't resist touching the carving, his proud face, his flashing eyes. He was so alive, and so achingly familiar. *This is exactly how he looked in Asgard,* I thought, *after the Trial of Æsilynd. When Óðinn let him go. Wild. Dangerous. Free.*

I moved to the blue plastic tarp. Hæmir's voice echoed in my mind. *Are you sure you want to do this?* I pulled the tarp back.

At first glance, the two prone stones under the tarp were exactly the same as they looked on my computer. I balled my fists in frustration. What the hell had I missed? What the hell was I doing out here?

There was the stone with the assembly of the gods - Óðinn in the center, flanked by Thor and Týr, and some strange monster figure in the lower left.

Some strange monster with curving tusks.

I've seen that before, I thought. *I've seen that exact*

room, with those exact people. Óðinn, offering me money, my doctorate, and -

A husband, kids, whatever you want, Thor said.

I would marry you, if you would have me, Hæmir said.

I turned to the final stone. On the left side of the carving was a row of figures, including Óðinn. On the right was Loki, bound and on his knees. And in the middle was a woman, standing, with her feet wide and her arms upraised. *Warrior position.*

It was me.

"Oh, shit," I said.

* * * * * * * *

Hæmir walked out to join me at the stones. I barely noticed he was there. I sat in the cold, volcanic dirt, staring at a picture of myself carved into stone over a thousand years ago.

"Shitshitshitshitshit," I muttered.

"Come on," said Hæmir, helping me to my feet. "I'll buy you a beer."

Twenty minutes later we were sitting at a table in the Slyndennär Inn. Hæmir put a beer in front of me and, after a moment's consideration, I drank almost half of it in one gulp.

"I think I just triggered Ragnarök," I said, more to

my beer than to Hæmir.

Hæmir laughed, bright and cheerful. "We all know exactly what's going to happen, but we never knew when. We didn't know what would spark it. And it turns out it was you!"

He reached across the table and clapped me on my shoulder. "Loki's little fuck buddy goes off to Asgard to save him and ends up triggering the one thing he's spent centuries trying to prevent!"

"You're disturbingly cheerful," I said, shrugging off his hand.

"It did make me feel better about you rejecting my marriage proposal," he said, with a radiant smile. "We wouldn't have had much time to enjoy each other."

My hands began to tremble. "You mean - Ragnarök is going to start -"

"Not immediately," he said. "The troops still have to assemble."

My shoulders relaxed.

"I'd say early next year," Hæmir said.

"Next year!" I flinched, and my hand knocked my beer. Hæmir caught it with unnatural ease. "Shit, Hæmir, it's already November!"

"Listen, Carol," he said, handing me my beer. "Mortals do survive Ragnarök." He took my fingers into his warm, rough hands. "I can make sure you're among those who go on to found the new world. The better world."

I pulled my hand away from him. "No." I said. "Listen, no, I can't. I've got a niece. She's just a baby. I can't - I mean - "

He shrugged and gave me his charming, lopsided smile. "So, she can come too. You can make a list."

"Hæmir, I am not going to make a list of who gets to survive the apocalypse!"

I slowly realized all the other couples at the Inn were staring at us, and I dropped my voice to a whisper. "I can't," I said. "I can't say one person is more deserving, one person is more worthy."

My eyes started to blur with tears, and I waved my hand around the room, to the bar, to the elderly couples at their tables, to the row of windows facing the North Sea. "I can't will the destruction of all this."

"Fine," he said. "But will it or not, it is coming."

CHAPTER THIRTY-NINE

A stabbing pain in my lower back woke me. I moved my head, and a stabbing pain shot through my neck as well. *Oh lovely,* I thought, opening my eyes. *I fell asleep at my desk again.* I stretched my arms above my head, moving my mouse to wake up my computer. The clock read 5:43 am. I looked at the last thing I'd written in my dissertation before falling asleep.

But the trickster figure cannot be reduced to a mere devilish trouble-maker. Indeed, it is the trickster's essential function to speak the truth: the destructive, the uncomfortable, the painfully obvious truth.

I yawned and glanced out the window. It was early February, and sunrise was still hours away. But if I took a long shower and then a slow walk, I'd make it to Medici just as they opened. I could start my morning with a proper cappuccino and an almond croissant.

The air was cold when I left the Flamingo, and it smelled like impending snow. My wet hair stiffened as it froze against my shoulders. I took a deep breath; the cold stung my lungs. The sky was a dusky, overcast gray, the streetlights shining valiantly in the gloaming.

Today's forecast, I thought, *snow, cold, and an increasing chance of Ragnarök.* I shivered in the wind. Suddenly it didn't seem very funny.

* * * * * * * *

"Stay with me," Hæmir said, as we drove through the gathering darkness back to the airport in Reykjavik. "I'll rent us a little house by the water. We can spend the last months of this age together." It had been three months since I returned from Reykjavik, and I still remembered the pleading, hungry look in his eyes.

"Come on," he said. "We can do things together you and Loki didn't even imagine."

I snorted. "Not likely."

His laugh sounded a bit forced. "It's the end of the world, Carol. It's the end of all the worlds. What are you going to do with the time you have left?"

I stared out the window. The lights of Reykjavik twinkled in the darkness, the last red streaks of the setting sun fading in the sky above them. The blinking white light of a single airplane hung suspended over the ocean.

"I've got a dissertation to write," I said.

When I got home from Iceland, I pored over everything I could find about Ragnarök. But I knew it all; some of it I'd even written. Loki escapes from his bonds. The gods hold a conference. Hyrm's horrible ship sails with the armies of the Jötunn. And they are, all of them, drawn to the battlefield, the final battlefield. Vígríðr.

Heimdallr blows the Gjallarhorn. Ragnarök begins. Óðinn's warriors meet the Jötunn in battle for the last time. Yggdrasil trembles, and there is no one in the Nine Realms who is unafraid.

Óðinn is killed by the Fenris wolf. Thor and the serpent Jörmungandr slay each other. The sun and moon are swallowed by wolves as Surtr's fire devours and destroys all of the Nine Realms.

"There's got to be a way to stop it," I told myself, over and over. Loki's voice echoed in my mind. *How would you prevent Ragnarök, mortal woman?*

But I could think of nothing; each event led inexorably to the next, beginning with the conference of the gods, the conference where Óðinn offered me a husband, and ending in hungry fire.

Sometimes I saw the fire, in my dreams. I stood before Yggdrasil, its branches swaying in the rich, dancing light. And then the fire began, on a far, distant branch, and it spread and spread until the air was thick with sparks, heat rolling off the tree in waves as all Nine Realms were consumed.

I'd wake shivering, and sometimes crying. And then, as the weeks stretched into months, I started to wonder what was happening, far away across the wide branches of Yggdrasil, as I wrote my dissertation and graded my students' essays. Had Hyrm's ship sailed? Were the armies assembling across the fields of Vígríðr? How much time did we have, all of us, before Heimdallr raised the Gjallarhorn to his lips and the Nine Realms were destroyed?

And where the hell was Loki?

* * * * * * * *

I shivered, wrapping my arms around my body. *Let it go,* I thought. I'd been telling myself that for the past three months, ever since I knelt in the black, volcanic dirt of Slyndennär, staring at a picture of myself carved into stone a thousand years ago. *Just focus on what you're doing.*

"And what I'm doing," I said, my breath forming white clouds in the frigid February air, "is walking to breakfast."

A tired, blonde waitress was just flipping the "Closed" sign to "Open" in Medici's front window. I pulled the heavy wooden door and let in a blast of cold air. The waitress gave me a look that was not exactly welcoming, but of course, surly staff is part of Medici's charm. I seated myself in a dark, wood paneled booth near the window and pulled out my copy of *The Implied Spider* and my notebook. If I could just find a bit more textual evidence to support my argument that -

I sensed him before I saw him. There was, perhaps, a slight crackle of electricity in the air, a quick gust on the back of my neck. Like a melting snowflake.

"Is this seat taken?" he asked from behind me.

I shook my head as he sat down, trying to remember to breathe.

"Loki Laufeyiarson," I said, hoping my voice didn't betray my pounding heart. "And what brings you to Midgard?"

"Happy Valentine's Day," he said.

"What?"

I reached into my pocket, grabbing my cell phone to check the date. But my fingers trembled pulling it out, and the phone crashed onto the floor, its dark plastic casing coming off the back. Loki and I both reached for it, and our fingers brushed. My hand came alive with electricity as I grabbed the damn phone and tried to jam the case back together.

"You're an asshole," I said, feeling my cheeks flush. "I haven't seen you in months. Not a word after I got back from Asgard. And now you show up and say happy Valentine's Day?"

Loki gave me a disarmingly handsome smile. *Damn,* I thought. *I forgot how stupidly attractive he is.* I tried to ignore the rush of heat between my legs.

"Hello!" The waitress was suddenly standing next to our table, her voice sounding fluttery. She was staring intently at Loki, her cheeks a bright red. "Can I get you anything?"

Loki smiled at her. "Just an espresso, if you please."

The waitress dropped her order pad. Then her cheeks turned an even deeper shade of red, almost a purple, as she bent for her order pad and backed away from our table. My phone dinged as it finally turned on. The display activated; 2/14 flashed in white across the charcoal gray screen. *So it is Valentine's Day.* I stared at Loki. My efforts to remain irritated with him struggled against the sheer relief flooding my body, the relief that he was still alive, that he had not yet gone to the bleak battlefield of Vígríðr.

"Did you really cross the Bifröst just to wish me a happy Valentine's Day?" I asked.

Loki's smile faded, and for a moment he looked old. Then the waitress arrived, her cheeks still bright, her hands trembling slightly as she placed Loki's small, white espresso mug on our table.

"Things are... winding down," he said, delicately.

"I've spent a millennium trying to prevent it. But it looks like Ragnarök approaches, now, despite my efforts."

I couldn't bring myself to look at him. "I know," I said. "I didn't realize it when I went to Asgard. But I know now."

I took a deep breath, preparing to say I was sorry. But when I looked at him, his high cheekbones and sparking eyes, his soft lips and flaming hair, I was not at all certain I was sorry. *He's free,* I thought, and I couldn't bring myself to regret it.

"I would like to spend some time with you," he said, turning to face the window. "Before the end. If you can bring yourself to forgive me."

"Forgive you?"

"The Trial of Æsìlynd. I would have spared you that." His eyes flickered toward me, then back to the window, to the empty street.

I sat in silence for a moment, watching the pale light of winter's early morning shift and tremble across his face. "Is that why you didn't see me in Asgard?"

"Of course," he said. "I thought you might accept Óðinn's offer. You might forget me."

"Did you really think that?"

Loki gave me a weak smile. "There was a chance."

"Óðinn's offer," I said, and an unpleasant thought occurred to me. "And how did he come up with that?"

Loki spread his arms, his palms up. "We discussed it."

"You told them to offer me a husband?"

"I told them to offer you everything," he said. "If the Trial of Æsìlynd is unsuccessful, the mortal is executed. I would rather see you married to Hyrm than - " His voice trailed off.

"But it was successful."

"And then you were punished for my crimes. By banishment, if I'm not mistaken," he said, his voice low, his eyes turned to the window. "I did not wish that for you."

I stared at his pale face, and I suddenly remembered how he looked, tied to the chair in Asgard, his mouth gagged, his body bruised and bloody, his eyes closed. And with that memory came a flash of deep anger.

"I don't regret what I've done," I said. "The trial was mine to demand. And I'm glad you're free." I paused, taking a deep breath. And then, because the world was ending, I said the words that were in my heart.

"I love you," I whispered, and I looked out the window to the empty street, the pale sky.

"As I love you," he said. "The trial would not have worked otherwise."

Our eyes met over the table, and it occurred to me there was one more thing I wanted to know, one final question I'd like answered before the Nine Realms were destroyed.

"Tell me about Sigyn," I said. "Tell me about your wife."

"I will." He put two twenty dollar bills next to his untouched espresso, stood, and offered me his hand. "Walk with me."

* * * * * * *

"I never meant to kill Baldur," he said as we left the warmth of Medici. It was so cold outside my first breath stung my lungs. I held Loki's arm.

"I loved Baldur. Everyone did. Every*thing* did. It was impossible to not love Baldur. But he was getting to be a cocky little son of a bitch. And -" Loki paused, taking a deep breath.

"A common enemy," I said.

He turned to me, his eyes wide. "That's right," he said. "I thought I could unite them, against me, if necessary. But how did you..?"

I smiled at him. "You told me yourself, years ago. The only thing that has ever united them is a common enemy."

He laughed, softly. "And it did work," he said. "Just not forever."

We walked half a block in silence, past hulking apartment buildings, fenced courtyards. The cold pressed down on us, and I held Loki's arm tighter than was absolutely necessary.

"But why?" I asked. "Óðinn, Hyrm, they seem almost like they're looking forward to Ragnarök. Why try to stop it?"

I felt him shrug his shoulders. "I'm not a warrior," he said. "A glorious death in battle has never exactly appealed to me. Besides," he raised his hand, gesturing to the street, the ice crystals sparkling off the sidewalk, the snowbanks in the gutter streaked with black and gray. "I like the Nine Realms. I'm in no rush to see them destroyed."

"Won't there be a... better world, coming after?"

Loki laughed. It was not a happy sound. "That's what they claim. But I've heard many promises that a better world will follow destruction and terror. It never quite seems to work out."

We stepped off the curb and walked along the pedestrian overpass leading to the park, our park, Promontory Point. The wind was fierce, howling down Lake Shore Drive, and we both fell silent until we were among the trees and rosebushes.

"I discovered mistletoe was the only thing that could hurt Baldur," Loki began, his voice soft, barely audible over the wind. "I carved the mistletoe into a weapon. A dart, really. And then I gave it to the person with the worst aim in Asgard - Höðr. He's *blind*."

Loki fell silent, and we walked along the lake shore. The waves were tossed with ice, crashing against the frozen pylons. My cheeks burned with the cold; my fingers and toes slowly went numb.

"I won't say I didn't deserve punishment," Loki said. "I discovered his weakness. I fashioned the weapon. I gave it to Höðr. Whatever my intentions, the spear pierced Baldur's heart."

He fell quiet again, and I glanced up at him. His eyes were far away, searching the distant horizon. "I deserved what I got. But Sigyn did not deserve to be punished. And my sons, they did not deserve to be punished."

Loki stopped, and I stopped next to him. He looked out across Lake Michigan, choppy with its shifting ice floes. I pretended not to notice the tears on his proud cheeks.

"They turned my son Vali into a wolf," he said. "And Vali the wolf tore his brother Nari apart. Then Óðinn and Thor bound me to a rock with my own child's entrails, and they put the serpent above me, to drip poison into my face."

I held his arm. The wind stung my eyes, bringing tears.

"And they bound Sigyn to that place, as surely as they bound me," he said. "That was my punishment. One child dead, one child imprisoned in a beast's body, perhaps eternally. And the knowledge that my wife, the woman I loved above all others, would spend the rest of her long life in a cave, catching poison in a bowl."

"I am so sorry," I whispered, my words sounding feeble and pathetic.

Loki shook his head and placed his hand on my arm, starting to walk again. "In the end," he said, "I was able to convince her to leave. To leave in the only way she could. The only way we both could."

I held my breath, the cold pulling at my jacket, slicing through my jeans.

"We drank the poison together," he said, his voice low and soft. "She had to hold the bowl to my lips. But it only killed her."

By now we were back at the pedestrian overpass. We were both silent as we walked over Lake Shore Drive, the wind ripping warmth from my body. *He killed her,* Lady Sif told me, in Asgard, when I asked about Sigyn. My tears made cold tracks down my cheeks.

Loki offered me his arm once we were back on the ground. I took it, holding him tightly.

"And then they let me go," he said, waving his hand. "Once Sigyn was dead, Óðinn and Thor showed up, cutting my binds. And I was free." He laughed bitterly. "Watching Sigyn suffer in the cave *was* my punishment."

I shivered violently, and Loki wrapped his arms

around me, kissing the top of my head. We walked the rest of the way to the Flamingo apartment building in silence. I keyed in the entrance code with trembling fingers. Then I opened the door, but Loki remained on the sidewalk.

"Come on," I said, holding the door.

"If you still want me to come in," he said.

My frozen cheeks managed a smile as I reached for his hand. "Of course I do," I said. "Of course I do."

CHAPTER FORTY

When the door to my apartment closed behind us, I suddenly felt shy. This apartment once felt like it belonged to him as much as it belonged to me. But that was a lifetime ago, and now I stood in the living room looking up at him, shivering, and not entirely from the cold.

Loki took my hands in his. "You're freezing," he said. "I didn't realize." His eyes turned dark in his pale face. "Again I've endangered you."

I shook my head and reached for him. "No," I said, forcing the words through chattering teeth. "I'm okay. I'm just cold."

"It's not - " He stepped away from me, his eyes fixed somewhere above my head. "When Sigyn died, I..." His voice faltered, and he took a deep, jagged breath, running his fingers through his hair. "Something inside me died as well. Forever, I thought. And then you... When we went to Yggdrasil, when I realized I'd put you in danger..."

His eyes closed. He looked lost, somehow, his confidence and pride gone. I reached for him, pulled his lips to mine, cold meeting cold. His hands wrapped around my waist and his mouth opened for me. My shivering stopped as my body relaxed against his chest, his achingly familiar tongue entering my mouth, the rest of the world falling away.

When we pulled apart I turned to rest my head against him, listening to the steady rhythm of his heart. "But I'm okay," I whispered. "I'm here. I'm here with you."

He was silent for a long time, his arms wrapped around me, our bodies pressed together. Then he took a deep, shuddering breath. "I wish I'd given you more," he said.

I laughed against his chest. "Loki, how many mortals get to see Asgard? Even if I can't tell anyone, even if no one will ever believe me. I walked the Bifröst. I saw Val-Hall." I turned to meet his eyes, but they were still distant, clouded.

"Still," he whispered, running his fingers through my hair and along my neck, "I should have given you more." His gaze moved toward the window. Away from me.

Óðinn's words echoed in my mind: *Money. Prestige. A family. All this I can give to you.*

Is that what you wanted to give me? I thought, and I reached for his pale face. As I touched his cheek, he shivered and his illusions slipped. I saw the scars radiating from his eyes, the jagged white bands crossing his full lips. I felt his real skin, rough under my fingers, for just a second. Then he shook his head and his face was perfect again, smooth, pale, and even.

"You don't have to do that," I said.

He smiled and turned away, looking out the windows of the living room.

"No, really," I said, running my finger along his lips, tracing the invisible scars. "I like you the way you are."

He looked at me, his perfect face unreadable. "You like me ugly?"

"I like you as you are," I said. "Please."

He hesitated, and then his illusions disappeared, and I saw *him*, Loki, the Trickster God of Asgard. His hair rose like fire around his very old and very wild face. Delicate white filamentous lines radiated from his eyes; his lips were crossed with thick, angry scar tissue where the dwarves of Níðavellir had sewn his mouth closed.

I leaned into him and kissed his rough lips. "You're very beautiful," I said.

I felt his chest shake against mine as he laughed. "And you are insane."

I smiled. "You gave me yourself," I said, meeting his wild eyes in his ancient, battered face. "That's what I wanted. That's all I wanted."

He bent to kiss me and then swept me into his arms

and carried me to the bedroom. My dusty tea candles flared to life as we lay down together on the pillows. His breath was warm against my neck as he leaned close to my ear. His voice low and trembling, he whispered words I did not know in a language I did not recognize. *But I've heard that before,* I thought. *Where have I -*

On my couch, I realized. *Before I went to Iceland.*

The last time we made love.

"What was that?" I asked, running my hands along his back and under his shirt. His body felt uneven beneath my fingers, the scar tissue knotted and torn over his muscles. He was silent for so long I thought he would not answer me.

"I am bound to you," he whispered, finally, his voice rough against my neck. "You are a part of me."

"Well, that's -" The words died in my mouth as I looked at him. His eyes were burning. I pressed my hand to his cheek, my thumb tracing the scars radiating from his eyes.

"I am bound to you," I said, meeting his gaze. "You are a part of me."

He smiled at me, his eyes filling with light. And then he bent his rough, uneven lips to mine, and my heart surged.

For the first time, we kissed with no illusions.

* * * * * * *

His unfamiliar skin shuddered and trembled under my touch. I ran my fingers along his neck, tracing his collarbone, and then down the curves of his chest, where the ridges of hard scar tissue rasped against my palm.

I pulled back from his hungry mouth. "You feel so different," I whispered.

He grimaced. "I despise this skin," he said, his voice low and rough in his throat. "And I'm not used to being t-touched - like this -"

He gasped as I kissed his chest, tracing his nipple with my tongue, gently closing my teeth around the hard skin. His breath was short and fast when I pulled away.

"I like touching you like this," I whispered. Our eyes met and he returned my smile, his fingers tracing my cheek.

He moaned and his eyes flickered shut as I climbed on top of him, tracing the arc of his muscles under the scarred lines of his skin. I moved my body down his legs, licking his navel, running my hands along his flat, muscular stomach and down his hips, feeling his body tighten under my touch. His cock was throbbing, ready for me. I ignored it as I bent over him, running my tongue along the inside of his thighs. His body trembled as I kissed the base of his cock, and then delicately traced its length with my tongue.

He cried out, his hands grabbing at the sheets, when I took him in my mouth. I wrapped my fingers around his shaft, kissing and licking the head, and his hips shook under me.

"Caroline," he gasped, "I can't - if you don't stop -"

I pulled away long enough to smile at him. "I'm not stopping," I said.

I moved my mouth along the length of him, slowly, savoring the way his body moved under my touch. And then, as his hips began to tilt and rock against me, I moved faster.

He cried my name as he came in my mouth, the sheets ripping in his hands. He tasted like salt and woodsmoke. His body was still trembling when I lay down beside him and wrapped my arms around him.

"Thank you," he gasped.

"Don't thank me yet," I said. "I'm nowhere near done with you."

He laughed, his face open and relaxed, his hand tracing the length of my arm. "I love you, mortal woman."

"And you owe me a new set of sheets, Loki of the Æsir."

He laughed again and turned to me, rubbing his head along my neck. His hips rocked into mine, and I could feel his cock twitching again, growing hard against my thighs. I moaned as he pulled his scarred lips over my neck, sending shivers across my skin. He reached for my wrists, pinning me to the bed as his lips moved over my chest, kissing and licking my collarbone. I gasped as the rough skin of his chest rubbed against mine, and then he circled my breast with his tongue, pulling it into his mouth, closing his teeth around my nipple.

"Oh, I missed you," I cried, wrapping my legs around his. "I missed you so - goddamn - much!"

His chest shook as he laughed, and then he pressed his face against my neck, breathing into my hair. "I missed your smell," he whispered, his voice thick.

He bent over me, his fingers following the outline of my waist as his mouth circled my nipples, licking and biting, and then dropped to the curve of my stomach. I shivered as his cool lips kissed my skin again and again. He pressed his cheek against my navel, breathing deeply. Then he gave me a wicked grin and dropped his head between my legs.

"Ah, fuck, I missed your taste," he said.

He buried his tongue inside me, and I cried out, grabbing at the sheets. His tongue flickered and pressed against the swell of my clit, and waves of pleasure rocked through me until my hips were trembling against his lips. He pulled back just long enough for me to moan his name, and then his mouth was against me again, circling and tasting until the room began to spin. And then he slowed, keeping me on the brink of release

428 | THE TRICKSTER'S LOVER

as he slid his fingers into my sex, rubbing his thumb delicately against the hot flesh of my clit. I moaned and writhed under him, gasping for breath.

"I need you," I cried, my fingers twisting in the sheets. "Oh, Loki, please!"

He bent over my thighs, his thumb still making lazy circles against my throbbing clit, his fingers moving inside me. He dragged his teeth and scarred lips across my hips, and then he closed his lips around the skin of my upper thigh and bit me. I cried out as sensation flooded my body, obliterating thought, destroying the distinction between pleasure and pain, and then his mouth was back on me, his tongue against my sex, and my body crashed and rocked under his lips, the sheets ripping in my hands as I screamed his name, my orgasm flooding my body, drowning me.

He kissed me as I lay trembling on the ruined sheets, and I could taste myself on his lips. "Sorry about the sheets," he whispered, his face soft in the candlelight.

I found I couldn't make my mouth work, so I just turned to wrap my arm around his waist.

"Although," he said, his fingers tracing the curve of my neck, making my skin flush and prickle, "I believe you said you were not done with me..."

I laughed in his arms and ran my fingers through his hair. "Kiss me," I whispered.

His lips touched mine and he kissed me, slowly and

intimately, until my body began to burn and tremble again, until I was gasping against his mouth, running my hands along the ridges of his scarred back.

"I'm ready," I said, spreading my legs beneath him.

He pulled back and buried his head in my neck, kissing my skin, breathing deeply. I reached down and he gasped as I wrapped my fingers around his stiff cock, guiding him into me. We both moaned as he entered me, our bodies joining together, gently and slowly. His arm trembled as it wrapped around my shoulders.

"Does it feel different?" I whispered. "When you're... like this?"

He drew a deep breath, his face against my hair. "Yes," he shuddered.

I wrapped my legs around his as he began to move inside me, his skin still cool against mine, even as our bodies slid and pressed together. His arm crushed me to his chest, as though he were trying to draw me into himself, to make us one.

"I am - bound to you," he whispered against my ear, his voice low and jagged.

"You are a part of me," I finished.

His body shook in my arms. I sighed as I opened myself to him, giving him everything, everything I had, everything I was. We trembled and rolled like the sea, clinging to each other as the waves crashed around us, swept away by something much larger than the two of us.

CHAPTER FORTY-ONE

We lay together on the ruined sheets, my head on his scarred chest, as the tea candles sputtered and went out on my dresser. His fingers trailed absentmindedly along my arm.

"So," I whispered, once my heartbeat finally returned to normal. "What's your plan?"

His chest shook as he laughed. "What makes you think I have a plan?"

"Don't you have a plan? To stop Ragnarök?"

He sighed, leaned down to kiss my hair. "Finding you. Apologizing. Spending Midgard's last days in your arms, if you would have me. That's my plan."

I tilted my head to meet his lips. "What about a common enemy?" I asked, after a slow, sweet kiss. "Couldn't that work again?"

He laughed softly in my arms. "And would you see me bound beneath the earth for another thousand years, mortal woman?"

I shuddered. "No. Of course not. But isn't there

something else?"

He shrugged, his hand tracing the curve of my cheek. "You said it yourself. Óðinn, Hyrm. They want this. There'll be no tricking them this time. Really, it's a wonder the Nine Realms have stood for this long."

I shook my head. "There has to be something we can do."

"Of course there's something we can do," he growled, grabbing me by my hips and pulling me on top of him. "We can fuck each other senseless. If I'm going to be pulled to the killing fields of Vígríðr, I want to go with your scent on my body, and your taste on my lips."

I opened my mouth to disagree, and he pressed his lips against mine. His heartbeat quickened under my fingertips.

As far as plans go, I had to admit, I'd heard worse.

* * * * * * * *

I fell asleep curled against Loki's chest, listening to the steady drum of his heartbeat.

Then I shivered with my entire body, as though I were pushing through a curtain of cold water. I blinked and I was in San Diego, standing in my parents' backyard. The California ash towered over me, moving in its own private windstorm.

I looked up to see dark, heavy storm clouds piled on

the horizon. *Trouble*, I thought. *Trouble is coming.* I could smell smoke, heavy, greasy smoke. Battlefield smoke.

The air was suddenly thick with sparks and embers, with burning leaves falling from the sky. I shaded my eyes and looked up, up along the trunk of the California ash. *It's going to burn*, I thought. *The whole tree is going to burn.*

Then it was no longer my parents' backyard. It was no longer my family's California ash. Now it was Yggdrasil. The World Tree. And the top of the World Tree was on fire.

My dream shifted, and I found myself back in my old studio apartment, my legs wrapped around Loki. He kissed me, deeply.

"We... overlap," I said, and he smiled.

"Yggdrasil," I said, my fingers interlaced with his. "That's a... a metaphor for the social structure."

Loki laughed. "No, it's a *tree*," he said. "It's an ash tree."

The dream shifted again, and I stood, alone, in my parents' backyard. The California ash loomed above me, the tree limbs turning and waving, dancing to their own private windstorm.

It's a tree, I thought.

It's an ash tree.

* * * * * * *

I opened my eyes, blinking in the darkness. I heard Loki's rhythmic breathing next to me, saw his scarred face in the blue glow of my bedside clock. I pushed myself up on my elbow, watching him. He'd once collapsed in my bed, after his magnificent battle, his illusions vanishing, revealing a body covered with blood and battle-wounds and scars. And he had slept next to me in Nowhere, when it was too dark to see his body.

But this was the first time he'd slept in my bed, actually slept. I watched him breathing, staring at his high cheekbones, the network of delicate white lines radiating from his eyes, the dimpled scar tissue above and below his lips. *He is so beautiful,* I thought, and it was suddenly very difficult to keep from touching him, from pressing my lips against his. Everything I'd ever read about Ragnarök came flooding back to me, and my breath caught in my throat.

"No," I whispered. "I'll stop it. I'll find a way." I blinked back the tears threatening to spill down my cheeks. "I will not let you die in Vígríðr, Loki of the Æsir."

I climbed out of bed, trying not to disturb him, and walked, naked, to the living room. I stood at the window, watching cars flowing along Lake Shore Drive. Watching the sky lighten against the surface of Lake

Michigan. Watching the waving, black arms of the trees on Promontory Point.

"It's not a metaphor," I whispered to my darkened windows, running my fingers through my hair. "It's a tree. An ash tree. And what do you do when something goes wrong with a tree?" Something flickered at the edges of my mind, something I couldn't quite grasp.

"You're up early."

I turned toward my bedroom. Loki stood in the doorway, his arms crossed over his chest, the scars on his face illuminated by the faint light of early morning through the living room windows.

"Shall I make breakfast?" he asked.

I smiled and walked to him, running my hands along the scarred ridges of his chest. "You mean steal breakfast?" I asked. "From Val-Hall?"

His face darkened and his smile vanished. "No, not Val-Hall. I can already feel the pull of Vígríðr. It would be... unwise to leave this realm, even momentarily."

My arms tightened around his waist, and I leaned against his cool chest. *Vígríðr,* I thought. *No. No. No. No.* Something flickered again, dancing on the edge of my consciousness.

"It's a tree," I muttered, pulling away from his chest and walking back to my windows. The sun crested above the lake, and the bare branches of the trees glinted in the dawn. "And when something goes wrong with a tree -"

I turned back to Loki. "Can you get us to Yggdrasil?"

He tilted his head. "You would go to Yggdrasil now? Even there, you'll not be able to escape the flames of Ragnarök."

"No, it's not about escaping. I mean, it is, but not just me. Look, it's a tree, right? And when part of a tree goes bad, well, you get rid of it."

Loki smiled at me, a sad smile that exaggerated the scars across his lips. "That's a nice thought," he said. "That's... clever."

"Well, damn, thanks for the ringing endorsement."

"But we would need to get to Yggdrasil. And no, I cannot travel there. Not without assistance, something like Óðinn's mead. Which I very much doubt I'd be able to acquire a second time. Especially now."

I turned back to the window, watching the trees along Promontory Point in the thin, golden light of the winter sunrise. Trying to remember my dream. I'd been watching another tree, another ash tree. A tree I'd seen my entire life...

"They overlap," I muttered, turning to Loki. "What if there's a place in Midgard that overlaps Yggdrasil?"

He raised an eyebrow. "Is there?"

"I don't know," I said. "But I know who to ask."

I picked up my phone and called my brother.

* * * * * * * *

Geoff answered after four rings, his voice heavy with sleep. "Carol? Is everything okay?"

I glanced at the clock. It was just past two in the morning in San Diego. "Yeah, hey. Sorry to wake you."

"S'okay," he said. I heard rustling as he adjusted the receiver. "What's up?"

"Uh, I need to know about the tree," I stammered.

"The what?"

I took a deep breath. "The tree in Mom and Dad's backyard. The ash. I think there's something kind of... special. About it."

Geoff laughed. "Figured that out all on your own, did you?"

"Geoff, this is serious!"

"Okay, I'm listening," he said, although he still sounded like he was laughing. "What's up? What do you need to know?"

"Um, this is going to sound kind of crazy," I hesitated. "If I say Ragnarök..."

"Awww, shit," he sighed. "I knew it. Norse gods?"

"Yeah." I glanced at Loki. His lean, naked body bent over the kitchen counter as he filled the coffee pot. My cheeks flushed, and I turned back to the window. "Norse gods," I said.

"Hang on. I'll get Di. She's got a bit more experience

with the whole saving the world thing." I heard more rustling as my brother sighed into the receiver. "Seriously, though. Norse gods? You've got some weird tastes, sis."

"Thanks, that's very constructive just now," I said. Then Di's voice came on the line. "Hi, Carol," she said. "Is this about the tree?"

I opened my mouth, then closed it again. "Yeah, I guess it is."

"We've been watching it," she said. "How much do you know?"

"Uh, I don't know anything," I stammered. "I mean, I know I triggered Ragnarök. And I'm really sorry about that."

"Ragnarök," Di said, and then she growled something low and oily that could only have been a string of curse words. After that she was silent for so long I looked down at my phone to make sure it was still working.

"I know the realms overlap," I said. "And I had a dream about the ash tree. I guess I just thought, if we could get to Yggdrasil, then maybe we could, well, do something. Put out the fire. Stop Ragnarök."

Di still said nothing, and a thick band of panic settled around my chest. "I guess I haven't exactly worked out all the details. But..." I hesitated. My throat felt tight, my voice high and wavering. "I have to do something. I can't lose him."

I heard a gentle sigh on the other end of the line. "I know," Di said, finally. "And you're not wrong about the ash   tree."

"I'm not?" I squeaked.

"The tree in that yard is a window," she said. "And stewardship of that tree was given to your family, to your grandfather, in exchange for several boons. Including extraordinary children." She paused. "That's how I met your brother. I had to clear up a bit of trouble some years ago."

I took a deep breath. I'd spent the last three months preparing for the end of the world, and still, this came as a bit of a shock. "So if it's a window... Can we go through it? If we can get to Yggdrasil, if we can find Vígríðr. Could we cut it off the tree?"

The phone rustled as Di shifted. "Maybe," she said. "I can't get you to the World Tree, but perhaps I can help in my own way. How soon can you be in California?"

I glanced toward my kitchen. Loki stood in the doorway, wearing a dark suit and holding two steaming coffee mugs, his face once again pale and smooth. "Soon," I said, hanging up my phone.

Loki crossed the living room and handed me a mug. "Well?"

"Hang on," I said. "I've got to get us tickets to San Diego."

"No need," he said, smiling as he reached into his suit jacket. He handed me a rectangle of white paper. It was a first-class Delta Airlines ticket to San Diego, departing from O'Hare at noon. For Caroline Laufeyiarson.

I raised my eyebrow. "Uh, this name doesn't exactly match my photo ID."

Loki laughed. "Yes it does," he said, his eyes sparkling.

I walked to my desk and fumbled in my book bag for my wallet. There was my California driver's license, my absurdly unflattering picture from four years ago. It read *Caroline Laufeyiarson.* "So, what exactly does this mean?" My heart jumped as I looked from *Laufeyiarson* to Loki's dancing eyes. "Are we..?"

"Get dressed," he said, cutting me off. "The cab's waiting."

I took one last look at the driver's license for Caroline Laufeyiarson and headed to the bedroom, pulling open the closet. I blinked, staring at rows of jeans and T-shirts. *We're going to save the Nine Realms,* I thought. *We're going to stop Ragnarök.*

What am I going to wear?

Loki walked behind me and wrapped his arm around my waist. "Pick something sexy," he whispered, his lips achingly close to my neck.

I smiled and reached into my closet, all the way to the

back. The red dress was a little wrinkled, but I pulled it on. *What the hell,* I thought. *The world is about to end. I might as well look sexy for once.*

CHAPTER FORTY-TWO

"Whoa," said Geoff. "Nice... dress."

"Thanks," I stammered, my cheeks burning as I shifted uncomfortably in my impractical black heels, staring at the concrete sidewalk outside the San Diego airport.

The passenger door of the Capello's Landscaping & Tree Surgery van swung open, and Di stepped out. *Something's wrong,* I thought, but it took me a second to realize what. It was Di's hair; she'd cut her beautiful, golden hair painfully short.

"You look lovely," she told me, taking both my hands in hers.

"Thanks," I stammered again, too shocked by her appearance to say anything else.

"Yeah," said Geoff, scratching his head. "Lovely. So, you ready?"

I nodded. "Geoff, Di, this is-" I waved at Loki, but he'd already turned to Di and taken her hand. He bent low, bringing her fingers to his lips. They greeted each other with words that were no human language.

"You know each other?" I asked.

"Love and lies," Loki said, with a smile. "We're quite well acquainted."

"Right," said Geoff, clapping his hand together. "Let's do this."

We climbed into the van and Loki's hand closed around mine. He glanced into the back, the dark tangle of extension cords, shovels, bags of soil, and heavy machinery. "Assuming I can get us to Yggdrasil, which is quite the assumption," he said, his voice smooth as still water, "you do realize no mortal tools can touch the World Tree?"

"Yup, we've taken care of that," said Geoff. "Don't worry about it."

Loki's brow furrowed in the golden evening light. He said nothing, but his grip on my hand tightened.

* * * * * * * *

The sky was an angry, bruised purple when we pulled into the driveway of my parent's house. "I think you'd better wait until it's dark," Di said.

"No," Loki said. "Dusk is a good time. It's a thin time."

Di said nothing, but I noticed a hard line appear between her delicate eyebrows. We climbed out of the van and Geoff opened the back, stepping into the darkness and then emerging again without a word. He held a simple folding bow saw in his right hand. The curving handle was a battered turquoise. It looked like the kind of ordinary tool a middle-aged suburban dad might use to cut down a Christmas tree, or to prune something unruly in his backyard.

The blade glimmered strangely in the fading light, shining with an odd, golden color, almost the exact same shade as Di's hair. No, it was the exact same shade. The blade was wrapped, over and over, with tight loops of Di's long, golden hair.

Loki raised an eyebrow. "That... might actually work," he said.

I reached for the saw, but Geoff turned away from me. "No," I said. "Geoff, I take the saw."

He shook his head, and I understood the hard line between Di's eyes. "Caroline, out of the two of us, who is actually a tree surgeon?"

"Geoff, this isn't a joke!"

"I'm coming," he said. "He can take us there, you can find the battlefield. I'll cut the branch."

"No," I said, my voice cracking. "You've got a family now."

Our eyes met in the fading light. "Exactly," he said. "This is my world, too, you know."

I felt Di's gentle hand on my shoulder. "Yggdrasil

will try to protect itself," she said. "This will not be easy. You'll need him."

I sighed and let go of the saw. Geoff moved toward my parents' house, the turquoise bow saw in his hands, and I followed him through the darkened front door in silence. I reached for Loki's hand as we walked through my childhood home, lacing my fingers through his. His skin was cold.

Di opened the sliding glass door to the backyard. Loki whistled, softly, as he stared at the ash tree. Its limbs were perfectly still in the gathering dusk.

"Impressive," Loki whispered, turning to Di. "Your work?"

"Not mine alone," she said, with obvious pride.

Loki muttered something low and thick in his throat, and Di nodded grimly. Then she raised her hands to Geoff's face, whispering something in his ear before turning to us.

"I have warded the area as best I can," she said. Her eyes flashed and, for the first time, I *saw* her. Not Di, the sweet, perfect, beautiful girl my brother brought home and married, but Aphrodite, an ancient and terrible force, undeniable as the tide.

I shivered. *What the hell are we doing?*

* * * * * * *

Geoff, Loki, and I walked across the dew-wet grass to stand before the California ash. I heard Di close the sliding glass door behind us. The ash seemed very ordinary, a regular tree in a regular neighborhood in the gathering darkness of a regular day.

Geoff sighed and shook his head, running his fingers through his hair. "Shit, sis," he said. "Had to be Norse, huh? That pantheon is seriously fucked up."

"Hey!" I smacked his arm.

Loki just raised an eyebrow. "Indeed," he muttered.

Geoff turned to him. "Can you get us there?"

"Or die trying," Loki said, smiling.

It was not especially reassuring. Loki's fingers tightened around mine, and I took a deep breath, focusing on the California ash. The ash that did not exactly move to the winds of this world. *Overlap*, I thought. *There are Nine Realms, but they overlap.*

And then we were moving. It was not instantaneous, not like closing my eyes in my apartment and opening them in Nowhere. It was not like walking the Bifröst through the swirling fog between the worlds.

It hurt.

I was pushing, pushing against something that did not want me. My body was cold, plunged into freezing water, and crushed, crushed against ice. I tried to breath, but my chest was broken, pressed flat between the freezing water, the sheets of ice that separate the worlds. My blood was solidifying, turning to crystals, ripping my skin. My heartbeats slowed-

Loki's hand crushed mine, and he *pulled.* I stumbled, falling forward, gasping and gulping the warm air of a California evening. *Shit,* I thought. *It didn't work.*

I opened my eyes. The soft grass below my hands was very green. Aggressively green. I raised my head and saw Yggdrasil. The air was thick, dancing with lights. *Fireflies,* I thought, raising my hand to brush them away. But they were red.

Sparks.

I looked up, up along the trunk of the World Tree, and I saw the flames of Ragnarök dancing on a far, distant branch. Geoff climbed to his feet next to me, the turquoise bow saw in his hands. His face was pale, his mouth a hard, grim line.

Loki was on his knees between us, breathing shallowly. His scars were livid, his flaming hair wet against his head. A trickle of blood from the corner of his mouth looked very bright against his gray skin. I reached for him, putting my arm around his shoulder.

"No," he rasped, shaking his head. "Don't waste time with me. Go."

I felt Geoff's hand on my shoulder. "He's right," he said. "Let's do what we came to do."

In the shifting, dancing light, Geoff looked strange and unfamiliar, like a marble bust in a museum. Sparks fell in his hair, on his shoulders. I took his hand and got to my feet, facing Yggdrasil. It towered over us, looking very, very solid. I craned my neck to stare at the interlacing branches. They seemed to go on forever.

"Are you sure about this?" I asked Geoff, my voice trembling as sparks flared and danced between us.

"Of course," he said. He put his hand on my shoulder and pushed me toward Yggdrasil. "Just take me to the right branch. Take me to the battlefield."

I bit my lip and looked over my shoulder. Loki was slowly coming to his feet; our eyes met in the strange, shifting light. *You will not die in Vígríðr,* I thought. And I raised my hands to the bark of the World Tree.

"I need to go back," I whispered. "Back to the battlefield. Back to the site of Ragnarök."

The bark shifted under my hands, moving like the skin of a great, living beast. It grew warm and soft under my touch, welcoming. The lines in the bark began to form images, began to form a face. A baby's face. I stared at baby Devi, sitting in her high chair at my brother's house. Then the bark rippled and I saw my mom sitting in front of Devi, laughing.

Come home.

It was a soft whisper, the heartfelt advice of a close friend, echoing in the back of my mind. *Come home, Caroline Capello.* I shook my head and turned to Geoff. The air was warmer, now, the smell of smoke more pronounced.

"Is this it?" Geoff asked, raising an eyebrow.

My heart caught in my throat as I realized we were no longer standing on the emerald grass. We were on a branch, an enormous branch, surrounded by snaking wood and shimmering leaves. I took a deep breath and looked down... I couldn't even see the ground. I couldn't see Loki. My head started to spin.

Geoff's hand grabbed my chin, pulled my face level with his. "Don't look down," he said.

I nodded, trying to catch my breath.

"Now, is this it? Is this the branch I need to cut?"

"No," I said, turning back to Yggdrasil. Baby Devi was still laughing in her high chair in the shifting, changing bark of the World Tree. And my hands - my fingers had vanished, sinking into the wood. I pulled them out, slowly. The World Tree was smooth and warm, yielding like a lover.

"Stop it," I said. "I need to go to Vígríðr."

The branch heaved once, as if sighing, and the lines began to shift and dance again. This time I was aware of motion, a fluttering in the leaves, a breeze across my arms, as Yggdrasil moved beneath us. Taking us -

"Vígríðr," I whispered. "Take us to Vígríðr." The bark flickered faster, a flurry of images, flashes of vision from the windows of a swiftly moving train.

And then I was staring at Hæmir.

His hazel eyes narrowed, scanning a distant horizon. He raised his hand, pushing his soft curls back from his forehead. I saw the faint shadow of stubble on his cheeks, and I remembered how it felt along my neck, the flush of heat he brought to my body. *Lovely Carol,* the silky voice whispered. I shook my head and closed my eyes.

"Is this it?" Geoff asked.

I coughed in the smoky air, trying to clear my throat. "No," I whispered. "Not here."

I looked down and saw my hands had disappeared, falling into the bark of Yggdrasil. My heart jumped and I swallowed, trying not to panic. Very slowly, I pulled my hands out of the wood. They did not come out quite so easily this time.

"Vígríðr," I said, staring at the lines in the bark.

The sense of motion came again, faster this time. Less comfortable. The lines in the bark spun so quickly I couldn't follow them; words, faces, voices. Oceans and stars, worlds spinning beneath my fingers.

And then I saw Loki. He staggered to his feet on the emerald grass below, far below Yggdrasil. He wiped the blood from his mouth, leaving a crimson streak across his cheek. As I watched, he closed his eyes and raised his hands, and oh, he was so beautiful, with his flaming hair and his soft, full lips -

Go to him, Caroline, the smooth, gentle voice

whispered in my mind. *Go to your love. Be with him, now, at the end of all things.*

"No," I growled, shaking my head. With a start I realized I was trapped. My arms had sunk into the tree up to my shoulders, and they burned as I struggled to pull them out of Yggdrasil, the bark leaving red, snaking tears in my skin as I pulled free.

The smoky air scratched and caught in my throat. Despite the heat coming off Yggdrasil in waves, I felt cold, cold sinking into my arms and legs. *What if that's the last time I see him?* I thought. *What if that's my last -*

Geoff's arm tightened around my shoulders, and I leaned against his chest until I could breathe again. "Lemme guess," he said. "Wrong stop?"

My shoulders trembled as I laughed. "You could say that."

Geoff coughed, then pulled back and met my eyes. "Fourth time's a charm?"

I nodded and forced myself to turn back to the World Tree. "There's nothing more you can offer me," I said, putting my scratched and bleeding hands against the bark. "Take me to Vígríðr."

Yggdrasil shuddered once, shuddered violently, and then fell still. I saw black, jagged mountains scraping overcast skies above a cold, desolate forest. The air was filled with smoke, heavy, greasy smoke. In the far distance, I heard the clash of metal on metal.

I sighed and let myself fall into the World Tree.

CHAPTER FORTY-THREE

For a moment I was aware of a split, aware of myself in two places. I fell into Yggdrasil, and yet I stood, motionless, in the branches, with Geoff's arm on my shoulder.

And then the vision disappeared, and I opened my eyes in a forest, choking and coughing as I tried to breathe. The air was bitter cold and thick with greasy smoke. The rocky, broken ground beneath me sloped steeply, dropping into darkness below, rising to heavy, overcast skies above. I looked up into the swirling gray darkness, and I couldn't see the summit of the mountain.

I remember this place, I thought, wrapping my arms around my chest. *After my exams, when we drank Óðinn's mead together.*

"Oh, come on," I yelled into the heavy skies. "You couldn't just take me to Vígríðr? I have to climb this fucking mountain again?"

My voice echoed off the rocks, and I shivered. *Maybe*

this is close enough, I thought. *Maybe Geoff can just cut the branch here.* An echoing, hungry howl rose from the trees somewhere behind me and I jumped, slipping on the rocks. I caught myself on my hands and knees and stood again, trying to stop shaking.

"Come on, Caroline," I muttered. "This isn't really the kind of thing where you can just do 'close enough.'"

I started climbing, scrambling up the rocks on my hands and knees when the pitches grew steep. The trees fell away quickly, and the rocks were soon covered with a thick, ashy layer of hoarfrost. I was soon shivering so violently that my movements became clumsy, uncoordinated.

"Had to wear a goddamn dress," I muttered, stopping to lean against a boulder and trying to rub some heat back into my arms. "You had to wear a goddamn sexy dress."

I looked down, concentrating on the rocks in front of me. *One step at a time,* I thought, falling into a slow, careful rhythm. Climb. Rest. Climb. Rest. And then my foot slipped and I fell, sliding down the rock face until my kneecap stopped me. White stars exploded across my vision and I screamed, rocking back against the mountain, my hands wrapped around my leg. I took a deep, hissing breath and pulled my hands away from my knee. They were bloody.

"Shit," I said. "Shit. Don't be broken."

I slowly flexed my knee. It hurt; I heard my heart pounding in my ears, and I felt dizzy. But it worked. My knee still worked. I reached down and pulled off my stupid black high heels.

"Worst shoes ever," I muttered, throwing them down the mountain. They seemed to bounce for a long time before being swallowed by the dark forest far below.

I closed my eyes and wiped grimy tears off my cheeks. "Boots," I told the mountain. "If I survive this, I'm going to buy myself a nice, sturdy pair of hiking boots."

Then I looked up. The mountaintop seemed no closer, and my chest felt tight. I took a few deep, gasping breaths of the cold, smoke-filled air, but they made me cough so violently I gagged, pressing my body against the jagged granite boulder as my shoulders shook.

What if I can't do this?

I thought of the last time I'd seen baby Devi, asleep in her rocking swing under the lemon tree in my brother's backyard. Of Mom and Dad. Of my friends in Chicago, Debra, Steve. Would Ragnarök destroy them instantly? Or would the sky open slowly, pouring Surtr's flames across Chicago as the wolf Skoll devours the sun? Would they have time to cower in fear, to run for shelter as the earth began to tremble under their feet?

My shoulders heaved and trembled, and my head spun in the thin, freezing air. My knee throbbed as my fingers dug into the rocks, and I wedged my body into a crack between the boulders. I closed my eyes, leaned my forehead against the rocks, and tried to think of nothing at all.

Loki. I smiled, remembering his eyes, his lips.

"Happy Valentine's Day," I whispered to the darkness.

Was it just yesterday he'd surprised me in Medici? Just yesterday we'd walked together in the freezing cold of Promontory Point, and then come together on my bed, destroying the sheets, clinging to each other? My fingers curled around the pendant between my breasts, and my heart clenched. *I wish we could be together,* I thought. *I wish we could be together at the end of the world.* I remembered his face in the dim, blue glow of my alarm clock. Loki Laufeyiarson of the Æsir, asleep in my bed. His high cheekbones. The gentle curve of his soft, scarred lips.

I opened my eyes, blinking in the smoky air.

"No," I said. "No. I will not let you die in Vígríðr, Loki of the Æsir."

I pulled myself out of the crack in the rocks and stared at the mountaintop. It looked no closer. I swallowed hard against the rising panic in my chest, and I kept climbing.

* * * * * * *

I heard the heavy beating of giant wings a moment before I saw two huge shadows on the rocks. Hugin and Munin. Thought and Memory. Óðinn's ravens.

"Hello, boys," I panted, not looking up from the rock face. "Here to lend a hand?"

Their feathers ruffled in the wind as they landed on either side of me. I ignored them.

"Well, this looks like fun," Hugin cawed.

I laughed, and it turned into a cough. I had to stop, gripping the rocks, as my shoulders heaved and my lungs fought the smoky air. "Thanks," I finally wheezed. "Your insight is invaluable, Hugin."

"And you should have taken the deal when you had a chance," he said, cocking his head as he stared at me.

"Oh, fuck you," I said, pulling myself up the next rock.

And then my entire body shivered, like I was pushing through a curtain of cold water, and I was back in the Slyndennär Inn, wrapped in Hæmir's strong arms. "Lovely Carol," he said, his breath warm on my neck. "You are not alone now."

"Stop it!" I said. I bit the inside of my cheek, dug my fingers hard into the cold rock. Still I could hear Hæmir's voice echoing in my head. *Lovely Carol...*

"Fuck you, too." I glared at Munin. He looked at me with impassive, black eyes. "Get out of my mind, Memory," I said, shaking my head.

The motion made me dizzy, and I slipped on my frozen toes, twisting my ankle in a blinding shock of pain. I screamed as the rocks rushed up to meet me.

My face felt frozen and numb against the frost-covered granite. A giant raven sat above me, regarding me with shiny black eyes. *Hugin,* I thought, blinking. *It's Hugin. Thought.*

"Can't go on," he cawed. "Don't worry. I'll eat your eyes." He hopped closer to my face, lowering his sharp, black beak.

My heart surged with fear, and I scrambled to my knees. My ankle howled in pain as I pulled myself to my feet. "Listen, Hugin," I growled. "I will crawl up this goddamn mountain if I have to."

I took a deep breath, then pulled myself up and around the closest boulder. *There,* I thought. *Just do that ten million more times and you'll be at the top.* The ravens followed, hopping and landing just out of reach above me.

"You can tell Óðinn," I panted. "You tell him I'm not stopping."

I heard the heavy beating of their wings as they both left the mountainside. I watched them go, my cheek resting against the cool rocks. Then I turned back to the mountain and kept climbing.

Both ravens were waiting when I finally dragged myself to the small, flat clearing at the summit. My ankle throbbed, and it was increasingly difficult to breathe in the cold, thin air. "Hugin," I panted, nodding to the ravens. "Munin."

They said nothing as I turned to look across Vígríðr.

The battlefield spread for miles below me. And it was ready. It was *hungry.* The pennants of the Æsir waved in the gloom, their tents spreading to the horizon. I heard the clash of metal as the armies sparred below me. One final practice. *Hidy,* I though. *Hidy is down there. Hidy and Frank and Phil. Óðinn and Thor and Týr and Heimdallr.*

Tears bit at my eyes again and I turned to the horizon. There, in the distance, was the gleam of light on water. An ocean, perhaps. And in the middle of the water, pressed against the shore, was a strange block of a mountain.

No, I thought, with a shiver. *Not a mountain.*

My ship, Hæmir said. The Naglfar. Carrying the armies of the Jötunn with the armies of the inglorious dead from Niflhel.

"Hæmir," I whispered.

My heart clenched painfully in my chest, and I almost screamed. *If only there was something I could do,* I thought, frantically. *If only I could talk some sense into them –*

CAW!

I jumped as Hugin landed next to me. "Not that it's any of my business," he croaked, "but if you're going to do something, best do it soon."

I nodded. "Hæmir," I sighed, shaking my head. "Hæmir, you great, fucking idiot. You wanted this. You wanted to be down there."

You'll die down there, I thought, although I could not bring myself to say it. *But Loki won't, goddamn it.*

Loki will not die in Vígríðr.

I tried to stand, felt a hot stab of pain in my ankle, and sat down again on the cold, broken rocks. Below me, far below me, a horn sounded. The sound built and built, until I was shaking with the reverberations, shaking on the top of a broken stone mountain above Vígríðr. Shaking with my hands on the World Tree.

Heimdallr's horn. The Gjallarhorn.

The horn's last notes faded. Ragnarök began with the sound of thundering hooves as the armies of Val-Hall rode to meet the armies of the Jötunn. The mountain trembled with clashing metal.

I closed my eyes and took a deep breath, ignoring the ravens, ignoring the battlefield. Ignoring the screaming. I reached for Geoff and Loki, and I *pulled* myself through the cold between the worlds. I pulled myself back, back to my brother and my lover.

Back to Yggdrasil, to the trunk of the great World Tree.

* * * * * * * *

I felt heat first, a rush of heat along my face and arms. Then I felt Geoff's hand on my shoulder. "Here!" I yelled.

I opened my eyes and turned to face him. We stood in front of a tree branch so huge it was more like a wall, the curve of the trunk almost invisible behind the branch. Sparks rained down on us, burning holes in my clothes, burning holes in my skin.

What the hell are we thinking? My vision began to blur, and I blinked back tears as the sparks seared their way across my arms. The air had a violent, acrid smell that was somehow familiar. *My hair,* I thought, dimly. *My hair is on fire.*

"Can we really do this?" I yelled, my voice hardly audible over the roar of the flames.

"Course," Geoff said. "I'm a professional."

His hand left my shoulder as he raised the saw. Di's golden hair shimmered in the angry red light. Then the blade of Aphrodite's hair met the bark of Yggdrasil and the world exploded.

CHAPTER FORTY-FOUR

I was very cold. So cold it hurt. So cold I wanted nothing more than to just fall back asleep, back into oblivion. But somewhere there was an alarm, a high, loud cry going on and on and on. *Air raid siren,* I thought. *But that's impossible, because I'm -* I forced my eyes open. My ankle throbbed with a dull, red pain. Heavy storm clouds bore down on me. The freezing wind smelled of the ocean; salt water and cold.

Where am I?

I tried to move but my body refused. Someone moaned, deep and low, close to me. I blinked, took a deep breath, and tried again to turn my head. My ear grated against stone. My brother lay next to me, his body curled tight, moaning in pain. But my brother has blonde hair, almost white from the sun. And this brother's hair was burned black. And his face was black, black with ashes and blood, not like Geoff, not like my handsome brother.

I tried to reach Geoff-not-Geoff, this whimpering,

moaning creature, but I couldn't make my hands work. I thrashed my head in frustration and saw Loki. His skin was pale, so pale I could almost see through it. No, I could see through it - I could see through him to the lichen and grass and rocks beyond.

He was not breathing.

Adrenaline stabbed through my body, forcing my arms to work. It took all my concentration to drag my hand, slowly, across the black and broken stones. Finally I felt Loki's cool fingers, and I grabbed them.

"Don't you...*dare*...go to Vígríðr," I whispered, my voice rough in my frozen throat. Loki's hand twitched against mine, and I could no longer keep my eyes open.

* * * * * * * *

"Hello?"

There was a voice, now. A voice yelling over the air-raid siren. I tried to ignore it, all of it. The sirens. The voice. *Rest,* I thought. *Just let me rest.*

"Hello!"

I've heard that voice before. I tried again to find the blackness of sleep, but the siren and the voice and the throbbing in my ankle made it impossible.

"Hello? Hæmir?"

Annajär. Hæmir's graduate student. *But that's impossible.*

I struggled to move my arms, pushing myself off the ground. The siren was still wailing. I forced my eyes open and saw the back of a squat, stone church in the fading light. It was dusk, dusk over the ocean, over a beautiful little town of whitewashed stone houses sheltered by rocky cliffs.

I know this place. Lokisfen.

I was sitting in the remains of Loki's sacred grove. In Iceland. I turned to see my brother, curled in on himself and trembling violently, his face and arms horribly red and black. My fingers were still wrapped around Loki's hand. It was cold, very cold, and he was not breathing.

"Help." I tried to scream, but it came out a wracked whisper.

Panic flooded my body, and my heart started hammering.

"Help!" I tried again, but it was barely louder than a whisper. I could hardly hear myself over the wailing siren.

I heard a shout behind me and then footsteps, running footsteps, and Annajär suddenly knelt in front of me. *She's wearing lipstick*, I thought. *And a dress.* She looked very beautiful, and very young.

"Carol?"

Then she saw Geoff, and her eyes widened as I heard what could only be a long string of Icelandic curse words. She took off her coat and began to wrap it around Geoff, her eyes wild and afraid. I opened my mouth to explain, and the earth shook.

Yggdrasil trembles, I thought. *Yggdrasil trembles, and there is no one in the Nine Realms who is unafraid.*

Next to me, Loki gasped for breath.

* * * * * * * *

Once the earthquake subsided, Annajär and I dragged Geoff to his feet and pulled him toward her dark blue Skoda. He screamed in pain every time we moved, every time we brushed his body. It wasn't until Geoff was in the passenger seat of Annajär's Skoda, semi-conscious and moaning, that I noticed something was wrong with the ocean. The sheltered little harbor was different, the water flat in the fading light. The brightly colored fishing boats seemed very low, and very far away. Some of them were even listing to their sides, caught on something. Caught on the bottom of the harbor. *But I shouldn't be able to see the bottom of the harbor,* I thought, a sick feeling growing in my stomach.

And then I saw the black wall of water in the North Sea. It was moving. Quickly.

Annajär and I stood next to her Skoda in Loki's sacred grove and watched as the tidal wave slam into the town of Lokisfen. *The siren,* I realized numbly. *It was a warning.*

The black water tossed and shattered the fishing boats, devouring the docks. The first rows of whitewashed houses simply disappeared. The water covered the village green, lapping greedily against the second story windows of the outer rings of houses. Cars floated and bobbed in the tumultuous darkness, their alarms howling above the air raid siren. I heard a woman screaming, and I gradually realized it was Annajär.

Loki, I told myself. *I have to get Loki. We have to get to a hospital.*

I turned to Annajär. She was staring at the swirling mess of dark water that used to be the village of Lokisfen. And she was screaming. I grabbed her face with both my hands.

"We need... to get... to the hospital," I rasped. My cold, dirty hands left black smudges on her cheeks.

She nodded, tears leaking from her eyes. "Hæmir told me to be here," she said, her voice dazed. "He told me to meet him here. Today."

"Good," I said, the words tearing at my throat, my ankle burning with pain. "We need... to get..." I turned to Loki, gesturing with my hands. "Him... to the car."

For one terrifying second I was afraid Annajär wouldn't be able to see Loki, but then she nodded and walked toward him. I limped after her, gritting my teeth as I dragged my ankle behind me. Loki lay motionless on the grass of his sacred grove. He was breathing, barely, but he still seemed transparent and unreal. When I wrapped my arms around him, he weighed almost nothing.

"Stay with me," I whispered, my lips against his ear. "Don't you dare leave me now."

If Annajär heard me, she gave no indication. We lifted Loki, just as we'd lifted Geoff, and we dragged him together. Hot tears made their way down my cheeks as I forced my shattered ankle to keep working. I pulled Loki into the back seat, relieved to hear Geoff still moaning in the front.

Annajär stood in the gathering darkness outside her car, trembling violently in her colorful, flattering dress. "Hæmir said to meet him here," she said, her voice soft and dreamy and distant.

Hæmir.

If Loki is here, the wards around Iceland have been abandoned, I thought. The one keeping him out must be gone. Hæmir must now be Hyrm, leading the armies of the Jötunn to their glorious deaths on the fields of Vígríðr.

I took Annajär's face in my hands. "Hæmir... was just here," I lied. "He's gone... back to Reykjavik. I need you..." The world began to grow dim and I had to stop, resting my head against her shoulder.

"I need you to go to Hæmir," I said. "You need to

drive to Hæmir. In Reykjavik. Can you do that?"

She nodded, her blue eyes full of tears. "I can drive to Hæmir," she said.

"Good." I climbed into the back seat of her Skoda and the world went black.

* * * * * * *

I woke in the darkness to the sound of a woman singing. I blinked and pushed myself to sitting. It was very dark in Annajär's car, and it smelled of smoke and blood. An unbroken line of taillights stretched before us. It looked like they were not moving.

I listened. My brother was still breathing, although his breath sounded shallow and labored. My fingers were intertwined with Loki's and, when I put my hand to his chest, I felt his breastbone rising and falling. Barely. I squeezed his hand and felt his fingers twitch against mine.

"Annajär?" I said, hesitantly.

She stopped singing. "Oh, hello, Carol."

Her voice was disconcertingly cheerful. I wondered if she was in shock. Or perhaps she'd lost her mind; perhaps the sight of the tidal wave destroying Lokisfen had left her completely unmoored from reality. *Doesn't matter,* I thought, gritting my teeth, *as long as she gets us to the goddamn hospital.*

"Where are we?" I asked.

"We're not far now," she said. "So many people!" In the dim light of the dashboard I saw her brow furrow, and I thought I'd better change the subject.

"Thank you," I said. "Hæmir will be glad you helped us."

"Yes," she said, nodding. "I'm doing what Hæmir asked."

"You're a good friend," I said as the black edges of the world started closing in again.

"I am Hæmir's friend," she said, and then she began to sing again, softly, in Icelandic.

CHAPTER FORTY-FIVE

Reykjavik was a disaster of blaring sirens and flashing lights; the roads were almost impassible. It looked like the hospital was doing triage on the sidewalk where Annajär parked her Skoda and opened the doors. Geoff was able to limp out of the car, following my voice. Loki was still unconscious, but he felt reassuringly heavy in my arms.

"Thank you," I told Annajär, holding her pale hand in mine. "You saved our lives."

"I'll tell Hæmir you are here," she said.

I watched her car drive away, the tail lights flickering. The sidewalk was cold against my bare legs. I drifted in and out of consciousness as my body slowly went numb, and I stared at the distant stars in the dark sky, holding Geoff with one hand, holding Loki with the other. Sirens howled in the distance. The night air smelled of smoke.

Someone shook my shoulder. I turned to see a young nurse with violently dark circles under her eyes. She spoke again, but I couldn't understand her. I shook my head and realized she was speaking Icelandic. And expecting an answer. I dug in my pocket and was surprised to find my wallet and cell phone. I handed her my California driver's license with shaking fingers. *Caroline Laufeyiarson.*

"My brother," I said, my voice rasping. "He's burned. He needs help."

I pointed to Geoff, and the nurse stood, waving her arms. Two young men brought a stretcher, and my brother moaned as they wrapped him in a gray blanket and rolled him onto the stretcher.

"Name?" the nurse asked me.

I stared at her. She gestured toward Geoff, who was being carried through the doors of the Reykjavik hospital. Then she waved a clipboard at me. I tried to hold my hand still long enough to write GEOFF CAPELLO. I noticed with detached interest my arms were covered with angry, red burns. The nurse vanished after the stretcher, and Loki and I were alone on the cold sidewalk, surrounded by the injured. I lay down, wrapped my arms around him, and closed my eyes.

* * * * * * *

Gradually I realized someone was talking to me, his voice a rambling mixture of English and Icelandic. I opened my eyes. The sky above Reykjavik was streaked with pink and filled with dark, spinning sparks. I blinked, rose to my elbows, and realized they weren't sparks. They were birds. The sky was filled with birds, hundreds and hundreds of birds, their undulating murmurations stretched across the dawn.

Loki was curled on his side next to me. I moved my hand to his chest and felt the faint thudding vibration of his heart, the rise and fall of his breathing. Then I turned toward the voice and realized an old man had joined us in the night. The right side of his face was covered with dried blood.

"Never, never, never," he said, shaking his head. "Never anything like that."

Then he turned and looked directly at me, his single blue eye dancing. "Thought it was Ragnarök for sure this time."

"I think it almost was," I said, my voice trembling.

The old man laughed and continued in Icelandic, his voice so thick and fast I couldn't follow his words. He was interrupted by a tall nurse with a dark, spreading stain across the front of his uniform. I hoped it was coffee.

"Name?" he asked, pointing at me.

"Caroline Laufeyiarson," I said, without thinking.

"And what is problem?"

"I think I broke my ankle," I said. Then I glanced at

my blacked, blood-streaked arms. "And burns," I added.

The nurse made a note on his chart. "And your husband?"

"Fine," Loki said from behind me. He did not sound fine. He lifted himself on his arm, wincing. "Please. Her first."

The nurse nodded, made a note on his chart, and began talking to the man next to us. Loki collapsed against my shoulder, his head resting on my neck. He whispered something that might have been "alive." Or it might have been "love."

* * * * * * * *

After ten hours on the sidewalk, my ankle was reset and put in a cast, and the burns on my arms and shoulders were cleaned and bandaged. I thought the doctor might say something; something about my recovery time, about whether or not I would be able to run again. Something about how, exactly, Caroline Laufeyiarson of Chicago came to be in Lokisfen with a broken ankle and red, angry burns along her arms and shoulders, just in time for the earthquake and the tidal wave.

But the doctor said nothing. He was older, his dark hair streaked with silver; like everyone else in the hospital, it looked like it had been days since he last slept. His face was grim as he warned me, in slow and articulate Icelandic, that setting my ankle would hurt.

It did hurt, and I screamed. But it was over quickly, and then he wrapped my ankle in a cast, silently and efficiently. I was given a single crutch and a tube of antibiotic ointment for the burns, and the doctor moved on to the next casualty.

"I am sorry," said the nurse, as she helped me balance on the crutch. "We need this room as soon as possible."

I limped into the hallway and fished my cell phone out of my pocket to try dialing Di again. I got the same strange error message I'd gotten all morning: "All circuits are currently in use. Please try again later. All circuits are currently in use. Please try again later." I sighed, shoved the useless phone back in my pocket, and hobbled through the chaos of the Reykjavik hospital. I tried not to look at the injured bodies jamming the hallway, but I could not shut out the sound of their moaning, their crying.

Yggdrasil trembled, I thought. *Were we too late?*

I finally found Geoff on a bed in one of the long, white hallways, his torso and face wrapped in gauze, his arm connected to an IV. His eyes flickered when he saw me.

"Did it work?" he whispered. I could barely hear him over the hum and buzz of equipment.

"It worked," I said. "Yggdrasil shook, but she held."

He closed his eyes, and I reached for his hand. "You

were very brave," I whispered as his chest began to rise and fall in sleep.

"Your brother?"

I turned to see a nurse standing behind me. She was young and tall, her blonde hair piled above her head in an efficient bun. I nodded at her, trying to keep the tears in my eyes.

"He'll be fine. He's very strong," she said, giving my shoulder a sympathetic squeeze.

"Yes," I said, blinking furiously. "He is."

* * * * * * * *

The sky was a deep, rich velvet outside the hospital windows by the time I found my way back to the overflowing waiting room. The television screens had all been dark or filled with static this morning, but now they were flooded with images of devastation. There was shaky cell phone footage of the tidal wave that destroyed Lokisfen. There was a dark chasm in Reykjavik, near the airport. There were fires in Paris. I saw a flickering image, over and over, of Big Ben listing dangerously toward the Thames.

Loki was wrapped in a hospital blanket, shivering violently. He gave me a weak smile as I grabbed his cold hands. "Still here," he whispered.

"Me too," I said, trying to force my lips to smile for

him.

I held Loki until his shivering stopped and he fell back into an uneasy sleep, his head leaning against the wall, his body hunched in the waiting room chair. Then I stood and hobbled to the sidewalk to try my cell phone again. To my great surprise, it worked.

Di's voice was clear and strong. "You succeeded," she said, before I could speak.

"We were too late," I said, my voice trembling. "The earthquakes - there are so many people in the hospital. People have died!"

Di's voice was suddenly deep and resonant with authority. "Caroline. You prevented the destruction of the entire world. Of all worlds."

We both fell silent. The phone shivered in my cold hands. Already, I noticed, the air above Reykjavik was clear. I could no longer smell smoke.

"Mom and Dad...?" I asked.

"Fine," said Di. "And their house stands, as does ours. I've told them Geoff was injured extinguishing the fires from the natural gas rupture."

"How did you...?" I stammered. "We're in -"

"Iceland," she said. "When he wakes, please tell my husband it is not his face I love."

Then the line went dead, and I struggled on my crutches through the hospital doors. When I made it back to the waiting room, Annajär was sitting next to

Loki.

"You need a place to stay," she said. It was not a question. "Come. You can stay at Hæmir's."

"I can't leave my brother," I said.

"Is very close," she said, her face impassive. "You can be here every day. Come, I drive you."

Loki put his arm around Annajär's shoulders, and I followed. Hæmir's apartment was only two blocks from the hospital. Annajär let us in, and I did not comment on the fact that she had the key to his apartment on the same ring as her car keys. His apartment was smaller than I'd expected, and sparsely furnished. *But then,* I thought, *this was never his real home.*

"There's food in the fridge," she said. "But we lost the power. It may not be good." She paused. "I'll check back tomorrow."

"Thank you," I said, leaning awkwardly in the doorway, trying to keep the weight off my cast.

"Don't thank me," she said, stiffly. "It's what Hæmir asked me to do. He left a note - If Carol shows up, give her shelter."

I sighed. My head was swimming, and there seemed to be nothing I could say. I looked over my shoulder. Loki had already disappeared into the bedroom.

"Carol?"

I turned back to Annajär. Her face was suddenly very pale, her blue eyes huge in her beautiful face. *Poor*

Annajär, I thought. *Visited by the Jötunn Hyrm.*

"Will he come back?" she asked. "Hæmir? Is he coming back?"

No, I thought. *He'll die on the fields of Vígríðr. As he wanted.*

"Perhaps," I said.

She closed the door gently behind her. I lay down next to Loki and slept while the world began to rebuild itself outside Hæmir's apartment.

CHAPTER FORTY-SIX

Geoff was scheduled to be released one week after we were admitted to the hospital. I visited him every morning, wearing the baggy men's clothes I'd pulled out of Hæmir's closet and slowly getting more competent hobbling on my single crutch.

My arms itched and my ankle ached and throbbed. The nurses at the hospital said they were very sorry, but they could not spare painkillers for something as minor as a broken ankle. I'd used all of Hæmir's aspirin within two days, and the corner grocery store said they had no idea when they'd have more of anything, let alone painkillers. I changed the white bandages wrapped around my arms every morning and every evening. By the second day the burns had faded to a pale pink, and I decided I could probably ditch the antibiotic ointment and the bandages.

I spent most of my time lying on Hæmir's bed, my ankle propped on pillows, watching Loki breathe. He slept for two full days, his face pale, his scars livid. I did not dare touch him or try to wake him, but I traced the patterns of his scars with my eyes. *I love you,* I thought, not quite daring to say the words aloud. *I love you.*

I was staring at him when his scars faded and his eyes opened. He smiled at me.

"Your ankle?" he whispered.

I tried to laugh, but it came out a strangled sob. "Don't worry about my ankle! You've been unconscious for days. Are you - " My throat tightened, and my voice faded. I grabbed his hand and held it tight.

"You saved the Nine Realms," he said, his voice rough, barely more than a whisper.

"Not exactly by myself," I said, bringing his hand to my lips. I kissed his fingers gently, my heart an aching knot in my chest.

His eyes closed and his lips curled into a smile.

"You brought us back, didn't you?" I said. "You pulled us from Yggdrasil to here."

He laughed. It sounded like the effort hurt him. "Honestly, I didn't think it would work. I got lucky. The wards were gone, so I could reach the one place in Midgard that once belonged to me." Then his eyes opened once more, and he smiled at me. "I would kiss the mortal who saved Yggdrasil," he said.

"You saved me," I said, running my hand along his cheek.

I leaned toward him, closing the distance between us,

bringing my lips to his. Electricity surged through my body as our lips touched, and I couldn't believe how much I'd missed this, how much I'd missed him, missed the feeling of my body coming alive under his touch, his soft lips, his cool fingers. I sighed into his mouth, hungry for him. I felt his heartbeat quicken under my hand, but I pulled away, afraid of asking too much from him.

"Are you okay?" I whispered.

"I'm alive," he said. "I'm alive when I should be dead, and I'm with you when the world should have ended. Yes. Yes, I'm okay."

I kissed him again, hungrily, pressing my body to his until I was straddling him, my hands running over his chest. I kissed him until I forgot about the dull throb of my ankle, until my body filled with his heat and my breath caught in my throat. His head tilted back, and I caught his lower lip, gently, with my teeth. His lips smiled against mine. I released him and leaned back.

"I really want you," I whispered, rocking my hips against the heat of his erection. I pulled off Hæmir's huge turtleneck and flung it to the floor. But when I looked down, Loki's face had turned pale. "If you're, uh, up for it," I said, and I stopped grinding into his hips.

"Your arms," he said. "Oh, Caroline."

I froze. *The burns,* I thought. *I don't look... I don't look good anymore.*

"They're not so bad," I said, but my voice trembled and I felt cold. I watched Loki's graceful fingertips trace the tight, pink skin along my wrists, the dozens of coin-shaped burns from the sparks, the angry, snaking lines along my biceps where I'd yanked my arms out of Yggdrasil's bark.

"I mean, I can always wear long sleeves, right?" I said as my eyes filled with tears, and I turned to stare at the far wall.

Loki laughed. I blinked and turned to face him. He was naked; no clothes and no illusions. Thick, angry scars crossed his chest, his lips. His arms.

"They're nothing at all," he said.

And then he reached for my head, pulling my mouth to his. He kissed me fiercely, his lips hard against mine, his tongue deep inside me. I shivered as his hips moved under me, his cock pressing against the seam of the jeans I wore.

"I desire you," he growled as we pulled apart, my body flushed with his heat. "Did you really think your *arms* would change that?"

For the second time that afternoon, I found myself blinking back tears. "I love you," I whispered.

"Of course you do," he said. "Now take off those atrocious pants."

I rolled onto my back and did what the Trickster God of Asgard suggested. It was a bit awkward, and not especially sexy, to pull Hæmir's baggy pants over the cast, but Loki watched me with hungry eyes, devouring my body as if pulling oversized men's jeans past an ankle cast was the world's hottest strip tease. By the time I'd finally kicked off my underwear, I was so wet and ready for him I was aching.

"How do you do that?" I said, my voice thick. "How can you make me so goddamn hot without even touching me?"

He shrugged and rolled to face me, revealing the full length of his arousal. "You think you don't do the same to me? Now get over here. Let's enjoy being alive when we should be dead."

I straddled him again, taking him into me, gasping with pleasure as my skin shivered under his touch. I tried to slow my hips, tried to savor the feel of his body rolling under mine, but I couldn't hold back for long. I'd missed him too much; I'd spent too many hours staring at his still, sleeping face, wondering when he would wake. If he would wake.

I tilted my head back and abandoned myself, taking everything I could from his body, from his hips, from his mouth and hands. I rode him with a wild, fierce hunger, demanding everything, holding nothing back.

I came over and over, collapsing against his cool chest, catching my breath as his hips moved slowly against mine, only to find that I wanted him again, wanted more and more of him. His hands tightened around my waist as he moved against me, controlling himself, bringing me over the edge again and again until we were both slick with sweat and trembling, my body spent but still craving him. When he finally came inside me he cried out, his voice echoing around the room, his hips lifting me off the bed.

We collapsed across the rumpled sheets, arms and legs tangled together, breathless, hearts racing. Loki closed his eyes and was silent for so long I thought he'd fallen back asleep. But when I moved to reach for the blanket his eyes opened, and he kissed me softly on my forehead. I pulled the blanket over both of us and nestled against his body, my head resting on his chest.

Loki sighed as he ran his fingertips along my forearm, gently tracing the new scars. "I should have protected you," he whispered.

I tried to laugh, but it caught in my throat. "I should have protected *everyone*," I said. "I was... I was slow, climbing the mountain. Finding Vígríðr. I was too slow."

He stopped my words with a long, sweet kiss. "Shhhhh, Caroline," he said as we pulled apart. "Yggdrasil stands because of you, mortal woman."

I shook my head against his arm. "But the earthquakes, the tsunami. Loki - "

He pressed his finger to my lips. "Quiet. You did not

cause this."

I sighed and closed my eyes, breathing him in. "They're calling it the Quakes," I said. "I saw it at the hospital: 'An unprecedented cataclysmic global seismic event.' It's the only thing on the news."

"I love you," Loki said, moving his head to kiss my hair. "And now, please. Shut up."

I smiled against his chest. For the second time that afternoon, I did what the Trickster God of Asgard suggested.

* * * * * * *

I jolted out of sleep, blinking in the darkness. There was a sound - knocking? Yes, there it was again. Someone was knocking on the door. Loudly. I tried to untangle myself from Loki's long arms without waking him. He shifted slightly in his sleep, then sighed, and I smiled at him. His long hair lay tangled across his face, and I was tempted to pull it back, to bend over him and wake him by kissing the scars across those soft lips -

Knocking. Again. I sighed and slipped out of bed, feeling in the darkness for the jeans and turtleneck I'd been wearing. I tried to pull them on as I hopped toward the front door.

"Coming," I called, after I closed the bedroom door behind me. "I'm coming."

The knocking stopped. I looked down, made sure I'd zipped up the jeans. *Okay, good.* I reached for the crutch I'd propped against the bedroom door and made my way across Hæmir's small living room.

It was Annajär. She looked a bit more composed, or perhaps just better rested. Her arms were heavy with grocery bags. She gave me a curt nod, and then she noticed what I was wearing. A shadow crossed her pretty face.

"I'm sorry," I said. "My clothes were basically destroyed. I didn't know what else to -"

"Is no problem," she said, her cheeks flushing. "I brought you some clothes. Also some food. You are hungry, no?"

My stomach clenched at the mention of food. "Yeah, I am," I said. "Please, come in."

Annajär handed me a loaf of bread and some cheese as she put away the groceries. She knew where everything went, I noticed, and I wondered again exactly how close she'd been to Hæmir. *Close enough,* I thought, my heart clenching painfully. *Close enough to miss him.*

"And how is your... friend?" she asked, glancing toward the closed bedroom door.

"Oh, he's great," I said, with a sigh. Then I caught myself and shook my head. "I mean, he's recovering. Nicely."

"And your brother?"

I put down the hunk of bread I'd been devouring. "He's doing well, too. I think. But they haven't taken off the bandages yet, and I - I don't know what's under there."

Annajär put her hand over mine. "Your brother is what's under there," she said, smiling. "Just your brother."

Then she put a plate in front of me, and a glass of wine, and we had dinner together in Hæmir's apartment. Like friends.

CHAPTER FORTY-SEVEN

I stood in Geoff's hospital room on the day he was released. I held his hand while the doctor slowly removed the last of his facial bandages.

"I am sorry," Doctor Kjærstad said. "The facial scarring was extensive."

"Di says it's not your face she loves," I told Geoff for the hundredth time, my voice trembling as I squeezed his hand.

In the years to come, my brother would tell people his scars matched the flames of the fire he'd fought. Di said they looked like fireworks, or a map. Baby Devi would come to know that pattern of scars as the face of her father, nothing more, nothing less.

But I always saw only one thing when I looked at Geoff's face. Yggdrasil. My brother had the World Tree burned across his cheeks, on his lips and nose and forehead. Every branch, every root, in twisted, taut red and white across his handsome California tan.

"How bad it is, sis?" he asked, his voice slightly

slurred as he moved lips that had been twisted into unfamiliar shapes.

"You look like a warrior," I said.

Dr. Kjærstad looked tired as he handed Geoff a large mirror with a pink plastic handle. Geoff held the mirror to his face, examining himself for a long time, touching the scar tissue around his eyes and across his cheeks. Then he turned to me and twisted his battered lips into a smile.

"Like a warrior," he said.

I stood outside the thin, pale green curtain dividing Geoff's hospital room while he pulled on the jeans and T-shirt I'd brought from Hæmir's closet. And then I handed him my phone so he could call Di.

"Hey, honey," I heard him say through the curtain. "So it's, uh, it's pretty bad."

I decided I didn't want to hear any more of my brother's conversation with his wife, and I went for a hobbling walk through the endless, white halls of the hospital, my heart aching; the scars on my arms were nothing compared to his face.

Geoff's room was silent when I returned. I could see his silhouette through the curtain. His head was in his hands.

"Everything okay?" I asked through the curtain.

The hospital sheets rustled as he stood. "I'm fine," he said, pulling back the curtain and handing me my phone. His eyes were red. "And everything is good back home."

I nodded, not wanting to push him. "You ready to go?"

"Yup," he said. "And, hey, whose pants am I wearing?"

I shifted uncomfortably. "Uh, that's kind of a long story."

The limbs of Yggdrasil twisted around Geoff's cheeks as he smiled. "So. What happens now?"

I shrugged. "We go home. We fly out tomorrow. You've got a ticket to San Diego."

Now he looked impressed, raising what was left of his eyebrows. "You got plane tickets? I thought half the Reykjavik airport was destroyed by the Quakes?"

I smiled and shrugged again. "It wasn't a problem."

I'd spent almost two full hours on the phone, arguing with every single person at every single airline I contacted. The woman at United actually yelled at me. "Haven't you heard of the Quakes?" she said. "You're not going anywhere."

When I was ready to cry at the thought of missing my dissertation defense, Loki opened the front door and walked to me, kissing my neck and handing me three white rectangles of paper. Airplane tickets. First class. For Geoff Capello to San Diego, and for Caroline and Lucas Laufeyiarson to Chicago

"Nice," Geoff said, patting me on the shoulder. "I'm impressed, sis."

The receptionist behind the front desk of the hospital was smiling, although she looked ready to fall asleep on her feet, and she spoke perfect English as she walked Geoff through the signing-out process. Her brilliant blue eyes kept drifting up to the scars across his lips and forehead. I hoped he didn't notice.

Geoff took my arm as we left the hospital. "And your, umm... Your friend? Loki?"

I laughed and squeezed his arm. "He's fine. He's at the apartment." I smiled. "He's making dinner."

* * * * * * * *

Hæmir's apartment smelled amazing when I pushed open the door. Loki smiled at us from the kitchen, where he was opening a wine bottle.

"I have to apologize," he said, wiping his hands on a towel. "The options in the store were quite limited."

He walked toward us and then stopped, bowing low before Geoff. "You saved the Nine Realms," he said, his voice resonant and formal. "I am indebted to you, Geoff Capello of Midgard."

Geoff looked slightly uncomfortable. "Uh, yeah. Don't mention it," he said, running his fingers through his hair. "So, what's for dinner?"

Loki smiled. "The best I could manage," he said.

It was fantastic, of course. He'd made a curry out of canned chicken, bananas, rice, and coconut milk. Annajär joined us just as we sat down to eat, carrying an enormous bottle of brennivín in a cheerful yellow shopping bag. She embraced Geoff with both arms, standing on her toes to kiss his scarred cheeks.

"I was so afraid for you," she said, holding his shoulders. "I am so happy to see you!"

He shrugged. "Happy to see you, too," he said. "Thanks for saving my life."

She put down the bottle of brennivín and went to Hæmir's kitchen, bringing back four tumblers. "Now," she said, "you leave Iceland tomorrow. And so, you must drink brennivín tonight. It's tradition."

Loki made a face as Annajär poured four very full glasses. "Brennivín is one of the foulest drinks in the Nine Realms," he said.

Annajär frowned at him. "I saved your life," she said. "You drink."

She raised her glass, and we all followed suit, knocking back huge slugs of the oily anise-flavored liquor. Geoff and I both coughed, and Annajär laughed.

"Ugh, it's as bad as I remember," I said. My eyes were watering.

"Oh, keep going," said Annajär, cheerfully. "It gets better."

I took another sip and decided she might be right. It did seem to burn a little less the second time.

And by the time we finished the bottle, sitting together in Hæmir's living room and all laughing hysterically, I'd decided Loki was wrong. Brennivín was *awesome*.

* * * * * * *

I woke to someone shaking my shoulder. I raised a hand to push them away, and soft fingers caught my wrist. Cool fingers.

"We do have a plane to catch," Loki whispered.

I opened my eyes, squinting against the sunlight streaming through the blinds. I didn't remember coming to bed, and it looked like I'd slept on top of the covers. In my clothes. *Charming*. I could hear the hiss of the shower running, and I hoped Geoff would leave some hot water for me.

"How are you feeling?" Loki asked.

"I'm okay," I said. My tongue was thick and dry in my mouth, but I didn't feel too bad.

Loki raised an eyebrow. I sat up and my hangover hit me like a sledgehammer. My head throbbed and my stomach churned in protest. "Oh, shit," I groaned. "You might have been right about brennivín."

He kissed my forehead. "I'll make another pot of

coffee."

* * * * * * *

I'd had three cups of coffee and two pieces of toast by the time we boarded the Boeing 747 that would take us to O'Hare, and I was just starting to feel like a human being again. Geoff told me he was feeling totally fine and he'd had way crazier nights, but I noticed he moved slowly, and he closed the window shade in the plane, shutting out the painfully bright sunlight.

The smiling, blonde flight attendant brought us orange juice in heavy glass tumblers while we waited for takeoff. Loki raised his, and Geoff and I turned to meet him, bringing the glasses together as solemnly as the airline seats would allow.

"To the Nine Realms," Loki said. "Long may they stand."

We clinked our tumblers of orange juice and drank together as the massive engines hummed to life beneath our feet.

Home, I thought. *We're all going to make it home.*

EPILOGUE

It would take more than an unprecedented cataclysmic global seismic event for the University of Chicago to interrupt their schedule, and so I defended my doctoral dissertation on May fifteenth, the date that was scheduled almost a year ago.

My family flew to Chicago on May fourteenth. I met them in Baggage Claim at O'Hare International Airport, which was still a disaster of plastic sheeting, scaffolding, and heavy construction equipment after the damage done by the Quakes.

"Doctor Capello!" Dad yelled to me from across the airport, waving his arms.

"Dad, you can't call me that yet," I said, hugging him. "I need to actually defend my dissertation first."

"Hey, doctor, can you have a look at this weird rash I've got?" my brother asked, smiling at me through his Yggdrasil scars.

"Gross, Geoff. I'm not that kind of doctor."

"Oh, he knows, he knows," said Mom, waving her

hands. "Doctor of Philosophy, we understand. And you're going to be a professor! At U.C. Santa Barbara, right?"

I rolled my eyes. "Mom, I didn't like the Santa Barbara position. I'd be stuck teaching intro classes for the rest of my life."

"I know," she said, with a sigh. "What about Stanford?"

I smiled involuntarily. "Well, I have to get the interview first."

"Oh, you will," Mom said, patting me on the cheek.

Then Di handed me baby Devi and I spent the rest of our time in Baggage Claim kissing my niece on the neck and making her giggle uncontrollably.

* * * * * * *

It took a long time to get the Capello family onto the El, and to drop off luggage at the hotel where Mom and Dad were staying, and to finally get everyone to the Flamingo in Hyde Park and then into my apartment. I ordered deep dish pizzas and we sat around the cherrywood dining table, drinking wine, playing peek-a-boo with Devi, and talking about the Quakes.

"They're rebuilding the Hotel del Coronado already," Dad said, pulling out his phone to show me the pictures.

I moved Devi to my other knee and leaned in, looking

at his pictures. The earthquakes and resulting tidal surges hadn't been as destructive in San Diego as they were further up the coast, in San Francisco or Seattle, but the old Hotel del Coronado had been swept into the Pacific like a sand castle. Coronado beach looked the same as ever, with a broken hole of crumbling concrete and wood behind it. Funny the ever-changing beach could survive without a scratch, while the historic hotel was destroyed.

"Honey, I don't know how you can live with a kitchen that small," my mom said, emerging with a roll of paper towels under her arm. She started to wipe off the table.

"Oh, Mom, I can do that," I said.

"Nonsense," she said. "I'm sure Di and Geoff would like some help giving Devi a bath. And oh, this table is lovely!"

* * * * * * * *

Baby Devi finally fell asleep in the center of my bed, curled against Di. I shut the door to my bedroom and joined Geoff in the living room.

"Did they make it back to the hotel?" I whispered.

"Yup, just got a text. Mom said everything is lovely."

I smiled. The third bottle of wine had been a good idea, then.

"How are you?" I asked, glancing at my brother's

beautiful, battered face. His scars had tanned somewhat, making the twisted patterns of Yggdrasil's branches across his cheeks and forehead look a bit softer.

"Not bad," he said, with a shrug. "Dad's talking about me taking over."

"No way? Taking over Capello's Landscaping?"

He nodded. "He says he's getting too old for this. We've been busy, crazy busy. All the damage of the Quakes, you know."

"I wish we could've done more," I said, softly. "I wish we hadn't been so late."

"Don't talk like that," said Di. She closed the bedroom door behind her and stood next to Geoff, putting her hand on his shoulder. "You saved the worlds."

Geoff smiled at her. *He's still handsome,* I thought. *Scars and all.*

"Let's get some rest," Di said. "Big day tomorrow, right, Carol?"

* * * * * * *

Devi, Geoff, and Di slept on my bed, so I spent the night before my dissertation defense on my couch, watching the lights of Chicago, the cars along Lake Shore Drive, the inky darkness of Lake Michigan. For a moment I thought I saw the glow of fireflies in the trees and rose bushes along Promontory Point, but it may have been my imagination.

I smelled woodsmoke just as I was falling asleep.

"You know," Loki said, his cool hand soft on my cheek, "I have a perfectly good bed."

I smiled at him in the darkness. "It's okay. I'd like to stay here."

He kissed me, gently. "Sleep well, then."

"See you tomorrow," I said as he disappeared.

* * * * * * * *

My dissertation defense had two elements. First, I gave a public presentation of my thesis; second, I'd be given a verbal exam by my dissertation committee. I took a deep breath as I opened the heavy, oak doors of Swift Hall the morning of May fifteenth with my entire family in tow. My heart hammered jaggedly as we walked upstairs to the large, high ceilinged room where I'd give the public presentation. Loki was already there, sitting comfortably in the first row. He stood when I entered. I took another deep breath.

"Mom, Dad, I'd like you to meet my, uh, friend. My boyfriend."

Loki crossed the space between us and shook my father's hand. Then he took my mother's hand and kissed it. She raised an eyebrow at me but said nothing.

"I'm very pleased to meet you," Loki said, smiling.

Dad returned his smile. Mom pursed her lips, appraising him cooly. I could almost hear her thoughts: *Expensive suit. Handsome. But wild eyes.*

I felt Loki's hand on the small of my back, and I turned to him. "I'm glad you're here," I whispered.

"I wouldn't miss it," he replied.

"Oh my God, is that Lucas?"

I turned to see Debra in the doorway, her mouth gaping. "Lucas? I haven't seen you since - what - the night of Carol's exams?"

Loki took her hand and kissed it, making Debra blush. "Lovely to see you again, Debra."

Debra smiled at me. "You are a lucky woman," she said. Then she turned to my family. "And you must be Carol's Mom and Dad! And is that little Devi?"

Steve arrived next and muttered a good luck as he shook my hand. He seemed a bit pale, but then again, his own defense was in less than a week. Kara came in at the last minute, squealing over Devi and promising my entire family free coffee whenever they made it to Higher Grounds. Then the room grew silent as Professor Loncovic walked to the podium, turned the microphone on, and introduced me.

The notes in my hands trembled slightly as I looked out over a room that held nearly everyone I loved, nearly everyone who had influenced my life, who had seen me through the last five years. Hæmir's lopsided smile flickered in my memory, and my heart clenched for a moment. *You made your choice,* I thought, taking a deep breath as my eyes found Loki's calm smile and wild eyes. *You made your choice, and I made mine.*

And then I began to speak.

* * * * * * *

But the public presentation was just a show, really. The actual defense came afterward, when I entered a locked room with the members of my committee so they could rip my dissertation to shreds, asking me to defend every single claim I'd made in the five hundred pages I'd written.

My hands trembled again as I hugged my family and turned to follow Professor Loncovic down the stairs to the small, private conference room for the actual defense. Loki walked with me, pulling me close in the quiet hallway.

"Forgive me if I'm wrong," he whispered as we walked together, "but are you not the mortal woman who told Óðinn the All-Father to go fuck himself?"

I laughed, and then tried to turn it into a cough. "Technically, I think I just said 'fuck you,'" I whispered.

"You'll be fine, then."

"And no magic," I said as we stopped outside the

door.

He brought his hands to his chest, a wounded expression on his face. "I would never - "

"I mean it," I said. "I do this on my own."

"You don't need magic."

"Thank you," I whispered. "I'll see you when this is over."

I walked into the conference room and pulled the door shut behind me. Professors Loncovic, Cohen, Najjar, and Singh sat along a long, wooden table. They each had a copy of my dissertation in front of them. None of them were smiling. I was suddenly reminded of the conference in Asgard, with Óðinn, Týr, and Thor. With Hrym the Jötunn.

And then I remembered Yggdrasil, the air thick with sparks. I remembered breaking my ankle in the mountains that ringed Vígríðr, telling my brother where to cut the World Tree to separate the battle of Ragnarök from the Nine Realms.

This is going to be a walk in the park, I told myself, and I took a deep breath.

* * * * * * *

When I pushed back from the table and stood to leave the conference room four hours later, I was Caroline Capello, Ph.D.

Professor Loncovic stood in the doorway and shook my hand solemnly, then pulled me close for a hug. Then I was laughing and trembling and shaking hands with Cohen, Najjar, and Singh, thanking them for everything. Loki walked over to us, putting his arm around my shoulders, and then I introduced Lucas Laufeyiarson to my dissertation committee and the entire world suddenly felt very surreal.

It was early evening when I finally left Swift Hall; the spring sunlight was thick and golden. My family was already at the tapas restaurant where we'd reserved a table for the celebration, so Loki and I walked together, hand in hand, to catch a taxi. The scent of the blossoms on the crabapple trees was heavy in the air, and the little insects of early spring danced in the syrupy light, which seemed so heavy I felt I could almost reach out and touch it.

I wrapped my arm around Loki's waist, breathed deeply, and was convinced, absolutely convinced, Hæmir had been wrong. There could be no better world after Ragnarök, because there was no better world, no better world than Midgard in the spring.

In the taxi, Loki handed me a flask filled with something that was sweet on my tongue and burned going down. His hand worked its way up my thighs and I leaned to kiss him, and we did not stop until the taxi driver banged on the plexiglass window.

"Hey! We're here! You not leave, I keep the meter running!" he yelled.

I left the cab laughing, my head light, my heart full.

My parents had reserved an enormous table in the center of the restaurant, and it was covered with bacon-wrapped dates, olives and cheese, calamari, salted cod, chorizo, and skewers of pickles. And sangria. Lots and lots of sangria. Everyone cheered when we walked in the room. They all stood and called me "Doctor" about a hundred times, and I drank an entire glass of sangria while hugging friends and family.

Debra told me she was proud to have me as a colleague. Kara said she always knew I'd defend in under seven years, and Steve hugged me and said he hoped he'd do half as well during his defense. Di told me I was very brave, and I could tell from her eyes she was not referring to the dissertation defense. My brother kissed my head and squeezed my arms and said he was proud of me. Dad hugged me and clapped me on the back and told me he always knew I would turn out all right. Even baby Devi hugged me and gave me a sloppy, drool-filled, baby kiss.

And then Mom held me with tears in her eyes. "Caroline," she said, grasping my hand so tightly it almost hurt. "I am so proud of my wonderful daughter."

"Thank you," I said, to everyone, over and over. "Thank you."

And then we finally sat down to eat.

"So," Dad asked, raising his glass of sangria toward me, "what is Dr. Capello going to do next?"

Loki smiled at me, his wild eyes dancing.

"Marry me," he said.

ACKNOWLEDGEMENTS

A great many people helped to make this book a reality.

First, I'm grateful for my friends, professors, and colleagues at the University of Chicago, none of whom should be held accountable in any way for what I've done with my education.

Thank you so much to my phenomenal beta reader and friend Laura Duffy for your support and cheerleading. I'm also indebted to Moselle Green for the beta read and the encouragement. Cate Courtright at The Book Medic gave very helpful feedback, and this novel is much stronger thanks to her input and expertise.

I'm deeply grateful for the Buffalo Writers Meetup Group, especially the Wednesday evening contingency. Thank you for telling me when you were confused!

My fellow Buffalo writer Gaia Amman walked me through the independent publishing process. Her website, gaiabamman.com, is invaluable. You should check it out.

I'm very thankful for Teresa Conner, my virtual personal assistant, who helped me figure out what to do with this book once it was finally finished.

My sister came up with a wide variety of wildly inappropriate pen names and served as a sounding board for all sorts of different problems. Thanks, sis. Don't tell Mom and Dad.

Peter Tiernan told me I should start writing again. You were right. Thanks.

Thank you to Kit Foster for making everything look pretty!

Thanks to my kids. Sorry, you'll never be old enough to read this.

And finally, thank you again to my very patient husband, who spent many hours embroiled in conversations about what imaginary people might say or do in highly improbable circumstances.

Made in the USA
Middletown, DE
07 February 2021